Books by Andrei Codrescu

Hail, Babylon! In Search of the American City at the End of the Millenium
(1997)

Valley of Christmas (CD: 1997)

Alien Candor: Selected Poems (1970–1995) (1996)

The Dog with the Chip in His Neck: Essays from NPR and Elsewhere (1996)

The Blood Countess (1995)

Zombification: Essays from NPR (1994)

Road Scholar: Coast to Coast Late in the Century (1993)

The Muse Is Always Half-Dressed in New Orleans (1993)

The Hole in the Flag: An Exile's Story of Return and Revolution (1992)

The Disappearance of the Outside (1991)

Belligerence (1991)

Raised by the Puppets Only to Be Killed by Research (1989)

The Stiffest of the Corpse: An Exquisite Corpse Reader (1988)

At the Court of Yearning: The Poems of Lucian Blaga (1989)

Monsieur Teste in America (1987)

A Craving for Swan (1987)

Comrade Past and Mr. Present (1987)

In America's Shoes (1983)

The Life and Times of an Involuntary Genius (1975)

The History of the Growth of Heaven (1973)

License to Carry a Gun (1973)

Messiah

a novel

Andrei Codrescu

simon & schuster

c. 1

SIMON & SCHUSTER

Rockefeller Center

1230 Avenue of the Americas

New York, NY 10020

SIMON AND SCHUSTER and colophon are registered trademarks

of Simon & Schuster Inc.

Designed by Karolina Harris

Manufactured in the United States of America

1 3 5 7 9 10 8 6 4 2

Library of Congress Cataloging-in-Publication Data

Codrescu, Andrei

Messiah: a novel/Andrei Codrescu

p. cm.

I. Title

PS3553.03M47 1999

813'.54—dc21 98-39032

CIP

ISBN 0-684-80314-3

If the words in this book are right
it is because Laura Rosenthal—
their lector and doctor—
gave herself over to their care.

A grievous vision is declared unto me; the treacherous dealer dealeth treacherously, and the spoiler spoileth. Go up, O Elam: besiege, O Media; all the sighing thereof have I made to cease.

— ISAIAH 21:2

Seen the arrow on the doorpost
Saying this land is condemned
All the way from New Orleans to Jerusalem.

— BOB DYLAN,
"BLIND WILLIE McTELL," 1983

For those who were in the world had been prepared by the will of our sister Sophia—she who is a whore—because of the innocence which has not been uttered.

— NAG HAMMADI GNOSTIC GOSPELS

Chapter One

Wherein Felicity Le Jeune, a young native of the city of New Orleans, finding herself at a crossroads of life, seeks solace from the Virgin

s Marie-Frances Claire Le Bec, ninety-six years old, dozed like a wilted sprig of mint on her deathbed, her granddaughter, Felicity Odille Le Jeune, waited impatiently for the end, wondering where on earth the old woman had found so much green chiffon to pass away in.

Felicity also wondered if she should attempt to wake Grandmère, to give her a message to carry to God.

Felicity's spiky short hair, baggy clothes, pierced nostril, and eight-hole black work boots were the manifestations of the "be more manly every day" discipline she'd practiced for years. The goal of the regimen was to achieve maximum teenage boyishness by the time she turned thirty, and to maintain it indefinitely, or until the angel now hovering so patiently over Grandmère came to take her, too.

Poor Grandmère. How she had worried about proper attire, clean undergarments, correct posture, and myriad other Victorian details. For all Felicity knew, her grandmother Le Bec was the repository of the last complete set of nineteenth-century manners to exist on the planet; this was perhaps why, in her dying hour, she did not recognize the granddaughter who in comportment and manner of dress was the perfect denial of her life's work.

city clicked the stud in her tongue several times against the back of
th. It sounded like typing. Christmas Muzak poured out of the stat-
speaker on the wall, the management of Charity Hospital having apparently decided, like the rest of America, that Christmas began the day
after Thanksgiving. From a bed behind a ratty curtain, an invisible patient
coughed. Patients in every room started coughing at once, as if linked by a
pull chain. The machine registering her grandmother's increasingly feeble
life signs pinged three times in a row.

A glassy brown eye rolled upward, away from Felicity. Grandmère was
awake.

"Is it Christmas?" the old woman asked.

"No, Grandmère. It's only the fourth of December."

The glassy brown eye focused briefly on the shape by the bed.

"Doctor," she asked Felicity, "has Reverend Mullin arrived yet?"

Reverend Mullin! The hound of hell! Felicity sometimes thought of
Mullin as a dog yapping at her heels; at other times she saw him as a snake
emerging from under her pillow just as she was about to fall asleep. She
had been only thirteen when Grandmère had the dream that had bound
her to Mullin—and ended Felicity's childhood. The night before Easter
1985, Grandmère had dreamed that Jesus himself appeared to her and ordered her to dispense with the paraphernalia of the popes and leave the
Catholic Church. She found herself kneeling in a pasture, and his body,
emanating light, filled the entire horizon. His index finger pointed to a
huge television that rested between two mountains. The face of an angry
man was on the screen, and written in black letters under the face were the
words THE MINISTRY OF THE UTMOST GOD'S TEMPLE, 15600 VETERANS
BOULEVARD, METAIRIE, LOUISIANA, JEREMY "ELVIS" MULLIN, PASTOR, TELE-
PHONE 999-9999.

"*Mullin is your only hope, Marie-Frances, and the hope of your spawn!*"
thundered Jesus, even as the mountains crumbled, leaving only the TV.
Scared to death of losing her soul, Grandmère pleaded in vain with the
raging Savior. Begging for mercy, she recalled her devout childhood, her
mother's faith, the baptisms of her children, her pilgrimage to Medjugorje
with a busload of white people from Chalmette, and the Carmelite convent where her virtuous great-great-grandmère had been raised. (She still
had in a trunk the lacy tear-stained handkerchiefs into which her ancestress had poured her grief at being shut away in the convent by her own
mother, the light-skinned mistress of a white French Creole aristocrat.)
But Jesus was stern, unequivocal, and above all, specific. Broaching no dis-

sent, he commanded her by name: *"Marie-Frances Claire Le Bec, you must be born again, or you shall never see the Kingdom of God."* A spiral gust of wind sprang out of the numbers on television, and Grandmère tumbled like a leaf back into her bed.

Next day they drove out to a suburb that no one in their family would have admitted was part of New Orleans, to partake in the barbarian Baptist rites.

"The Reverend Mullin," the old woman insisted. "Where is he, Doctor? Is he here yet?" The glassy eye rolled around like a marble.

"Not yet, Grandmère. I'm Felicity, remember? I want you to take a message to God."

The old woman's eye focused on her for a stern second. "I have to be light before Jesus. I can't be going up there laden with doctor's notes."

"I'm not the doctor, Grandmère. It's Felicity. Your daughter Eliza was my mother; she ran away with a trumpet player to New York. You raised me, remember?" The bleary eye closed, but Felicity persisted. "Felicity, whose happy childhood you sabotaged with rules and regulations, whose adolescence you thwarted with visions of hell, and whose young womanhood you fucked up by giving away the only money that ever came your way. Felicity. Fe-li-ci-ty."

Felicity bit hard on her lower lip. She was so angry it was all she could do to keep herself from karate-kicking one of Charity's long-suffering walls.

She remembered holding tight her grandmother's hand, as they sat squeezed in a mass of fluttering souls sweating profusely in their Sunday best. Mullin's cologne wafted down from the pulpit like an ill wind.

"Feel the Spirit," whispered Grandmère, and Felicity imagined that the Spirit had to be the reverend's cologne. It flowed from his outstretched palms as his voice thundered down on them:

"They say that we spend too much money on television! They say one hundred million dollars a year is too much to spend on spreading the Word of the Lord! When that miscegenated freak, Prince, makes one hundred and thirty million! It's Friday in the world, but Sunday is coming! Jesus said, 'I've come to take away your sins!' Verily, brothers and sisters, I say! Whenever I look up to that TV camera I see my man tellin' me: 'Take it all away, Jeremy!' and truly it's Friday in the world, but Sunday is coming!"

It so happened that Prince, soon to be the graphic formerly known as Prince, was at the time Felicity's favorite person in the whole world. She wasn't sure what "miscegenated" meant, but she suspected it had something to do with color. People all around them swooned and fell. A blind woman lifted her tear-streaked face to the TV camera and called on America to watch her see. The snow-bright girls in the choir lifted up on the wings of a heart-ripping "Hallelujah!" and floated on the Spirit-scented air! All but one, that is: a disgruntled angel in the first row who tapped impatiently with her foot in the direction of the preacher and scratched her neck with cherry red fingernails. Maybe she loved Prince, too.

In the parking lot after the service, surrounded by pickup trucks with guns in their gun racks, Grandmère told Felicity that God was both color-blind and considerate enough to have made much blacker people than Prince and themselves. She said that Felicity was a lucky girl. God had also seen to it that all those rednecks in the pickups praised the Lord instead of hunting her and her Prince down. Felicity, who had always thought of herself as Creole, not black, got an odd sensation in the pit of her stomach. She did not like Reverend Mullin at all. Later, she found out that Mullin's God and the hunting of blacks were not mutually exclusive. One of the reverend's faithful sat on Angola's death row, drafting another appeal to the Supreme Court. He'd killed two black men because the voice of God told him to. The upcoming race war, he wrote, would prove he was right.

"Damn it, old woman. I said I got a message for you to take to God!" Felicity was angry, but she also felt guilty. She'd been told that Charity Hospital, Huey Long's legacy to Louisiana's poor, was filled to the rafters with the dying of the city. Why they had all decided to leave their earthly existence this very afternoon of Saturday, December 4, 1999, in the very last month of the second Christian millennium, was a mystery to Felicity, but maybe they knew something she didn't. Maybe she could persuade another poor soul to take her message to God. She hoped that her saying "damn" would not preclude delivery.

"One last time, Grandmère, are you hearing me?"

The old woman didn't move.

Well, that's just like her. Even dying, the woman was proper and hard. No matter. Felicity would give her the message anyway, and she would have no choice but to take it with her. Saying anything to her now was like pinning a note to her departing soul. There was no time left to unpin it.

"Tell God," she whispered, "to grant me an orgasm."

There was a commotion in the hall outside the hospital room, and Felicity knew that the devil had arrived. Reverend Jeremy "Elvis" Mullin, the great poo-bah of the United Thieves of Love, the horned and hooved one who had stolen Grandmère's soul, barged into the room. Doctors and nurses trailed behind him with notepads, asking him for autographs. Mullin was a celebrity.

"Fuck you, hypocrite and thief," she muttered as Mullin approached the dying woman's bed. "You stole Grandmère from me, you slimy bag of shit. You stole her Catholic soul from the church and from her mother and all my ancestors. Hell isn't big enough for all the pliers and drills reserved for your torment. You'll go to Catholic hell for sending Grandmère to Baptist heaven."

Felicity shut her eyes so as not to look at the tight-panted, leather-jacketed, slick-haired reptile, but she could still smell him. His expensive cologne—Jurassic—barely masked his sweaty pelt and slinking scales.

Felicity felt herself shoved aside—Mullin displaced people by sheer presence. She was forced to look at him: a knobby man with an oversized silver cross strung about his thick neck. His manicured hands were soft and pudgy; Felicity imagined them crossed behind his back while she locked a pair of handcuffs too tightly around his wrists.

Mullin knelt beside Grandmère's bed, and taking the silver cross from around his neck, held it near the tiny wrinkled fig that was her face.

"Jesus waits for you, woman! He is beaming down his welcome on you. Lord Jesus, take Marie-Frances Claire Le Bec into your arms and take her soul to your keeping!"

It was a command, rendered forcefully enough to make the whole hospital room shake. Even Felicity, enjoying the fantasy of dragging the cuffed minister on his knees through the mud, felt the power of his performance. She looked out the hospital window and saw a fat, coffin-shaped cloud slither over the Mississippi River. She knew that it was filled with all the souls leaving the city of New Orleans that very minute, and it was just waiting to pick up Grandmère's. Indeed, the cloud made directly for the hospital, and for a moment the view turned white. Then the cloud, with Grandmère's soul aboard, took off for the river again.

Felicity felt another hole opening inside her, adding itself to the others: her father, Mama, Miles . . . She was as full of holes as she could be, like a piece of wormy wood, or a golf course, or an aborted flute. These were her images; she knew them well. She felt empty and holey and less substantial than the green sprig of the century-old corpse in front of her. "Take me too, Lord," she whispered. "Fill me up and make me whole, even if you have to kill me."

"What was that, daughter?" inquired Mullin unctuously, wiping the cross on his silk sleeve before hanging it back around his neck. "Can I comfort you?"

"Not on your life, motherfucker!" Felicity replied crisply.

Felicity left the room, shutting the door behind her in what she hoped was a dignified exit, and nearly knocked over a janitor angrily mopping the corridor.

"It's like goddam Saigon in 'seventy-three," he muttered. "Everybody pushin' and shovin' to take the last choppers outta hell. And me gonna do all the mopping!"

She needed to think. The Tulane entrance to Charity Hospital was a circus: mothers with coughing children clamored to be admitted; a man with a flowering wound wrapped in a T-shirt around his arm staggered right past her; two wheelchairs collided; a gaunt patient in yellow pajamas was leaning on her walker biting into a half-peeled orange; a junkie was throwing up on the steps. When Felicity gained the street, she saw an old toothless woman sitting on top of a broken TV looking at her gnarled bare feet.

"These feet," she said to Felicity, "walked they whole life." Felicity nodded. So had her Grandmère's. The old woman had walked every-where, disdaining streetcars and buses.

It was drizzling by the time Felicity got to Basin Street. She turned onto North Rampart. Try as she might she couldn't get Mullin out of her mind. He sat there at a crucial intersection of their lives, scorching the past with his flaming yellow eyes. After her dream, Grandmère started cleaning house. The next Sunday, when Felicity would have normally put on her crisp white dress and her black patent leather shoes for morning Mass, she found neither in her closet. Missing too was the picture of Saint Cecily wrapped in her hair above the dresser. Gone from the parlor were the seven lithographs of angels, the holy water from Lourdes vase, the cherrywood rosary hanging over the sofa, the statue of the Blessed Virgin Mary, and the autographed picture of Father Hannan.

But worse things were in store for her yet.

Less than three weeks after they started being Baptists, Grandmère won the lottery— $2.1 million. Felicity, still only a pubescent sprout, had just become aware that the poverty they lived in made it impossible for her to buy clothes and CDs and go to the movies like her friends. When

Grandmère announced the winning numbers, Felicity had nearly fainted from happiness. There was a pounding in her ears: *To the Mall! To the Mall! To the Mall!* To this day she knew the numbers by heart: 363-54-2122. She had written them at the top of her diary, a yellow book with a lock that she still had somewhere.

Next day, Reverend Mullin preached against the lottery and said that it was "the devil's money." Grandmère prayed for guidance. Monday morning she tore up the lottery ticket. After she tore up the lottery ticket, she tore up everything of sentimental value in the house, including the photo albums containing the only pictures of Felicity's mother and one picture of her dad in uniform. Felicity had often looked at her pretty mom standing under a big oak in City Park and tried to imagine herself inside her tummy. But now that picture was gone, except inside her head.

Felicity couldn't actually remember Grandmère tearing up the lottery ticket. That is what Grandmère had told her, and she had imagined the scene in such vivid detail. Felicity stopped dead in her tracks and leaned against the whitewashed wall of Saint Louis Cemetery. What if Grandmère hadn't actually torn the ticket but given it to Mullin instead? She closed her eyes and saw again the smug face of the evangelist. It was possible!

When she opened her eyes, two fat tourists, big guts spilling out of their T-shirts, were breathing beer on her. One of the T-shirts displayed pairs of breasts with the captions *Figs, Melons, Pears.* The other tourist was sipping from a straw that curled behind his ear from a beer can on top of his hat. His shirt said, *New Orleans Crawfish: We Suck Da Heads and Pinch Da Tails.* He held out a brochure to Felicity.

"Says here this useta be Storyville, Basin Street, the red lights district, girls, music, action!" He popped his fingers. "Where is Basin Street?"

Felicity knocked the brochure out of his hand and stared into his piggy eyes. She enunciated very slowly: "Once this was Storyville. Now it's a motherfucking freeway going through a fucking cemetery. You want to know what happened to the black whores, you go ask the fucking feds who put a fucking freeway through here."

They backed away; the freak looked like she was packing heat.

The light drizzle turned to rain as she entered the French Quarter at Saint Philip Street. It soaked her clothes and streaked her face and would have mingled with her tears if she'd been crying. But she was not. The cottony cloud that had collected Grandmère's soul had vanished in the leaden sky. The houses along Saint Philip Street looked dumbly at her from behind shuttered windows. They were full of as many ghosts as they could hold; wisps of white smoke wafted from their dormers. Felicity passed a store window with a large glass jar filled with colored liquid in which floated a two-headed pink lizard. Felicity forced herself to look at it. It was Mullin! The two-headed abortion was unmistakably made of the same substance as the evangelist. Felicity knew for sure that her Grandmère hadn't torn up that lottery ticket. She had offered it to Mullin on his silver collection platter, and the reptile had used the money to grow in hideous power. Her money, Felicity's money, her adolescent allowance, her college fund, her inheritance. Why else would a world-famous TV devil respond to the summons of a poor old woman dying in Charity Hospital?

Because he owed her. Because she hadn't torn up the lottery ticket—she had given it to the United Ministries. Why hadn't she seen this before? She had been robbed. She remembered the new domed tabernacle Mullin built in Metairie, and the giant plaster Christ he'd erected on the shores of Lake Pontchartrain the following year.

Felicity began to sense a cruddy substance emanating from the foul history of the Creole cottages on either side of the street. The former homes of slave-owning colonials stood rigidly inside their courtyards. They too had risen from pillage, extortion, slavery, gambling, and whoring. The longer she walked, the more convinced she became that Mullin had stolen her money.

When Felicity reached the corner of Chartres Street she realized where she was heading. Without thinking about it, she was walking toward Saint Louis Cathedral, where she'd often gone as a girl.

She kept her eyes fixed on the misty spires of the cathedral, which kept receding in the rain like a ship. It didn't help that when she looked toward the river, a real ship loomed over the levee, floating so high in the river it threatened to sail right into the Quarter. She had known all her life that the city was below sea level, but she never stopped being startled by the sight of ships over her head. New Orleans was a bowl, hugged tightly by the Mississippi River. The levees that kept the river out were no match for a hurricane or a great flood. Felicity imagined herself floating like a gardenia in a porcelain bowl. It was only a matter of time before the people and buildings were washed away. "We are doomed," she said out loud; "it's the only thing that keeps us going."

Two wet pigeons looked down on her from the facade as Felicity passed through the ironwork fence and walked through the open door of the old church. A gold-ringed, speckled gray marble holy water font greeted her. It looked smaller than it had when she had had to stand on tiptoes to look at the "blessing water." The water, Grandmère told her, contained one of the Holy Mother's tears, and the tears of all the brokenhearted women of New Orleans, of which, she added ominously, "there will never be no shortage." Little Felicity didn't know what she'd done, but she'd stood accused and guilty anyway, apologizing silently for her mother and praying for her safety in that unimaginable Yankee city.

The bank of votive lights in the foyer was ablaze. The sign below it read: *Large 2 Dollars, Small 50 cents.* Oh, large, definitely large. Felicity chose the brightest and largest.

The smells of her girlhood surrounded her: old books, melted wax, incense, damp old people, roses. A chandelier, like a crown with long crystal teardrops, hung from a long chain above the altar. As she walked up the center aisle she saw a few worshipers abstracted in prayer, kneeling or asleep. They had always been here, part of the furniture since the days of her childhood, lost in an endless conversation with God or one of his host. Poor Grandmère. Maybe Mother Mary hadn't abandoned the old woman, though she'd forsaken the faith of her birth. Maybe the Holy Mother had kept up her end of the conversation, even after Grandmère had fallen silent, sure that one day the dialogue would resume. And that day was today; it had finally come. Perhaps at this very moment the two were deep in conversation. For her part, Felicity had never stopped speaking to that part of her soul which had shined so brightly in her early years. When she had decided to stop believing, she stopped addressing her interlocutor by the names she had learned long ago, but the talk went on.

Felicity carried her fat light to the left of the altar, where she planted it at the feet of the Holy Mother holding the infant Jesus like a precious pastry. She knelt in a pew before the Virgin and raised her eyes to the beatific face. The words ECCE PANIS ANGELORUM were written on the ceiling. *Behold the bread of angels!* God sat blessing the Lamb above the altar, while just below a motley crew of early Louisiana colonists partook of the divine light.

"Dear Blessed Mother," said Felicity, "please take into account all the extenuating circumstances and help me!" Even as she spoke, she knew that she'd have to do better than that. "Dear Mary, is there no way for this string to be broken? The old woman's dead and all she's left me is another hole. More than half of me is gone, dear Mother, and there won't be much left if you don't help me."

That wasn't quite right either. If she'd had long hair she would have let it hang loose over her eyes and prostrated herself in the manner of penitents. Her hair was short, her language was petty, her belief shaky at best. Perhaps she'd be better off gone; there was no reason for her.

"All gone, all gone," lamented Felicity, "and me so young. And that preacher devil stole my lottery ticket!"

"Get off it," said the Virgin. "After what my son went through, the lottery just sounds comic."

"Can I help it?" Felicity said, chastened, "that I only have two modes? The despondent and the comic?"

Felicity wanted to be selfless and admirable like the Holy Mother herself, or the Magdalene with her hair loosened on the Via Dolorosa, or Saint Catherine of Alexandria with her wheel. Saint Agnes with her lamb. Saint Ursula, martyred at Cologne with eleven thousand virgins. The nuns had given her an obdurate store of images.

Felicity was aware of the strong smell of urine. A bum was kneeling in the pew behind her, bent in exaggerated humility. She felt a compulsion to pat the top of his dirty head. We are one, *mon clochard*, she murmured between clenched teeth. There is no difference between us. I will sleep with you, look for lice in your clothes, wash your intimate parts. Felicity saw herself cradling the destitute creature. As she nearly touched his head, she saw that the bum's suffering pose was disguising the fact that he was fishing white envelopes from the back of her pew.

"Hey," she said.

The bum straightened up and slunk away in a hurry, dropping an envelope. Felicity picked it up. *Donations to the Christmas Campaign for the Restoration and Renovation of St. Louis Cathedral, New Orleans, La.* There were a few crumpled dollars inside. Felicity dug in the hip pouch zipped to her shorts and took out a five. She put it in the envelope and was about to return it to the box when she had another thought. She dug deeper in the pouch and came up with a Post-it note and a pen. She wrote on it, *363-54-2122*, and tucked the note in the envelope.

"Restore the cathedral, Mother of God, and restore my lottery ticket, and restore me to wholeness, and give me back all my loved ones, and take Grandmère to you!" concluded Felicity.

She stood up to go. "Oh," she added, "and grant me that orgasm."

That was her whole wish list.

As she rose from her knees she knew what she had to do. Her uncle, Major Notz, who lived in the Pontalba Apartments to the right of the cathedral, was the man for the job. Major Notz had always been there for her and, though he was not actually a blood relative, had been a kind of father to her. An army buddy of her dead father, he had appeared one day at their house with presents and affection, and had persisted in caring for Felicity against the formidable opposition of her grandmother, who had hated the major from the very beginning. Felicity needed his comforting bulk now.

In her absence—how long had she been gone?—Jackson Square and, indeed, the whole sky had undergone a miraculous transformation. The sun was shining through the drizzle, and the once nearly empty square was teeming. Several tattooed and pierced young people, called "Shadow people" by the *Times-Picayune* but known familiarly as "Shades," lay playing cards under the mounted statue of General Jackson doffing his hat. The painters and fortune-tellers were back at their easels and cardboard tables. Behold humanity, Felicity thought, and smirked. Half of them want their portraits done; the other half want to know the future. And the other half provide it. That's three halves, and there you have it. Expressionist math. Felicity was an expert at it ever since she'd decided, at age thirteen, that nothing adds up.

A mime with rain-streaked makeup, huge breasts, and hairy arms stood on a crate. A hand-lettered sash identified her as Miss Bra '99. Two tourists made faces to try to make her move. When they walked away, Miss Bra '99 came off her pedestal and took a few dollars out of a bucket at her feet. She ducked behind the Lucky Dog vendor, lifted her short skirt, and took a roll out of her panty hose. An unmistakable bulge remained. She added the dollars to the roll, stuck it back in, and climbed up on her box. The Lucky Dog vendor sold a hot dog to a midget who stared intently at Miss Bra. Why, thought Felicity, would anyone want to be such a sad parody of woman? Why, indeed, would anyone want to be a woman? Period. She had never sung, "You make me feel like a natural woman," and she had experienced a genuine vertigo of nausea when she watched a television commercial for some female hygiene spray featuring a white woman belting out that song.

Holy Mother, holy, holy, bla, bla. She was moved by something both hilarious and infinitely sad. What times I live in. It was enough to make her wish she had been born in the fourteenth century, a nun sweet on Jesus. Anytime but now. Anyone but me.

Still, there was a tiny dot of mellowness in her wretchedness. Perhaps there wasn't anyone to blame, really. Grandmère died thinking Jesus was holding her. For a moment, Felicity was even uncertain of Mullin's evil. Perhaps what had befallen her was in the nature of a hurricane, a natural disaster. Mullin had perhaps been only an unwitting agent.

Neah. She had a vivid fantasy of dismembering Mullin and feeding him piece by piece to her neighbor's rottweilers. Yum-yum. Preacher meat. Raw and bloody. That made her feel better.

Chapter Two

Wherein a tender-aged orphan named Andrea is delivered to Saint Hildegard Hospice in the city of Jerusalem, to the bafflement of the sisters there

N **i g h t** comes early to Jerusalem in December. The sisters at Saint Hildegard Hospice, in the German quarter, were decorating their Christmas trees and discussing the impending snowstorm. "The sun," Sister Maria said, "hasn't been out in a month."

"When I was a young girl in the Carpathian Mountains, we never saw the sun in the winter," Sister Rodica mused. "My father used to say that the sun went away because we were bad, and that if we didn't say our prayers it would never come back again."

The Ursuline sisters of Saint Hildegard's came from a dozen nations, many from the German-speaking countries of Europe, but some from as far as the Sudan. Mother Superior required them to speak German, but they often lapsed and whispered to one another in their maternal tongues. The sisters had been raised for the most part in Catholic orphanages and had chosen quite early to stay within the church, but they felt particularly nostalgic now, around Christmas, when memories of their birthplaces became insistent. The scents and sounds of their childhoods were as varied as the hues of their native skies. Just now, decorating the trees and speaking to each other in Romanian, the two Transylvanian-born nuns tasted something heavy and sweet on their tongues, like *coliva* at a wake. The cake, made from nuts and honey and festooned with hard candy, was baked only for funerals, and it was redolent of Carpathian pinesap.

The buzzer at the outer gate sounded like an old-fashioned bronze knocker, eletronically generated. The sisters hastened to the TV monitor to see who was calling at this hour. It was after ten, the time when the convent shut itself off from the outside world. Two bulky shapes wrapped in raincoats stood there under a black umbrella. The rain glittered on the dome of the bumbershoot.

"All the guests are in. Maybe it's a delivery," Sister Maria speculated.

They studied the two shapes sparkling under the security light fastened to the Gothic *G* in the name of the blessed Saint Hildegard. One of the shapes was bigger than the other. In fact, one of them looked like a child. The sisters had strict orders from Mother Superior not to allow any strangers in. This was, after all, Jerusalem at the end of the millennium. "Every nutcase in the world is here, dragging a lit fuse behind him," she had said, and it was true. Just in the past week, three terrorists had been captured in their neighborhood.

"Let's ask what they want!" Sister Rodica's curiosity got the better of her. *"What do you want?"* she shouted into the intercom, though there was no need to shout.

"I brought the child," the man said.

The sisters looked at each other. The child? That was strange. They knew nothing about a child arriving here.

The nuns buzzed them in. The strangers dragged mud into the foyer. Their faces were covered by scarves, and water poured off the hoods of their raincoats. The man gazed at the two trees and exclaimed in wonder. "Fifteen years I don't see any Christmas trees! Now I see two!"

He pushed the wet bundle next to him forward. When the creature pulled back the hood and lifted the wet scarf, they saw that it was a girl, sixteen or seventeen years old, skinny and starved looking. She had enormous green eyes, and in her hand she clutched a cardboard tube.

"This is where I get off," said the man. "The tube has all the papers and things. She's clear with immigration."

Before they could ask him any questions, he had pulled his hood back up and was out the door. There was only a widening puddle where he'd been.

Sister Maria took the cardboard tube from the girl and laid it on the desk. Sister Rodica took away the dripping scarf and hastened to get a towel from the linen closet. Sister Maria inspected the girl thoughtfully.

"What is your name, child?" she asked in German, while Rodica dried the girl off with the towel. "Come here, next to the fire, where it's warmer. Sit down."

The girl sat obediently where she was told and allowed the nuns to remove her wet shoes and dry her feet with the towel. But she didn't talk. She just looked at them with those bright green eyes. Something about her suggested to the sisters that she had come from very far away. If she was okay with immigration, as the man had said, perhaps she was Jewish. The Law of Return guaranteed all Jews the right to live in Israel. The sisters' own situation was more precarious—Jerusalem was administered by a plethora of confusing immigration policies.

Sister Rodica tried speaking to her in Hebrew, to no avail. Then Sister Maria tried English.

"Andrea," the girl answered listlessly.

"That's a pretty name," Sister Rodica assured her.

"It's an angel's name," confirmed Sister Maria.

The girl understood English. But the accent made it unlikely that she was American. It was Slavic or Caucasian, darkly flavored. The sisters wanted to peek inside the cardboard tube, but they feared their mother superior. The abbess had retired for the night and could be extremely unpleasant when wakened. The sisters decided to consult her in the morning, at which time they would also investigate the cardboard tube and the mystery of Andrea's identity.

Meanwhile, they fussed over their guest. They brought her a snack. Andrea sipped the tea and ate the sandwich, and when she was done, she said, "Thank you," in English. But when Sister Rodica invited her to help decorate the trees, Andrea shook her head and shuddered, as if the idea was truly distasteful to her. She also refused to go to bed when the sisters offered to see her to a room. She indicated with a shrug that she was content to stand in front of the fire and watch them work.

The rain intensified outside, and small bursts of hail pelted the convent roof and window.

Just as Sister Maria stood on tiptoes on the top rung of the ladder to hang the star, the lights went off. Somewhere down the dark corridor, one of the guest room doors opened, then closed. Sister Maria froze, holding the star. It was very dark, but she could see Andrea's eyes looking up at her, two luminous points. The sister would have crossed herself had it been possible. When the twinkling lights resumed, she hung the gold star and quickly descended the ladder.

"Did you hear that door? Sounded like the Dark One himself," whispered Sister Rodica. "Did you hear how first it opened then shut . . . pat— tap . . . pat . . . tap."

Sister Maria could still see Andrea's luminous eyes. A door opening and closing was the least of all the strange things! The convent was three hundred years old—there were twenty guest rooms, which were always occupied by visiting clergy or researchers. It was not at all odd for the electricity to fail, especially if more than five guests plugged their laptops or hair dryers in simultaneously. It was even less unusual for doors to open and close without discernible reason. Dozens, possibly hundreds of ghosts lived here. Once the headquarters of the mysterious Order of the German Templars, the convent was famous for its spirits. Both sisters had heard and seen ghostly presences, shimmering ectoplasmic forms that vanished quickly or slowly. One night Sister Maria had seen a red tongue of flame issue from the center of one of these hapless ghouls. But it had not been as disturbing as Andrea's green eyes glittering in the dark.

It wasn't so much her eyes as the feeling that overcame the sister, a mixture of awe and animal fear. She didn't have long to think about it, however, because a door opened in the corridor and the cross-legged form of a naked man with long flowing white hair, floating about a foot over the octagonal stones of the floor, rounded the corner. His eyes were closed under bushy silver eyebrows, and his penis lay delicately on his left thigh. In the twinkling Christmas lights he looked more fantastic than frightening.

"Mr. Rabindranath!" Sister Rodica exclaimed reproachfully. "Not now! Not just before Christmas!"

Gently, as if she were shooing away a butterfly, she stood before the form and agitated the air with her palms. Mr. Rabindranath floated in the opposite direction.

"When he's like this, he can neither hear nor see," Sister Rodica explained. She shooed him back around the corner to his room. There was a thud, a door shut, and Sister Rodica reappeared, blushing to the soles of her feet. She felt personally responsible for Andrea's marred introduction to Saint Hildegard's.

"I'm sorry," she said in German, adding in Romanian, "You poor child! To see such a thing your first night in Jerusalem!"

"I know about Hindu meditation techniques," Andrea said flatly in Hebrew. "Does Mr. Rabindranath often lose control of his meditation?"

"Only twice since he came to stay with us last year," replied Sister Maria in German, crossing herself. "They say it's a religion. From what I've seen, it's of the devil!"

But perhaps the Evil One had enabled Andrea to speak such perfect, musical Hebrew. Sister Maria herself knew only just enough of Hebrew to shop in the markets and to deal with repairmen. "Did you hear the child, Rodica?" she whispered.

"I did," said Sister Rodica cheerfully. Having understood that the child spoke good Hebrew didn't startle her in the least. Nor was she unduly bothered by Mr. Rabindranath's display. She just hated to expose someone of Andrea's tender years to a man's ugly privates. She knew that people, including many of the scholars currently in residence, worshiped in all sorts of ways. Mr. Rabindranath himself, embarrassed by one of his earlier displays, had explained this at some length. His own levitation was something called *samjama*; his spirit separated from the body, and the body, left on its own, became very light and ceased to obey the laws of gravity. For thousands of years, yogis engaged in *samjama* had startled people with this by-product of their practice. Mr. Rabindranath related other unusual practices to Sister Rodica, who would have liked him to stop but was fascinated nonetheless. She found out that some Hindus liked to walk barefoot on hot burning coals, that in Africa some tribes cut their faces and incised their privates to please their gods. In the Sonora Desert Yaqui shamans copulated with eagles. There was no end to the kingdom of heathenism, and if the truth were known, there were some Christian practices that made the sister blush. Before Easter, on Via Dolorosa, people on their bleeding knees crawled up the hill with a cross on their backs. And Mother Superior scourged herself late at night with a leather whip. Flagellation was one of their order's secret rites.

Mother Superior woke, as was her custom, at 3 A.M., and, after her prayers, walked to the lobby, where the Christmas trees sparkled gloriously. She stood a moment admiring them. They were the most beautiful in all her years in Jerusalem. Then she saw the cardboard tube lying on the reception desk. She took off the plastic cap and slid out a scroll. It was written in Latin, and addressed to Sister Ingeborg, the mother superior's predecessor. Sister Ingeborg had died, aged ninety-seven, the previous year.

Forgive me for not writing to you in the lingua franca—which one, I wonder—but as you doubtlessly know, the situation in Bosnia does not ease communication. I have just seen a transport of orphans out of Sarajevo. His Holiness has assured me that these children will be placed in the care of the Holy See. They are all God's children, but among them is an extraordinary child I trust to your personal care. Her name is Andrea Isbik. She was born a Muslim, but like many Sarajevans, her family were agnostics whose children were educated by the communist state. Her mother may have been Jewish. At least, we were able to make a case for this to the U.N. commissioner for refugees, who arranged her emigration to Israel after a brief stay in Rome. For seven months after her parents were killed she was kept in a Serbian POW camp unequaled for brutality and horror. The girl has experienced things no child should ever have to. She will not speak of her time there. For five months after she was released she lived in my house and demonstrated a miraculous (I do not use this word lightly) aptitude for languages and philosophy. She speaks her native Bosnian dialect, Turkish, Albanian, and Serbo-Croatian, as well as English, Russian, German, and Hebrew (these last two she learned from me). She is a seemingly simple child who might appear poorly developed to the casual observer. She is, I assure you, both brilliant and blessed. I have sent her to you in memory of that day long ago when you said, "I will do anything for you, my dear Father Eustratius!" I now hold you to your word.

Your elder by one year,

Eustratius

Sarajevo, A.D. 1995

In addition to this letter, the tube contained the girl's birth certificate, a lyceum registration form, a letter from the U.N. commissioner for refugees, the Israeli reply, a transcript of school grades, a faded photograph of a little school girl with her mother and father, and a rosewood rosary intended as a gift from Father Eustratius to Abbess Ingeborg.

Mother Superior was touched. She did not know the nature of the promises the priest and nun had made to each other, but she imagined the scene a half century ago in a Vatican portico: Abbess Ingeborg and Father Eustratius bowed together in prayer. Her predecessor had been a Montenegran princess before taking the veil.

Mother Superior was baffled by the formality of the old priest's letter. Saint Hildegard Hospice had long had a school for orphans attached to it. The world was a broken place; orphans came to the school from the civil-war-riven countries of the former Soviet Union, from Africa's wars, Pakistan's starvation zones, Asia's dust bowls. No child would have been turned away. There was hardly need for such an elaborate reminder of a past debt. But maybe that was simply a way to underscore how special this girl was.

Mother Superior was also confused by the date. The old priest's letter was dated four years before. Where had Andrea Isbik been for four years? And how old was she? These mysteries had to be investigated before any decision was taken about allowing her to stay. Four years was a long time. The hurt child of 1995 was now a young woman, and surely different from the girl Father Eustratius had known.

Sister Rodica, happy that Mother Superior wasn't angry at her for opening the gate after ten, led her to the small storage room where she had made a bed for the girl. Andrea was still sleeping. She had thrown off her covers during the night, and sprawled unself-consciously naked under a black crucifix, a pale admixture of child and young woman. The two tiny buds atop her small breasts were blood red. The rest of her was skin and bones. Her brownish red hair didn't quite reach her sharp shoulder blades.

Mother Superior smiled. "This one needs to be fed," she pronounced. She looked around at the clutter in the room, where things no longer useful to the convent had been stored for the past four hundred years. Large trunks full of forgotten belongings were piled on top of one another like a child's blocks. Dusty shelves crammed with worn books, dented chalices, and torn habits climbed to the ceiling.

"One day we'll have to let some air in here," she sighed.

The little room stood atop a maze of tunnels that had once served as an escape route out of the city. The nuns of the order were buried in the tunnel walls, beginning with the founders, who were directly below the room. The graves of centuries-dead Sister Marias and Sister Rodicas stretched out toward the old walls of Jerusalem. The entrance to the catacombs was below Andrea's bed, an old hospital cot with two blankets on it.

Chapter Three

Wherein a distraught Felicity is consoled by her uncle with a great dinner and a job

h e spacious proportions of Major Notz's apartment did little to disguise the impression of his formidable bulk. He came to the door dressed in a crisply pressed World War I British naval officer's uniform. As usual, he exuded smoke, a lit pipe in hand. At home he always smoked pipes. In public, cigars only.

"Goodness," said Felicity. "It's Lord Nelson at Trafalgar."

"Close, close. World War One. Come in, my dear, come!"

The major folded his adopted niece in his tremendous arms, bathing her in a comforting effluvium of smoke, both new and ancient: the trapped air of his youth, essence of cigarillos, homegrown backyard tobacco, butts relit from overflowing ashtrays, now mingled with the luxury tobaccos of prosperous middle age. His aroma was one of her primal delights. Felicity liked to imagine each of these varieties smoked in one of the myriad perilous situations that constituted the major's past. Cigarillos in Cuba, training a squad of assassins to take out Castro. Hashish-tipped cigarettes smoked on horseback, crossing the snowy mountains, smuggling guns to Afghan fighters. Hand-rolled in a Siberian jail. Lipsticked filter tips left smoking in whorehouse ashtrays in Istanbul.

These scenarios were the fairy tales of her childhood. Uncle Notz had often put her to sleep with bedtime stories probably still considered highly classified by the National Security Agency. Many evenings they sat in Grandmère's jasmine-scented yard, Felicity planted on his enormous lap, while he whispered these stories gravely in her ear. They snuggled this way well into her fourteenth year, when Grandmère noticed that Felicity was growing breasts. Vestigial, it's true, but breasts. This having been noted, Felicity had to content herself with sitting on a lawn chair facing her uncle and listening to his stories from this unaccustomed position. She did get some revenge on Grandmère, though, because now, instead of sinking into the warmth of Major Notz's comforting flesh, she sat with legs uncrossed in the hope that he might catch a glimpse of her pubescent down, which, unlike her breasts, grew early and luxuriously. But Notz continued to tell his bizarre tales undistracted late into the mosquito-slapping summer evenings, ending them inevitably with a huge sigh: "The world just can't go on like this, it can't!"

On her birthday and Christmas he gave her games like Chinese checkers and a Rubik's Cube because "the world is complicated, dear Felix, and you have to learn it to undo it." Oddly enough, because he abhorred television and missed no opportunity to excoriate it, he gave her a home version of the television show *Wheel of Fortune.* He made her a present of the game with instructions to "get deep into words, because there are word magicians out there who do with words what they can't even do with bombs."

On the other hand, Grandmère watched television continually, particularly religious programming. Felicity did her homework for years to the Christian Broadcasting Network until, mercifully, the major gave her a Sony Discman and a complete set of Beethoven's symphonies. Just how much television she absorbed before blocking it out is an open question. Probably more than she needed, and less than she wanted. She read *Twenty Thousand Leagues Under the Sea, A Connecticut Yankee in King Arthur's Court, A Thousand and One Nights, The Count of Monte Cristo, The Idiot,* with the television on—and Captain Nemo, Scheherazade, the Yankee, and Raskolnikov crossed wires with Oral Roberts, Jeremy "Elvis" Mullin, and Jimmy Swaggart and came out slightly drunk with hallelujas and smelling of fried chicken. The books, too, were gifts from the major, who was a river of goodwill, a cornucopia of important ideas.

On Sundays he took her out to Antoine's or Galatoire's for pompano or soft-shell crab. She always dressed up for these occasions and tried to be ladylike, though she couldn't always control her feet, which swung back and forth under the table in their shiny black patent leather shoes.

At fifteen she lost her appetite for both food and life, and decided to quit eating and living. She was diagnosed manic-depressive and was declared officially depressed by the school psychologist. The major told her that it was not a disease but merely her body's way of sympathizing with suffering. She was at that age of extreme sensitivity, when the material world seems crass and evil. He taught her to sip peach nectar and honey with a glass straw from a thin rose jar. At sixteen the psychologist added attention deficit disorder (ADD) and borderline personality to her profile and put her on Ritalin and Xanax, and then Zoloft and Prozac. The major predicted that the pills would change nothing. At first, the pills changed everything. She became, by turns, calm, attentive, vacant, unemotional, sociable, adaptive, cunning, clever, clumsy, suicidal, bewildered—and addicted to oysters. She rode an elevator of personal attitudes and changes until she became stable within a long-term depression brought about by lithium salt. Throughout the whole of her journey through the hells of American adolescence, Major Notz stood patiently by, first with peach nectar, then with the whole range of his considerable gourmandise. He led her from oysters to other mollusks, then to shellfish, to merlitons, star fruit, and tiramisù. He snorted indignantly at the ogres of psychiatry counting out her pills, but did not interfere until she had herself realized their inefficacy.

So you could say he raised her. But Major Notz didn't just say that he raised her. The major believed that he had raised her to be something special. Something so special, in fact, that he hadn't yet revealed it to her. She had disappointed him. He'd wanted to send her to Princeton to study engineering and ancient languages, but Felicity had other ideas. Her journey through the shifting sands of her psyche and her reading of Dostoyevsky had made her interested in psychology. She had also read Conan Doyle and Agatha Christie, authors who'd made her interested in unraveling criminal mysteries. "Ultimately," she told the major, "I will discover the crime that led to all my unhappiness, and the guilty will be punished. Isn't that *special?*"

She said it in that special Southern way, and it infuriated the Major. That was not the "special" he meant, and never in *that* way. They argued strenuously. The major had only contempt for psychology. "People," he shouted, "no longer have any inner lives! You want to know what's in them, watch commercials!" He felt somewhat less hostile to detective work and to her understanding of it, if indeed she meant it to be a seeking for clues of "vast crimes, so vast they have gone unreported!" He seemed to refer to crimes other than the one crime she had in mind, but she let it slide. She let slide also his remark that "the drawback to solving crimes is losing precious time for committing them."

She had no idea what he meant by that, but they forged a compromise. Felicity went to the University of New Orleans, and the major approved and paid for her study of psychology. She enlisted in the Police Academy, completing the course without taking the police exam. Six months after graduation she'd received her PI license, but one year later she was still waiting for a "vast crime." She had converted the front room of her street-level apartment into an office, and waited there like Sam Spade, playing with her brand-new nine-millimeter Beretta, taking admittedly ladylike sips from the bottle of Maker's Mark she kept in the empty left-hand drawer of the desk. It was a good thing that the last installments of the survivor benefit that had accrued to her after her daddy's "accidental" death in an undeclared Central American war still had eighteen months to go.

"Am I still your special one?" Felicity half teased him now as she followed him down the hallway, lined with the uniforms of several dozen armies. Major Notz's was the most comprehensive collection of military uniforms in the South.

"Why, sweet pea, whatever might cause you to ask such a thing?"

Felicity sank with what she hoped was some grace into a leather fauteuil in the living room. In front of her, silver Roman centurions faced a legion of brass Persians on the chess table. She decided to get to the point of her visit.

"She's dead, Uncle."

"Oh, child."

The usually loquacious major fell uncharacteristically silent, unable to offer either condolences for the old woman, whom he'd hated with a passion, or congratulations to Felicity, who was now unencumbered and ready to embark on her mission. Which he hadn't yet revealed to her.

"I feel for you, child," he finally said, and patted her spiky bleached head. It melted her tough front, and she burst into a long sequence of sobs, the longest of her entire life. Sobbing was no longer in her repertoire: she despised "weepy women." But these sobs were not just for Grandmère; they were for her parents, for Miles, for herself, for the whole world.

Notz listened attentively, as if hearing a piece of rare music, nodding his head now and then at a difficult passage. When Felicity subsided, he handed her a monogrammed kerchief and patted her head again.

"I will cook for you. Divine substances. The Creole cuisine of your forebears. We'll send Marie-Frances Claire off with a meal of Catholic splendor and tropical excess."

Major Notz rose like Zeus and headed for the kitchen, followed closely by his niece. Like the rest of his rooms, the kitchen was partly a museum. Hanging on the brick wall above a large fireplace shone copper and gold sieves from around the world. A collection of ladles was arrayed longitudinally between two narrow windows, and a mahogany bookcase held cookbooks in fifteen languages. The major pulled open a nearly hidden drawer below the range and extracted a stack of papers.

"Mmm. Mmm. Mmm." After each of these significant "mmm's," the major made a little note. Finally, he phoned in an order to Langenstein's for a pound of turtle meat, one mild goat cheese, six soft-shell crabs, one can of cucumber relish. This done, he checked a cabinet and concluded that he had sherry and white truffle oil.

Felicity followed his deliberations with interest. From the high stool behind the range she could see down the hall to the major's bedroom. The walls were entirely lined with well-kept bookshelves containing, as she knew, volumes on comparative religion, occultism, philosophy, and manuscript reports of various kinds from one of the hundreds of secret associations Major Notz monitored or belonged to. On the counter in front of her was a red apple. Felicity picked it with a fingernail to make sure it was real (she had bitten into a wax one before) and then took three bites.

The major glanced over. "Always three bites. Why?"

"The first is knowledge, the second shame, the third rage."

"Well said, bright eyes."

The major probed the truffle oil with the corkscrew of his thick Swiss army knife. Felicity loved that knife. She remembered the time he had removed the little tweezers and zinged it in her ear. It hummed perfect C, like a tuning fork. Like the other minutiae to which the major attended, this was not without significance. He told her that this perfect C had saved his life when he was held hostage in Lebanon, when he discovered that the chief guerrilla holding him had been a Cal State music student. He also contended that this note was a key element in an occult musical phrase, a Rosicrucian code known only to high initiates.

"You are very special indeed. At this moment of sorrow for you, your life is in fact beginning." He sniffed the tip of the oiled corkscrew and grunted approvingly. "You remember the grand mission I once predicted for you?"

"Well, I'm still in the dark. Mission impossible. My mysterious benefactor has revealed nothing to me yet."

"That's true. It's up to you to discover it. However"—the major raised a very fat and very long forefinger above the knife—"you have to begin training intellectually and emotionally."

Felicity gave a skeptical snort. "Right now I feel like shit. I used to think that one third of me was gone; now I'm sure there is only half." She clicked her tongue stud against her teeth.

The major disliked vulgarity. "Dirty words are potent. If you trivialize them by casual usage, you deprive yourself of a weapon. In your line of work you need every weapon you can get."

"Jesus Christ! Grandmère just died. My boyfriend overdosed a year ago almost to the day. My so-called profession has so far earned me about three hundred bucks a month. I took pictures of six guys getting . . . well, committing adultery in their ten-year-old cars, I found somebody's dog, and I think I solved the great mystery of a twelve-year-old kid breaking into parking meters. If this is my great destiny, I think I'll jump in the river and drown!"

"Things always look darkest just 'fore dawn," said the major. "As a matter of fact, there is a little job I would like you to do for me."

"Nepotism, Uncle?"

"It's the way of the world. If you look on my desk you'll find a file. It's an old case. I would like you to go over it again, see if anything was overlooked."

On the desk, a Louis XIV escritoire, she found a manila file. It contained clippings from the *New Orleans Times-Picayune*.

Felicity remembered the story. Five years before, a young actress named Kashmir Birani disappeared in New Orleans. She had been the hostess of *Kismet Chakkar*, India's *Wheel of Fortune*, and her grandfather Sajat Birani had been India's most popular movie star in the fifties and sixties. Her distraught mother and father came to New Orleans and searched the dives their bohemian-inclined daughter had frequented. They even employed psychics to find her, to no avail. A report that she had drowned in the river turned out to be bogus. She was never found. The police had pursued leads in the French Quarter, where Kashmir had been friendly with the street musicians. She had befriended a trumpet player who called himself Bamajan.

The name rang a bell. Felicity had known someone by that name, a friend and occasional accompanist of Miles's. Someone from the drug side of the scene. Miles had kept quite a few of his friends from her. This one left a chill behind him. She had met him only once, leaving the apartment, though she'd listened to him play beside Miles. He was methodical, with a precise but dark style that complemented perfectly Miles's romantic complexity. The *Times-Picayune* didn't pay him much attention, beyond the brief mention. The articles described the Indian star as a voracious reader and jazz lover who periodically fled her glamorous life with a backpack full of books and her journals. She had been writing a novel at the time of her disappearance, but the manuscript had never been found. One item surprised Felicity so much she nearly dropped the clipping. The bohemian actress had apparently spent some time singing in Reverend Jeremy "Elvis" Mullin's First Angels Choir. It was bizarre. Why would a hip girl like Kashmir attend Mullin's tacky, self-righteous Christian tabernacle, where everything she must have enjoyed was denounced?

The copied newspaper photo of Kashmir was bad, but one could still make out large black eyes, pronounced eyebrows, a full mouth. She must have been quite beautiful. Felicity had trouble imagining what had attracted this pampered, upper-class, glamorous girl to the scuzziest dives of New Orleans. She had known a few Indian women of Kashmir's class in college—they were spoiled, argumentative, and witty. They dressed in expensive, fashionable clothes. Kashmir had been made of something else. Felicity could imagine the route by which the girl might have arrived at a love of jazz and Beat books; American hipsterism had circumvented the globe. There were even Samoan beatniks. But Mullin? How had she found him?

Mullin. She'd really love to get Mullin. "Okay, I'll take the job, but what's your interest in this case?"

"It's a long story. I'll tell you over dinner."

The major introduced the dishes with a flourish. He set them on the damask-covered dining room table and lifted their silver lids one by one.

"Turtle soup with sherry," he intoned, revealing a satiny broth signed with a squiggle of amber sherry. "Mixed wild greens with warm goat cheese. And the pièce de résistance: soft-shell crabs with wilted greens rémoulade aioli!" The major held the lid up long enough for her to see the perfectly poached soft-shell crabs steaming on their green mounds, swimming in the red rémoulade. "And, of course, bread pudding with whiskey sauce!"

Felicity was moved—the meal was a replica of her sixteenth-birthday dinner at the Grill Room of the Fairmont Hotel. She still had the menu in a cheap frame tacked to her bedroom wall. The major's creation was perfect in every detail. Aromas filled the air as the early winter evening fell over the rooftops of the Vieux Carré, turning the room deep purple. They ate slowly.

"Your interest in the Vanna White of India?" Felicity reminded him between spoonfuls of velvety soup.

"A long time ago . . . ," began the major.

Damn. One of *those* stories. Despite her impatience, Felicity couldn't help but be charmed. The major's stories were hypnotic.

"A long time ago, a small number of secret societies began to make plans for the future of the human race. And when I say a long time ago, I mean almost directly after the expulsion of the apple-chomping couple from the garden."

"Major," Felicity protested weakly.

"Be patient. I won't drag you through the history of the occult network underlying human events. I'm just providing a context, or maybe a metaphor. In this case, Judeo-Christianity is both the context and the metaphor. Some of these secret associations pursued their aims through contacts in the spirit world. . . . You believe in the spirit world, don't you, darling?"

"No," Felicity said flatly.

"No matter. I'm using 'the spirit world' provisionally. Another metaphor. One of these societies, whose name may not mean much to you, was the Knights Templar. High initiates of that order embarked on the study of coincidence, chance, and chaos. Their techniques gave them access to what they called angelic informants."

"You mean angels?" interrupted Felicity.

"Special angels. Informants. Not all angels inform. Some of them obfuscate. They are a lot like people. May I continue?"

"Sure." Felicity was beginning to feel grumpy.

"The Knights Templar knew the hidden symmetry that underlies existence, just as atomic structure does matter. They knew that nothing is unrelated, that creation is a cosmic wheel, and the wheel is subject to the laws of chaos."

"Does it matter?"

"Darling, how do you like the soup? Too much sherry?"

"Not at all." The soup was divine. "These knights, what did they do? Bring sherry to Louisiana?"

"They were warriors and scholars. They insured the safety of pilgrims to the Holy Land, established the world's first banking system, and were seemingly wiped out of existence by the pope and the French king. In reality, they retreated to secret hideouts until recently."

"And now they are bringing sherry to the Third World!"

The major ignored her. "They are now waging a great battle, perhaps *the* final battle, against a host of enemies relaying their messages through television. One of these evil forces may be deploying the power of the Language Crystal, a sophisticated linguistic mechanism that reprograms the left-right brain. Based in Sanskrit, the Language Crystal can operate in all Indo-European languages, which is but one reason why I wanted you to study languages."

This mild reproach, delivered without rancor, stung Felicity. "Well, Uncle, I can find your Vanna without speaking Sanskrit. I'm sure her English is quite adequate." She ripped a leg off her crab and bit into it. The crunchy, peppery snap was satisfying and resonant. The forces and spirits were far from such immediacy.

"I don't think I shall ever grasp a spirit as fleshy as this crab," improvised Felicity, with her mouth full.

The major smiled; improvising parodies was one of his mannerisms. Felicity had picked it up when she'd been about ten. But now he was attempting to teach her something extremely important, and her flippancy was inappropriate.

"Darling, please try to concentrate. Forget about what is in front of your nose for a moment. There is a symphony going on within the din of our daily noise. We speak words that contain divine sounds, we write words within which lie hidden meanings. You can puzzle out the true nature of your life by simply hearing or seeing common words. Take your name, 'Felicity.' It means 'happiness.' "

"Yeah, right."

"But within it," continued the major without hearing her, "there is also a 'city' and 'fel.' You might say that 'a city fell' to bring about the 'happiness' you embody. What city? When? You see, the simple act of breaking your name into syllables has already yielded a mystery. This is a only a bit of light from the Language Crystal. Now imagine the brilliant power of the crystal brought to bear on our sacred texts, on our officials' speeches, as well as on our daily talk. The hidden meanings will be revealed at once! The Language Crystal, which has passed through many hands in the past, may be active again."

"Whoa," exclaimed Felicity. "You mean this crystal is an actual thing, like the Grail? A real gem?"

"Possibly."

"Wait a minute, Uncle. What you just did with my name is in anyone's power to do. Everybody's got a crystal like that in their own brain. All you need is to squint a little, or mishear."

The major put up his immense white palms in a gesture of peace.

"I won't argue this. A small piece of the crystal probably does lodge in everyone. But the Language Crystal itself is a much greater force, an unparalleled object. Suffice it to say that its uses seem to have been forgotten until now. This Indian Vanna, as you call her, may have inadvertently produced sound combinations in Sanskrit that proved to be quite potent, and she activated the old sound machine."

"But television is a visual medium," Felicity argued, sensibly.

"That's exactly it! Everyone is looking for significance in the images, but the visual is only a cover. Humming beneath it is the Language Crystal."

Felicity was only too familiar with the major's contention that conspiratorial groups were working to influence events in preparation for a cataclysm that would end human history. Now he was insisting on a new element of the story, and Felicity was quite put off. Her world was in pieces, and the thought of the worldwide conspiracy did little to soothe her.

She spoke sharply: "Which am I supposed to find? The crystal, or the girl? Is the disappearance of this unfortunate girl cosmically significant?"

Notz said tersely: "We must do everything in our power to recover the crystal."

"Anything? Loosen the plagues? Nuke the metaphors?"

"Maybe. The crystal is no metaphor."

A brief silence filled with sherry, crab, and poetry passed.

"Oh, Uncle!"

"Darling," the major sighed, "I could trace for you, step by step, the quite reasonable chain of events that lead from Edenic hyperspace to the nuclear age to Kashmir's disappearance, but I'm not sure—"

"Edenic hyperspace?"

"A description of the state prior to the one that most traditions insist is now ending. The point is, in helping me find Kashmir you will begin to fulfill the mission I've always imagined for you. More crab, darling?"

Felicity was irritated—her mentor had chosen the wrong time to try to involve her in his obsessions. All she was interested in was Mullin's con-

nection to the disappearance of the TV star who liked jazz and Jack Ker-
ouac. What did occult traditions, humming crystals have to do with it?
And this End of the World business, she was sick of it. The newspapers
were full of apocalyptic hokeyness.

"Somehow," she said bitterly, "the end of the world is contingent on my
finding the vanished Vanna. Am I reading this correctly?"

"In a way." Notz was not satisfied with her grasp of matters. By this
time, she should have seen more. Then again, she didn't have a psychic adviser who could see simultaneously into the past and into the future as he
did. The channeler Carbon was due later that evening for a channeling
session.

"Must be Vannageddon," she teased.

"Put crudely, yes." The major was displeased. "You aren't listening very
well. This Vannageddon, as you call it, is a specific event, followed by specific aftermaths, and it concerns everyone, especially *you*."

"No, Uncle, it doesn't concern me right now. Maybe you should be
talking to that fundamentalist Bible freak, Jeremy 'Elvis' Mullin. He'd tell
you it's all in the Bible. The four horses and all. The Antichrist. The Second Coming. Probably even Vanna White."

"The Second Coming," Notz insisted, "what do you know about it?"
Oh, no, Felicity thought, now he's going to quote that hoary old Yeats
poem.

Sure enough, the major began to recite:

> Surely some revelation is at hand;
> Surely the Second Coming is at hand.
> The Second Coming!

I'd love to come just once, Felicity complained silently.

> Hardly are those words out
> When a vast image out of *Spiritus Mundi*
> Troubles my sight: somewhere in the sands of the desert
> A shape with lion body and the head of a man,
> A gaze blank and pitiless as the sun,
> Is moving its slow thighs—

That, she couldn't help noting, was pretty sexy. Her own thighs felt
suddenly quite soft. How long had it been since she had slowly moved

them apart, submitting to the head of a man with a lion's body? Probably never. Miles was skinny, with the body of a scrawny cat, and Ben had been no lion either, although his head was quite leonine.

> while all about it
> Reel shadows of the indignant desert birds.
> The darkness drops again; but now I know
> That twenty centuries of stony sleep
> Were vexed to nightmare by a rocking cradle—

The cradle was not to be. She had decided a long time ago that she would not bring into the world something to die. Sometimes she thought that her elusive pleasure had perhaps retreated from her after she'd made this decision. She had denied death life; and death, displeased, had taken her orgasm. Hey, Death, Felicity called, give it back, bitch!

> And what rough beast, its hour come round at last,
> Slouches toward Bethlehem to be born?

Dear Uncle. He always was, in an unpredictable way, predictable. Felicity loved his voice, rich as bread pudding with whiskey sauce.

"And if," Notz went on, still in the voice of the poem, "a cradle can rock the centuries, may not a wheel spin them? Why not the Wheel of Fortune watched by millions? The wheel of chance from which are born phrases and clues, things and mysteries? The gyre in a falconer's hand? *Kismet Chakkar?* Could not such vulgar wheels display the signs to the multitude? Well, answer me, what could be better?"

Felicity couldn't argue. Grief had made her gluttonous, and she felt as stuffed as a merliton. The food, spreading its delicious warmth through her, was making her sleepy.

"The point is," the major was saying, reverting to the proper subject of the conversation, Felicity herself, "that I believe you when you say that there is only half of you. Love, and the loss of it, leaves huge holes in us. Christ, who reputedly loved everyone, was like a sieve by the time he died, nearly transparent. You may not understand this yet, but one of my gifts is to look at a person and be able to determine just how much of them there is. Most people, trust me, have had extraordinarily large chunks removed. Their souls are miniscule, like commas in the compact *OED.*"

"So . . . am I going to be whole? Or what? Where is my missing half?"

"Your other half is coming," said the major, peering into his bread pudding as if he saw someone in there.

"I hope you don't mean my better half. I hope it's not this Indian babe, anyway," Felicity said gloomily. She didn't know if her uncle understood her sexual dilemma. In truth, she didn't either. She had successfully seduced a girl she'd met at the Rubyfruit Jungle, but the encounter had confused her. Her pleasure had been as elusive as when she'd sought it with Ben Redman, whose uncomfortably large penis had distressed her terribly. Ben, dear Ben, her first boyfriend, was a high school jazz connoisseur, veteran of medication identical to hers, now rabbi extraordinaire. With Miles she'd felt something approaching physical satisfaction, but his junk habit had made physical intimacy a rare occurrence. It's a good thing she wasn't as paranoid as the major, or she'd believe she was the victim of an evil conspiracy.

Felicity was nearly asleep as she filled her mouth with a spoon of bread pudding that exploded there with pungent sweetness.

"Your mission, then," concluded the major, ending off a long speech she'd barely heard, "is to *wait* for specifics."

"My dear Uncle," Felicity said formally, "I would be very grateful to you if at this dramatic moment in my life and at this late hour, you would tell me the truth as simply as you can."

"Of course, darling. Everything in creation is subject to a sequence. Before anything *is*, there is something else, and before that *something*, there is something else. You are familiar, I am sure, with theological attempts to pin everything on a Prime Mover. I have no opinion about that. What I do believe, however, is that the sequence moves according to a will that *wills* it to go on. I have undertaken the modest task of exercising *my* will to take part in the sequencing of creation."

"Is that all?" said Felicity. "Isn't that, I don't know . . . presumptous?"

"Doubtless. Which is why one must make sure that nothing is left to chance. We must be well informed."

Felicity wasn't sure she understood. But she was too tired to investigate such loftiness. Before they called it a night, they needed to discuss the funeral.

"The old woman ought to lay in state at her own house," the major said.

"There is hardly anyone left, Major. All her contemporaries are dead, and nobody in the family spoke to her after she left the church and tore up that lottery ticket."

"Be that as it may, the woman embodies the twentieth century. You can't quickly dispatch such a person."

"She's not a book, Uncle. She's a corpse. And anyway, what's so great about the twentieth century? Stony sleep, was it? Good riddance, I say. I don't see the point of any nostalgia. Anyone who survived it must have had either plain dumb luck or a deal with the devil."

The major couldn't suppress his smile. "How you talk—and there is only half of you! I shudder to think of the complete creature."

"I would like to bury her tomorrow, Major." Felicity was determined. "I don't want that slimeball, Mullin, there, but I suppose I'll have to let him officiate. Grandmère trusted him."

For the sake of propriety then, but also for reasons of a residual affection (Felicity's) and grudging respect (the major's), they had more wine and recalled the old woman in all her crazy steadfastness. She had taken uncomplaining and strict care of Felicity after her mother's desertion. She had faced poverty with a big black purse, from which an inexhaustible supply of small change always poured forth. She had refused Notz's money, though he managed, through Felicity, to help. Marie-Frances Claire Le Bec stood up to authorities and was feared in many lousy city offices. She had been a talented seamstress, skilled enough to copy even fancy clothes. Before the conversion to Mullinism, she had cooked meals for the nuns, taking a pot of red beans and rice every Monday to our Lady of Perpetual Succor Chapel.

Felicity closed her eyes, swimming through the major's words like a nymph through seaweed. A shadowy figure that was her missing half was swimming toward her from very far away. The world's secret societies were weaving their nets above and below her, and Felicity let herself be lulled by the story just as in the old days, when she'd been a special little girl with a special great mission in a future so unimaginably wonderful only sleep could make it bearable.

Notz carried his niece to the guest bedroom and laid her down on a baldachin bed that had belonged to Teresa de Avila before her vision. After, she lived an ascetic life and slept on the stone floor of the convent cell, where she wrote mystical love poetry. Major Notz delighted in collecting artifacts belonging to saintly converts of the upper classes who left their luxuries behind for lives of poverty. The major saw himself as a specialized bird of prey who followed behind the saints, hunting their abandoned belongings. He would have given anything to own something of Gautama's, but his belongings, like those of Muhammad, had long ago been worn out by the superstitious pawing of followers seeking miracles.

The major surveyed the sleeping form of his rebellious niece and tried to hold at bay the affection that always threatened at such moments. He could not allow himself the all too human indulgence of sentiment if she was going to fulfill her destiny and his plan. Viewed from above, there really wasn't that much to the girl. She had bony knees, and her long, skinny legs looked like they needed a shave, and her feet needed scrubbing. Her eyes were shut too tight, and her breasts pointed up like two Mongol mini helmets. Even in sleep she seemed coiled up, ready to strike, unable to leave the world completely behind.

"My angry little Messiah, my Dulcinea-cum-Christ," murmured Notz, as if that were a dish he might whip up.

Chapter Four

Wherein the sisters of Saint Hildegard Hospice are
seen to wonder about the girl Andrea,
her habits, and her charm

 l t h o u g h they couldn't say exactly what was wrong with the girl, something clearly was. She was sick. Sometimes she shone as if she had a fever. Her eyes looked past everyone. When he first saw her, Father Hernio pronounced: "I have seen this in the eyes of other youths. She has the virus of indifference!"

Father Hernio had been observing the Shades and neotribals who gathered in Jerusalem's bohemian coffeehouses. Some of them had bones in their noses and earlobes. Their faces and bodies were sometimes completely covered with tattoos. One man had fifteen bronze studs in his face, like a pincushion. Another had a complete brain tattooed on the surface of his shaved head. And some had what appeared to be an entire body inscribed over their own. These disfigurements, thought the priest, implied a degree of faith in the future. Such skins could certainly not be discarded when the body died. Surely they would be dried and preserved. But the body art also implied an absence of faith in present-day life. In the eyes of these youths Father Hernio detected the virus of indifference.

But the sisters knew that Andrea was not sick from indifference; she was traumatized by what she had seen and experienced. There was a difference! Sisters Rodica and Maria busied themselves feeding Andrea, as if fattening her up was as great a task as teaching orphans, which they also did.

Andrea stubbornly refused to communicate beyond the occasional "Thank you," in English, but now and then, as she had in the case of Mr. Rabindranath, she delivered an opinion in Hebrew.

But if her mind did not permit her to trust her new home, her body had no such scruples. A week of the good sisters' ministrations resulted in all sorts of new curves and little plumpnesses where before there had been only skin taut over bone. Her cheeks changed from deathly pale to a marble-pink hue, and her hips and even her behind showed promise of womanliness.

Sister Rodica sometimes felt awkward in Andrea's presence, particularly when she failed to observe any modesty. The young woman commenced to project an unabashed carnality that wafted off her like attar. She loped like a feline when she walked, and the sweater over the nightgown she sometimes wore to bed was no impediment to her newly assertive breasts. God forgive her, but Sister Rodica acquired a permanent blush. In comparison with Andrea's troubling young flesh, Mr. Rabindranath's penis— which, since the first incident, had floated into the foyer one other embarrassing time—was like a discarded section of garden hose. While watering the convent's ten thousand roses, Sister Rodica had smiled at the comic hose in her hand. But Andrea was another matter, particularly since the sister had undertaken to teach the Bosnian girl about the life of Christ, a task that required standing close enough to bask in her animal heat.

In reproach to Andrea's unconscious sensuality, Sister Rodica dwelt unduly long on the story of Mary Magdalene's inability to enter Mother Mary's house in Gethsemane.

"The Magdalene tried three times to enter Mary's house, and three times she failed. The weight of her sins pulled her back." And: "Mary's purity stopped the Magdalene three times. Three times."

"Then why," asked Andrea, proving that she was a diligent student, "was the Magdalene the first to see Jesus after his resurrection?"

"He forgave her," Sister Rodica said, and thought to herself: Just like a man; I bet Mary didn't. And then she crossed herself, feeling blasphemous.

"I forgot, I just plain forgot about Mr. Rabindranath! I heard he did it again today," said Sister Maria, barging in and interrupting Sister Rodica's cautionary tale of the Magdalene. "I didn't see him actually floating, but I heard him chanting verses, and I smelled burnt milk coming from his room!"

"That," said Sister Rodica petulantly, wrinkling her nose in distaste, "was absolutely forbidden by Mother Superior, but he keeps doing it!"

"Part of his religion. Milk is offered to Pasupati, an ithyphallic god!" Andrea said in English.

"What is . . . ithy . . . ?" Sister Rodica asked, her red cheeks blazing.

The answer didn't relieve her embarrassment.

"A god with a big erect penis!" Andrea blurted.

The nuns crossed themselves. Andrea was clearly improving. Humor, Sister Rodica knew, was proof of recovery. Soon, Andrea might be able to leave the guest house and live with the other children, in the convent dormitory. There was, however, one impediment. Andrea was extraordinarily messy. To the sisters' heightened sense of discipline and cleanliness, the girl's behavior was nothing less than shocking. She managed to scatter her few items of clothing widely and disrespectfully. The trunks and shelves in the storage room might have been crammed, but even in that state they projected a German sense of order. One of her socks ended up suspended from the light fixture on the ceiling. One of her shoes fell from the windowsill into the garden. She never put anything away. She moved constantly, leaving whatever she happened to be holding wherever she put it down. She then spent nervous minutes searching for the lost item. Most shocking, she had absolutely refused to bathe more than once. She sprawled when she talked to people, often exposing more flesh than was seemly. Her clothes were wrinkled, bunched, and twisted. Her hair took on astonishing shapes, covering half her face. Often she chewed on a stray lock, pursing her lips in unconscious delight. She gave the impression of a storm, but she was so youthful, so fresh, and so unconcerned that everyone inhaled her scent deeply rather than turning away. And of course, Sister Rodica's reproaches rolled off her like water off a mirror. At least that is how Sister Rodica, rather fancifully, put it to herself.

Sister Rodica prayed as hard as she could for two things: one, that Andrea would soon regain her health and begin to forget the terrible things that must have happened to her in the camp, and two, that the inappropriate attraction she felt for the girl would be channeled immediately into stronger faith. Sister Rodica, like most of the other nuns, was refusing to consider the mysterious gap of four years in Andrea's biography. She believed that her memories of war were still fresh, which explained the girl's absent behavior.

Sister Maria was fascinated by Andrea as well, but for other reasons. She could not forget the girl's luminiscent eyes looking up at her the night she had arrived. Her eyes had never again achieved that feverish intensity, but Sister Maria felt to the depths of her soul that Andrea was not an earthly being. She would have been hard put to describe what kind of being she believed Andrea to be. She was certainly not an evil being, not one of the legions of Satan's minions; but neither was she holy, in the way Maria conceived it. Holy was modest like beeswax, sweet like honey, having the sound of crystal. Something with wings and flesh woven of mild light. Everything about Andrea bespoke fever and a stormy upcoming womanhood. Something hummed like an engine behind those green eyes, something bigger than the sister's imagination. And Sister Maria was more offended by Andrea's compulsive messiness because she, among the many neat German nuns, was the neatest. Her habit was so crisp it sounded like snapping leaves when she sat down. Not one of her lustrous black hairs showed underneath her wimple. Her shoes were polished to even perfection, and her rosy fingernails were rounded, pared, and ever clean. In Andrea she saw a repudiation of everything she spent her life perfecting.

Sister Rodica confessed her carnal feelings to Mother Superior, who admonished her to pray harder. The abbess was familiar with this important moment in the development of a young nun. It was the first of many critical tests of faith to come. She comforted the young woman with a tale from the life of Saint Teresa de Avila, who had spent much of her life inflamed by a passion she was finally able to transcend. The abbess promised to initiate Sister Rodica into the mysteries of flagellation. The Knights Templar, who had once lived in the confines of Saint Hildegard's, had been self-flagellators, too, and had bequeathed their blessed whips to the convent. One of these surely had Sister Rodica's name on it. The time had come to begin her journey of communal identity.

The younger nun certainly hoped so. Every day she found it harder to keep her feelings contained. They migrated like a swarm of bees to the surface of her skin and threatened to break out. She had prayed for relief on her bare knees on the stone floor, but her limits were being sorely tested. She craved the lashes of that purifying whip like water for thirst.

"Andrea," Mother Superior said, "has been sent to us for a very special reason, which we have not yet fathomed. Father Eustratius, blessed among men, named after the one who was martyred with Saint Orestes"—she had looked it up—"had an agreement with the blessed Mother Ingeborg to protect the soul of this orphan. You, Rodica, are now full of sinful and wicked thoughts which might endanger and spoil our gift. You must not attend to Andrea any longer. She will be the sole charge of Sister Maria."

This was a great blow to Sister Rodica, who cried herself to sleep that night. In the morning, though, she decided that it was for the best. Who knows where her attraction might lead? Saint Hildegard had been a virgin, a poetess, and a prophetess who had rebuked popes and princes, bishops and lay folk. How could Rodica ever aspire to stand in the sight of that great woman if she couldn't even gain control of her flesh? She looked forward to the Templars' whip, and in preparation, she lashed herself with a switch across her thighs and back until her body was like a wire mesh under her clean habit.

Sister Maria's confession, that Andrea might be otherworldly, was received more thoughtfully by Mother Superior. The possibility that Andrea might be an angel of some kind agreed with her own reasoning. Sister Ingeborg had been dead one year to the day when Andrea arrived. It was certainly miraculous. There was also the matter of the debt Father Eustratius mentioned. On the other hand, how could a Bosnian Muslim girl be an angel? She'd never even been baptized!

"Watch her carefully, Sister," Mother Superior advised the nun. "We can only hope and pray."

Sister Maria complained also of the girl's disorderly habits, which seemed impossible to correct. This was another proof, in her opinion, of demonic influence.

"It is possible," Mother Superior said, "that the girl completely lost her sense of boundaries during her sufferings. She may not know where she herself begins and ends, so she has no respect for anyone else's privacy or property."

This explanation satisfied neither woman, but it was the beginning of an attempt to understand the baffling creature who had landed in their midst.

Chapter Five

*Wherein Felicity Le Jeune sees Grandmère to her
final resting place, observes Reverend Mullin
in flagrante delicto, has an encounter with the
real America at Home Depot, stumbles on an
extraordinary Web page, and gets to practice her
profession by facing a very dangerous situation*

 h e burial of Marie-Frances Claire Le Bec attracted far more mourners to Saint Louis Cemetery No. 1 than Felicity had imagined would attend. Nearly a century of life had produced a great number of acquaintances. Most of the family had forgiven her defection from the church. Several relations of Felicity's, people in their seventies and eighties, came dressed in severe black and stood stoically by the Duclos–Le Jeune crypts. All in all, almost a hundred people huddled under the gray sky, while Mullin poured forth an insincere eulogy. Even some of the nuns had come, and Felicity wanted to rush over and kiss them, but something in their eyes stopped her. My God. They are disapproving of *me*. For a moment Felicity saw herself as they saw her: the girl arrested in sixth grade for spitting at a rent-a-cop who turned out to be epileptic. The high school junior who spent a night in lockup for trying to prevent the ousting of a homeless couple from the doorway of the mayor's house. The senior who chained herself to a tree the city was trying to cut down, and had to be freed with a blowtorch before being arrested. The fifteen-year-old who ate nothing but peach nectar through a straw and became so thin you could see the blue veins under the light cocoa skin. The simultaneously hyper and slurry speed and downer queen who teased every boy in her class in alphabetical order but never consummated the act

with any of them, though she signed all her notes "The Erotomaniac."
The college freshman who took off her clothes to protest the opening of a
Pizza Hut in the French Quarter.

But Sisters, Felicity cried telepathically in her own defense, these were
all acts of conscience. I have never joined a group and have nothing but
contempt for the throngs of delirious world enders and would-be saviors
who clog the streets and obstruct traffic, in whose ranks the old woman you
are burying ended up. That corpse has done more grievous harm than all
my acts of adolescent sickness and rebellion! But the nuns just turned their
heads and looked into the wind. A tear made its way down Felicity's cheek.

Felicity looked away, too. Charred chicken bones, half-smoked cigars,
used condoms, and shot glasses full of rum littered the graves where voodoo priestesses were reputedly interred. They believed in your Catholic
juju, too. I still remember all the crap you taught me, Sisters. I remember
that the soul is a garden, and prayer waters it in four ways: by irrigation, by
the waters of a stream, with a bucket from the well, or just rain. That's my
way. Just rain. Falling when it wants.

The major had paid for a coffin Grandmère would have hated for its os-
tentation. Felicity could imagine her inside the satin-lined box, calculating
the bags of groceries the $2,300 might have bought. Mountains of pota-
toes, carts full of round steak, beans for a lifetime, crawfish for seven years,
a river of catfish, a Niagara of milk. Grandmère's life had been evenly divided between food and God. Now she would have only one concern.

Standing at the major's voluminous flank, Felicity was aware of her
itchy black stockings and the ill-fitting black dress she had worn once before, at Miles's funeral. She congratulated herself for not wearing any
panties, though a chill breeze touched her now and then and she was shivering. She noticed two strange men standing behind Mullin. One of them
looked Pakistani or Indian, and the other had a brutal face.

"Mullin goes about with bodyguards," whispered the major, reading
her mind.

After the coffin was slid into its burial oven, Felicity said a silent good-
bye and couldn't help but admonish the old woman for leaving her with
the unpleasant task of sorting through a century of junk for disposal to the
Salvation Army. Grandmère had crammed trunks full of clothes and scraps
in the attic and had kept every cracked dish. In addition, there were thousands of dusty religious tracts and bundled-up church newsletters. Anything that might have been of value to Felicity she had destroyed after she
found Mullin.

When the service ended, Major Notz offered his niece a cup of hot chocolate at the Croissant d'Or, but Felicity declined. There was to be an elaborate repast for Grandmère's soul at the Autocrat Club, and she wanted to stay at the cemetery for a while to tend to her other dead.

Stacked in layers in their crypts like ancient loaves of bread eternally baking in the tropical sun were the people Felicity came from. Family legend had it that the bricks used to build the tombs came from the French Opera House, which had stood at Bourbon and Toulouse Streets and was destroyed by fire in 1866. "Our bricks are filled with music," Grandmère had said once, in a rare lyric moment. In New Orleans the dead led quite a lyrical existence, and were always present. Unlike the dead elsewhere, it was not possible to bury them in the ground—the water table was less than a foot below the surface. Felicity had heard of coffins floating out during floods and returning to the houses of their kin, who hadn't had them properly entombed.

At the bottom of the crypt was one Monsieur Robert Armant. She gazed at the eroded angel and the rusted iron cross on his marker, then took out a lace handkerchief and began to carefully scrub the name on the stone. Reasonably satisfied with the amount of grime she had removed from her great-great-great-uncle's grave, she next paused on the name of one Louis-Philogène Duclos, a more distant relative, whose begrimed inscription carried this ambiguous note: *Ci-gît Louis-Philogène Duclos, Enseigne dans les Troupes des Etats d'Amérique, Fils Légitime de Rodolphe-Joseph Duclos et de Marie-Lucie de Reggi. Né le 18 Août 1781. Décédé le 4 Juillet 1801.* This side of the tomb was smothered in leaves. A banana tree was growing straight out of its back. A bunch of black bananas threatened to fall on her ancestor at any moment. The ambiguity of the grave marker rested in the single word *légitime*, which signaled to anyone cognizant of New Orleans ways that Louis-Philogène had been the product of a Creole mistress's liaison with a French nobleman. Questions of legitimacy were debated to this day in Felicity's milieu, though, blessed be Saint Expédite, the intensity of the debate had diminished in the recent past.

Felicity had never attempted to hide her origins. Her café-au-lait skin was lighter than that of her Italian or Jewish friends, but she had never resorted to the easy palliative of the *passe-blanc*, passing for white. It was difficult to maintain her identity, and had she left New Orleans, she might have lost the incentive for doing so. But she had lived all of her young life with her grandmère in the neighborhood where she was born, a faubourg once called the Mistresses' Quarter. The faubourg retained the sadness of its former inhabitants, beautiful light-skinned women who had spent their lives watched over by anxious matriarchs, awaiting the rare visits of their married, aristrocratic lovers. Weeping willows hid the low, well-kept houses leaning into one another like veiled sighs. Grandmère's home, now hers, was a nineteenth-century building with a shady porch where Felicity, a little girl in a hammock, sometimes thought she could hear the monotonous plaint of a young woman going crazy behind the cypress beams. The sadness of the house seeped into her, and she kept it at bay by reading, reading, reading, endlessly reading the books the major brought her. Felicity thought about that young woman's lament now. She found her present situation akin to that of the light-skinned girl who had been bought at an Octoroon Ball by a rich man and virtually imprisoned in the house in the bloom of her youth. True, no one had chosen Felicity in this fashion, and her leash was much longer. Still, there was something helpless in the way her life had unfolded.

The last grave Felicity stopped for was new. She embraced the tomb drunkenly as if it were a man. It had been a man. Her man. Her love lay buried here in Saint Louis Cemetery No.1 with veins full of poppy juice. HE MADE SWEET MUSIC, the chiseled epitaph said. He had indeed. She'd paid for the inscription herself, and the words had been all hers. But Felicity didn't listen to his kind of music anymore. She had buried the tapes of Miles's brilliant piano improvisations in a trunk locked with seven locks, buried under a house that had another house on top of it. And she had shipped the trunk and the houses all the way to China, just to make sure. Now she went to the Rubyfruit Jungle, trying to persuade herself that she was a dyke who preferred, musically speaking, the killing din of Dada technorap to the uncertainties of jazz. This was deliberate musical genocide.

Done with her dead, Felicity drove to the Autocrat Club, where Grandmère's kin were mourning over mountains of food provided as part of the funeral package by the Treme Social & Pleasure Society, which had also interred her. Grandmère had faithfully paid dues to the club for forty years in anticipation of this occasion. Felicity made the rounds, hugging frail old folks and shaking hands. Then she got herself a plate of pork roast and a bowl of étouffée and ate at a back table watching Jeremy "Elvis" Mullin glad-hand the crowd like a politician. When Mullin made his noisy celebrity exit, Felicity got up and followed him.

Reverend Jeremy "Elvis" Mullin drove angry. It was already evening. He headed out of New Orleans down the river road, driving his gold Caddy west past the smoking cauldrons of Hooker Chemicals, Dow Chemical, B. F. Goodrich, E. I. Du Pont, Union Carbide, Texaco, Exxon, Uniroyal, Nalco Chemical, Freeport-McMoran, and Rubicon Chemicals, glowing in the night like a party of devils along the Mississippi. They were his rosary beads, his Mardi Gras necklace.

He could feel the coming of the Rapture in his bones. The ascent of the faithful to the Kingdom of Heaven was imminent. They would be taken from their homes, cars, or wherever they might find themselves. The Rapture, the prelude to the End. It was so delicious he could taste it.

The fate of those left behind after the Rapture did not concern Reverend Mullin, though he allowed himself the wicked enjoyment of imagining it. He saw the unbelievers crashing into one another on roads full of the abandoned vehicles of the risen. He saw airplanes fall to the ground after the Christian pilots ascended. He saw them burning in their houses, unattended by the firemen now in heaven. He saw them scrambling in the wake of the righteous. Let them. The Lord would sort them out, wheat from chaff.

As he rolled past the smoking behemoths of Louisiana's chemical corridor, he could see like Jesus right into the pitch-black hearts of the doomed and abandoned—the atheists, the agnostics, the media vultures, the Satanists, the blasphemers, the pope's miracle seekers, the soft-slippered morticians of dying secularism. Although he couldn't place her precisely in any of the general categories, Mullin saw clearly the face of the dykey girl who'd shamed him at her granma's deathbed in front of doctors and nurses. She may have been in a category all her own, a sexual deviant with a reserved spot in the Lake of Fire.

But something was bothering the reverend. His followers had become restless of late, impatient for the End, eager for the Rapture. He had to give them dates for the End events, but he wasn't going to do it until all his schedules were met and Lord Jesus spoke to him.

As the flaming towers of oil refineries flashed past, Reverend Mullin savored the brilliance of his plans. He would eventually give believers the date by which to put their affairs in order and give themselves wholly to Jesus. After that, in a matter of days, God's plan would unfold as foretold.

Mullin maneuvered the Caddy into the parking lot of a shabby motor court and beeped his horn. A girl-child sauntered out of a doorway, looked casually around, and then got in the car. Innocence had mostly fled the world, but here it was, in the depths of this cauldron of vice, shining unbent and unbruised.

"Did you bring me rock?" asked the girl. This was the third time that the preacher had sought her out. The first time he only wanted her to take off her shirt, and he'd paid her $10. The second time he had asked her to masturbate. After her awkward performance he patted her head and said, "Don't fear me, child. I am the rock," And she, in her innocence, had said, "Then bring me some rock next time."

But Reverend Mullin had forgotten. "I'm no purveyor of drugs, child," he said indignantly. "I'll give you a healing rock instead." He reached into the glove compartment and took out a Mexican marble egg he had bought in the French Market.

"Carved straight from the rock at Mount Golgotha!" he assured her. "Filled with the Lord's healing spirit."

"Bless it," demanded the waif, laying her palm on his thigh.

He mumbled a few words and passed the silver cross over the egg.

"Show me before I give it to you," he demanded.

She showed him. No more than thirteen, fresh as a dawn over the bayou, with skin as smooth as an unshelled pecan, she pulled up her dress and showed him the smooth horizon of a hairless mound. A thin fissure ran from the top of it to the dimples in her ass.

She reached for the egg.

"Find it, child," he asked.

The girl touched herself clumsily, and desire and gratitude surged through the evangelist. He felt his hardness through the black gabardine of his trousers. I am watching a doe munching on a sapling, he thought as her long fingers pulled back the flesh of her tiny pirogue and tossed about the little seed of her pleasure. Oh thank you, Lord, for the flower before me. And for the flower in me.

When the girl made a little moan of pleasure and withdrew a moist finger from her innocent film, Mullin leaned forward and took that finger in his mouth. With his other hand, he dropped a business card between her legs.

The girl picked it up and read: *Angel Choir of the Heavenly Abode of the Utmost Deity and Paradisiacal Tabernacle, Inc.* And there was a phone number.

"Call, child," he said, "and you'll get singing lessons and a job in the world's greatest choir. You'll sing the world to a beauteous and fiery end."

He was ready to pay her the usual ten bucks—the most he ever allowed himself to spend—and go off without complaint. He had recruited another soul among the fallen and was a little more like Jesus, therefore.

The girl was actually grateful. She did have a nice voice and wanted to sing. She did not want to be a whore. In gratitude, she wanted to give her benefactor something extra. She asked to "see" his. It was so innocent a request, so filled with the sticky memory of childhood, Mullin was flooded with sweetness. He unzipped his fly and extended his engorged member to the girl's gaze. She lay a hand upon it. Neither one of them heard the repeated click of Felicity's Nikon only a few yards away in the parked Plymouth van.

On the way back to the city, Felicity stopped for gas. When she pulled out of the Shell station, she thought that she recognized the brown, round face of the Pakistani in her rearview mirror. But then the red Olds fell back a couple of cars and she wasn't sure. Being followed had so far been only a theoretical possibility in her budding detective career. Of course I'm being followed, she thought optimistically; it is the essence of the work. I follow, so I may be followed. Dictum. She repeated this mantra to herself, glancing anxiously in the rearview mirror, but she didn't see the red Olds anymore. She was disappointed then. An unfollowed girl dick. Story of my life, she thought.

And then she saw the Olds again, two cars behind. Life, she told herself, is quite simple, until it becomes complex, then simple again. Why should I be surprised that my instinct is right? Mullin is a reptile, and as such he stands for a principle, the reptile principle. Her reptile radar was flawless. And what is a reptile? she asked herself, making a surprise left onto a suburban side street. The big red car followed.

A reptile is that which slithers while practicing the opposite of what it preaches. Most people lie, even Grandmère, bless her pure hard heart, but they lie innocently, as it were, out of necessity or self-preservation. A reptile lies with wicked pleasure; it spews oil as it lies; it creates conditions for evil. The Olds was now right behind her.

The road she had taken cut through the heart of a vast Caucasian enclave, the repository of the decades-long white flight from the old city of New Orleans. This relatively new boulevard, crowded with Home Depots, Wal-Marts, Taco Bells, and Burger Kings, was already cracked and uneven, shoved up by the unsteady mud below. The Olds was still with her, and she could see its occupants quite clearly. The Pakistani was wearing shades. The driver had stripped down to a T-shirt that revealed two densely tattooed arms.

PI Felicity wasn't carrying her gun—there hadn't been much point in taking one to a funeral. What did these goons of Mullin's want with her? Why did they follow their boss to his dirty little assignation? If I were a reptile, thought Felicity, would I have myself followed and observed in the act? Maybe Mullin was such a perverted reptile that he couldn't even enjoy filth without being watched. Or else these two had followed Mullin without his knowledge, for their own vile reasons, and had simply stumbled onto her. In that case, the creeps might not be out to get her. Maybe they just wanted the film.

Felicity pulled into the gravel driveway of a house that sat on cement blocks in a futile effort to avoid the next flood. An American flag jutted out above a door with a *David Duke for President* sticker on it. An RV that must have cost three times what the house did sat majestically in the front yard, bearing the sticker IN CASE OF RAPTURE, THIS RV WILL BE UNMANNED. The Olds came to a crunchy stop behind Felicity.

She waited as the two men got out simultaneously and walked toward her car. They were nearly there when the door of the house swung open and a bare-chested man bounced out and began firing a shotgun at them. Felicity ducked, and buckshot shattered her windshield. The bad guys ran back to their car and backed out, gravel flying. Felicity did the same. This time she followed the Olds, which was doing a determined eighty-five down the two-lane road.

In the parking lot of the Clearview Shopping Mall the Olds came to a screeching stop in the shadow of Home Depot. Felicity was right behind it, squinting through her shattered windshield. She nearly hit the rear bumper before she, too, stopped. A man pushing a shopping cart full of flowerpots so large they obstructed his view bumped into her as she jumped out of the van.

"America!" muttered the Pakistani, slamming the heavy door of the Olds behind him, "Everything bigger than anything! Flowerpots taller than a man!"

"Motherfucker!" Felicity called out in her toughest voice, rubbing her bruised flank. "Why the fuck were you following me?"

The Pakistani looked to his mate, an ex-con, who was still behind the wheel, hands limply out, cool as a cucumber with shades.

"You have something that belongs to us." He opened the door and got out. He was short, but the snakes tattooed up and down his arms rippled on solid muscle. "We saw you snappin'. We want the film."

Felicity grabbed her crotch in a classic American gesture of contempt: "Here is your film!"

That was a language the goon spoke, because he grinned, but the Pakistani did not understand. "Vulgarity!" he said. "America! Everything as vulgar as it looks!"

"Watch it, towel head!" said the ex-con. "This is my country. I'll stick a flag up your ass!"

"Good idea," said Felicity.

"So whatcha gonna do about it, gumdrop?"

"I tell you what I'm gonna do . . ." Felicity had spotted a security guard and waved him over.

The guard unsnapped his pistol holster when he saw Felicity waving at him and advanced toward the group. "What seems to be the trouble?" He was a fat black man—a baseball cap said SECURITY.

"These men, Officer," Felicity said matter-of-factly, "are making lewd propositions. This one"—she pointed to the Pakistani—"suggested that he would like to perform an unnatural act with the American flag."

The guard, his hand on the butt of his pistol, said gravely, "This is the parking lot of Home Depot. That's America, you unnerstand? You get your goddam foreign ass outta the Home Depot parking lot or I'll shoot your sorry curry ass."

"Yes, Officer," said the tattooed one, "I agree one hundred percent."

The pair reentered their vehicle. The thug said to Felicity, "I'll be seein' ya."

"I don't think so," said Felicity.

When the Olds crawled out of the Home Depot parking lot, Felicity thanked her savior and offered to buy him a beer; he would have accepted if he hadn't been working. They settled instead for a modest snack of dried shrimp and Hubig's cherry pie, purchased right at the counter of the giant superstore. Large men were solemnly purchasing tools, doors, ceilings, roofs, entire houses. Felicity and the security guard sat on two paint drums to eat and conversed a little.

"It's like a church in here," Felicity observed between bites of cherry pie.

"That it is. People pray hard, lookin' for the sink drain and the doggy door. They walks around lost, and then they finds what they was lookin' for. It's all they can do to stop theyselves singin' hymns."

"America."

"Hallelujah."

For a moment, filled with awe, girl dick and security guard sat in a silent salute to their country, and the Cathedral of Home hummed with the praise of the consuming masses. Now and then Wynonna Judd's voice could be heard bouncing off the lumber on the high shelves, shattered at intervals by the ecclesiastic chant of "Assistance needed on aisle four!" Felicity was almost happy. Perhaps what she needed was not a great mission or a phony glamour profession but to lose herself amid the purposeful people at Home Depot. Maybe she should find a husband here in the solid potbelly of America and have a couple of kids and remodel the rec room. Maybe the perfect anonymity of a burb would fill her holes. She peered into that future and saw herself sitting with a mug of decaf in a bright kitchen, nodding sympathetically as a litany of troubles poured out of her next-door neighbor. The pie smelled done and the Russians were knocking at the door, asking for work.

"Where do you live?" she asked Security, finding him as likely a husband as she could think of.

"At the airport," he said. "I have another job. I'm a redcap."

The idea of living at the airport made Felicity laugh.

"Whatcha laughin' at?"

"Flying." She was sure that this man with two jobs was her intended anonymous husband, if she ever went that route. Who knew? Maybe he could even give her that "bittersweet quake at the core of the nut," as she had read orgasm described by the poet Anna Akhmatova. Felicity had never experienced what she understood to be the common property of women everywhere.

"Do you have a business card?"

Security laughed. "What for?"

"In case I need my bags carried."

Felicity was moved and amused. There was a world of people without business cards that she could always disappear into if her life, which wasn't great shakes right now, got any worse. Here was an escape hatch, an alternative life. And because she was a modern girl she made a mental note to create a new computer file named ALT.LIFE.

Felicity thought about sex all the way back to her apartment. She concluded that there was nothing normal about it. Sex was based on a basic

lie—nature tricked people into having babies by making sex pleasurable—
so it was no surprise that everyone lied about it, in imitation of nature's
original deception. They lied about what they liked, who they liked, how
they did it, who they did it with. For a preacher like Mullin it must have
been even worse. No one really practiced what they preached. Everyone
lied, but Felicity felt incapable of it, an organic defect perhaps. She was
honest to a fault, doubtless the reason why she couldn't come. You had to
be a liar, she concluded, to climax in the "normal" way.

Felicity developed the film in the tiny bathroom she had turned into a
darkroom. While she waited for the prints to dry, she took off the funeral
clothes, particularly gratified to free her legs from the unaccustomed
stockings. She stood in the small bedroom of her apartment-cum-office
and studied herself in the mirror on the door. Without any doubt, long
legs and large eyes were her best features. Her pubis, too, had a presence,
separate somehow from her, like a little beastie in residence. Distaste for
the scene she had witnessed in the parking lot did not preclude a little
horniness: the image of the young whore putting her sticky finger in
Mullin's mouth had inexplicably aroused her.

Felicity swept off the bed the nine books she had been reading simultaneously, flopped down on her belly, and turned on her little laptop computer. SEARCH THE WEB, she commanded it, and then typed in TABLOIDS,
SCANDAL. Immediately, the *National Enquirer, World Evening News, Our
Mirror, News Uncut,* and *History Laid Bare* presented themselves for her in-
spection. She was quite sure that this was the way to go: she could already
see photos of the millionaire televangelist, fly unzipped, white worm out,
splashed over 10 million tabloid covers. She would bring about the end of
a reptile. She felt slightly guilty about the money she planned to extort,
but there was justice in it.

Felicity had never heard of *History Laid Bare,* but the name of the
tabloid appealed to her. History laid bare was exactly what she would provide. She clicked on the title.

History Laid Bare: The News from the Past. It wasn't exactly what she had
in mind. Her news was more like news from the future. A future, she told
herself, when all these phony TV men of the cloth will stand before Saint
Peter, pointing to their little peckers. What will you have to say for yourselves, Preachers, after you are unmasked by a girl dick? They'll be limp
for eternity! Downtown to the barbecue, all of you! I should have been a
poet, sighed Felicity.

She would have gone on to the *National Enquirer* if the menu listing the contents of *History Laid Bare* hadn't caught her eye. Among the items was an intriguing heading: *Make Love to People from History*. She clicked on it.

After a series of stern warnings forbidding persons under twenty-one years of age to enter, an image of Alexander the Great in a very short tunic appeared. The tunic was so short that it didn't entirely cover the perceptible nub of Alexander's manhood. He sat sidesaddle on an elephant superimposed on a map of Asia Minor. On the right side of the screen was a vertical strip titled *Temporary Avatars*. Five little cartoon figures were pictured below: a fat, squat Venus of Willendorf; a naked Greek discus thrower; an armless winged Roman Victory; a Carmelite nun in a high, pointed wimple; and General Patton. Felicity chose the nun and clicked on Alexander. A word balloon appeared over his head, and Alexander asked:

ARE YOU INTERESTED IN HISTORY?

Felicity typed YES, and the word appeared above the nun's head.

DO YOU BELIEVE THAT HISTORICAL PERSONAGES ARE STILL ALIVE TODAY? Alexander nudged the elephant and they moved closer.

The nun answered, YES.

IF YOU ANSWERED YES, WOULD YOU WANT TO MEET THEM IN THE FLESH? Felicity could now see Alexander's finely drawn cartoon hair.

YES.

IF YOU ANSWERED YES, TYPE IN THE HISTORICAL PERSONAGES YOU WOULD MOST LIKE TO MEET.

Whoa. Was this for real? Felicity stared at the screen as if it were the mouth of a bottomless pit. Easy, now. Who do I want to meet? The question is, what do I want to know? And who do I want to get it from? She could almost smell Alexander's elephant as it took another step forward, nearly dwarfing the nun. Felicity felt herself beginning to sweat. Well, one thing was for sure. It had to be women. Men had certainly had their say in books. If there was anything to be discovered by meeting "historical personages," it was stuff the books didn't talk about. Here was a chance to affirm, er, prove, test, well, figure out whether history was *his* story, afflicted by gender bias as the feminists claimed, and whether she was a true dyke or not. Especially if, as the site more than implied, lovemaking was part of the deal.

Felicity laughed at herself. Man, I can't believe I'm sitting here actually believing this crap. How many masquerades have I attended? One Mardi Gras I danced with Napoleon, made out with Josephine, shared a joint with Darth Vader, and traded hats with Baron Munchausen. How is this different?

She was familiar also with the game playing and masquerading going on over the Internet. Some of the virtual chat rooms were so realistic, people felt that they were living their real lives in there. By comparison, their so-called real lives, of work and human contacts, paled to insignificance. The virtual narcotic had spread everywhere in America, but a little less in New Orleans, where what cybernauts called "meat space" still throbbed, happily. Felicity, like many of her fellow New Orleanians, was highly skeptical of virtuality.

Still, Felicity was unable to shake the feeling that this cybermasquerade *was* somehow different. For one thing, the real people behind the avatars were tiny. She broke down and typed in a name: JOAN OF ARC.

They were old friends, in a manner of speaking. Jeanne d'Arc was the patron saint of New Orleans. And of old *Orléans*. Felicity's favorite work of public art in the city was the gold Joan atop her gold horse in front of Herod's Casino. Felicity had served on a committee to save the statue when the gangsters who owned Herod's tried to have Joan removed from her pedestal, on the pretext that she might upset the suckers. The committee had won, so Felicity felt that she herself had won a battle, like Joan. Besides, there was something sexy about the Maid of Orléans, and if lovemaking were to take place, it would certainly be a pleasure.

The next choice gave her trouble. Pursuing the somewhat sacred line she had already opened, she typed in: THE VIRGIN MARY (AKA THE MOTHER OF GOD).

She had in mind both the sad, stern Virgin in Saint Louis Cathedral and the bare-breasted Virgin with a positively mischievous look on her face in an Italian painting she'd seen at the New Orleans Museum of Art. If the Virgin really was a virgin, Felicity's awkwardness in lovemaking would be barely noticeable. After all, she'd had *some* experience.

Continuing her list, Felicity typed: AMELIA EARHART.

I always wondered what happened to Amelia Earhart.

Felicity was warming up now and had little trouble coming up with the next entry. There weren't many famous women in the dangerous business of espionage, but one had been a superstar.

MATA HARI.

Then the major's guest bed sprung to mind, and she typed, SAINT TERESA DE AVILA, whose mystical love poetry she had read, which had caused her to blush. "Thorn filling with blood, draining my heart," the saint had written. The words had caused her to shiver.

But having gotten this far, Felicity experienced a pang of doubt. Maybe the sole company of women was not such a great idea. The world was made of both women and men, and there were men with a lot of woman in them, just as there were women who were part, or all, man. In her profession, she could hardly afford to harbor any bias. Furthermore (here her pang became acute), what if she wasn't really a lesbian? What if she ended up wanting a man after all?

She scanned her skimpy American education for worthy men. Napoleon Bonaparte she knew as the emperor of New Orleans kitsch. Attila the Hun took his women on horseback while simultaneously chopping heads all around. George Washington had wooden teeth and couldn't lie, either. George Washington Carver was the man who invented peanut butter, the most perfect food. These men were not quite right. They suffered from either heroism or ruling-class selfishness. In high school Felicity had cut a lot of history to smoke pot with Ben. After that, history's men had become known to her only through haphazard reading. She had read, for instance, a biography of ALEXANDER HAMILTON, whose ideals and intelligence she had admired. She had even had a fantasy of being there at the duel with Aaron Burr and somehow deflecting the bullet. Like Wonder Woman.

Felicity relaxed and allowed a number of historical men she had read about to parade before her mind's eye. One man, smiling indecently, stood apart from the rest: the young MARK TWAIN.

A writer was definitely the kind of man she might be interested in. Finally, she typed in JULES VERNE, in whose submarine she had often traveled through the half-submerged city, with the taste of ashes in her mouth.

After she had entered all her objects of interest, Alexander the Great asked:

IF YOU COULD BE SOMEONE HISTORICAL, WHO WOULD YOU LIKE TO BE?

She thought about the great destiny Major Notz insisted was hers, and a wave of nausea and arrogance rose simultaneously in her throat. She was quite sure that she would never fit in either the shoes or the dresses of any historical personage. The only thing she did not lack was a profound feeling of unworthiness. Even the bum stealing donations from the church was more purposeful than her. The world did not know that she existed, and it had not the slightest reason for knowing. If Jesus Christ was, let's say, the most famous and most worthy person in the world—for the sake of argument only—then she was the absolute opposite of Jesus. However, and here Felicity allowed herself a tiny smile, there was no one in cyberspace who knew the difference. Therefore she could, if she so wished, be Jesus himself. She typed: THE MESSIAH.

Alexander said: YOU MAY NOW CREATE YOUR OWN AVATAR, USING PAINTBOX.

Felicity clicked on *Paintbox* and clumsily drew a creature with large breasts and a crooked nimbus over her head. She chose for her avatar a repertoire of expressions that included giving the finger, giving blessings, scratching her nimbus, slapping her hand over her mouth, frowning, and laughing with a hand between her legs. It was a pretty jolly avatar, and hardly messianic. She popped up next to the elephant, somewhere between Nineveh and Corfu.

DEAR MESSIAH, Alexander greeted her,

YOU ARE NOW READY TO MEET AND MAKE LOVE WITH JOAN OF ARC, THE VIRGIN MARY, AMELIA EARHART, MATA HARI, SAINT TERESA DE AVILA, ALEXANDER HAMILTON, MARK TWAIN, AND JULES VERNE. ENTER YOUR CREDIT CARD NUMBER AND EXPIRATION DATE NOW.

Felicity extracted a nearly maxed-out Visa card from her army surplus canvas bag and entered the number. An on-line address—*http://history.love.messiah*—appeared, accompanied by this cheerful message from Alexander:

CONGRATULATIONS!

YOU ARE NOW A MEMBER OF A SELECT GROUP OF PEOPLE WHO MEET IN ORDER TO PREPARE THE WORLD FOR A BETTER FUTURE THROUGH TRANSTEMPORAL LOVEMAKING. THIS IS A PRIVATE ENVIRONMENT WITHOUT RESTRICTIONS. YOU ARE FREE TO ENJOY YOURSELF TO THE BEST OF YOUR IMAGINATION. WHEN YOU ARE READY TO PROCEED, ENTER THIS ADDRESS AND YOU WILL FIND YOURSELF ON THE GROUNDS OF HISTORICAL EVENTS, WHERE YOU CAN MAKE LOVE WITH YOUR FAVORITE HISTORICAL PERSONAGES IN THEIR OWN BEDS, ON BATTLEFIELDS, ABOARD SHIPS, IN DESERT TENTS, OR IN SECRET CHAMBERS.

Alexander turned his elephant away and rode off into the mountains of Anatolia, which melted before him, giving way to a desert landscape of blooming cacti and cerulean blue sky.

"Damn!" said Felicity.

She saw herself putting her finger in Mata Hari's sensual mouth—she remembered her penetrating eyes in a portrait—and became aroused. It was absurd to think that some VR porn game might succeed where the throbbing flesh of actual humans had failed. But there it was, the thin film in her crotch, calling out.

Felicity logged off temporarily and sauntered to her darkroom. The prints were good—even the child whore's hairless snatch was graphically revealed. The detail excellent, down to the sheen of grease in Mullin's hair.

Felicity stuffed the pictures into a manila envelope and stuck it behind the framed print of Botticelli's *Primavera* hanging in the bedroom. Then she pulled on a T-shirt, got back on the bed, and pulled the warm laptop onto her naked lap, ready to make love with people from history.

The doorbell began ringing repeatedly, insistently. Felicity glanced at the clock radio—11:45 P.M. A little late for business. And she was on the verge of meeting Joan of Arc. She pulled on a pair of jeans and reluctantly put Joan on hold.

Felicity slid out the top drawer of her bedside table and took out the Beretta. She slipped it into the waist of her jeans. The cold barrel on her belly gave her gooseflesh. "Get bigger," she whispered; "you're not just symbolic." She cracked the door, secured by the safety chain. Standing there looking mournful were the Pakistani and his friend. Their faces, glazed by the streetlight, were moist and fleshy like wet pears.

"Can we talk?" whined the Pakistani.

She decided they were too stupid to be dangerous, and opened the door. The tattooed bodybuilder sat down on the only chair, and the Pakistani's eyes fastened on a framed photo of Mahatma Gandhi on her desk.

"We have a common hero!" he exclaimed, evidently pleased.

"What can I do for you gentlemen?"

"You fucking bitch!" growled the American.

"Beg your pardon?"

"What the gentleman means is, we would like the film," explained the other. "You give it to us, we leave. No problem."

"Let me put it this way, doll. You can give us the pictures or you'll never want to look in the mirror again."

"You're such a fucking cliché." Felicity took out her gun and pointed it at the man's shiny forehead. "Maybe I mess up *your* mirror, Jack. Take off your shirt!"

The thug wasn't particularly startled, but his partner launched into a stream of nervous chatter: "This isn't necessary. We were only asking. The film belongs to us."

"Take off your shirt!"

Deliberately, without taking his eyes off the gun, the one in the chair pulled the sweatshirt over his head. His torso was swarming with swastikas, hundreds of them, like a nest of spiders. They came crawling out of the hair on his chest and buried themselves in his armpits, and tattooed below each nipple in two vertical columns were the words WHITE and POWER.

"I'll be switched!" Felicity nearly dropped the gun. "A real live Nazi!"

"I'm sure he had to do such things in prison," the Pakistani sputtered.

"You can start with your names." Felicity clicked off the safety.

"Bamajan." The Pakistani instantly complied. "It means 'announcer of God.' A herald."

"Harrold? Bama? From Alabama? The Crimson Tide?" The Indian's accent was funny. But the name was weirdly familiar. Miles's junko partner had called himself that—he must have been God's announcer, too. *That* Bamajan, whom she hadn't seen in two years, was a trumpeter, so his name fit. He was also a heroin dealer and a pimp. The announcer of Satan, more like it.

"You can just call me Your Worst Nightmare," offered Mr. White Power, in his turn.

"Nice name. Look, we can do this one of two ways. I can shoot one or both of you for breaking and entering, or you can tell me your story nice and easy, and I'll tell the cops you were just playing."

Truth be told, Felicity had no idea what to do. She was afraid to pick up the phone and let her attention waver for even a second. The Nazi was coiled like a snake, just waiting to get to his piece. She couldn't just hold them indefinitely. The men were silent, seeing, she imagined, right through her.

"You got swastikas on your dick, too?" Her best tough-girl voice.

The Nazi rose to his feet. "With your permission." He undid the belt of his pants and they fell with a thunk to his feet. Felicity was sure that there was a gun in the pocket. He wasn't wearing any underpants. The lower part of his body, including his penis, was as densely tattooed as the rest of him.

"You look like a freakin' jigsaw puzzle!" Felicity was genuinely amazed. "Who assembled you? Hitler?"

The man made a move to pull his pants back up, but Felicity barked sharply, "No! Step away from them!"

Hitler's jigsaw puzzle did what he was told, and Felicity ordered Bamajan to shove the trousers toward her. She felt with her foot a wallet in one pocket, a gun in the other.

"You working for Mullin?"

"We do his bidding," answered Bamajan fiercely. "He is God's messenger. We are God's announcers. Gandhi was one, too. Be simple! Be simple!" He was becoming agitated.

"Okay, Announcer of God, take off your clothes!" Felicity had hit on a solution to the standoff.

The Pakistani didn't unravel so easily. He was more layered than your average American. Under his shirt he wore a kind of teddy with laces at the back. His flowery boxers were backed up by a pair of powder blue bikini briefs. His brown skin looked like just another layer of clothing, and for a moment, Felicity actually thought that he would remove another layer. There wasn't a hair on his body—his pubis was shaved clean, smooth as a pat of butter with a Vienna sausage stuck in it.

"Fucking pansy," laughed the Nazi. "We useta grease up guys like you and play pass-the-meatball."

When both men were naked and Felicity had their clothes in a bundle at her feet, she asked again for their story.

"I want to know who owns you, and I want it in plain English. And just to reassure your fucking bare butts, I'm a lesbian. You're ugly as shit to me, and it would only give me pleasure to shoot you. I'm a member of S.C.U.M., if you must know."

This speech unsettled Bamajan, but the Nazi just grinned.

Bamajan lowered his head, and covering his exposed parts with his hands, related quickly that he was in charge of protecting the Most Holy Reverend Jeremy "Elvis" Mullin; that he and millions of others around the world believed that Mullin was the reborn Redeemer; that he himself belonged to a Hindu sect, though he had been born a Muslim; and that the entire sect had converted to Mullinism in 1996.

"Mullinism?" Felicity stifled a laugh. "How many of you are in the city?"
"Ten—"

"Shut the fuck up, you rice cake!" hissed the Nazi, straight backed and stark naked, staring hatefully at Felicity.

"I'll get to you in a moment, Goebbels! Where'd you find this scum bucket, Bamajan?"

"Many of our followers are converted in prison."

"You talk too much, soy breath!"

Felicity'd had enough. "Get the fuck out, both of you! Turn around! Open the door! Out!"

The last she saw of them was their asses, one hairy white ass stenciled with swastikas and one round brown hairless ass atop two spindly legs. She called the police and reported two naked men prowling the neighborhood.

The real thing. Felicity was shaking, still clutching the Beretta. Sangfroid. Wait till I tell the major. Uncle, I was on the verge of a transtemporal sexual experience when I was rudely interrupted. Or even better: I was about to be bedded by Joan of Arc when a real, live Nazi invaded my office. Adrenaline pumped through her. She paced. She made coffee. She wanted to call somebody, but she no longer had any friends. Miles's crowd was into nightclubbing and drugs and staying up all night. In the daytime world she'd made few lasting acquaintances. Still, she wanted real, live, fleshy, friendly human contact now. She poured a cup of truly evil java and was startled by the thought that she had enjoyed the company of the two naked men. It had been a relationship, as they say. Was she this despondent, deprived, twisted?

Felicity was bothered by her body's evident interest in the disturbing images of the day—the whore's finger in Mullin's mouth, a Nazi's tattooed dick, a virtual fuck world. Why couldn't she get off like everyone else, in the missionary position, with a finger on her clit? In the normal world of men and women, orgasms were as bountiful as peanuts. Or were they? The images that aroused her despite herself came from that normal world, after all—the world of pedophile preachers, tattooed dicks, and techno-perverts. What if everyone was thriving on hellish and tormented imaginations made "normal" only by a common agreement to treat hell as if it were home? In the last five years, death had taken more than a dozen of her friends. Dying young from the sexual plague was so common now only the loved ones of the deceased mourned. The world no longer empathized. All the stores of common grief were empty, and the store of compassion, once abundantly open at the death of the young, was empty, too. What if another cargo had moved into those empty stores, crawling pornographic visions intended to blot out the pain with . . . quaking peanuts?

If such were the case, if the world was hell, salvation had to come from somewhere, and soon. The genetic puzzle was nearly unraveled; the tiny demons crossing the wires deep within were all named and numbered. In a few years, scientists had mapped the human genome, giving names to every tiny particle in the blueprint of life. And yet death strolled at leisure, picking the choicest of the young, without hurry, without panic. What gives death such confidence? I suppose, thought Felicity, that death knows something that makes it confident. What does death know? Maybe death knows that we all feel guilty about something. Maybe we feel guilty about knowing something that we aren't supposed to know. Like what am I not supposed to know that I actually know? Felicity searched the trembling bud knotted tightly in her sternum, a knot of knowledge, brimming with guilty puss like a boil. But it was nothing; it was only guilt about knowing . . . death. Felicity surprised herself with the circular banality of this discovery: death drew its power from her knowledge of death. As idiotic as the near tautology was the simplicity of the solution: death will be ended by one who knows nothing of it. An innocent, a freak, an idiot. This brought back a dim memory: *Felicity's a freak! Felicity's a freak!* She heard childhood voices chanting this but was comforted as soon as she heard them. Children! Of course. Children had no idea that they were living in hell. They felt no guilt knowing death. Children were freaks and idiots. She, Felicity, was almost as freaky as a child, guilty knot notwithstanding. She had not yet had an orgasm. She felt relieved, and proceeded to investigate the contents of her would-be assailants' pockets.

The naked men were picked up before Felicity had even examined very thoroughly the contents of their wallets. A young policeman knocked at her door. Felicity shoved the men's clothes behind the bedroom door and let him in.

Officer Joe Di Friggio hid his green horns under a studied frown.

"You the one who called?" He pulled out his notepad. "Willing to testify in court?"

She answered only the last question, saying that she preferred not to show up in court. She had merely glimpsed them out the window and done her citizen's duty.

"Isn't it illegal," she asked rhetorically, "to be naked on the streets?"

Officer Di Friggio looked doubtful. After all, this was New Orleans. Joe wrote down his number on the back of a ticket and handed it to her.

"In case you change your mind?" She reached for it and tugged, but Joe held on. "You never know about these naked characters," he said.

"You mean there are a lot of them?"

"Dozens every night." The patrolman grinned, still holding on to the ticket. "We pick 'em up like pecans in October."

"Your country upbringing," said Felicity, finally wrenching the ticket from him, "has given you colorful speech."

"Hate to disappoint you, but I'm from right down here in the Irish Channel. Only I'm Italian."

This was more than Felicity wanted to know.

"Are they dangerous?" She hoped this sounded sincere.

"Naked men," he snorted. "How dangerous can they be? Unless they was hiding stilettos in their behinds." Joe laughed, showing many white teeth. "Unless what they wear in front presents a threat to you."

"On the contrary," said Felicity. "I'm always surprised by the disparity between advertising and reality. But I do call the cops, just in case."

"Just in case what?"

"Just in case one of them lives up to the ads."

After he left, Felicity allowed herself to tremble some more. She double-checked the locks on all the doors before she stripped again. She pulled on the loose black denims of the Nazi and fastened them to her skinny middle with the belt of her bathrobe. She tried to imagine what it was like to have a penis covered with tattoos. Her trembling was compounded by a fierce arousal. She flopped down on her bed and turned on the laptop, ready to make love to people from history. Or anyone else for that matter.

Chapter Six

Wherein Andrea, the Bosnian orphan, is fascinated by a television game show

 n d r e a ' s improved health did not escape the notice of the hospice's guests. Some of the scholars began to follow her around; others arranged to bump into her at breakfast or in the library. The girl became a subject of discussion among the distinguished residents.

One plausible explanation for their common fascination was offered by Dr. Luna, the Mexican priest: "We spend our lives studying and watching, watching and waiting. When something or someone unusual appears, we agitate. To people such as ourselves, a girl like this is like a new language!"

The first sign that Andrea was returning from the mist she had been wandering in was when she began to watch television in the lounge after supper. She was especially interested by the game show *Gal Gal Hamazal*, the Israeli version of *Wheel of Fortune*. She sat transfixed through the entire half hour.

After watching the program for the first time, she was in much improved spirits and even told a little joke to the assembled guests.

"Did you know," she said in English, "that Christ came through Sarajevo carrying his cross? A man stopped him in the road and asked, 'Where did you find the wood?' "

"Poor child," murmured Father Tuiredh, "to have survived there."

It was the only mention of her past, and no one asked for more. The hospice's guests were happy just to be near the child. Time seemed somehow to have expanded, allowing them to complete in days research that had been dragging for months. They slept less every night and looked forward to breakfast with Andrea like restless children.

Watching *Gal Gal Hamazal* became a Tuesday evening ritual at the hospice. Television was forbidden to the nuns, but they had their ways. At the hour of the broadcast, Mother Superior was always secluded in prayer in a little-used chapel at the far end of the convent.

As the hour for *Gal Gal Hamazal* neared, the doors to the guest rooms began to open, letting out the motley assortment of residents. There was Father Hernio, a Filipino priest who ministered to six hundred souls in Berlin; Father Zahan, from Australia, a native Yuin, also a Catholic priest, who wrote books on tribal religions; Lama Iris Cohen, a Buddhist nun and the highest-ranked Westerner of the Tantric branch of Tibetan Buddhism; Father Magh Tuiredh, an Irish cleric who wore the embroidered name *Lugh* on his cassock; Dr. Carlos Luna, an Indian from Oaxaca, Mexico, wearing a bright sweater depicting the Aztec calendar; Professor Weng Li, from the University of Beijing; Earl Smith, a Hopi from Arizona; and Mr. Rabindranath, now decently clad in trousers and white sweater, smoking clove tobacco from a meerschaum pipe.

Each guest greeted Andrea and the sisters with varying degrees of effusiveness. Father Zahan smiled most widely and patted Andrea's hair. While the others sat modestly on straight-backed chairs, Lama Cohen made room for Andrea on the small couch by the rain-streaked window. The lama was hoping for snow. She had grown up in Vail, Colorado, and felt oddly nostalgic. Something about the Bosnian girl reminded the lama of a snowflake.

The little television sat on a small dais covered in red cloth.

Although most of the company had never watched *Gal Gal Hamazal* before the previous Tuesday, they anticipated it as if it were a precious ceremony vouchsafed only to a lucky few.

The vivacious hostess of the show, Gala Keria, appeared to wild applause. Green eyed and tall, with dark, shoulder-length hair, dressed in a black leather miniskirt and a long-sleeved white T-shirt poked by nervy nipples, she had a half-knowing, half-sad grin that made men and boys alike a little soft in the head.

The cohost greeted her ironically, announcing that he was, as always, utterly surprised by her wardrobe. He just didn't know what to think. The

audience applauded long and hard—whether in support of the host's bafflement or in favor of Gala's wardrobe was hard to say.

"Gala is like mercury," he effused. "I don't think we can hold her very
long. If you are beautiful, intelligent, and aged between eighteen and
twenty-five, start thinking about her job now."

Gala, unlike her American counterpart, did not simply turn letters.
When the three contestants were introduced—an engineer from Rishon
Le-Zion, a jeweler from Jaffa, and a soldier from Jerusalem—she patted
the engineer on the back, hugged the jeweler, and kissed the soldier, who
blushed. She then sauntered over to the blank puzzle board, inside which
hid the secret letters, and bowed. The category appeared. It was CREATION
AND CREATOR. This met with approval from both audiences: the studio's
and the hospice's.

"What better puzzle?" Father Hernio observed.

"The best!" agreed Lama Cohen.

The engineer spun the wheel; it came to rest on *800 Shekels*.

"*Mem!*" he said. "I would like *mem!*"

The studio audience now began chanting, "*Mem! Mem! Mem! Mem!*"

Sister Maria was astonished to see the otherworldly Mr. Rabindranath
begin to rock back and forth, silently mouthing "mem." All those present,
with the exception of Dr. Carlos Luna and Andrea, began to do the same.
Why, of course, thought Sister Maria; they are all chanters and vocalizers.
Most religious traditions use mantras and chants.

Beaming, Gala turned one of the squares and revealed *mem*. She smiled
radiantly. But she was not done. With a generous sweep of her pretty arm
she reached farther down the blank board and flipped over another *mem*.
The audience went wild. "*Mem! Mem! Mem!*" The little salon of the Saint
Hildegard Hospice positively quaked with the unleashed energy of *mem*.
And like the goddess Isis surveying one of her ceremonies, Gala whipped
up the frenzy, conducting the chant with her arms and her feet, dancing
with abandon. Sister Rodica was sure that the surge would never stop but
would break into chaos. She imagined the audience might tear out of the
studio, spill into the streets, hug strangers, dance, and shout, "*MEM!
MEM!*" with tears streaming down their faces, until the whole city was
one unleashed hora. But as suddenly as it surged, Gala stilled the wave,
and the engineer spun again.

Surprise, decided the wheel. This was an audience favorite; unlike its
counterpart in America, the Israeli *Surprise* was not always a good thing. If
the contestant guessed the letter correctly, the surprise would be a car or a

refrigerator. But if the contestant failed to guess, the surprise might involve a brief humiliation before the audience—such as a spanking by Gala herself or a verbal lashing by the host, with audience participation. The strongest punishment surprise so far had been a contestant's being forced to crawl on all fours and bark at the audience. Gala had climbed on his back and waved her scarf, driving the audience wild.

"*Lamed!*" said the engineer. "I want *lamed!*"

For a suspended moment, the world plunged into anxious silence. And then, like the sun breaking through clouds, Gala's marmoreal arm traveled graciously toward the board and revealed with the authority that only she possessed the existence of *lamed!*

The emotion in the room seemed to Sister Maria quite disproportionate to the activity on the screen. She had seen the show before but had never felt this kind of involvement. But Sister Rodica understood the frenzy; *Gal Gal Hamazal* was her favorite pastime in the whole world, because she was a great believer in wheels. The Carpathian village of Piatra de Moare, where she was born, had been built around a huge round stone that resembled a giant millstone. Consequently, everything in Piatra de Moare was round: the wells, the church, the houses. She missed her village so much she felt like crying every time she saw the symbol for *Gal Gal Hamazal* on TV. Until now she had never felt that anyone else shared her emotion.

To be honest, Sister Maria had always considered *Gal Gal Hamazal* a low-class sort of thing. Secretly she had contempt for what she perceived as Sister Rodica's simplemindedness. Sister Maria didn't tell anyone, but she had read more than the *Lives of the Saints!* And yet here were all these learned scholars as absorbed as four-year-olds in a new set of building blocks! Sister Maria was not a little disappointed.

"*Lamed! Lamed! Lamed!*" The audience on the screen and in the lounge of Saint Hildegard Hospice became one as nuns, mystics, and professors burst out: "*Lamed! Lamed!*" Sister Maria seemed to hear just below their childish voices another sound, a kind of lament: *Mene, Mene, Tekel.* Then other biblical laments surfaced momentarily and vanished like bubbles in a soda. Then, quite distinctly, the crack of a whip. Then more bubbles of sound, muddy, moaning, weeping. Then "*Lamed! Lamed!*" again. She was having odd sensations today. She looked at Mr. Rabindranath, absorbed in the pleasure of chanting the Hebrew letter, and couldn't quite associate him with the naked floater.

"I find it curious," Sister Maria burst out, unable to control herself any longer, "that distinguished scholars such as yourselves find this game so stimulating."

This seemed to amuse the company—it was just the kind of remark they expected a smart nun to make.

"It's like this, dear Sister," Mr. Rabindranath said, accepting her challenge for the rest of the group. "We are all devotees of the wheel. Every one of us lives by a wheel that contains and instructs us. I, for instance, believe in the great Wheel of Karma. Lama Cohen here meditates on the Tantric wheel, a very beautiful wheel with angels and demons on it. Dr. Carlos Luna even wears his wheel on his sweater. Father Zahan has written and meditated on the meaning of circular enclosures for the Yuin and Murring people, and as a Christian he is doubtlessly delighted to be in Jerusalem, the city of a thousand cupolas, circular ceilings, great rotundas—circles and spheres everywhere you look. In Professor Li's China, the circle is the symbol of heaven. The Tao is familiar throughout Asia, including Father Hernio's native Philippines. Father Magh Tuiredh's Celtic ancestors performed their rituals inside circular magic groves. And Mr. Earl Smith, from Arizona, can draw in sand the great Wheel of Creation on its cardinal point axes. Have I left out anyone?"

"I am a little familiar," Sister Maria said modestly, "with the wheels of some religions." In truth, she knew only less than a little but made a mental note to study. "Still, *Gal Gal Hamazal* is hardly a sacred wheel on the level of those you have mentioned."

"Don't be so sure." Mr. Rabindranath smiled a bit smugly. "It may be a new religion for the masses in our time."

Sister Maria remembered with distaste the tapered brown flesh of his flaccid penis, and she also wasn't sure what he meant: was TV the religion, or the Wheel of Fortune itself?

"Anyway," he continued, "the child seems to enjoy the show very much. You are a very pretty girl, Andrea. If Gala Keria were to resign, you could do her job."

Andrea gave no sign that she heard him. Nonetheless, there was a murmur of assent, and a lightning-quick glance passed between the people in the room, or so it looked to Sister Maria. But the next moment she thought she must have been mistaken. How could so many people exchange a look among themselves so fast? It was physically impossible.

But the conversation distracted Andrea enough so that she never actually found out the answer to the puzzle CREATION AND CREATOR. The engineer appeared to have won. She sat in glum silence for the rest of the show, participating in neither the chanting of the Hebrew alphabet nor the childish joy of the spectators. Was she really pretty enough to take Gala's place? Andrea had not the slightest idea. She hadn't thought for ages about her looks. She would have liked to wear glasses, but her vision was perfect. She was always surprised by masculine attention, which, she imagined, was something every girl received. She had always given in quite easily to men's urgent pleas and didn't think much of it. When they began acting like lovesick puppies, she avoided them. She had told Sister Rodica that during the months that she'd been "in transit," as her jailers had called the time when she'd been in the camp, she had become quite indifferent to what happened to her body. Sister Rodica's heart filled with pity for the girl, not much younger than herself.

The solution to the category BOOKS turned out to be *The Bridge over the Drina*, a book Andrea had read in school shortly before her entire world became one of its unwritten chapters. Written by the Bosnian Ivo Andrić during World War I, it was the story of the history of a bridge that linked Bosnia to the world. Andrea had cried when she'd read the book because she'd felt its truth like a bitter seed on her tongue. But for all his knowledge, even Ivo Andrić would have cried in disbelief when his bridge over the Drina was blown up by Serbian nationalists in 1995. That was the year when my life ceased, thought Andrea.

The next category was SONG, which turned out to also be one of her favorites, "Your Precious Love." She had sung along with her fraying cassette of Marvin Gaye's *Motown Hits* until her voice cracked.

For an extra 500 shekels the jeweler was asked to sing the song, and amazingly, he did. "Heaven must have sent your precious love . . . And you gave me a reason for living . . . you taught me the meaning of living . . . Heaven must have sent you from above . . . Heaven must have sent your precious love."

The final category was MOVIES. The engineer solved the puzzle: *Elmer Gantry*. Andrea had seen this, too, and had found Burt Lancaster riding on his horse over a mountain ridge a frightening image.

The exhausted audience chanted a final *"aleph, lamed, mem, resh"* and watched with bright excitement as a Yamaha motorcycle, a GE refrigerator, and a Subaru pickup truck rotated on stage.

Andrea felt sorry for the soldier, who hadn't won anything. "A refrigerator!" she said contemptuously. "What a silly prize."

"Not silly." Father Magh Tuiredh spoke up unexpectedly. "The refrigerator is the White Goddess!"

"How is that, Padre?" asked Lama Cohen, amused.

"There she is, large and white and unavoidable, at the center of every household in the modern world. You cannot ignore her; she draws everyone to worship. You open her door and look in long and hard by that little light. Giver of sustenance!"

"How blind are our poets!" exclaimed Professor Weng Li. "Chinese poetry has observed the ignored detail for four thousand years. I do not believe that we can find a single verse dedicated to the new White Goddess, the refrigerator."

"Not even during the Cultural Revolution?" wondered Dr. Luna. "It is well known that your poets wrote about the Four Modernizations: the modernization of agriculture, industry, culture, and sports."

Professor Li looked quizzically at Dr. Luna. The hint of a smile crossed his face. "Scholar of our recent history, I see."

"Conversations with my Cuban friends. My unsavory communist youth." Dr. Luna bowed.

"Well, at least I know who Robert Graves is!" Sister Maria was huffy. It seemed to her that she was being made sport of. She hadn't actually read Robert Graves's *White Goddess*, but she had heard of it.

Sister Rodica didn't understand much of this scholarly discussion. For her, *Gal Gal Hamazal* held personal and secret meanings. She was also—though it would have made her blush to admit it—a little in love with Gala Keria. And to complicate things, she had found Dr. Rabindranath's comment to Andrea extraordinarily apt. Andrea *was* pretty enough to apply for Gala's job! The nun felt the need to pray: she needed to banish both Gala and Andrea from that overwhelmingly warm place in her solar plexus, a place that was doubtless the devil's nest. It was still only a small nest compared to the spacious rooms given over in her to the love of God, Jesus, and the Holy Mother, but it could grow, she was certain.

Chapter Seven

Wherein Felicity initiates a transaction with Reverend Jeremy "Elvis" Mullin

Th e Napoleon House stands at the corner of Chartres and Toulouse Streets. The old building sports a cupola from which a citizen wielding a telescope might survey ship traffic on the Mississippi. Legend has it that the house was built by a group of conspirators who'd hatched a plan to spring the emperor Napoleon from Elba, the island of his exile. The cupola had been constructed as a vantage point from which to watch for the ship carrying Bonaparte. It was hoped that the emperor would recover his brilliance in the New World and lead the heroic conspirators to unparalleled heights of glory. Unfortunately, Napoleon died before he could be sprung, and the Napoleon House became a tavern. It seemed to Felicity that every noteworthy and historic building in New Orleans became a restaurant eventually.

The propensity to plot was as intrinsic to the city as the sticky, muggy, sultry, sexy weather. The French Quarter boasted numberless establishments where for centuries plots ranging from the takeover of small Latin countries to the assassination of presidents had been hatched with varying degrees of success.

Felicity had considered writing a guide for mystery lovers that would take them to the places conspirators had met in the past. She knew the exact locations from Major Notz, who delighted in pointing out ruined courtyards and ancient doorways where dashing and eccentric men had made preposterous plans to introduce order into chaos. One of these men had succeeded in proclaiming himself emperor of Nicaragua for a whole week before his armada of fishing boats was annihilated. Adventurers destined for Cuba, Mexico, and Central America first had their visions in the strong absinthe of New Orleans cafés. Felicity dreamed of setting off for exotic ports, but adventuring required moolah, which she lacked. But not for long, if everything went right.

The interior of Napoleon House was dark and inviting, kept deliberately in a state of careful decay, with faded paintings of the emperor on the walls. Beethoven's *Eroica* enveloped the room, the only music allowed here that wasn't opera. In the courtyard a Canadian couple shrieked, having sighted their first New Orleans roach. The size of small black hearses, the roaches of New Orleans, called palmetto bugs by their poets, enjoyed dropping into the plates of Yankees. The place was perfect.

Reverend Mullin had not enjoyed reading the letter summoning him to this meeting. It had been written by someone hostile to Jesus. The message began, civilly enough, "Most Esteemed Reverend," which was then crossed out and changed to "Your Satanic Majesty."

> ~~Most Esteemed Reverend~~: Your Satanic Majesty:
>   The Eye that sees everything was wide open yesterday. While taking in various acts of banal wickedness performed by the ignorant motorists of our state, the Eye was arrested by a huge outrage. This concerns you.

The reverend paused. The amateur writer who had penned these lines was obviously in need of remedial English. A long time ago, he too had suffered from a prolix style, but as his vision clarified, Jesus had made his speech crisp and effective.

> The Eye saw you engaged in sexual concourse with a minor.

That wasn't so bad. But the message was. The reverend felt anger and fear fill his chest. He'd survived blackmail attempts before, but there was something novel here. The tone of the note was impertinent and shameless. More than money was at stake.

> You were wallowing in filth with an abandon that became even more evident when we developed the Eye's pictures. We now have a pretty good idea of what you mean by morality when you preach the fires of hell and scare the shit out of old ladies and children.

The letter ended abruptly with a summons to a meeting at Napoleon House that afternoon. It was signed "The Messiah."

Felicity, too, had misgivings about the style of her missive. She realized that a cool blackmailer would write an impersonal note, but Mullin enraged her. Besides, she didn't want to appear to be too well read; it might put the reptile on his guard. Let him think she was a simple girl, like Joan of Arc. Which she was, though maybe not as strong; it was hard to imagine wearing heavy armor day after day. Joan must have been a sturdy woman, her body solid muscle. And inside? Inside? What was inside Joan of Arc? A bright emptiness? White light? Faith and anger? Concern for her horse?

She was drinking her second Irish coffee when Mullin showed up, half an hour late. He wore a light-colored business suit and carried a stylish burgundy leather briefcase. He seemed to have grown denser and meaner, like a big cat. He squinted into the dark and then spotted Felicity at the corner table. He should have known. The moment he saw that young punk in her grandmother's hospital room he knew that this was no innocent girl. He saw the sparkling sapphire in her ear and the silver glare of her bracelets, and in his mind's eye, an old snake hissed at him. You need a special music, young cobra! he silently hissed back. The music of the angel that drains the venom from your fangs.

Mullin sat down heavily and lay the entire weight of his authority-filled gaze on her not-unpleasant face. Her bright red lipstick contrasted fetchingly with the magenta streak in her spiky blond hair. Even the discreet ring at the right corner of her lip had a certain flair. Mullin was susceptible to women and snakes, whence came his wariness and his guile.

Major Notz had once told Felicity that the secret of worldly success lay in allowing people to underestimate you until they relaxed sufficiently to reveal their weaknesses. At that moment, you strike. She hoped that Mullin would buy it.

The manila envelope of compromising photographs lay on the table between them.

One of the bar's phlegmatic waiters appeared, and Mullin ordered water.

"What's the matter? Too cheap to have a beer?" spat Felicity.

"Let's get to the point, young woman."

"Call me Messiah."

"There are certain limits . . . on earth, in heaven, and in conversation. I'll do business with the devil, provided we proceed with civility."

"Sorry," said Felicity. "Fresh out. We'll have to go with impertinence."

When his water arrived, she couldn't resist pointing out that New Orleans tap water was so impure it was known to glow in the dark. "They say that every glass of water that comes from the Mississippi at New Orleans has been drunk at least six times." She was in no hurry, and Mullin's visible distress pleased her.

"It will get worse," Mullin said darkly.

Since the girl seemed unwilling to get down to business, Mullin reached for the envelope. Felicity's small right hand, chunky rings on each finger, slammed down sharply on the back of his hairy hand.

"Now, now," she chastised.

Mullin was startled by her strength, but it wasn't physical pain that enraged him. It was that she dared *touch* him at all. No one touched him without permission. In this respect he was like the pope, infallible, out of reach. It was perhaps the most important reason why he'd become a man of the cloth. His worshipers might kiss his sleeves or his shoes, but never his flesh. Mullin closed his eyes tightly, seeing the seas redden.

Felicity, too, was taken aback by the violence of her gesture and by Mullin's weird reaction. But two Irish coffees made her fast. "Okay," she said quickly, in a somewhat conciliatory tone. "I have here pictures of the entire sequence of your debasement."

Mullin put a finger to his lips and glanced around. He reached for the envelope again, and Felicity let him have it. He took the stack of photographs halfway out and flipped through them. Then he asked quietly:

"What do you want?"

"It's a long story," said Felicity.

The reverend sat back in his chair.

"Well," began Felicity, "in the beginning was hell. After Grandmère was robbed by your televised pitch, this little girl lost her bearings. I would call it abuse, but the word is tossed around so much, I'll just call it extortion. And it wasn't just emotional."

Felicity described the loss of her heirlooms, lingering with sadistic pleasure on each object, hoping to make Mullin squirm.

"Every night I went to sleep seeing two faces, my mother's and Saint Cecily's . . . and I prayed the rosary. I had a little chest of keepsakes. My Communion dress with the lacy border was in it. A picture of my dad in a silver frame. A prayer book inscribed to me by my favorite nun, Sister Amelia, my history teacher. A lucky fava bean I got from a Saint Joseph's altar. A lace handkerchief dipped in Lourdes water."

Mullin did have a moment of discomfort. He reached for his water.

"Man," Felicity smirked, "I got a bundle of pain from you, Preacher. Endless Sundays having to listen to your malicious damnation of things I loved. Prince! Guess what? God loves Prince. He doesn't love you! *You're* a freak."

Mullin listened to her litany but in the end did not recognize himself in her words. The awesome figure Felicity was describing was someone he admired in the way one admires a fine portrait of oneself. In his pulpit, on-stage before people, Mullin had no thoughts. God spoke *through* him. Alien words came out of his mouth, and the faithful loved and rewarded him. It was not in defense of himself but of that divinely inspired messenger of God that he'd built an elaborate mechanism, set to destroy any intruder, any threat to his domain. This girl, with her sob stories of adolescent despair, was about the size of a flea. He needed to deploy only one millionth of the power of his mechanism to erase her completely. Which he would do, he thought, as soon as this charade ended.

And then Felicity got to the point.

"Grandmère won the lottery. Two-point-one million dollars. And you took it from her, Jeremy Mullin!"

During the silence that followed, Felicity kept her eyes steady on the preacher. She had presented her case as fact, but now she wasn't so sure. Perhaps the crazy old woman had torn up the ticket after all.

"I did?" Mullin stirred from his dull resentment. "She gave *me* no money, young woman." He paused. "She gave to God's work."

Felicity strained hard to keep herself contained.

"Marie-Frances Claire did her part to battle sin."

"Sin?" said Felicity. She pointed to the manila envelope. "You'd know a lot about sin." She stared into his eyes for a long minute. The reverend's eyes were pools of darkness. At the bottom of each one stood Satan, masturbating. "The way I see it," she said slowly, "you owe me . . . two-point-one million."

Mullin started. He leaned across the table and joined the fingers of his hands.

"There ain't no fucking picture in the world worth two-point-one million dollars."

"Sure there is. Haven't you heard of van Gogh?"

"Negotiable?"

"Not."

"Everything is negotiable, except your eternal soul."

"You sold yours a long time ago."

"Hell is real, young woman."

"Yeah. And you know how you get there, Preacher? By insulting heaven. Heaven is like a bank account. It's full of pleasure. Everybody's born rich. But if you take too many loans and dip too much into other people's accounts, you'll find it empty when you die. And that's what hell is: heaven empty of its treasure."

"Well said. Too bad you don't have the calling."

"It's a matter of principle, scumbag. You owe me two-point-one million dollars. No more, no less. No interest, you notice. I'm being kind."

Officer Joe Di Friggio hadn't stopped thinking about Felicity since the night they met. The two characters he'd nabbed at her request had told the judge some cock 'n' bull story about being mugged outside the Harness, a gay bar notorious for orgies. Which explained their nakedness. Only, the Harness wasn't anywhere near Felicity's apartment. Joe wasn't gay, but a few years before, he had allowed himself to be photographed clowning in his police uniform at a party. Subsequently, a poster of shirtless Officer Joe in his leather jacket, cap tilted rakishly on his head, billy club raised, had been distributed without his permission. The beefy pinup had been a hit. Joe was unable to find out who the photographer was, but when the poster first appeared, he went on a rampage. He tore it off the walls of every gay bar in New Orleans, but the poster reappeared every time. After a while Joe gave up, consoled by the fact that the billy club half hid his face. He had been raised to look on homosexuality as an abomination, and it bothered him that gay men all over the city might have been aroused by his uniformed body.

Joe had called Felicity to update her about the case and found himself asking her out for a date. At first she had claimed that she was too exhausted to flirt. Then she had consented and had suggested that they meet at the Napoleon House.

The French doors of the restaurant swung open to let in a couple of Japanese tourists. Towering behind them was Officer Joe Di Friggio. Very punctual. Inviting Joe to her meeting with Mullin had been a spur-of-the-moment idea, but now she was glad that she had.

It wasn't the kind of place Joe would have chosen for a date. The tall blond cop was just this way of pudgy, an inevitable development in the city of fried oysters. He liked noisy bars or quiet Italian places with Harry Connick Jr. on the juke.

Felicity waved him to the table. Joe didn't look pleased to find that she was not alone. "Sit, Officer, sit."

Felicity made room for Joe on the small bench and made introductions.

"Patrolman Joe Di Friggio, this is my spiritual banker, Reverend Mullin."

Joe knew who Mullin was. He'd seen him on television. What kind of girl would bring a preacher to a date? He needed a beer, but he was in uniform and didn't want to drink in front of a man of the church drinking water.

"It's the strangest thing," Felicity explained to Mullin. "I looked out my window the other night and saw two naked men. One was some kind of Pakistani with a round ass, excuse my language, Padre. The other guy was tattooed with swastikas, everywhere, even on his—"

"Okay, yeah." Joe was embarrassed on behalf of Felicity.

"Joe here responded to my nine-one-one call," Felicity concluded demurely.

Mullin was very still. He was being set up, and the worst part was that he had no idea what Kross and Bamajan were doing in the picture. They'd never said a word about any of this. He'd given them their leave after the old woman's funeral. Why did they follow Felicity? Unless they were following him and saw her take the pictures. They obviously couldn't be trusted anymore.

"Well," said Joe after he'd ordered a sandwich and a root beer, "in my line of work I see everything."

"And I don't?" said Felicity.

"Yeah, I forgot." Joe grinned. He had read her shingle: FELICITY LE JEUNE, INVESTIGATIONS. He had also looked up her PI license.

Felicity handed the reverend and Joe her business card: FELICITY LE JEUNE, GIRL DICK, 888-6547. "So you won't forget again."

Mullin stood up. "That's the number I call, then."

"That's it. You've got two days," Felicity answered cheerfully, and the reverend hurried out, perspiration staining his light-colored jacket.

"What was all that about?" Joe asked, taking a bite of the sandwich he'd ordered—a big, round muffuletta stuffed with ham, provolone, salami, and olive salad on a bed of lettuce and pepperoncini. A truckdriver friend of Felicity's told her that he'd bought a muffuletta in New Orleans and eaten it all the way to San Francisco, and still had half left when he got there. It was that big. Felicity could eat only a half.

"My grandmother died. Reverend Mullin has some of her things."

"Rich s.o.b.," mumbled Joe between bites of his sandwich. "I hear he's worth about a billion dollars."

"That's TV for you. You and I get on TV, Joe, we'd make a bundle."

"Sure, honey buns. And what would we be showing 'em?" Joe wiped some olive oil from his chin.

"We could show them your gun. Catch criminals live. And alive."

"TV is everything these days," said Joe thoughtfully. "I only watch reruns of the *X-Files* and *Star Trek: The Next Generation.*"

Felicity had to confess to a certain handicap. Half the references normal people made went right by her. They were all from TV. She now remembered, with a guilty twinge, the job that Major Notz had given her, to search for the Indian TV star who had disappeared in New Orleans. Events had been unfolding at such a dizzying rate she had hardly had time to breathe. But a job is a job. She had seen *Wheel of Fortune* only once. She had no idea what might be going through the mind of someone who turned letters for a living.

"You ever see *Wheel of Fortune,* Joe?"

"Used to watch every night. My mother and her sister, the retired nun, watch it every evening. They say they are better at seeing the answer than most of the people they got on there."

"What did you get out of it?"

"I don't know. It's fun to try to guess the words. I like Vanna White, too. I was gonna write her a proposal letter, but then I met you." Joe winked.

Felicity wondered if Joe was actually dumb enough to write a letter like that. She didn't think so, and she liked the smell of the young cop, a mix of light sweat with some cheap deodorant, leather, and gun grease.

Joe asked her to go dancing that night after his shift.

She ignored his question. "I'm wondering if you could help me out with something, Joe. And stop winking; I hate that," she said when Joe winked again.

"Okay," he said. "I'll save the winking for Vanna."

"A few years back an Indian girl named Kashmir Birani disappeared in

New Orleans. There was a lot of talk in the paper at the time, then nada. The case is still unsolved. Could you get me a police file, something on the status?"

"Who wants to know?"

"A client. Will you do it?" Felicity looked into his eyes. No, Joe wasn't dumb at all. Someone serious stared back.

"If it means something to you."

Chapter Eight

*Wherein the hospice guests play a game with
ramifications beyond the convent walls*

 **h e** guests of the hospice, rejuvenated by Andrea's
presence, found other ways to pass the rainy evenings
during Advent. Mr. Rabindranath proposed that they
play a writing game. Each of them was to write something on his laptop computer. They passed the little machine back and forth, and they all typed in a few lines
without reading what the others had written. When they printed out their
collaboration, they found this:

God of plagues, where are you going?
We burn paper boats and bright candles to light his way to heaven.
If it is multicolored and shining, one has fallen prey
to the numerous ghosts of death.
There came a rain of resin from the sky.
There came one named Gouger of Faces: he gouged out
their eyeballs.
There came Sudden Bloodletter: he snapped off their heads.
There came Crunching Jaguar: he ate their flesh.
There came Tearing Jaguar: he tore them open.
Ye are like horses fastened to the chariot poles, luminous
with your beams, with splendor as at dawn;

like self-bright falcons, punishers of wicked men, like hovering
birds urged forward, scattering rain around.
The Flute Elder tells me that the world must return to its first
state of purity, that all plant and animal life as well as all mankind
must be cleansed and return to a harmonious life.
Maelrain taught that even in Lent one should take meat if there
was famine in the land and the alternative was starving.
A native priest, Tamblot, incited the natives of Bohol to repudiate
the Christian faith and return to the religion of their forefathers.
Many shells fell on homes and from their charred flesh rose
a desire to travel far and to be me.

Lama Cohen remarked that this odd little composition seemed to be
mostly about magical creatures and food. Each of them had put a little
fragment of their people's sacred texts into the composition. The subject
gave them cause for reflection.

"What would happen," speculated Dr. Luna, "if each of us were to bor-
row an angel from our mystical traditions and tell others of his adventures?"

"A species of bedtime story?" Dr. Li asked ironically.

"I can see that," Mr. Rabindranath said enthusiastically. "In the Hindu
tradition we are encouraged to retell the adventures of Krishna and even
to invent them. It is believed by some that our inventions become part of
Krishna's life, retroactively."

"Yes. We Hopi believe in stories. Our kachinas come to life when we
weave their stories. Spider Woman made the world. She was a weaver of
stories. She made them up and things happened."

"In the beginning was the Word," said Father Tuiredh.

Lama Cohen was confused. "Wait a minute. You are proposing that we
each employ an angel from our particular tradition to work for us?"

"In a manner of speaking," said Dr. Luna.

"Are there unemployed angels?" asked the lama. "And if there are, do
we have to right to use them in this way, for storytelling, for pleasure?"
She was troubled. "What if they are needed for bigger jobs than serving
the whimsy of bored scholars playing childish games . . ." She didn't say it,
but everyone could finish her sentence: "to entertain a silly young girl."

No one was sure whether angels should be plucked from their duties
and made to have adventures by the mere whim of humans. Father
Tuiredh argued that angels were always present, millions of them, and

each one already had a precise and taxing job. The very subject they were discussing was probably being recorded by an angel; at least half of them were in the business of recording everything for God's judgment.

Dr. Li said that this sort of surveillance made Western myths about the Chinese secret police laughable. These Christian angels were nothing but microphones.

Dr. Luna questioned the ability of angels to perform in three dimensions because, he said, angels are made of light and are totally flat.

Professor Li, who was in a most critical mood, declared that the creatures were fictional and was promptly attacked by the rest of the company, who made whirring noises of wings and threatened to bury him under a great deal of iconographic evidence.

In fact, few of them could agree on what angels looked like. For Lama Cohen they were not even remotely human looking. She passed around her prayer wheel, from which hung a variety of creatures, ugly and beautiful, but definitely not human. Dr. Luna's angels looked abstract, like squiggles of silver ink on black paper. Mr. Rabindranath insisted that every angel looks exactly the way one imagines it.

The discussion distressed the sisters so much they refused to participate. They loved angels: they had seen them in icons, in their prayers, and in their dreams. Making up fanciful things about them was as much as to try to reorder divine providence. Only Satan would want to do that. Sister Maria said so, but stopped short of accusing the company of being in collusion with Satan, though she thought it might be the case.

"All right," said Father Tuiredh reasonably, "we tell stories about our angels. But what's their *mission?* Providential beings must have a mission."

"They just wanna have fun," said Lama Cohen, "just like girls."

Andrea, who hadn't yet said anything, smiled broadly and exclaimed: "Cyndi Lauper!"

No one seemed to agree as to what these angels' mission might be, or even if they needed to have one beyond being the subjects of the good scholars' stories. Mr. Smith thought that maybe their job was to probe humanity with a view to deciding the exact hour of its termination. Mr. Rabindranath said that the so-called End of the World was only a transformation, one of many, and that these angels, whoever they were, ought to merely smooth the passage. Father Tuiredh argued that angels were messengers and that the most they were capable of was passing on decisions made elsewhere.

Lama Cohen had a practical solution that in the end satisfied almost everyone. She proposed that for the purposes of their story, the angels, who might be privately imagined by each as they wished, should be involved in preparing a great Meeting of Minds from all ages of history. These Minds would then deliberate the fate of the world. This would give the angels a great purpose and would cause them to have adventures that would entertain the company.

"But why should they be angels, then?" Mr. Rabindranath asked quite logically. "Could our characters not be saints, or gods, or simply brilliant minds? As long as their goal is to unite many intelligences, they can be whatever figures suit us."

The company agreed, and this version was adopted because it did not limit anyone to the controversial genus of angels, and it gave each one a chance to think about important things and imagine silly adventures without fear of offending anyone else.

Everyone retired for an hour of meditation to obtain a figure for storytelling, whatever that figure might be. At the end of the hour, the hospice guests reconvened.

"I have chosen an animal," Lama Cohen announced. "Turtle. In some Buddhist traditions, the turtle outwits everybody. And not just Buddhist tradition, of course. The turtle and the hare. In one story, the turtle learns to fly but gives it up because it prefers slowness. Turtle is going to speak Brooklynese."

There were murmurs of surprise. Sister Rodica asked the lama how she'd chosen the turtle. Lama Cohen said that at first she had thought that she might employ Einstein or the fourth Dalai Lama as the character of her story, but then she realized that she would be depriving this character of choice because he would be a prisoner of her story. Instead, she had chosen the turtle to act as an intermediary between heaven and the Great Minds.

Father Tuiredh said that something similar happened to him. He had thought of Saint Patrick or James Joyce, but an angel called Magdbeh, who had taken the form of a butterfly, appeared before him. In some representations Magdbeh was a butterfly-child who touched people and renewed their innocence. Innocence was essential to salvation. "Therefore," he concluded, "my hero is Magdbeh the Butterfly."

Mr. Earl Smith had considered the Rain kachina or Richard Nixon, who had been a great friend of the Hopi people, but then chose Coyote, the Trickster, whose adventures had always intrigued him and on whom he had once written a paper at the University of New Mexico.

Father Hernio had thought about choosing Ignatius Loyola or Saint Sebastian but settled instead on Monkey, who in the Philippines was always getting into trouble, on the side of good. Monkey had the ability to exist simultaneously in several worlds at once. This, it seemed to Father Hernio, was an angelic quality, and it had the further advantage of protecting him from a charge of blasphemy, which he might have leveled against himself had he chosen a martyr of the church.

Mr. Rabindranath had paraded before his mind's eye a long and colorful procession of Hindu scholars, saints, and deities but realized, to his surprise, that he preferred a folk character called Salamander. This too had the advantage of protecting the gods, who, while not as surrounded by literalism as the Christian saints, were nonetheless fearsome if wronged.

Dr. Luna, using pretty much the same logic as Mr. Rabindranath, arrived at the figure of Crow, one of his favorite story heroes. He imagined Crow preening his feathers and reflecting on the nature of reality.

Professor Li chose Fox, a magical being capable of numerous transformations, whose deeds and power were little known in the West.

Pressed to participate, the sisters said that they could not possibly bring themselves to invent anything that would be offensive to Holy Scripture. Told that perhaps they didn't have to invent anything but that they could participate by just retelling sacred stories, Sister Rodica allowed that she might bring to the gathering stories of Saint Teresa de Avila, who had been a poet and storyteller herself. But then she changed her mind and said that she might use a Romanian folk character called Pacala-Tandala, who was so clever he sometimes lost his sense of good and evil. She then changed her mind again and said that in Romania it is impolite for a host to tell a story. Only guests had that privilege.

Sister Maria also held firm. She said that for her there was only the Holy Mother and that whatever mention she might make of the Mother of Christ would have to be received with utter respect by the company. One did not speak lightly of the Mother of God. The nun exuded such sincerity the wily scholars were momentarily abashed.

Andrea couldn't think of anyone, human or animal, whose figure she wanted to use. She said that she hated mythical creatures who could get themselves out of every difficulty, which was impossible for most people, and the only angels she had met were evil ones, camp guards who had power of life and death over people. She also insisted, with uncharacteristic eloquence, that all stories are sad because they end.

No one argued with her about that, but Dr. Luna suggested that the endings of stories were only an illusion, that stories went on long after both telling and teller were finished. "Otherwise," he said, "how would the world go on?"

Dr. Li, an atheist, joked: "Perhaps Andrea is our subject. She doesn't need to employ a character to tell stories because she is the intended audience for all our stories."

The remark struck those present deeply, though it was spoken in jest. They officially proclaimed Andrea chief listener. The chief listener, they said, listened to everything and was comforted in this way by a single unending story, because whenever a teller finished a story, another would begin, and so on.

There now remained only the question of where the story was going to unfold, so that the action would not spin out all over the place. There had to be someplace where the Meeting of Great Minds would be held, even if the journeys of their magical creatures traversed many regions and climates.

"Why, Jerusalem, of course," said Mr. Rabindranath.

But the others objected. That was too easy. How about the holy sites of their own countries? Oraibi, on the Second Mesa? Or the Taj Mahal? Or the Palace of the Great People's Congress?

They couldn't reach an agreement, so Andrea suggested: "Let's spin the globe."

There was a globe in the library, and so it was done. Andrea closed her eyes and spun the globe. When it came to rest, she put her finger on it, and the place it landed on was New Orleans, Louisiana, in North America, a place none of them knew anything about.

The story of the guide beings and of the Great Minds who would meet in New Orleans to decide the fate of the world began that very night at Saint Hildegard Hospice in Jerusalem.

Chapter Nine

Wherein Felicity meets Amelia Earhart, the famed aviatrix, in cyberspace and becomes friendly with Joe, the cop

B e f o r e her date with Joe that night, Felicity decided to make contact with Joan of Arc and ask her how to proceed in her righteous campaign against Mullin. She had always admired the warrior girl, who had never backed away from a fight. She had written a history term paper on the patron saint of New Orleans.

Felicity logged in to *Make Love to People from History*, identified herself, *Messiah*, and requested Joan.

"I'm sorry, Joan is not here," said a figure in jodhpurs with aviator goggles, who opened the door of what looked like a motel room in Los Angeles. A dusty palm tree could be seen in the courtyard.

"Who is this, please?" Felicity asked politely.

"Her roommate, Amelia."

"Amelia who?"

"Amelia Earhart."

The famous aviatrix had disappeared in 1937 over the Pacific Ocean on the last leg of her around-the-world flight, the first for a woman. All sorts of theories surrounded her disappearance, and some said that she'd been captured by the Japanese and executed before the end of the war. Others claimed to have seen her alive in China. One report had Earhart living in the United States under an assumed name. It was generally believed that she had been a spy. Amelia Earhart had been another one of Felicity's adolescent obsessions, and the subject of another term paper. She'd read a book written by two flight engineers who had analyzed in detail the condition of the plane and had concluded that mechanical errors and fatigue had most certainly caused an accident. According to them, the plane and its two passengers were at the bottom of the Pacific Ocean. But Felicity never believed it. The mystery of the vanished Electra twin-engine had preoccupied her for a whole year.

"Great," typed Felicity. "You're one of my old crushes."

"Thrilled," Amelia responded. "Interested in flying?"

"Not really. I've lived in New Orleans all my life. Never had the urge to get in a flying box. No control."

"Would you like to come in?"

Felicity scratched her crooked nimbus, then walked through the door into a room strewn with the aftermath of a serious drinking party. Empty bottles of scotch lay all over the floor. Women's lingerie was strewn over the furniture. Amelia made no apology. She sat down on the couch and bade Messiah sit next to her. Felicity remained standing.

"What attracted you to me?" Amelia lit a cigarette.

Felicity thought for a moment before answering. "Your drag. You know, your goggles, your scarf, your leather jacket. The look. Aviatrix. Cool. And your disappearance. The mystery. You pushed the envelope. That's a phrase they coined after your time. Your courage. I would like to push the envelope, too."

She'd said too much. The trouble with having taken typing. There was a prolonged silence in the world of the aviatrix. Then the reply: "You hit on it with the scarf and the leather. We are basically a leather-and-silk-restraints club."

"We?"

"Charles Lindbergh, the Germans, the Red Baron, the explorers. Our taskmaster is Fred Nietzsche. It's 1937 around here all the time. The music is Wagner. We are naturists. I flew naked once or twice."

"Is dying young part of the deal?"

"Definitely! That's what explorers are: scouts into humanity's future feelings. Humanity's future feeling in 1937 was for death. There was a thirst for death, a passion for it. We were drunk with water from the fountain of death."

"It wasn't so pretty by 1945."

"Well, no, that's the trouble with the masses. They vulgarize the work of elites. Death was an art for us. The fucking peasants and bureaucrats turned it into a production quota."

"The world seems to be on the verge of something like that now, Aviatrix," typed Felicity. Messiah sat cautiously down on the far end of the couch.

"Big time. Disgusting. Death without heroism. Piles of bodies. But let's get back to you. Why do you call yourself Messiah, anyway? You want to save the shithouse?"

Felicity blushed. She typed: "Blushing. I have no idea. There are a lot of phonies running around claiming to be the Messiah, so I thought I'd subvert them. I *could* be the Messiah. You do believe in God, don't you?"

"Guess what?" replied Amelia Earhart. "I don't. I'm dead, but I haven't seen hide nor hair of God. Besides, the Messiah is a Semitic notion."

"Are you an anti-Semite?" Felicity challenged.

"Definitely! Can't be *Übermensch* without a worthy adversary. Jews are the *worthiest*."

"Okay. You're a racist. Get ready to pop your goggles. I'm black." Messiah gave Amelia the finger.

"Sigh. I must treat you like a slave, then. Take off whatever rags you are wearing and prepare for a whipping." Amelia stood up, reached behind the couch, and picked up a horse whip.

The game had gone too far. Felicity wondered whether the flush of excitement that hardened her nipples was worth losing her on-line dignity. Why had she told her the truth? She could have been anything. After all, who knew that this cyber-Amelia wasn't black? Or Jewish? Self-loathing, Felicity knew, was the muddy source of a lot of sexuality.

"I'm not into subjugation. Why don't we try it the other way? I could beat your little blond ass instead."

Amelia took a long time to answer. "I am only a locus. I am only an occasion. I have no body. I can provide you with a fantasy, but it has to be consistent. I cannot be both superwoman aviatrix and masochist. It's not in my logic." She put away the whip.

Felicity wrote: "I'm sorry. Would you recommend someone more poetic, gentler, sadder? I don't think I can deal with Nietzschean will freaks right now. I'll call you sometime, okay?"

"Roger that. Try Ovid. Roman poet. Exiled. Very sad. Over and out." The motel room dimmed, and Messiah found herself alone in the desert with the blue sky.

Felicity took a very long shower and mourned her blasted integrity. Her distress was compounded by a new awareness of her unconscious megalomania. Messiah, my ass. As the water pummeled her dark little Creole ass, she considered what opportunities she was missing by remaining so stubbornly honest and provincial. She could pass for white and fuck cyber–John Wayne. She could pretend to be a man and Amelia Earhart would be hers. She could be anything she wanted to be in the brave new world of cyberidentity. New Orleans had taught her that much; life was a masquerade, and disguise was essential to the enjoyment of the flesh. Carnival—*carne vale*, the farewell to the flesh—was the essence of her city.

The phone must have rung while she was showering. The message on her machine was delivered by a flat female voice. "The party you met this afternoon would like to complete the transaction by the end of the day tomorrow. Another call will follow this one, to set the time and place." Mullin was biting.

Felicity primped slowly. She had no appetite. If Joe intended to take her out to dinner before they went dancing, she wouldn't even be able to look at the food. In Miles's days of drugs and roses, everything she looked at made her hungry. The world was a luscious menu. A kind of acid had been slowly eating away at her since Miles's death. It was making the colors fade and turning her appetite into rage. Felicity removed some of her rings and rummaged through her closet for something more conventional than her usual punk uniform. She settled on her only dress, a sleeveless black linen number. The mirror returned to her the image of a little girl playing dress-up.

When Joe Di Friggio appeared at her door, he looked like a special delivery package from Chippendale's. His Italian suit was too perfect, he reeked of cologne, and a thick gold chain was visible beneath his open-collar silk shirt. She almost asked him if he'd ever danced for money.

Joe gave her a tightly furled red rose and a computer disk.

"The Kashmir Birani file. I downloaded what we have."

Felicity was touched. She locked the door behind her and surveyed the magnolias and withered azaleas on both sides of the street. Two Shades stood smoking on the sidewalk, looking glassy eyed on the world. She was fond of the Shades, who had appeared out of nowhere one day and now occupied public space all over New Orleans. They were tattooed all over, except for the face, with body parts that coincided in all respects with their own. They had feet tattooed on feet, hands on hands, and so forth, but since the drawings were of necessity smaller, the shades looked as if they were cradling a body that had somehow adhered to their own. It reminded Felicity of a Robert Johnson lyric: "I'm closer to you, baby, than Jesus to the cross."

They were very much like herself. The only difference was that they were poor runaways who'd escaped diagnosis and were self-medicating instead. The first time she had pierced her nipple, it had been an alternative to suicide. She'd been taking Zoloft, an antidepressant that had made her serene enough to consider the ultimate antidepressant, death. A tattoo artist, a friend of Miles's, had dropped by and, after hearing her rambling defense of suicide, had offered to pierce her nipple. "A foretaste," he said, "of invasive self-assault." It had worked. From that time, she'd pierced herself every time she'd wanted to die. Every ring in her body was a memento of the urge to end it all.

"Bums," Joe commented tersely.

"They're okay. Benign vegetarians. They've committed themselves to this earth." Felicity threw a kiss in their direction.

Joe put a police light on top of his Camaro and parked right in front of Café Sbisa on busy Decatur Street.

"You eat like a bird," said Joe, watching her push a shrimp around with her fork. Café Sbisa was dark, mirrored, discreet, old-fashioned, steeped in bay leaves and sea salt. Waiters slick as Dracula, their manner at once familiar and haughty, bent close to whisper the specials, and perhaps to smell her hair and check out her tits. There was a crooner at the piano upstairs, not exactly Harry Connick Jr. but definitely smoky and Italian and a little edgy, slightly chipped like her fluted champagne glass.

"You got class, Joe."

Joe was proud. Actually, Sbisa was a bit over his budget, but his cousin Tony worked here. All his cousins were waiters. In New Orleans the waiting profession was hereditary. Tony had done some time for spousal abuse, but the sentence had been drastically reduced when fifty waiters had shown up in court to testify to his good character.

"Like a bird," he repeated, looking with regret at the shrimp diablo à deux.

"Actually, birds eat all the time. Who were those naked men, anyway?" She sipped some more champagne. "The preacher isn't here. You can tell me the rest of it."

"They gave the names Fabricius something and Cleo something. Just cruising for a good time, and bam. There's a lot of that these days. We pick 'em up stuck in daisy chains, with bottles up . . . excuse me. This is not dinner chat."

"Gay bashing," said Felicity.

Joe had no sympathy with political correctness. "We call 'em queers where I come from. They go fishing with worms, they catch gators some-times."

"Surely you don't think homosexuality is unnatural," she teased.

"Afraid I do. Men and women were built for something specific."

"Yeah. Consuming shrimp diablo à deux."

"This Kashmir Birani case . . . is it a good-paying job?" Joe enquired, changing the subject.

Felicity sensed again that there was a deeply serious man behind the surface of pretty-boy cop. "Not really. I think my uncle hired me out of pity. I've been doing nothing but domestic bullshit since I hung up my shingle."

Joe was watching her mouth. No shrimp had yet passed that plump red lower lip. The upper quivered slightly. A kiss, thought Joe, will make it stop.

"You follow people, right?" he said.

"Sometimes they follow me." She lifted a forkful of diablo, then set it back down. Her tongue briefly probed her upper lip. The crease above was narrow but distinct. Miles used to say, "The angel that put his finger there was one skinny motherfucker."

"I'd follow you," said Joe, with an expression of greedy interest.

"What if I told you I was gay?"

"I would say, no way."

"You think it's curable?"

"Don't believe in it. Two holes don't make a whole, if you'll pardon me."

"So what do you call lesbians, Joe?"

"Doughnut slappers." He grinned.

"I'll have to remember that one," Felicity said acidly. "What if I told you that I was black?"

Her compulsive honesty again. Felicity wondered if relentless honesty was a disease. Perhaps she ought to avail herself again of one of the many kinds of pills that had adjusted her not so long ago. But they hadn't been specific enough. What she needed was a pill to curb honesty. A pill to make a date go smoothly. A pill to make her hungry. A pill to make her ignore blatant unfairness.

Joe looked her over carefully.

"I'd say my interest is doubled."

"You don't believe in same-sex love but you're all for interracial dating."

"Something like that."

Felicity would have liked to dislike Joe, but she couldn't. She was ashamed for having accepted this date only because she wanted the Kashmir Birani file. It was dishonest. Not only was she compulsively honest; dishonesty made her ill. She decided to level with Joe.

"Joe, I only came on this date to get the Birani file. I'm telling you this so that you can hate me now, instead of later. I've been having a tough time lately."

To her surprise, Joe was not upset. He reached over and touched her hand. It was a warm, friendly gesture. "Everybody's having a tough time these days. Something is going on in this city. You can tell me whatever you want. I don't have any evil designs. . . . Well, maybe one."

Felicity laughed but felt like crying. She found herself telling Joe the story of Miles, her boyfriend, killed by the mean city.

Joe listened very carefully. He'd worked Vice undercover and was familiar with a lot of characters. The musicians' milieu was well known to him. He'd listened to some great music in the city's clubs while stalking one dealer or another. When Felicity finished describing the horrible night after they'd come home from Tipitina's and Miles had taken his final shot, Joe reached across the table and took Felicity's hand again.

"I used to work Vice. I know the dealers. You want me to find the scumbag who sold him the shit?"

Oh, no, thought Felicity, liking the feel of his wide, rough palm over her fingers; I hope he doesn't tell me. She had decided not to pursue the likely purveyors of Miles's bad heroin—she was afraid that a lot of good musicians might be implicated. What was the use? They made beautiful music, but they had sad hearts and made mistakes as large as their lives.

"You worked Vice undercover? Then how come you're a patrolman, Joe? Did you fuck up?"

Joe didn't smile. He had been assigned to undercover on a trial basis and had done an excellent job. Then he'd found out that in Vice he was expected to keep his mouth shut and protect some very bad people. But he couldn't do it. If he did, he could never look at his mother again, or face his parish priest. So he'd gone back to patrol. It meant that he probably couldn't afford someone like Felicity. So be it.

"Do you know a guy named Bamajan?" Felicity asked, hoping to change the subject back to Kashmir.

"Dealer to musicians. A trumpet player. Did your boyfriend know him?"

"They were buddies."

"Maybe that's your man. He sold him a hot shot."

Now I have another fucking job. Thanks a lot, Felicity thought unhappily. Was Miles's pal the same Bamajan involved in the disappearance of the Indian TV star? If Bamajan really meant "announcer of God," she suspected that it was a generic name for adepts of yet another weird cult. New Orleans was full of them. Some cults were just covers for drug dealing. She knew that Miles's Bamajan was now a street musician, playing for tourists on the riverfront. This Bamajan was just a junky, one of a million pulsing veins in the night.

"I don't think I want to know," she said softly. "It doesn't change anything."

Joe patted her hand. "I think I understand. If it was me, though, the motherfucker would be dog food. The city is full of scum like that."

"And you'd like to clean it up, right? Remember the law, Joe?"

Joe grinned. Asking a New Orleans cop to remember the law was like asking a nun to give head. Joe wasn't dirty himself, but he knew his colleagues were less than clean. New Orleans cops had been busted for murder, rape, drug dealing, battery, insurance scams, shakedowns, and myriad smaller offenses. The department was a sea of lawlessness.

Felicity got even more depressed thinking that this nice guy, this regular Joe, might be dirtier than the floor at the Acme Oyster House, where they threw the shells at their feet.

"Do you ever read them their rights before you blow them away, Joe?"

"I'm a religious man, sister. I read them the last rites in every case."

It was a joke, but she wasn't amused. She suspected that if she had to choose, she'd feel safer with the Bamajans than the NOPD. It was a screwy city in a screwy country in a screwy time, and dangerous as shit. Felicity had once counted up her dead or dysfunctional friends. Seventeen dead, six of those gunshot victims, eight suicides, and three had crashed drunk in their cars. That left out those who'd tried starving themselves to death, had killed one or both their parents, or who were permanently addicted to one thing or another.

"What's the matter? Did I offend you?"

"I don't know, Joe. Let me ask you a silly question. You ever think about America? I don't mean, like, do you vote, or do we have the best of everything, or any of that. I mean, honestly, up from the street. What do you think goes on?"

Even as she said these things, Felicity blushed for their banality. But Joe was not put off. Quite the contrary. He often thought about things like that.

"It's Rome," he said, "in the last days. Our society is falling apart from the inside because we've lost our faith in God. It's a battle between good and evil, and all the prophecies are going to come true."

"Jeezus, Joe. You don't really believe that crap."

"Crap?" Joe was offended. "You some kind of secular humanist?"

"You could say so. One time in college I went to hear a lecture about America's great destiny, or some such. The speaker was this racist from something called the Identity Church. 'America,' he screamed, 'is waiting for the white Jesus!' Then he raised one arm in a Hitler salute and crossed himself with the other. Ever since, whenever anyone says that they are waiting for Jesus or the End Times or something, I see this weasely motherfucker with the '*Sieg heil*' and the cross. In fact, whenever someone says, 'I'm waiting for someone,' even if it's just the plumber, I picture this 'someone' as a fucking Nazi. You follow me, Joe?"

Joe did. He'd refused to be part of groups like that, though he'd been invited many times. Everyone from the KKK to the American Nazi Party to Amway had tried to recruit him. He'd turned them down, not necessarily because he disagreed with some of their points but because he was an old-fashioned Christian. His mother had taught him not to boast about his faith. Humility was a virtue. Joe was embarrassed by the shouters and the screamers. But how to explain this to Felicity?

"I'm sorry," he said.

"More bubbles, please." She couldn't seem to get drunk.

What the hell was wrong with her, anyway? She couldn't even enjoy an uncomplicated date without being turned off by something that offended her sense of right and wrong. Joe was a good guy. She remembered something her friend Ben Redman had said years before when she said she believed that most people were good.

" 'Brutus is an honorable man. So are they all, honorable men,' " Ben quoted Shakespeare in response. Ben was the only human being on the planet with whom she could discuss matters of principle. They had also discussed the minutiae of their psyches and the changes wrought on them by the drugs they were being prescribed; they cautioned and urged each other at the approach of delusions; they questioned reality, never leaving well enough alone.

"Let's talk about movies." Joe had watched the darkening of her mood and was beginning to doubt the success of the evening.

"Haven't seen any lately. But the world's pretty bad. Wonder who directed it," said Felicity. Her own life seemed like a movie just then. She was watching, but not very well. There was something provisional about her life, as if she had borrowed it from someone else. It allowed her to do anything and everything, but from a distance, like a movie.

Felicity asked him to take her home.

Chapter Ten

Wherein we hear stories told by the guest scholars at Saint Hildegard Hospice

Tu r t l e needed a job," said Lama Cohen. "He had been lying around hibernating all winter, then spring came and he was starving. He went up to an old hermit who had lived in a cave without any food or water for about sixty years, and asked him if he had a job for him.

" 'Why,' said the hermit, 'I have a job sitting. I don't eat or drink, and I never talk. Now you come up here, ask me for a job, and have me say all these words, which are going to exhaust me.' And the hermit got so depleted from speaking that he died.

"The turtle was astonished. I just killed a man, he thought; maybe I should be a soldier. So he went to a rich raja who had a palace with towers that reached the clouds.

" 'I want to be a soldier,' he said. 'I have endurance, and my shell is very hard.'

"The raja said, 'These are peaceful times and I don't need any soldiers, but I have another job for you. I heard that holy men all over the mountains have been dying in their caves. One after another, after not eating, drinking, or speaking for many years, they suddenly fall over and die. It is well known that these hermits have treasures hidden in their caves. Your job is to go to the caves of the dead hermits, find their treasures, and carry them back to me on your strong, hard back.'

"So Turtle went to all the caves, and crawled over the dead hermits who turned to dust as soon as he touched them, and looked for treasure. He didn't find any. But the spirits of the dead hermits, who had been watching him search, were laughing. So when Turtle went back, they jumped on his back and rode with him to the raja's palace.

"And so it came to pass that the raja's palace became filled with the spirits of holy men. The raja himself died eventually, but because he was no holy man he became a servant spirit, who fetched food for the hermit spirits. Turtle remained alive because turtles live a long time, but also because the spirits needed him to carry them to a meeting of Great Minds. The word in the spirit world was that a Meeting of Minds that was going to decide the fate of the visible world was going to be held in New Orleans, Louisiana, in the United States of America. They all wanted to go there, mostly for the meeting, but also for the local music, of which the spirits had heard great things."

"A fox," Professor Li began, "was caught in a trap by the great Confucius. She knew that Confucius would not kill her before they had a good philosophical discussion, so the fox stayed awake all night thinking of clever things to tell the great man. But in the morning Confucius didn't feel very well, so he told the fox that she was free to go, provided that she returned the next day for a philosophical discussion.

"The fox was very smart, and normally she would have taken off for the woods never to return, but the thought of a conversation with Confucius was just too irresistible.

"The next day she returned, and Confucius told her: 'I am going to die in three days. One thousand years from now my spirit will be summoned to a great meeting. Please tell your children to tell their children to tell their children about this. After a thousand years have passed, one of your heirs will ferry my soul to the meeting. Until then, I have a piece of advice for you. Don't wait around for philosophical discussions. Choose freedom every time. Otherwise, as you can see, all you'll get is a job.' "

"I can see how this is going," said Earl Smith. "Every clever animal on earth is going to make arrangements with the most clever Minds to go to New Orleans. But it's a small city, so there is no way that all these Minds will fit, particularly if they come tended by thousands of spirits, not to speak of wildlife. Unfortunately, it may become necessary for some of the Minds to miss the meeting. Some of these animals and their precious cargo of souls will have to be diverted. We would not want the great meeting to become the great cacophony. "To this quandary, Coyote has the solution. He is not only clever; he has absolutely no qualms about doing terrible things, if they are necessary and amusing," Mr. Smith concluded with a grin.

"I can live with that," said Andrea.

"In other words," declared Father Hernio, "Coyote is declaring a war of wits on everyone else."

"For the sake of narrative interest," said Mr. Smith humbly. "It appears that Coyote was very bored one day. He was tired of all the physical gags that had so amused him in the age of silent films. He wanted to improve his mind. He presented himself to the film department at UCLA and demanded to be instructed. He found the instruction pretty dull, so to amuse himself he sometimes caused the spirits of his favorite filmmakers or actors to take over the bodies of his professors. The stodgy academic lecturing would find himself all of a sudden possessed by Orson Welles, or John Ford, or Cary Grant, and begin an extraordinary display that thrilled the students. The spirits of Welles, Ford, Max von Sydow, Marlene Dietrich, Cary Grant, and others were terribly annoyed by Coyote's antics. They pledged to revenge themselves at the earliest opportunity. When the decision to convene a Meeting of Minds in New Orleans was taken, the great film artists decided that Coyote would ferry them to New Orleans and perform the functions of guide, butler, cook, chauffeur, and maid. Coyote hated this assignment, but he pretended to go along. He put on a chauffeur's uniform and opened the door of the spirit car for the filmmakers and actors. He drove and drove for what seemed like a very long time, and then he stopped.

" 'New Orleans!' he called out.

"The spirits got out and looked around; they were inside a cave covered with movie screens on which all their movies played at once.

" 'What is this place?' cried the annoyed cineasts.

" 'Plato's cave!' replied Coyote, and vanished into thin air, leaving the greats of the film industry to find their own way out of Plato's cave. Unfortunately, this is nearly impossible, which is why film people will be underrepresented at the meeting."

"That's not good." Andrea shook her head disapprovingly. "I'm afraid this big meeting is going to be all serious people, men with beards. I like movies."

"Well," Earl Smith said, "based on my experience with the film indus-try, I have to admire Coyote."

There was a brief intermission while Sister Rodica went to the kitchen to fetch lemonade. After everyone had filled their glass, Father Tuiredh reas-sured Andrea: "I am going to tell a story about young people without any beards, who will also be present at the time of this meeting." He then launched into his tale:

"Magdbeh the Butterfly had once been a boy, during the reign of King Albdhir the Magician. Ireland was experiencing unprecedented prosperity because of his magic, and there was no lack of fried mutton leg, mead, and entertainments. As it often happens during good times, the boys and girls were very bored, mad at their parents, and always causing mischief. One day, Magdbeh was loitering about the marketplace, making rude com-ments to his friends about the well-fed people buying meats and fruits, when a messenger arrived from the king."

Father Tuiredh brought his hands to his mouth and spoke through his fingers like a megaphone: " 'Hear ye all, hear ye! King Albdhir is bored!' Magdbeh and his friends applauded. That's how they felt, too. 'King Albdhir has decreed a Metamorphic Lottery!' When they heard this, the young peo-ple applauded even harder, but the older folk were worried. Nobody had any idea what a Metamorphic Lottery was, and the messenger did not explain.

"A big wheel was erected at the center of the city, and every citizen of the kingdom was given a turn at spinning it. Whatever number the wheel stopped on became that person's number. The king's scribes wrote down everyone's number next to their name. Magdbeh drew the number 999, a number considered very propitious by the king's astrologers. And so it was. Magdbeh won first prize in the Metamorphic Lottery. Everyone else won, too, but theirs were smaller prizes. The whole kingdom rejoiced at such luck, and few people slept that night, waiting for dawn, when the ac-tual prizes were going to be revealed.

"The king appeared on his balcony before all the citizens of his king-dom, who bowed their heads in silence, waiting for him to speak."

Father Tuiredh paused and looked at the rapt faces before him. He gazed longest at Andrea. He didn't speak again for a long time. His audi-ence was growing impatient, fearing that the father had brought them along this far in the story only to leave them in suspense. But Father Tuiredh continued:

"The king announced that Magdbeh, the first-prize winner, had the choice to be transformed into any creature he wished, for that was the meaning of the word 'metamorphic.' Magdbeh was speechless with wonder. While everyone, including the king, looked at him, he thought about all the creatures that he could become. He liked wolves and bears and birds, but he liked butterflies best.

" 'A butterfly!' "

"No sooner said than done. He became a butterfly with gold spots on his black wings, and he lifted up into the air and landed on the king's crown. Magdbeh was a butterfly in all respects but for his eyes, which remained human.

"The king then distributed the rest of the prizes, which consisted of transforming every man, woman, and child in his kingdom into another creature. Only the first-prize winner had had a choice, so the rest of them became whatever the king wished. Some he made into wolves, others into fish, others into birds, and yet others into worms, roaches, and horseflies. When the king was finished, there were no more people in Ireland, but there were so many wild creatures that there was no room on the island for all of them. The king filled the sea with round drums and he set the creatures in them, launching them on the currents. This is why most of the creatures in the world now stand still when they hear Irish music. They used to be people in Eire once.

"Magdbeh traveled farther than all the rest of them, floating from place to place. Whenever he settled briefly on anyone's hand or shoulder, he left his image there. In the long centuries that followed, many great people sported the image of a butterfly on their skin. If Magdbeh rested more than a minute on someone, that person would feel light, happy, and refuse to participate any longer in the dense and weighty problems of the world. Thus were born tribes of wanderers known by various names, but having in common an airy disposition, a love of floating, and an aptitude for music, dance, and joy. Today, the tribes of Magdbeh the Butterfly are known as Shades. Magdbeh himself is in the city of New Orleans, settling randomly on whoever tastes sweet to him."

The company sat in charmed silence for a time, and then Andrea asked, "Where do the people who live in Ireland now come from?"

"A lovely question, child," Father Tuiredh replied. "I am not rightly sure, but some say that they came from the east, following the apostle Luke. King Albdhir converted and gave up magic."

"Well, I am quite certain," said Father Hernio in a tone of feigned annoyance, "that Monkey did not come from Ireland. He came from the Philippines, and his story is quite native."

Father Tuiredh conceded graciously that there might be an animal or two that did not come from Ireland.

"Monkey was always Monkey," stressed Father Hernio, "but one day he had the opportunity to put his monkeyness to good use. He was eating a banana, when he saw a girl sleeping under his rubber tree. It was a vision of ugliness, this hairless creature stretched in the moonlight, still as a bumpy carpet. He came down to investigate. He flicked his tail over her nose, but she didn't wake up. She's probably sleeping because she is too ashamed of being hairless, thought Monkey; I will help her. Monkey plucked a branch from the top of the monkey tree, which was the tree the first monkey came from. The leaves of the monkey tree, when properly applied, had the effect of making a monkey out of anything, even a stone. He wrapped the sleeping girl in the leaves of the monkey tree branch and then waited the required three days, singing the first-monkey song."

Father Hernio paused and puckered his lips.

"Yes, yes," Lama Cohen said. "Sing the song, Father."

"I have a terrible voice," Father Hernio confessed.

Everyone hastened to assure him that he was forgiven, so in a terrible voice, Father Hernio sang the first-monkey song:

> Father Sun, Mother Earth,
> thank you for my fur,
> thank you for my eyes,
> thank you for my tail.
> How can I thank you for my fur?
> All creatures love Monkey.

Everyone applauded, and Father Hernio said: "The song was very old and it didn't work as well as it used to in the old days, when in combination with the leaves, it could make a monkey out of anything. The saddest part of its not working was that the sleeping girl didn't get any fur. But it worked well enough to wake her up infused with monkey spirit. She didn't just wake up, she leapt up. She snatched a banana from Monkey's stash, ran around the tree, climbed it, and threw bird eggs at Monkey's head.

"The hairless monkey girl lived in the forest, watched over by Monkey, who saw to her education. But one day she strayed onto the beach and was captured by American pirates, who thought she was human. She was taken across the ocean and then to New Orleans, where her odd behavior was attributed to her life with the pirates. She was forcibly socialized and taught Victorian manners, especially the right way to hold a knife and fork.

"She was very unhappy. Every day she thought about her friend Monkey and had long telepathic conversations with him. During one of these, he told her that her salvation would come from Salamander.

"It hasn't happened yet. Somewhere in New Orleans lives a girl with agile thoughts and restless limbs who can never sit still either in her mind or in her body. She is Monkey. She will not find peace until she kisses the salamander."

"I think that this is my cue!" exclaimed Mr. Rabindranath, who had become so excited during Father Hernio's story it was all he could do to keep himself from levitating. "But I must ask, Father, why no Great Minds were involved in this story."

"It's my little tribute to Charles Darwin, in acknowledgment of the pope's latest position on evolution. If man did indeed evolve from monkeys, with God's help, then all great minds were monkey first. The girl in New Orleans, by being monkey, is the ancestress of all the Minds."

"Very well. I beg your forgiveness, Sisters, for parts of Salamander's story. He is Hindu, and as you know, our religion is most physical."

Sister Rodica blushed, and Sister Maria said: "My ears will be tremendously selective, Mr. Rabindranath."

"Salamander was the daughter of Princess Rani and Arjuna the Warrior. She grew up learning music, dance, and horticulture. Her garden in Kashmir sat between two peaks of the Himalayas and contained all the flowers and fruits of India. The river watering the garden was the river Birani, and rare fish lived in it, and also a guardian monster named Chakkar, who was rumored to look like a handsome man, only he had fish scales instead of skin, and eight—forgive me, Sisters—phalluses instead of one.

"Salamander had never seen Chakkar, but her imagination was stimulated. She found most of the princes who had been courting her lacking. One evening, as she sat sighing and watching her silk sari billow in the gentle breeze on the riverbank, she heard a man's voice behind her.

" 'Do not turn around, resplendent Salamander! I have loved you since you were a little girl and first came to rest here by my river. I am Chakkar.'

"Salamander wanted nothing more than to turn around, but Chakkar warned her again. 'Anyone who sees me will become a lizard.'

"Salamander and Chakkar met every night after that, but she never looked at him. At first he stood a short distance behind her, but their desire for one another was great. One night, just before dawn, Chakkar embraced her from behind, and Salamander let her body fall into his arms. The fish scales did not discomfort her, because they were warm and felt just like skin, but Salamander found it difficult to adjust her slender body between Chakkar's eight erect phalluses. It was hard to know where to put her arms. At last they found a comfortable position and settled like this into one another's arms for many nights.

"But Salamander wished more than anything else to see Chakkar's face and to embrace him from the front, like any normal lover."

Sister Maria coughed. "Mr. Rabindranath, is it possible to gloss over some of these, uhm, technical details?"

Mr. Rabindranath shook his head in dismay. "The essence of Indian stories resides *in details*, dear Sister. Have you ever seen the Taj Mahal? A myriad small details."

"I have seen a depiction"—Sister Maria was stung—"and I am sure that it took *a very long time* to build it."

Mr. Rabindranath bowed slightly. "Point well taken. One evening, after their many nights of delight, Salamander could bear it no longer. She turned around and faced her lover. She looked into his deep black eyes full of moonlight and beheld for the first time the full splendor of those male members whose texture and weight she knew intimately by touch.

"At that moment she began to change. Her soft skin rippled and roughened. Even as Chakkar cried out in distress, his lover became a lizard.

"They held each other for a long time, crying. At long last, Chakkar spoke: 'There is only one remedy, my love. You must journey into the future to the city of New Orleans and meet Monkey Girl. If you kiss her, you will regain your lovely form.'

"With these words the guardian monster leapt back into the waters of the Birani River and was gone.

"Princess Salamander journeyed to New Orleans many times over the centuries, ferrying the Great Minds of India there—the writers of the sutras, yogis, poets, and magicians. But every time she made the crossing, she found that she was in the wrong future, that it was too early to meet Monkey Girl. She left her precious cargo, which spread many Indian spiritual practices across America, and returned to Kashmir. She is now readying herself for one more trip. This time she will take there the great Mahatma Gandhi."

"What happened to Chakkar?" Andrea wanted to know.

"He strokes his sad flesh, waiting for her return."

Dr. Carlos Luna said gently: "The night is almost over. Perhaps we should wait until tomorrow for the story of Crow, the prophet of chlorophyll propulsion."

Everyone protested. No one admitted being tired.

"Very well, then. Crow was fed up with the gloomy symbolism that poets kept saddling him with, so he decided to show the world that despite his color and morbid face, he was a benefactor of humanity. He thought long and hard about this, while sitting on a high-tension wire just outside New Oraibi, Arizona. It occurred to him that the humming wire he gripped with his feet was the lifeline of the modern world. Through such wires flowed the juice that kept American homes lit at night, turned America's engines, powered its computers, and crowned its festivities. The juice, he knew, was wrenched from the heart of the earth, pulled from the fury of rivers, and forced out of atoms. Crow also knew that there were many other juices that humans had not yet discovered, juices that resided like milk in nature's bountiful complexity.

"Crow presented himself to the U.S. Patent Office in Washington, D.C., and declared that he intended to file a patent for a new juice he called 'chlorophyll propulsion.' The man in the office laughed. 'In the first place,' he spat, 'you're a hundred years too late. In the second, you're a crow.'

"Crow took great offense at this. 'In the first place,' he croaked, 'tell me who filed the patent a hundred years ago. And in the second, time means nothing to me because I am Crow. You, on the third hand, are human, which means that time is everything to you, and you will die.'

"The clerk was furious, but he supplied Crow with a name anyway: 'Nikola Tesla.' He sneered. 'He beat you, Crow.'

"Crow left the patent office in a bad mood and went to a bar. He watched television for a while, then he got an idea. He would go see this Tesla and ask him how he had had the very same idea, only a hundred years earlier.

"Crow found Tesla playing chess with Mark Twain.

" 'Not now,' Tesla said when Crow tried to interrupt.

"Crow is still there, watching the two men play chess. He knows that when the game is over, Tesla and Twain will be summoned to a Meeting of Minds in New Orleans. At that time, Crow will accompany them and find out everything he needs to know."

"Dr. Luna," said Mr. Smith, "not only is this not an Aztec story, but it doesn't even take place in Mexico. It takes place in Arizona, where I live!"

"Are you offended?" Dr. Luna enquired, quite worried.

"On the contrary, my dear man. I am pleased. If more people took the trouble of placing their stories in each other's homes, the world would be greatly improved."

Chapter Eleven

Wherein Major Notz is seen discussing grave mat-
ters with the representative of a Japanese cult.
His discussion with Felicity. The major's psychic
adviser channels Hermes, who has news
of the utmost urgency.

 **a j o r** Notz was involved in a tricky bit of busi-
ness, negotiating to buy a small nuclear device
from a representative of the Japan-based cult Solar
Apotheosis. Mr. Yashimoto, a diminutive man with
large round glasses, sat in Notz's best chair, a piece
that had belonged to Paul of Tarsus before he became Saint Paul.

"New Orleans winters are damp and nasty affairs," the major explained.
"It never snows, but it can be cold all the same. The citizenry goes into a
kind of shock, responsive only to strong drink."

Ostensibly, Mr. Yashimoto had come to New Orleans as part of the
popular Japanese game show *Where Are You?* The program flew contestants to well-known places in the world without revealing the destination.
They were blindfolded and led to a landmark like the Eiffel Tower—or in
this case, Bourbon Street in the French Quarter—and asked, "Where are
you?" If the contestants guessed correctly, they won a prize. If not, they
were punished. Yashimoto had guessed wrong on purpose. He had known
the destination beforehand, but for security reasons he'd played the fool.
He had been punished by being forced to drink five hurricanes in a row,
poured down his throat by a Bourbon Street bartender who recited the ingredients as he made each drink. Mr. Yashimoto was supposed to repeat

the list of ingredients until he remembered them all, after which he would be released. Finally, after the fifth sickly sweet cocktail, he repeated correctly all that the man had poured into him: three rum, two dark, one light—Jamaica, Puerto Rico, Barbados. Grenadine. Pineapple juice. Shot of 151 . . . Three islands, one light, two dark . . . And so on.

Now he was trying to understand what the major was telling him, and he was beginning to sober up. He watched the major's giant fingers come together as he quoted Revelation, chapter 18: " 'And the merchants of the earth shall weep and mourn over her; for no man buyeth their merchandise any more. . . . For in one hour so great riches is come to naught.'

"That, my brother, is the truth, and this is the hour of truth. We are ten branches of the order. You, our Solar brothers, are one; our god-workers in the Mojave, another. We join up in the testing of Dark Angel, and we all profit."

Mr. Yashimoto was authorized to negotiate for the sale of the weapon, but also for a place in the American desert, where Solar Apotheosis intended to test a more advanced device. Major Notz, it appeared, was offering a test site but no cash.

"All right," said Mr. Yashimoto, no longer drunk, "Our brothers of the Golden Dawn in Britain and Russia are prepared to contribute three million. The purchase price of Dark Angel is ten million dollars. In one week."

"How much are the Solar brothers prepared to contribute?"

"Development of Angel One took all our resources." Mr. Yashimoto extended his empty palms.

Major Notz smoothed the shoulder of his Roman toga, once the property of Peleus Serenus, military governor of Dacia Trajana. Seven million was a bit much. He mumbled, "The Bible reminds us every week, 'For the love of money is the root of all evil.' "

"Yes," Mr. Yashimoto mumbled in return, "but until the millennium, when we use money no more, we need—"

"I know, I know."

The device in question would be a trigger, setting off its bigger siblings in the storehouses of the secular state. It was, the major blushed to think, a clitoris, meant to stimulate a larger charge.

The doorbell interrupted them. Two short rings and one long.

"Ah," said the major. "My angel has arrived."

Felicity was unhappy to find her uncle with a visitor. She regarded the Japanese man with hostility as he bowed low. There was a trace of recognition in his eyes, as if he had met her before.

By way of introduction, the major explained: "Mr. Yashimoto is the representative of Solar Apotheosis of Japan. They are working to usher in the millennium. My niece, Felicity, is one of the workers of peace. I think you might have a lot in common."

Fuck, no, thought Felicity. Is he pimping me out? But Mr. Yashimoto did not as much as glance at her shapely thighs. He bowed again and took his leave.

"I will be waiting for your call at the Royal Orleans, Major. I think the television producers have plans for us tomorrow. It was a great honor, Miss Felicity."

"Where are you?" grinned the major, referring to the game show.

"Midpoint," Mr. Yashimoto said soberly.

"We are Roman today, I see." Felicity chose her favorite seat in Notz's collection, a chair purported to have been Churchill's.

The major excused himself "to slip into something more comfortable" and returned dressed in a crisp Soviet naval captain's uniform.

"When life gets interesting, Uncle, it does so all at once! What's that smell?"

"Oh, I put some soup on. I was hoping I could tempt you."

The smell of sour cherry soup was wafting from the kitchen. The sour cherries had come from Vladivostok, a present from the New Orleans chapter of Russian Freemasons.

But Felicity still had no appetite. Why was it that whenever she couldn't stand the idea of food she was offered delicacies, but when she was hungry nobody called and she had to settle for toast and peanut butter?

"Uncle, isn't Ovid one of your favorite poets?"

"Yes, precious. What, did the toga remind you? Ovid is one of my favorite poets for these reasons: he was exiled among the barbarians at Tomis, on the Black Sea, after having spent a frivolous youth in Rome. There he wrote the *Tristia* and achieved a deep understanding of life in exile. Perhaps he even tasted sour cherry soup in his banishment."

"He diddled the emperor's wife, didn't he?"

"Felicity!"

"Well, that is why he was exiled. What would you ask him if you could meet?"

The major warmed to the game. "I would ask him if he had any inkling that his condition, that of exile, would become the status quo of all humanity two thousand years later. But, of course, he would have."

Felicity wondered how exactly Ovid's condition was everybody's. She had been born and raised in New Orleans and had never left home yet. But she could see how the major might be right, even about her. Most days she felt so far from the people and places in her past she might as well have been in Tomis among the barbarians herself. There had been a time when she'd felt at one with her world, but she had been only a little girl then. Since then, the distance had been growing. Sometimes she heard people speaking as if they were underwater. At other times, they shrank, as if she were viewing them from the wrong end of a telescope. She saw the gaps between what people said and did as huge chasms. There was even distance between her own words and what she meant by them. The fabric of her life was full of holes being continually torn.

"I would also ask," continued the major, "how Ovid would revise his epic *Metamorphoses* if he were alive today."

"I will ask him," said Felicity.

The major raised a furry eyebrow and looked intently at the small gold earring decorating her left eyebrow. "How might you mean that?"

"If you have any questions for Saint Teresa, I can ask her too . . . and a few others." Felicity was having fun now, tweaking his interest.

"Saint Teresa?" Major Notz was instantly alert. "You slept in her bed just the other day, child."

Felicity explained how she had stumbled on a Web site where people representing themselves as figures from history conversed with one another. While she knew that they were simply adopting a disguise, she had been terribly impressed by their depth of knowledge.

"Of course," she added, "my knowledge of history being next to nothing, I am easily impressed."

The major was thoughtful. Was it possible, though improbable? He'd thought for some time that cyberspace would be an ideal medium for spirits. Everything there was disembodied. But until now he had found little proof that the medium was anything but a repository of information and a way for people with too much time on their hands to chat aimlessly. But if the membrane of cyberspace had been penetrated, there was a new dimension to consider.

"Who can say if these voices were not genuine?" he asked, almost of himself.

"If that were the case, Uncle, the old woman we buried might be available at keyword *grandmère*."

"Well, it might take a certain savvy for a spirit to enter the medium. Maybe one has to be dead awhile."

Felicity caught the seriousness in his tone and became a little apprehensive.

"I think it's just a game."

"Perhaps."

The major watched as the rosebud of her understanding began to unfurl. He had been watering that flower all her life.

"So, you think that these characters are real?"

"Our world is a sieve. We mingle with spirits continually. Some are fraudulent, some are real. I spend a great deal of time questioning phantoms." The major was silent. This was one of his very difficult problems. He employed a channeler, but he had concluded that this old-fashioned, nineteenth-century method of contacting the beyond was cumbersome and confusing. Perhaps cyberspace was a truer medium.

"Okay, I have another question. The great plan you have for me, my destiny . . . is it inevitable? I mean, is it going to happen no matter what I do?"

It was not as abrupt a transition as Felicity thought. The major grew alarmed. "Child, what have I been telling you all these years? Of course not. It is all up to you. I can help you in limited ways. My job is to see to it that order prevails." And he added, almost as an afterthought, "Even in destruction."

Felicity did not understand. "Destruction? I want no part of destruction. What is my job?"

"Christ, Felix. Which 'why' would you like me to answer?"

"Destruction. Isn't it enough that people die? They always died. More will die. Isn't this the way life continues? Destruction is without end. What's the point in producing either more or less death than occurs anyway? I hate the fiery ends all these preachers promise."

The major understood her objections. The child had seen her share of death. But the time had come when she needed to understand the drama unfolding at this point in history.

"The essential terms of human existence have changed, Felix. One hundred years ago, in an age of strong monarchs and rulers, the question was which one of them would control the path to the divine. In our age, the question is, how do we transform mere rudderless humans from passive consumers into militant saints?"

Felicity experienced a sort of vertigo. She felt as if she were being examined about everything she knew.

The major continued, ignoring her panic. "The growing tide of con-sumers are about ready to devour the earth. Unless these consumers, through a miracle, become saints who will refrain from consumption, we won't have much of a planet left. Which is why we are going to intervene. We'll consume a few million consumers before all is consumed. Your job, love, is to convince them all to give up their greed for sainthood in the lit-tle time remaining."

"Excuse me? Who's 'we,' anyway?" Her bristly hair stood like a shocked porcupine.

"Your humble heralds, Felicity, are trumpeting the message every-where."

"That's crazy. You sound like Mullin." She had always thought her dear uncle eccentric, but this was insane. She had taken his stories of conspiracy to be fairy tales. They had helped her sleep when she was a child. She felt now as if she were waking from the sweet sleep of childhood into a night-mare. She loved her uncle, but there was no love in his vision of her des-tiny. And she realized that her love for him stood somehow in the way of his horrific vision. Not sure now that he would understand, she said, "I still believe in love. You can't stop love."

"Example?" the major demanded sarcastically, clipping the end of a new cigar. It was worse than she thought. He didn't *want* to understand.

"Example. The Mississippi and the Atchafalaya."

She thought about the levees and dams that shackled the Mississippi River. A century of control by the Army Corps of Engineers prevented the Mississippi from joining with its love, the young, swift Atchafalaya. If they joined, the Mississippi would shorten its way to the Gulf of Mexico by 120 miles, leaving New Orleans high and dry. New Orleans without the Mis-sissippi! One day, she exulted, Old Man River will break out to get to his love. *Amor vincit omnia*. Likewise, the earth will deal with her devourers in good time.

"The cherry soup is done."

She had wanted to tell her uncle about her next day's meeting with Mullin, before he had sent her to these dark speculative grounds. She had thought that the major might protect her in case Mullin meant to do her harm. But now she didn't feel that it was appropriate. A crater had opened in front of her, and she had to be careful of her next step. Her anchor had come loose. It was too much to think about. She'd handle Mullin on her own. She consoled herself—childishly, she knew—with the thought of the money she'd soon have. She relished in advance the surprise on the major's face when she presented him as a gift Saint Sylvester's crib or John the Baptist's coffee mug. Perhaps he would then return to the self she had always known and loved. Tomorrow, she told herself again, I will be worth $2.1 million.

After Felicity went home, the major, in a state of uncharacteristic agitation, called his PA (psychic adviser), Carbon, to arrange a consultation. Carbon arrived promptly at Notz's door, as he always did when his favorite client called. He was a most unlikely-looking psychic, nearly as fat as the major but towering over him at six feet six inches. He dressed in the battered leather uniform of a biker, with spike-studded boots, brass-ring knuckles, and leather hood. An unruly red beard framed his cheeks and spilled forth from his chin like a waterfall. He was an eclectic practitioner, performing past-life readings, regression, aura adjustments, tarot card readings, palm readings, dream interpretation, healing massage, and above all, channeling. Major Notz had availed himself of all these services at one time or another, but he prized above all Carbon's ability as a medium. He channeled a variety of spirits—some were trustworthy and accurate, others were lying scum, but as Carbon said, why should the spirit world be any different from this one?

"Carbon," said the major after the psychic settled his bulk in a carved armchair Notz had acquired in Domrémy, France, where Joan of Arc had been born, "I need you to ask Hermes, or his equivalent, to look into the future and apprise me of my niece's activities. What is her direction?"

As was his habit, Carbon pressed his huge leathered hands against his eyelids, and his head relaxed, falling forward into his beard. A high and oddly operatic voice issued from his ragged throat.

"Greetings, Major. It is said that the angels are awkward and don't like to be called into meetings. Some of them are large and fluffy like bread pudding, while some are no bigger than an incense stick and just as bright. For the most part they know their jobs because their missions are built in. But some have not had a mission assigned, and all they do is play all day long. Angels with a mission regard these unassigned angels as grown-ups regard children. They are all, actually, unidimensional, so that even though there are millions, maybe trillions of them, they are no thicker than a thin sheet of paper, or a flake of phyllo. The more substantial, thicker beings in charge of the angels walk about in a state of terminal annoyance at having to keep track of so many. But by far the worst job is that of the Namer."

"Why are you giving me a lesson in angels?" Major Notz demanded, not pleased at all. "And who are you, anyway?"

"I'm Hermes, the messenger," said the piqued entity, equally put off. "If you wanted Pythia you should have said so. It's not like we aren't busy, Miss Human."

The major was willing to make peace. "Tell me, how serious is Felicity's involvement with entities from the past, these things called cyberbeings?"

"If you are willing to listen. As I said, the hardest job concerning angels is naming them, so the Namer is an important figure. It is said that in the waning days of the twentieth century an angel will fly into the city of New Orleans on a delicate mission. His name will be Zack, short for Hezekiah. It is not the most resonant name for an angel of such importance. On the day of his naming, the Namer on duty was absentminded and cranky. He had been recalled from a job tending the waters of life and death to fill in for a Namer who'd run out of inspiration.

" 'Name him yourselves, nard-sotted bureaucrats!' he groused when the shiny, still-wet angel pupa was brought before him. 'Heaven's getting as specialized as the baculum of a dog! Now there are Bearers and Bathers and Namers and God knows what else, but I'm sure he doesn't! And to what purpose? You name them Ezekiel or Isaiah, but in the end they turn out to be just ornamental putti on pink puffs! Not a real Isaiah or Ezekiel in the bouquet! It's worse than earth!'

"It is said that after these dismissive and terrible words, the Namer wrote with the light of his finger on the soft chamois of the pupa and sent him off to do the jobs of the universe. As it turns out, his first big job, after a basic training period of eight angel *mok*, which corresponds to the time it takes a sequoia to grow from seed to a height of one hundred feet, is rather momentous. He is to insure the flawless unfolding of a formidable Council of the Minds, who will meet in New Orleans in order to decide whether to bring on the End of the World in the manner described by John in Revelation or in some other form."

"Wait *one* minute!" shouted the major. "What Council of the Minds? How many? Who are they?"

"I warned you, listener," hissed Hermes, "don't interrupt. I don't know how many, nor does the poor angel in charge of them. As I speak, he is selecting them, cursing his fate. What is certain is that they will arrive here at any moment, so be prepared. Your mental abilities lag far behind the brilliance of this event. Of course, that isn't my concern. It is the angel Zack I feel pity for. In addition to setting up the Council of the Minds, a very tall order if you truly knew the chaotic state of the spirit world, Zack has to recapitulate, in essence, two thousand years of religious quarreling, in order to insure that the Messiah is ready to proceed when the cleansing is concluded."

"The Messiah," whispered the major. "Well, at least we are in familiar territory. But this council—"

Hermes didn't hear him. He went on: "Then there is the question of the Evil One, the one you call the Antichrist, pretending to be the Chosen One, and the credibility gap that the impersonation will open. Simply engineering the meeting is a big job, but what the Minds will do is a mystery. It does not seem that there is enough earth time to tend to both the Messiah and the Antichrist. Angels are simultaneistic, but what about reincarnated Minds? Do they operate in angelic, or earthly time? Zack will have a time problem, given that the council will be composed inevitably of Minds with differing points of view and different historical contexts, who would quarrel for an eternity if not guided somehow. Zack suspects that the whole thing may even be some unspeakable divine trick, since these Minds have already been quarreling for eternity in the heavens. What will be so different when they incarnate?"

"He could turn down the job," grumbled the major. "Get a superangel or something. Somebody experienced."

"It was proposed. It is said that nobody in their right mind wanted the job. Most angels are in their right mind; otherwise they wouldn't be angels. They would be archangels or saints. Young angel Zack is in for a hell of a ride. While he does feel sorry for himself, he demands not to be pitied, because, as he would point out to you, there are perks and mitigations, not the least of which is visiting the city of New Orleans itself. Also, hell is watching with the keenest interest: if the ride is rough enough, they will put it on the menu with the shrimp diablo."

The major wondered at Hermes' intricate knowledge of his city's fair cuisine. Was Carbon poking through, or had Hermes consulted the Bayonna Restaurant Web page on the Internet?

"One might argue, as his Namer did, that the selection of this inexperienced and potentially incompetent baby angel proves that the Ultimate does not give a rat's ass about your world. Whether it ends or not is of no great concern. One of the Namer's favorite earthlings, Buckminster Fuller, said that humans are an 'information-gathering function' in the 'eternally regenerative universe.' If they fail to do the job, another functionary will take over. Mushroom spores, for instance. Or fire ants. Humans are entirely too self-important. Still, charging a novice with the fate of Fuller's fellow creatures is ironic."

Hermes fell silent. Notz couldn't help but admire the spirit's sense of humor. The communication contained important news. The Council of the Minds came as a total surprise to him, complicating his already complicated task. But for Felicity, he would have had no clue how these Minds would be arriving in New Orleans. The cyberspace site Felicity had stumbled on was one of the nodes through which these Minds were landing. The city was a train station at the moment, with trains full of the illustrious dead pulling in for their great meeting. Felicity's cyberentities were collecting information prior to their incarnations. Watching the tunnel mouth of her Web site was a good way to observe the beginning of the invasion. But the Internet was doubtless only one of the means by which these entities traveled. There were others, and they had to be found. Carbon had become indispensible.

Chapter Twelve

Wherein Sister Rodica leads Andrea and the distinguished guests on a pilgrimage to the holy places. Andrea and Lama Cohen commune at the Wailing Wall.

O n e night Father Hernio asked Sister Rodica, "Sister, are you going to conduct one of your tours to the tomb of the Holy Sepulchre tomorrow? I would very much like to accompany you, to refresh my memory of the holy sites."

All the others, with the exception of Father Tuiredh, who pleaded business elsewhere, declared that they would like to go as well. Andrea, whose Christian education was lagging because Sister Rodica had been so inexplicably distant, also expressed her desire to go. She liked the hospice's guests, and now that the stories had started, she had a thirst for more. In some way, the inmates of Saint Hildegard's were a lot like the inmates of the refugee camp, who for lack of anything better to do endlessly discussed matters both profound and trivial, or passed the time playing writing and singing games. They knew full well that none of their discussions made any difference to their true activity, which was *waiting*. In the camps, they all waited for the day when they would be set free. Or killed.

Andrea was not sure what the scholars were waiting for, but she liked the attention that they gave her—they made her feel she was someone important.

That night she dreamed of the Mendeleyev table of elements, only each square contained a suffix for her name, like *ani, ita, ska, ina,* or *isha,* instead of the elements' abbreviations. Thus she knew that she was dear to each one of the hospice's guests who called her privately by an endearment. Andreani, Andreita, Andreska, Andreina, Andreisha . . . these were her diminutive selves, each one with a weight and a function, just like the elements.

After this dream, Andrea thought more about the possibility of being a television star like Gala Keria and wanted to hear more about it (blush, blush) from the disgusting Mr. Rabindranath. She remembered the young soldier from the first *Gal Gal Hamazal* show that she had watched. If she had been Gala she would have found a way to let him win, too. And if not, she would have taken him to her bed and folded her big wings over him. In her sensual fantasies, Andrea often sported a pair of fluffy white wings like the Roman statue of Victory at Ashkelon.

Next morning bright and early, the company met for breakfast. The nuns set before the guests baskets of fresh rolls, cheese, salami, and soft-boiled eggs in egg cups. Black tea and strong, sweet Turkish coffee in small porcelain cups were served. The guests enjoyed this simple Transylvanian repast, though only Earl Smith ate the salami. The rest were vegetarians. Mr. Rabindranath only drank the tea.

"Are you going to eat your salami?" Earl Smith asked Andrea.

"No, please help yourself!" She looked mildly surprised.

Mr. Smith laughed. "You'll never find a Native American vegetarian! Only fake Native Americans are vegetarians in America! Hippies, that is."

Andrea chortled uneasily. She had been under the impression that American Indians ate corn. But all she knew about Indians came from friends of hers, hippie musicians who had lived in a loft, slept on mattresses on the floor, and called themselves Indians. They wore feathers in their hair and had leather pouches around their necks. Faux natives! Mr. Smith explained that Indians had once hunted bison, called buffalo in North America, and that now they were enamored of filet mignon. They ate plenty of corn, too, and beans, and garnishes and sauces. When they went to the big cities they ate Chinese and Mexican cuisine. Take molé sauce, for instance! Andrea had never heard of molé, so she endured a detailed description of this rich chocolate-and-hot-pepper sauce, which had been used, Mr. Smith claimed, to obscure the rather gamy flavor of human flesh. Mr. Smith smacked his lips to everyone's amusement except Andrea's. Human flesh was not one of her favorite subjects.

The group had to take a series of crowded buses to get to the Damascus Gate. On one, Andrea found herself hanging from an overhead support, pressed against a frowning granny with a large bag clutched to her chest, and flanked by Mr. Smith and Sister Rodica. In addition to lurching, stopping suddenly, and weaving erratically, the bus was full of talk, buzzing like a beehive.

"Thank God for telephones!" a man said emphatically.

"Amen," came from different quarters of the bus.

"I sat in the basement with my gas mask on and called everyone!" said the woman with the shopping bag, giving both the nun and Andrea a look of contempt. "One Scud fell right next to my daughter's doctor's office."

Sister Rodica tried not to look at the woman's arms, two sticks of bone clutching the shopping bag. She knew what she'd see: the fading blue numbers. They were everywhere in Israel, ghostly, fading digits of the Holocaust, the phone numbers of hell. But she could feel the woman's eyes on her and the old man's voice—"Thank God for telephones!"— echoing in her ears.

Sister Rodica was offended on behalf of Andrea. She resented the unending lament of the Jews who felt free to broadcast their suffering loudly at every opportunity, especially when she, a sister of the German order, was around. Sure, it was their country, but the horrible fire that had burned those blue numbers on the woman's arm had gone out over a half century ago, more than forty years before Andrea was born. The Iraqi Scud attacks on Israel had long been over. The telephones, which had been lifelines keeping Israelis in touch while they sat in their bomb shelters with gas masks on, had long since turned back into instruments of idle gossip and business. What about all that had happened to Andrea? Her horrors were so fresh she still wouldn't speak of them. The sister had seen the fading scars of cigarette burns on Andrea's thighs and on the underside of her arms. Horrors that most young Israelis thought happened only to their grandparents had happened to this girl. But she had no one's telephone number. Sister Rodica blazed with indignation even as she became Andrea's knight in shining armor. She pressed against the girl, as if to protect her from the old woman's arms and the old man's raspy voice.

Sister Rodica's heavy cloth bag pressed against Andrea's side, filled with what felt like marbles. She leaned into the nun's ear and whispered, "What's in your bag, Sister?"

Even in the buzzing hive of the bus, the nun's blush was noticeable. "Chestnuts," she whispered back.

Sister Rodica, it turned out, had some business to conduct in the Arab quarter. She sold chestnuts from the convent garden to Arabs in the bazaar. Andrea later noted with some admiration what a tough bargainer the sister was. She rejected indignantly one offer of 25 shekels for a bag and stood her ground for ten minutes before going to the next stall. This was no mean feat; the merchants of Suk Khan ez-Zeit had been bargaining for four thousand years. While their shelves groaned with unsold spices at this unfortunate juncture of history, they had no doubt that long after the world of the twentieth century had evaporated, they would still be here, bargaining with whatever life-forms inhabited the planet. The spice market was too important to end with the world.

It was an overcast and windy day—Sister Rodica could smell snow on the blades of cold wind that agitated her habit. She loved this smell, the smell of her childhood. In her village, snow came down for weeks in winter, until only the round roofs of the houses were visible. Her father and the other men would clear paths through the snow to the church and to the tavern. During the long winter nights she listened to the singing of the men in the tavern drifting up to the icy pinpoints of the stars. The girls and women sat at home, weaving at their looms and telling scary stories. Smoke from their wood stoves hung in the air above the houses like question marks.

Of the convent's guests, only Earl Smith, Lama Cohen, and Andrea truly knew snow. For Earl Smith, the silence of the Second Mesa after a snowstorm represented the sum of all that was good in the universe. He had often mounted his horse and gone a mile or so out of his native village of Old Oraibi, just so that he could be alone in the vast whiteness of the mesa. This was the center of the world, as foretold in the Hopi prophecies. At no time was the truth of this more apparent than after a snowstorm, when creation was fully awake. If he looked hard enough, he could see the great Wheel of the Cosmos, composed of stars, turn above him. The message he waited for had always been partially hidden. But on the Second Mesa, part of it was visible. One snowy night, an elder of the Spider clan had come to him in a dream and said, "Go to Jerusalem!"

"The place of the Christians?" he asked, bewildered.

"And of the Jews, the Moslems, and Israeli television," the dream elder had replied.

As for Andrea, the less snow she saw, the better.

The Damascus Gate was crowded, as usual, with Arab money changers, idle Palestinian boys, and religious Jews handing out pamphlets. Sister Rodica went ahead of the group and cut resolutely through the jeering youth like the prow of a Christian ship. The Arabs glared at her, their faces masks of scorn. A small group of young Orthodox Jews with machine guns over their left shoulders made kissy noises in her direction.

"Sometimes the Orthodox Jews throw stones at the sisters," Father Zahan told Andrea, "and shout after them, 'Go to heaven, you like it so much!' But the sisters just forge ahead."

Sister Rodica turned, her round face filled with happiness. "There is nothing better than suffering for the Lord!" she said.

"Maybe!" Mr. Rabindranath said, "but there is an art to it!"

"There surely is an art to throwing stones in Jerusalem!" Father Hernio said ironically. "Here we are, a stone's throw away from the first Station of the Cross."

"And the Intifada," said Mr. Smith

"And the tombs of Absalom and Ezekiel, both of whom threatened, if I am not mistaken, to leave no stone standing in Jerusalem!"

"Better not talk of stones in Jerusalem!" said Lama Cohen. "I'm superstitious."

Everyone laughed. In the narrow streets of the Old City bazaar, stones took on personalities. Every one of them had been thrown at least once, soaked in blood many times, kissed and worshiped, washed, touched, rounded, spoken to. The stones of Jerusalem! There were as many of them as there were words in all the languages of the world, or maybe more. And they had lasted longer, cried louder, and seen more history than just about any stones on earth.

While Sister Rodica disappeared briefly into a dimly lit vault of the Suk Khan ez-Zeit to bargain, Andrea and Father Zahan inspected the wares of a shriveled little man whose stall stood below the seventh Station of the Cross. Among the walnut icons of Mother Mary and her son, which opened like little books, and Moslem prayer cards, and hand-carved Crusader chess sets, and silver icons of Saint George, there was a round black box full of white bone dice inscribed with characters the father had never seen. They looked cuneiform, Phoenician perhaps. His curiosity was piqued.

"Oh, it's only a game," the merchant said, waving his hand to signify that it was of little consequence. "Perhaps I can interest you in a tea set."

"I believe I once saw something like this in Australia," Father Zahan persisted. "It is a divination game of some sort, is it not?"

The merchant admitted that it was but claimed that he had no idea what language it was or what the characters meant. "Why bother? Why not buy a nice silver rosary? Or the best coffee *ibric* in all of Jerusalem? My very own *ibric*, from my ancestors!"

"Your ancestors, the Turks?" laughed Father Zahan. The brass coffeepot was of Turkish design.

"Anything you want; forget these . . . these dominoes!"

Intrigued by the spectacle of a *suk* merchant unwilling to part with his wares, the father insisted. The father and Andrea managed to wrest the game from the distraught dealer for 20 shekels.

"I think it is some sort of story game. The players build a story with the words," the father remembered. "The players arrange the dice to tell a story."

Andrea was given the honor of schlepping the box.

At the entrance to the Church of the Holy Sepulchre, Sister Rodica stopped to introduce the marble column to the left, its Crusader capital incised with knights' crosses. A crack ran through the bottom of it, and graffiti dating back to the eleventh century were carved into the marble. The sister ran her hand lovingly along the crack, and her eyes filled with tears.

"When the heathen first conquered the Holy City, the marble cracked here." She ignored the Bedouin with the filthy beard who stared at her with fiery eyes. "You can touch an open wound to this crack and it will heal, even a bullet hole. But if you're a heathen and touch it to blaspheme, a wound will open in you and you'll never be able to close it."

Andrea thought it safer not to touch the crack. But the others lined up like children at a petting zoo, and one after another they stuck their fingers in the miraculous marble, hoping for their spiritual wounds to close. One thing she noticed about her companions was that they were filled with mischievous pleasure and were ready to do any foolishness on a moment's notice. Learned men! snorted Andrea to herself, no better than children! And woman, she added, remembering Lama Cohen. But maybe this was faith, this joyful childishness. Faith wasn't grave and ominous, like the bearded Serbian priest assigned to reeducate camp inmates. In any case, she didn't think that she had any faith, either joyous or grave.

The Church of the Holy Sepulchre, begun by the emperor Constantine's craftsmen in the fourth century, was filled, for Sister Rodica, with miracles. Under the Martyrion, in the crypt known to the Crusaders as the Chapel of Saint Helena, steps led down to the foot of the cross. It was here that Constantine's mother, Helena, was instructed by a dream to dig for the True Cross, on which the Savior had been crucified. The ledge where she had sat throwing shekels to the diggers while she supervised the work was like the vault of heaven itself for the sister. She lifted up her tear-filled eyes and uttered a prayer. They were standing before Mount Golgotha, the hillock of Calvary. Behind glass was the virgin rock on which the crucifixion took place. It was deeply cracked, having given way at the moment of Christ's death. Hanging from an arch above it were oil lamps representing every Christian denomination in the world. Set in the middle of the arch was the representation of a crucified Christ, a Semitic-looking man with a short beard. Below the cracked stone of Golgotha was the cave where the skull of Adam rested.

"The blood of Christ," said Sister Rodica, sniffling, "washed away the sins of Adam." She knelt on the Greek altar at the Twelfth Station—ground zero of the crucifixion—and put her hand into a hole in the stone floor. When she stood again, her countenance was beatific.

"Go ahead," she urged her charges, "put your hand there and feel the redeemed skull of Adam. If you have faith, you will feel the peace of Jesus Christ."

Andrea kneeled, closed her eyes, and felt with her hand in the dark. Beneath her fingers the smoothly polished stone gave off a cold tremor, a sort of low electrical current. It traveled up her fingers and quickly spread through her shoulders and head and numbed her lips. It felt like the touch of the cattle prod the Serbian guards had used to make the inmates fall in line. Her heart opened like a flower, and sobs flowed involuntarily from her. She tried with all her strength to reverse the current, to send back this energy to the vibrating darkness below the cross, but she could not. She felt sorrow for her mother, her father, Sarajevo, the world, everything she never thought about anymore. She felt sorrow for everything but herself. About herself she felt nothing. Andrea withdrew her hand and lifted her eyes to the Byzantine image of the crucified man. But instead of Christ she saw Gala Keria, the hostess of *Gal Gal Hamazal*, looking down on her with anxious pity.

She straightened up abruptly and her backpack flew open. The divination game spilled out and also a heavy round object that rolled on the marble floor. Conscious of the press of pilgrims behind her, Andrea groped blindly for the boney letters and collected them. The other object, a heavy gold pocket watch, had come to rest at the very edge of the sacred opening leading to the skull below Golgotha. She clutched it and felt its ticking with relief. She had taken a fancy to it the moment she had seen Father Tuiredh withdraw it to study the hour. It had taken quite a bit of work and waiting to separate the watch from the suspicious Irish padre. Now that she'd recovered it, she was gripped by panic. Had any of her companions seen it?

Filled with dread, Andrea stood up, but her group seemed to have vanished into the shadows. Andrea lowered her eyes back to the ground, away from the figure that had replaced the Christ image. She saw that she was standing on a circle within a gold twelve-spoke star that announced to the world the birth of the Christian faith. But this wasn't her faith: she was sure that she had none. The world called her a Muslim, but her parents had followed another star altogether, the red star of communism. Of course, she told herself as tears flowed down her cheeks, even if there was *nothing* here, the collective strength of two thousand years of worship would suffice to charge the stones.

"This is the center of the world," announced Sister Rodica, reappearing. "At Easter a light comes directly from God. It hovers for one minute in the air and heals the sick and lights the candles of those who believe. All on its own, blessed Mother of God. No matches are ever used here."

"But plenty of fire power," said Lama Cohen.

Andrea saw that in addition to her group, several Israeli soldiers, mere boys, stood listening to the explications of their guide. Several chewed gum, and at least one looked Andrea up and down with a transparent purpose in mind. They carried enormous machine guns with oversized chambers. Her tears dried as quickly as they had welled up. Thank you, God, for the world, she said to herself. Without it, endless ennui and self-pity would reign.

A Japanese tourist posed his entire brood at the foot of the cross and got busy snapping them. Thank you for Japanese tourists, God. An Armenian monk, his long beard flowing nearly to the ground, hugged a column. A Copt wept into his Bible. An American family huddled close, uncertain of etiquette. And Andrea thanked God for all of them.

"Until Jesus came, Paradise was closed," the American paterfamilias proclaimed matter-of-factly, as if Paradise were some kind of store.

"Well, thank God it reopened," said the wife. "Should we go to the icon of the Holy Mother to get some oil now?"

Sister Rodica lifted her eyes again in suffering, but this time her suffering was connected with the gum chewers, the Japanese, the Americans— all the unbelievers. It was her trial to cut through this uncouthness to the ever-bright core of her faith. The oil in question, in which she later dipped her handkerchief, flowed continually from the icon of the Holy Mother at the foot of the cross.

There were other icons of disciples and martyrs who opened and closed their eyes in the dimly lit underground chapels. From the wounds of some flowed heavy-scented myrrh; drops of blood streaked down the smoky images of others. Sister Rodica knew every miraculous wound, every square inch of the mysterious sepulchre. But she lingered longest before those mysteries connected to the Mother of God and Mary Magdalene.

She pointed out to her flock images of the two holy women and, as always, shook her head at the exalted position the prostitute held in the panoply of saints. Pray as hard as she might, she still could not understand why Jesus appeared first to the Magdalene after his resurrection. She imagined the round stone rolled away by God from the tomb of Joseph of Arimathea, and the Magdalene looking deep into the emptiness of the tomb. God help her, Sister Rodica had seen in some of the icons of Mary Migdal more than a passing resemblance to the very earthly Gala Keria!

Just above the small cells of the Ethiopian monks, whence issued a deep murmur as of the earth rumbling, there was an image of the sinner walking meekly behind her donkey. The light-enfolded form of the resurrected Jesus filled the horizon. The woman's downcast eyes did not hide the sensuous turn of her lower lip. Her *familiar* lower lip! Sister Rodica turned and there behind her was the very same lip, drawn in but inescapably sensuous. Sister Rodica clamped her hand over her mouth. First Gala. Now Andrea.

Andrea looked to see what had startled the nun and was confused by the mixture of dread and desire she found in her eyes. Nonetheless, she also felt a strange joy and returned the gaze, just as she had when the lusty soldier had looked at her. The desire of others made her feel (she who had felt nothing for so long) *good*, and she thanked God with all her intense young body.

Sister Rodica reserved her greatest passion for the Stone of Unction, the bed of stone where the body of Christ had been prepared and anointed for burial. The nun fell to her knees and kissed the myrrh-scented stone, putting her lips where tens of thousands of women in search of healing had put theirs. Kneeling nuns were rubbing the stone with holy oil.

Andrea felt drawn to share in all that Sister Rodica took such joy in showing her. She wanted to give in to her feelings, good or bad, sorrowful or joyous. She knelt, this time carefully clutching her knapsack, and set her lips firmly to the stone. She felt the same numbing energy that had flowed from the skull of Adam—this time it was bitter and heavy and spread from her lips through her bones like a strange sleep. She felt drowsy at first, then full of light, but still heavy, as if honey, not blood, flowed through her veins. Over the Stone of Unction stood the Oratory of Saint Mary, where the grief-stricken Mother had cried with the pain of all womankind. Dried rose petals rustled on Christ's stone bed. It is useless, thought Andrea, to search the dried leaves of book knowledge to explain what is happening to me.

Andrea looked around for Father Zahan but couldn't see him. She found instead the round face of Dr. Luna, his black Mayan eyes full of sympathy. It seemed to the girl that his eyes were unfathomably deep, like the wells where virgins were sacrificed to the gods. She was ashamed of the inappropriate image, but Dr. Luna's kind eyes forgave her.

"On this place," he said softly, "Hadrian ordered the erection of a statue of Venus. She stood here over the tomb of the Nazarene, encouraging the pleasures of the flesh and demanding the sacrifice of virginity. Not for long, though. Soon Rome forgot its heart, and worshiped only Fortuna. The Wheel of Fortune was their *only* game. But following Fortuna destroyed them. The empire lost its strength to soothsayers and charlatans who promised worldly wealth and happiness."

"Was Fortuna *always* wrong?" Andrea questioned Dr. Luna, who seemed to her very wise.

"No, she was quite often right. But she was only a pointer, a guide to deeper realities. The wheel does not determine what will happen; it merely describes it. I fear that we, like the Romans, have also forgotten this."

It was a cryptic remark. Andrea did not understand. Did he mean that Christ had died so that people might believe in things other than luck?

Dr. Luna tried to explain. "The Wheel of Fortune was the ancient world's greatest mystery and its greatest downfall. What had been divination became gambling. The divine fled, leaving only despair."

About despair she knew. And about luck. She supposed that she was lucky to have survived and to have come to this beautiful city. But she had not left her despair behind.

Andrea and Dr. Luna emerged from the church and rejoined Sister Rodica's little band of pilgrims.

From the church of the tomb they backtracked for a short time through the Suk Khan ez-Zeit, stopping a moment to peer at the Gate of Judgement.

"This was the gate through which Christ passed on the way to Calvary," Sister Rodica informed them matter-of-factly.

The only view of the gate, 5 shekels' worth, was through a hole at the back of a dusty Arab shop. A tiny man crouched in front of the shop, holding a cardboard sign with the words *Gate of Judgment* hand-lettered in five languages.

"An interesting position," commented Father Hernio. "To have exclusive vantage point to another's religious shrine, and then to charge the infidel for viewing it."

"But that's not unusual in Jerusalem, Father," said Lama Cohen. "Every religious site here is built over another, with only so much room left to peep through." She measured with thumb and forefinger an inch or so. "This city is like a huge pornography shop, the kind of place where you put in coins to watch from behind a window the, er, pardon me . . . *mysteries.*" Lama Cohen's irony was not disrespectful, but typically Buddhist. To Buddhists, she often explained, the created world was sheer illusion. Her former Jewish self concurred with this worldview.

But if she expected the others to be shocked, she was mistaken. The company under the direction of Sister Rodica was steeped in knowledge and wisdom so vast few things upset it.

"Some cultures consider tumescence the only proper response before the gods!" Mr. Rabindranath offered, winking at Andrea.

"To show the gods that they were potent, fruitful, and were going to multiply," Dr. Luna said.

"If anybody here is going to talk erections," said Father Zahan, "it should be me. I wrote the church's official position on wet dreams. Alas, I am past the age where they hold anything but ceremonial interest."

"What is the church's official position?" enquired Lama Cohen.

"Primarily, a refutation of the previous position, which insinuated that succubi actively tempt sleepers. Our position now assigns no blame. A certain, well, *appetite* is considered quite healthy. Not an excessive appetite."

"Blessed be the randy, for they shall sup on ash," concluded Father Hernio, rubbing his tour-weary lower back.

But Sister Rodica had one more errand to attend to. She wanted to buy myrrh, the healing substance that seemed to ooze from every icon in Jerusalem. The only merchant who trafficked in myrrh was a wizened Palestinian named Faisal, who in the past had traded an ounce of the precious liquid for two bags of chestnuts. But nowadays he was charging a pretty shekel.

No one knew exactly how he obtained the stuff. Some speculation had him slipping phantomlike into the Holy Sepulchre through an opening known only to him and milking the holy icons. Others claimed that he had uncovered a cache of ancient vials filled with the holy balm. No one but Faisal knew which was true.

Even more astonishing was that Faisal also dealt in the substance known to the Hindus as soma. Mr. Rabindranath, shrugging apologetically, followed Sister Rodica into the shop and waited patiently while the two haggled. After Faisal wrapped the precious vial of myrrh in a page of Arabic newspaper sporting the face of Yasir Arafat, Mr. Rabindranath stepped forward and launched into his own negotiation. Soma made it possible to communicate with the god Indra, and Mr. Rabindranath, who was normally afraid of Indra, needed the counsel of this powerful trickster god just now.

The trader was amused by his customers' slight embarrassment. Buying their balms and sacraments from a Muslim! He himself felt pure in the transaction. That he was a true follower of Muhammad he had no doubt. But first and foremost he was a trader, exercising the prerogative of his ancient profession. He was a trader, an archetype. There was no older, surer identity. Muhammad had been a trader, too, before Allah revealed his divine wisdom to him. Other religions' avatars had started out as scholars, teachers, disillusioned rich men, or personified elements. Only Muhammad, praised be Allah who had created him, had trade in his blood. Muhammad was a prophet of an age of commerce, a most modern prophet. Faisal stroked his sparse beard and wrapped up the lekiethoi bottle with five drops of soma in it. The world might be ending, but he was in no hurry. Mr. Rabindranath watched him impatiently but respectfully. Faisal looked capable of procuring anything, and one day he might just need *anything*. Hindus were mean traders, too.

They exited the Damascus Gate—on top of which an Israeli soldier with a cannon-sized machine gun briefly appeared, surveying the swarm of Arab boys loitering in the *suk*—and found themselves at the bottom of the hill that followed the wall of the Old City to the Western Wall. A mule laden with gasoline cans came toward them, followed by a Palestinian man with his head wrapped in his kaffiyeh. They crossed his path at the foot of the Via Dolorosa. From that intersection, the panorama of the Holy City unfolded before them: the slopes of the Mount of Olives; the Garden of

Gethsemane; the hillsides overlaid with tombstones; the Dome of the Rock, the Omar Mosque covered in gold and glittering with Muhammad's dream of heaven; the Tower of David; the lead roof of the Al Aqsa Mosque; and in the distance, the giant white harmonica that was the new Mormon Temple—yes, even the youngest religion of America was here, waiting, waiting, waiting—and on the horizon, etched like fine hairs, countless construction cranes at work on the ever newer Jerusalem.

On the right, at the top of yet another hill of tombstones, stood the Golden Gate, bricked in and shut down. It was through this gate Jesus first entered the city, and it was said he would return through it. Jews believed that through this same gate the *true* Messiah would one day come to raise the dead from the stones of the city. God had told Ezekiel: "This gate is to be kept shut, and is not to be opened! No one shall enter by it because the Lord, the God of Israel, has entered by it; therefore it shall remain shut."

Throughout the centuries many false messiahs had tried to breach it. The Turks were the last to render the gate impassable, though they, too, awaited the coming of Mahdi, the avatar of Islam.

"It is sealed now, but it will burst open with the power of the True One," Father Hernio commented.

Andrea suddenly felt a surge of anger.

"The True One?" she repeated bitterly. Her tone surprised the priest.

"Why so bitter, dear?"

Andrea decided, because she had grown to trust the priest and all her friends at the convent, to tell them a story from her past.

"Once when they loaded us on a prison truck, I asked the Serb officer overseeing the transport, 'What's your name?' We were forbidden to talk to the Serbs; I don't know what I was thinking. Before the war, he would have liked me, but I wouldn't have looked at him. I was from the city, you see, and he was only a peasant! But now he looked back at me like I was a rat, and answered, 'The True One! I am the True One!' I knew what he meant. He meant that he was my conqueror, and that made him the only true person. So I said, 'Maybe *I* am the True One.' He hit me with the butt of his rifle, but the blow only landed on my shoulder. It missed my face."

The scholars listened silently to the girl's every word. It was the longest speech they'd ever heard her make. After a time, they walked on. Below them was the long row of the tombs of the kings and the prophets, the waterfalls of stone that were the tombs of Absalom and Ezekiel, whose calls for the destruction of Jerusalem had been heeded time after time.

God, keep that gate shut a little longer, Andrea prayed silently to she knew not which God; I am too young for the End.

Finally, Sister Rodica guided the group to the Church of the Tomb of Mary, where the Virgin lay in her crypt, surrounded by icons and jewel-encrusted lamps. The scent of incense and oils so permeated her clothes that for the rest of the day, when Andrea breathed deeply, she felt a painful intoxication.

It was here that Sister Rodica, overcome by emotion, declared in a weak voice that she was done for the day. The tours were never routine for her; no matter how many times she conducted them, the Holy Spirit filled, conquered, and finally exhausted her. Father Hernio kindly offered to take her back to the hospice in a taxi. The rest of the pilgrims continued up the hill to the Western Wall.

The Wailing Wall, Hakotel Hama'aravi, is all that remains of the Temple Mount. The focus of Jewish longing throughout centuries of exile, it is a wall of memory. In her short lifetime, Andrea had witnessed the fall of some mighty walls: the fall of the Berlin Wall and, in ironic counterpoint, the breaching of the walls of Sarajevo. All the hopes that accrued to the fall of the Berlin Wall were scattered savagely, like drops of blood, by the siege of Sarajevo. She had grown to love walls in her childhood, the tufty medieval walls that she climbed with her friends in the summer—and to hate them for keeping her in. Or out. But here was a wall that stretched both horizontally, through the longing of Jews everywhere, and vertically, through their history. It was a big wall, but not as big as the wall that could have been made from all the bones of Jews trying to get back to it.

To reach the wall, tourists and believers passed through metal detectors manned by armed soldiers. Beyond them, women were directed to the right, men to the left. Andrea and Lama Cohen walked slowly toward the wall. On a ledge high above them a cluster of fur-hatted Jews, clumped together like a flock of crows, held a sign that read, PREPARE FOR THE COMING OF THE MESSIAH! Doubtless they had been there since the destruction of the Temple, sometimes visible, sometimes invisible, but always in black, mourning and waiting.

As the group that had been led by Sister Rodica approached the wall, it began to snow. Lama Cohen lifted her arms to welcome it. For the most part, the lama had achieved a state of equanimity that it was her duty to maintain, but before the remains of the Temple her Jewish soul burst out. She had thought that she was done with the emotional trappings of her birth—when she looked in the mirror she saw only the even silver of her calm. She had burned most of her desires, which rested like fine ash at the bottom of her self. But now, tears, which she hoped Andrea did not see, met the thickly falling snow in this place of memory and lamentation.

The snowfall became a storm. Andrea pressed her head against the cold stones. Tens of thousands of tightly rolled strips of paper containing prayers moldered in the cracks. Andrea pressed hard, as if the wall held something other than cold rock.

Lama Cohen, almost invisible in the blizzard, pressed not just her forehead but her entire body against the wall, and imperceptibly at first, then harder, she began to rock back and forth in the traditional Jewish manner. Only, there was nothing traditional about it: she was a woman and a Buddhist. She smiled through her tears, remembering a story a doctor friend had told her: every day, dozens of people hurt their elbows, heads, and knees at the wall. Overcome by violent emotions, some pilgrims literally bashed themselves against the stone. The doctor called it the Jerusalem syndrome, an imprecise moniker that applied also to an entirely different condition that sometimes afflicted visitors to the Holy City: they believed quite suddenly that they were the Messiah. At that very moment, at Kfar Shaul Psychiatric Hospital, one hundred messiahs suffered their imprisonment without complaint, each one certain that he was the True One.

A trickle of something warm reached Andrea's lips; she stuck out her tongue and tasted it. It was a drop of her own blood; she had scraped her forehead on the rock. The drop of blood tasted salty and sweet. Seized by a desire to taste more of her own blood, she rubbed her forehead against the stone until another drop, hot and full of life, snaked down her face and found her tongue. She remembered the trickle of her mother's blood, a squiggly line drawn whimsically in the snow, as if by a child. Andrea tasted snow and blood and felt the coldness of the Jews' wall—and the bright white flower opened in her again. She looked to her left, where Lama Cohen had wrapped herself in a snowy shroud. The girl reached out and felt for her. The two fell into each other's arms, their tears mingling. It was an unusual moment for both: for Andrea it was the first time that she had felt a woman's warmth since her mother's death. For Lama Iris Cohen it was a breach of the Buddhist practice of detachment, a reversion to the sentimental impetuosity of her race.

Close to her fifteenth birthday, the first winter of the siege, Andrea had been laid out with a fever. She watched the first snowfall of the year through a small circle cut in the black crepe that covered the window. She watched the fat snowflakes float down, hoping that her mother would return soon with firewood. Normally this was Andrea's job, but she hadn't been able to get out of bed. She had lain there listening to the soft explosions that punctuated Sarajevo each evening. She had learned to discern certain patterns: if the last volley was rapid small-caliber-arms fire with a cannon boom at the end, everything was going to be all right. If the volley lasted past the boom, she was filled with anxiety. After the first boom, they had to leave their rooms and descend quickly to the basement. Sometimes she spent whole days and nights in the basement, pressed on all sides by the anxious bodies of their neighbors.

But this night the boom didn't come. The machine-gun volley was followed by nearby shouts. By the time Andrea ran up the stairs to see what the shouting was about, her mother had been covered with a blanket. A trickle of blood seeped from under the blanket onto the snow. Her father, who arrived soon after from a shelter where he was repairing a broken water pipe —even though there was currently no water—did not allow her to see her mother. She had been hit in the face by the sniper's bullet.

Later that night her father went out on a detail to check out shell damage to the streetcar line. He never came back. He and the other men were killed by an exploding mortar.

For the rest of that winter, Andrea lived with neighbors. She stayed indoors, afraid to go out into the snow. The stairs leading down to the basement were the closest she came to breathing the outdoors. The whiteness was a shroud. But it was not her mother's hastily shrouded body that haunted her. One day months before, she had seen the body of a young woman whose head had been blown apart. A stray dog was eating the brains. No one took notice. Corpses had become as common as broken windows in Sarajevo. Andrea watched the skinny yellow cur eat until he was satisfied.

When she got home, choked by the horror she had witnessed, her father had met her with a joke.

"Christ," he said, "is carrying his cross in Sarajevo. Someone stops him and asks, 'Where did you get the wood?' " Andrea had laughed. She was glad that she had.

"I came to Jerusalem," she told Lama Cohen, "because they told me that it never snows here. It isn't true. But I know that Jerusalem has seen more death than even Sarajevo. Maybe, even though it snows here, it's a wiser place."

Lama Cohen caressed Andrea's hand, sweeping the snow from it. "You are right. Each stone was washed in blood. Yet the city endures."

But she said to herself, This child is complex and strange like an obscured prayer wheel. I cannot yet read her soul.

The sentimentality that had earlier possessed her left her suddenly like a small bird made of snow and tears. The lucidity of the meditator returned, its merciless light revealing and harsh. But she felt for this child with the keenest empathy.

The hospice pilgrims regrouped outside the security checkpoint. They all seemed wearier and older.

"To the Omar Mosque?" suggested Father Zahan.

It was a rhetorical question. The place of Muhammad's dream of heaven, adjacent to the spot where Abraham had nearly sacrificed his son Isaac, would have to wait for another day.

In the taxi they took back to the convent, Andrea felt as though her body had changed shape. She felt longer and thinner; even her hands and fingers had grown outward, like the branches of a tree. Inside, she felt a mission forming, something bright and full of stories. Above all, she felt affection for everyone in her party, even Mr. Rabindranath and his yucky penis.

Chapter Thirteen

Wherein Felicity meets the poet Ovid and an old friend, Martin Dedette. Reverend Mullin arrives at certain dates crucial for humanity.

 **r e a l l y** need to get a good night's sleep, Felicity told herself as she typed in *http://history.love.messiah* and logged on to *Make Love to People from History*. Next day's meeting with Mullin was crucial. Felicity lay naked on top of her bedspread. It was a mild night; there was a breeze redolent of sap and river mud coming in through the skylight that was always cracked open. The little computer screen shone like the friendly beacon of a lighthouse. I am a little ship, thought Felicity. I am sailing far into the past. I am sailing past all the history I don't remember from school. Past America, past Europe, past the Civil War, past the Wars of the Roses, past Charlemagne and Attila the Hun.

She found herself floating past a scalloped shoreline dotted with the dark shapes of the tents of Attila's men. She thought about her loneliness, and the loneliness of everyone who ever lived. Loneliness was at the bottom of everything. Humanity was as lonesome, she thought, as each of its individuals. She looked up at the stars, and anguish pierced her like an arrow. She thought of Ovid, the exiled poet. Something about the author of the *Art of Love*, the *Metamorphoses*, and the *Tristia*—lover, seducer, exile—spoke to the melancholy that had settled unaccountably in her soul. It was a sadness different from her everyday sadness and feeling of loss. It was more primal, a single sad note playing since the birth of the universe. Miles had said, "The sound of the big bang is B-flat."

Of course, Ovid wasn't just the sad poet of exile. He had been a lover of the empress, a wit of his day, a courtly and sophisticated man. On meeting someone named Messiah, a concept with which he was likely to be insufficiently acquainted, he might have asked questions she couldn't answer. Perhaps she should be someone more humble, a temple vestal or a prostitute. But someone like that might not interest the great poet either. Most likely he would prefer someone witty, verbally brilliant. A storyteller. The greatest storyteller of the ancient world, Felicity remembered, was Scheherazade, who had saved her life by telling stories for a thousand and one nights. Yes, that was more like it.

Felicity decided to change her nom de guerre from Messiah to Scheherazade. It was less grandiose, and Ovid would like it. She would tell a story good enough to entertain a great poet. She would make up stories just as she had before going to sleep in her childhood, when she had been inspired by the major's fantastic tales.

Felicity used the Paintbox more skillfully than last time, creating Scheherazade as a slender waif wrapped in billowing veils. Her eyes were half closed and her heart-shaped mouth slightly open, as if she were already in the middle of a story. She was better looking than the Messiah, more feminine, and, Felicity thought, more like herself.

She typed in: OVID.

Time meant nothing to the author of the *Art of Love*. He lounged on a crude wooden bench in a tattered toga. Rough-looking sailors were drinking on other benches. A slim-keeled trireme was beached in the middle of the room, filled with Greek amphoras. Scheherazade stepped around it and came face-to-face with the poet. He didn't seem surprised.

"Greetings, Scheherazade. Some friends and I were sitting here in this café in dusty Tomis. I told them about you, and they all wanted to meet you. These boys have seen the whole world. They've sailed their boats to the isles of Hellespontus, the coves of Tunis, the Golden Horn, and known every kind of woman: the sirens of Cyprus, the fish-tailed wenches of the Irish coast, the croc-headed temple whores of Egypt, vestals at Delphi, patrician Roman wives, and also many boys, from the long-limbed lads of Corfu to the snake-muscled porters of Asia Minor."

"What do they want with me, Ovid?" Felicity decided that modesty was called for, though she looked nothing like a vestal virgin.

"Like I said, they've heard tell about you, Scheherazade. They heard that your stories are as strong as snake venom, but they do not kill. They heard that your stories arouse a man's manhood more than anything else; that the touch of your voice causes men to ejaculate rivers of effluvium, more than any other woman or boy ever could. It is said that following your stories, men are given the sweetest, deepest sleep—close to death and yet not death. These are restless men, Scheherazade—they have traveled the world because they cannot sleep. They have enjoyed and labored at women and girls and boys in the hope of sleep. You're their last chance, sweet Scheherazade."

"And you, Ovid, are you still lonely by the shores of the Black Sea, among the savage Gets? Haven't you sampled their women and boys? Won't you tell me their customs? I need stories, too, Ovid, like any poet. I do not make my stories out of whole cloth. I weave them from the stories of others. When one is fortunate enough to have for a friend the poet of the *Metamorphoses*, one should listen."

"You flatter me, sorceress from the future, and flattery is half of arousal. My manhood already chafes against the rough wool of my Getian breeches. Yes, I have sampled their women. They say that Orpheus himself hails from these parts. I can see why his lyre played such lovely tunes. The Get women of the patrician class wear short tunics like the harlots of Rome. Their legs are long and bronzed, and they wear sandals made from tree bark. Their toes are flexible like fingers—they can pick up things from the floor with their toes. One of the local refinements is for an Alexandra or a Clestea—they give themselves Roman names, the poor monkeys—to wrap her long toes around a man's phallus while tickling his piss hole with the big toe. I am well made, by Jove, and I can tell you that I scarcely believed it when the toes of such a wench went all the way around my manhood. Their fingers, though long and supple, cannot do that. The pleasure was doubled when I had two of these lasses, barely sixteen and already refined in pleasure, service me with their toes. It is said that the Gets are descended from wolves, and they are hungry indeed. At their festivals they daub themselves with red paint and run naked in the meadows, shooting their arrows into the sky to irritate their god, Zamolxes. When he is well irritated he sends down lightning, thunder, and rain. It makes their paint run and causes them to become frenzied. Their bacchanalia last for weeks."

Ovid lay down on the bench, and Scheherazade sat beside him and put his large head on her silken lap. The poet's head was heavy; his coarse hair scratched her. His forehead was deeply lined, and a faraway light burned like a fever in the black depths of his eyes.

"I was sold into slavery to a barbarian ship, Ovid. The sailors took their pleasure with me for a month at sea. I have learned things I can scarcely describe, they were so painful and—I blush to think it—pleasurable. The barbarians liked to take me in clusters, leaving no part of my body unattended. I lay on deck naked with sore gums, bunghole, and cunt, rubbing salves on all my body. Only my mind was free to soar, and in my mind I saw all the pure things of this world: small babes in arms, fields of flowers, rain on mosaic tiles. One day, one of the barbarians took me for his own and kept me all to himself and to his cabin boy, a young lad of sixteen. I healed, but cannot forget all that happened to me.

"Did you enjoy my story, Ovid?"

"Yes. I am a poet but I don't make things up out of whole cloth, either."

Felicity wondered what Ovid would think of Amelia Earhart. She thought that the author of the *Metamorphoses* might appreciate the aviatrix—in his time, only the gods flew. But she decided to wait before introducing them. There was time. Ovid lived in eternity.

Felicity liked herself much better as Scheherazade. She felt that she was an untapped fountain of stories and that her elusive pleasure would eventually be found at the junction of one story with another. In this respect, she was very much like all the other spirits in cyberspace.

When Ovid fell asleep, she logged off.

At dawn, a thick fog lay over the winding bayou outside, dissolving the Lord's Plantation House in a milky substance.

"Good God," one of the girls said, "it looks like one billion sperms."

"Souls of the unborn," said another.

"Mixed in with fiendish souls," added a third.

"Superstitious bitches!" said another, bringing out a tray full of coffee mugs, each inscribed *Spirit Industries*.

Upstairs, in a suite of rooms overlooking the cypresses by the bayou and the beginning of the Mississippi pine forest, Reverend Jeremy "Elvis" Mullin was staring blankly at a computer screen, waiting for Jesus to inspire him with a date. Several dates, actually. The time had come for him to put his money where his mouth was. Dear Lord, prayed Mullin, they are massing at the gates and calling for me to give them your deadlines.

The schedule Mullin needed to clarify was complex. He needed dates for the coming of the Antichrist, for the Rapture, for the Tribulations, for Armageddon, and for the Second Coming of Christ. The first was the most important right now, because the believers awaiting the Rapture were getting restless. He could sense that the Antichrist, though he hadn't revealed his identity, was nearby. The reverend's senses were prickly like the spines on a frightened porcupine.

Mullin reviewed several dates in the little time remaining before the end of the millennium, in 2000. July 4 might be excellent for the arrival of the Antichrist, who, it was known, had already taken over the U.S.A. through the bankers of the Tri-Lateral Commission. He was now only waiting for the signal to do his job. At last report, he had taken the form of an Italian banker named Ovid Publicus, who drove fast cars, owned a multinational telephone company, an on-line computer service, several television stations and newspapers around the world, and fancied himself a poet. He was handsome and persuasive, and, it was said, nobody could either resist or stop him.

Well, that was one opinion, anyway. Another school of thought maintained that Ted and Jane Turner were together the entity called the Antichrist. Everyone from Madonna to Hector J. Crackheart, a recluse billionaire philosopher in Montana, had been nominated by one faction or another.

So, if this Publicus, or whoever the AC was, were to declare himself on Independence Day, that would be perfect. "Independence" would then signify the opposite, which was slavery to the devil. It would behoove the Evil One to manifest amid the fireworks. Mullin was a patriot, but the United States, in his opinion, had long ago ceased to be worthy of the love of true patriots. A new United States would be born from the ordeals of the Tribulations. A cleansed, purified, *white* America.

Mullin waited, but the Spirit gave him no sign. His mind and his computer screen were blank. The scent of gardenias floated in through the French doors, and from downstairs, the silvery notes of the girls' laughter. This could be Paradise, thought Mullin, if only it weren't hell. Only my heart knows the extent of the darkness. But let the story unfold as foretold and this *will* be Paradise.

Sufficient time had to elapse, Mullin calculated, between the coming of the Antichrist and the Rapture so that people would believe that the millennium, the age of peace, had indeed arrived. In that time, the Antichrist had to inspire in humankind a feeling of well-being and accomplish the

elimination of national currencies, replacing them with a world currency
bearing the number 666. The Dow Jones Industrials would reach 66,666
at the beginning of this cycle. How much time was sufficient? The reverend thought that, at the accelerated rate of current events, two months
might suffice. Which then could put the Rapture right around Mardi Gras
2000.

Mullin chuckled to himself. That would be perfect. The true believers
would leave behind this world of wickedness on a pagan holiday, one that
had already replaced Christmas in importance in Louisiana. It was very
important that events fall on symbolic days. The success of Christianity
had come about partly from the coincidence of holy days with older, pagan
holidays. This had been no accident, and the End would not be accidental
either.

Still, Jesus gave no sign.

Would everything be ready by Mardi Gras 2000? The reverend believed that the deadline could be met, if only Jesus would give the go-
ahead. The domes were prepared. Everything was a couple of rehearsals
away from completion.

There was a knock at the door, despite Mullin's order to leave him unbothered until twelve. His newest singer, the girl whom he'd baptized
Pecan, stood at the door holding a silver tray with a message and a cup of
coffee. The other girls, knowing his temper, had thought it prudent to
send up the newcomer.

Mullin read the message and frowned. Then he hit his chest with his
open palm and smiled. He took the coffee from the girl and slapped her
behind. Jesus had spoken.

The message read:

Your Satanic Majesty:
I have taken the initiative of establishing our encounter inside Saint
Louis Cathedral at 8 P.M. this evening.
The Messiah

God works in mysterious ways. He slapped his forehead. All the elements were *here*, though disguised in the parabolic way of the Lord: the
cathedral (home of the Antichrist popes), the business he had to conduct
(part and parcel of the Antichrist campaign against him), and the signa-
ture, "The Messiah" (which, though meant mockingly, was nonetheless
one of Christ's names). The note had come through Felicity's hand, but it

wasn't hers. It had been dictated by Satan himself. And here was his sign. Sometimes Jesus spoke loudest through Satan.

Pecan lingered, happy as a stray mutt who'd been given a pat on the head. The sting of the reverend's palm on her behind reverberated pleasantly through her whole person. She hoped that he would notice her again, but the reverend had returned to his computer. After a while she just tiptoed out of the room. Every day she had up to seven hours of choir practice. The other girls were better singers, but none of them, as far as she knew, had received any further sexual advances from Mullin after the initial splat of obscenity. Pecan vowed to become a singer so great the reverend would embrace her nightly.

Felicity sipped her midday double espresso with pleasure bordering on ecstasy. The Vietnamese personnel and the bohemian clientele of the Croissant d'Or coffeehouse looked exceedingly fresh, as if they'd been cleansed by a spring rain. She could feel their gentle vibrations making a cocoon of warmth against the foggy winter day outside.

From her seat she could see the white wall of the Ursuline convent. Proud locals claimed that their ancestors, French "casket girls," so-called because they arrived with all their possessions in one small trunk, or *casket*, had resided there upon arrival in Nouvelle Orléans in 1723. Felicity chuckled. There had been only a few casket girls. In truth, most of the early female colonists to New Orleans had been Paris whores. Each of the casket girls would have to have given birth ten thousand times over to account for the number of present-day New Orleanians claiming descent from these virtuous women. No one, it seems, descended from the many more numerous prostitutes. How like us, thought Felicity, to reinvent even our roots. Everything here steams up and becomes fabulation, smoke, jive.

Felicity abandoned herself to worldly reveries about what she was going to do with the money. There was no question in her mind that Mullin would pay up. His televangelical empire pulled in over $300 million a year. He wouldn't risk all that for a puny $2.1 million. But a puny two-point-one was enough to set Felicity's dream choo-choo chugging.

First of all, she would remedy the lamentable state of her psyche by purchasing a mansion with a grand ballroom, where her favorite New Orleans musicians would play. She could even schedule regular evenings of musical entertainment for the amusement of the poor. She would set aside the lower floors for Shades, who would shower and stroll naked there in their splendid tattoos, jingling their jewelry and chains.

But then her responsible, social self woke up, and she was ashamed of her selfishness. She overheard a couple at another table.

"You know," the man told the woman, "they say that Napoleon did actually make it to Louisiana. He died en route, and he's now buried right next to Jean Lafitte and John Paul Jones in the Berthoud Cemetery."

That bit of trivia set her thinking that in the city of grand plots and conspiracies, she ought to do no less. Her uncle's plan to convert consumers into saints was unsettling because if the conversion was unsuccessful, the alternative was the murder of several millions of people. And why? Simply because they craved Big Macs and Whoppers! Such greed would surely destroy the earth, but how could one ask people to give up beefburgers and pork sausages and become ascetic nonconsumers? Physician, heal thyself, Felicity thought indignantly. Stop eating beer-fed beef and Armagnac-dazed shrimp, and then maybe you can expect the masses to give up their burgers and fries. But if they don't—as surely they won't— you can't just kill them.

Perhaps her mission was to present her uncle with an alternative plan. Her uncle, with his encyclopedic knowledge of revolution, would guide her to success. She could organize a campaign to sabotage the chemical plants that poisoned the Mississippi River from Baton Rouge to the Gulf of Mexico. The factories would fail and move away, if not proclaim outright their shame and self-dissolve. New Orleans could secede from the Union and proclaim itself an independent Republic of Pleasure and Music and Poverty. The alternative to consuming the world would be *musical poverty*. In a state of dancing ecstasy, people didn't eat much. Thus, dancing led to sainthood.

But just as swiftly as she was overcome by this happy vision, a black cloud of anxiety appeared. The cloud was composed of the word DUTY. Felicity remembered that she *had* a job. She had been charged by the major to find the Indian girl. Felicity remembered that she was very likely the target of two very angry naked goons, and she suddenly thought it entirely possible that the scaly reverend might *not* hand over the cash without a fight.

"Felix!"

Very few people called her Felix. Martin Dedette was one of them. When she and Miles were a couple, the dapper fashion editor of the *Times-*

Picayune had been one of their best friends. They had clubbed and hung together for years. Felicity had actually slept with Martin once. Miles had really pissed her off one night when he'd gone to a party after his gig without
her. Martin had driven her home and she'd asked him in. It had been awkward, but she remembered Martin's vigor with some satisfaction.

Martin must have remembered something similar, because he grinned
suddenly. "Felix, you gone missing. I've called your old number one hundred times."

"That would be twice," smiled Felicity. She was glad to see him. She'd
given him up along with everyone else, perhaps with even more eagerness
than the rest. Their intimacy still embarrassed her.

"Who you been hangin' with?" Martin kissed her on both cheeks and
sat down at the little table.

"Amelia Earhart, Ovid, Saint Teresa . . . you know."

"Always the bookworm."

Dedette caught her up on his life, which was exactly the same as always.
He went to parties and fashion shows, wrote for the paper, changed
clothes, and went dancing every night. Had nine girlfriends but couldn't
remember all their names.

It was almost lunchtime. Dedette said, "What do you say we grab a bite
and a drink down Decatur way?"

"We could, Dedette, but I warn you. I don't do flesh anymore. I neither
eat nor touch it."

"What, you give it to the angels now, *cher?*"

"You might say that, sir."

It seemed to Felicity that Martin Dedette had been sent to her by providence. In her briefcase was a manila envelope containing a complete set
of Mullin prints. She had addressed the envelope to *Our Mirror*, the sleazi-
est of the tabloids. *Our Mirror* was a fearless and filthy weekly that had
been sued countless times. Everyone read it. Felicity had weighed the envelope and put stamps on it. She had thought long and hard about whom
she could entrust with the package, but no one had seemed quite right.
And now here was Dedette. Gullible, charming, obedient Dedette.

On their way to lunch, Felicity explained to Martin that Miles had
taken the keys to her body with him to the other world. While this wasn't
entirely accurate, she did feel that way most of the time. The few occasions on which she had allowed penetration she had thought of herself as a
witness rather than as a participant. Her spirit was infinitely more promis-
cuous than her flesh.

The park across Decatur was a Shade shantytown of cardboard shacks. A group of Shades lay on the sidewalk directly in their path. Martin and Felicity stepped gingerly around them so as not to upset an odd-looking altar composed of dog food cans, driftwood, petrified half-eaten beignets, and a cross glued together from mirror shards.

"Hey, wanna see us spell 'Fuck'?" called one of them.

Martin quickened his step but Felicity slowed down. "Yeah," she said. She felt clean and powerful. Queen of the underworld.

There was a howl of approving laughter from the Shades. The one who had spoken leapt to his feet and offered them a spot in the circle on top of some old cardboard.

"You can't be serious." Martin was distressed.

But Felicity had already sat down and crossed her legs. "I never heard them talk. I thought they had a vow of silence or something. Sit, Dedette."

Reluctantly, Martin Dedette, fashion editor, crouched down next to her. He pulled up his pants so as not to upset the perfect crease.

The Shades began to leap about like movie Indians, shedding their rags. Four of them, two boys and two girls, arranged themselves naked around Felicity and Martin. Their tattoos became oddly congruent. The faceless bodies tattood on their skin leaned sadly on one another like a fresco of the damned. The Shade who had first spoken took Felicity's hand and guided it over the surface of the four bellies, just below the navels. Her fingers deciphered the short text before she had actually seen it: F-U-C-K. Each of them had a letter incised there.

"What else does it say?" asked Felicity, enjoying the lightly scarred surfaces at her fingertips. "I like brailling," she said, making up a verb.

More Shades came over and arranged themselves in a pattern that Felicity touch-read as: F-U-C-K T-H-I-S W-O-R-L-D T-H-E T-R-U-E O-N-E C-O-M-E-S.

"Who's the True One?" Felicity whispered, overcome by the earnest warmth of all the young bodies stilled there in such ritual yearning.

"You are! You are!" The Shades broke off and started dancing around them.

"For chrissakes, Felicity!" said Martin, getting up.

"Oh, don't be such a fuddy-duddy! Don't you believe that I'm the One? Dance, Dedette, dance!" She rose, taking off her jacket, and joined the circle, twirling around and around until she collapsed on the ground laughing. And she still wasn't done.

"Let me teach you something, Martin Dedette . . ."

"Listen," she said to the Shade who had first spoken to her. "You've done everything, right?"

"Everything," he said sadly.

"Drugs, right? Sex, right?"

To each question the boy nodded yes and got sadder.

"Burnt," he said. "Totally burnt, man. Done it all. Where is the One?"

"Okay, you've done it all, but have you ever seen a sheep?"

"A sheep?"

"Yeah, a sheep."

The boy thought about this and then looked around. Several of them shrugged.

"No, I guess not."

"How many of you never saw a sheep?"

Nearly all raised their hands.

"How many of you never ate a mango?"

Nearly all the shadow children raised their hands.

"You ain't done shit," said Felicity. "When you've seen a sheep and eaten a mango, preferably at the same time, you come tell me you done everything!"

Felicity rose and brushed the dirt off her butt. It was only with great reluctance and after receiving a hug from each Shade that Felicity finally parted. She thought she felt their fleas jumping on her. Bourgeois bitch, she admonished herself. Jesus hugged the lepers.

To his credit, Martin was still waiting when she got up to go.

"Doesn't this beat lunch?" Felicity was glowing.

She walked buoyantly alongside the inexplicably morose M. Dedette. When they had safely crossed the street, he led her to the bar at Sbisa. After a double shot of Drambuie, his natural elegance and worldly ease reasserted themselves.

"God, Felicity, you'd do anything."

"You should know, Martin. I did it with you."

Felicity laughed and leaned back in her seat.

"Martin, I want you to do me a favor."

"Teach you how to swim? Reverse revirgination? Anything."

"It's serious." Felicity took the manila envelope out of her briefcase. "I'm involved in a tricky case. Would you mail this envelope if you don't hear from me by tomorrow afternoon?"

"Christ, Felix. Somebody gonna kill you?"

"I don't think so. It's just insurance."

"And what do I get for being a good boy?"

Felicity gave him a frankly obscene look, licking her upper lip suggestively. "I'll put my tongue stud in for you."

Martin Dedette, who thought of himself as worldly and unflappable, blushed. Even he knew what the pierced used their tongues for.

"Well, what do you say we visit with the Shades some more, wealthy Saracen?"

"There is no way, darling, I'm going back there. You're on your own. And by the way, what were you teaching me back there?"

"Innocence, Martin. Have *you* ever seen a sheep?"

Felicity found it difficult to explain what happened next, or why. Martin made some joke and whispered the punch line into her ear, tickling something in there. A dark funnel that began there wended its way into her chest and made her warm all over. Blame it on her ear; she always had an excessively sensitive drum. Suffice it to say that they found themselves back at her apartment with a bottle of Knob Creek bourbon, sitting on her bed.

Martin did have a long, brown body with dark nipples that Felicity fell on greedily. He undressed her with assurance, peeling off her jeans without a hitch and lifting her blouse as easily as blowing a feather. He didn't snag himself in her belly-button ring as she half expected him to, but licked it instead, passing his tongue expertly through it. He took long enough with her ring for her bristly pubis to catch fire, and when he passed from the ring to the groove at the top of her cunt, she squeezed her thighs together hard. Her effort was no match for Martin's nimble tongue. He found her clitoris quickly and pushed it in and out of its hood as if playing with a tiny monk. Felicity surrendered to his ministrations.

The thick bow of Martin's cock felt silky and delicious when Felicity put it in her mouth. She found the heavy knob with its slit lubricated by a drop of semen indescribably sweet.

It would have been a completely adequate experience if everything had ended here. But Martin was determined to complete the program by the book. He turned her around suddenly and lay on top of her. The heaviness of his body awakened in Felicity a strong urge to escape. She did not like being pinned down and tried to get out. Martin took this for just another twist in their love play and forced her thighs open with his hand. She moved her head from side to side to escape his mouth, which locked forcefully on her lips. Felicity wasn't sure when he entered her, but she felt suddenly suspended, impaled on the mast of a sinking ship that was her own body. She became vacant, leaving her body behind on the bed like a discarded coat. From that point on, it became only a matter of watching for the end, which came swiftly and seared her with an abundant stickiness.

It hadn't been Martin's fault, and Felicity tried to smile while she extricated herself from under his sweaty flesh. Martin looked pretty smug sprawled there, and it took her a good quarter of an hour before she persuaded him to get dressed.

"I have to go now. I really do," Martin mumbled, as if it had been his own idea.

Poor, poor dandy. After he left, Felicity showered at length and had another drink. Something was happening to her. When she'd been a kid, she sometimes looked quickly sideways and glimpsed some fairy or elf scramble away. She had to be really fast to catch them. Some such thing was going on now. Felicity sensed that the thick, wet air was full of quick, fishtailing presences just waiting for her to see them.

Alas, there was business to tend to. She would forget the whole episode and get on with the real stuff. She thought fondly of the Shades, who were so purposely asexual. It dawned on her that they might be of some help for what lay ahead.

Chapter Fourteen

Wherein Gala Keria, hostess of Gal Gal Hamazal, *surprises and shocks all of Israel. The scholars discuss the burning question of the Messiah.*

n d r e a and the scholars, upon their return from sightseeing, were met at the the convent door by Sister Maria.

"Have you heard the terrible news?" she asked, hurrying to help them out of their coats.

Through each mind flashed a different idea, but the images had one thing in common: death. This was, after all, Israel. War and terrorism had made death a familiar occurrence. In addition to that basic concern, at least three of them thought: *Armageddon.* This was, after all, Jerusalem. The valley of Megiddo was a stone's throw away.

More nuns appeared behind Sister Maria, and all started talking at once, making it difficult to understand just what had happened.

"The rabbis have taken her to the chamber of the bad books!" one nun blurted.

Another declared, "The American took her to be his slave!"

Finally, the good sisters slowed down sufficiently to make some sense. Gala Keria was missing, possibly kidnapped! The news bulletins broadcast on Israeli television and radio relayed the contents of an E-mail message to *Gal Gal's* producer, apparently from Gala: *The Fates may use the Wheel, but the Wheel will roll away!* This cryptic message stimulated everyone to heights of speculation.

"They say that she was taken by the devil to turn the wheel that will set the date for the End Times," speculated weary Sister Rodica, her voice touched by hysteria.

"They say that Hamas is holding her!" Sister Maria was both more realistic and politically aware.

Hamas had been increasing its campaign of political terror; there were explosions nearly every day. Only two streets away on Haik Efraim, a terrorist had blown himself up in a movie theater, killing fifty people. But kidnapping was not one of their tactics. Muslim martyrs preferred going up in a blaze, clutching their key to heaven.

Sometimes, after an explosion, only this key remained intact. Sister Maria had seen one pictured in the newspaper: a bronze key with small teeth on which the suicide's imam had scratched in Arabic the word HEAVEN.

Another sister had just returned from the city, where she had read the headline of a tabloid in a kiosk claiming, *American Billionaire Kidnaps Second "Wheel" Hostess.*

The first had been Kashmir Birani, hostess of the Indian *Wheel of Fortune—Kismet Chakkar—*who had vanished in the city of New Orleans five years before. The tabloid claimed that the billionaire responsible was no other than Dr. Edward Teller, the father of the H-bomb and the American Star Wars project. Sister Rodica, for one, believed it. She had been a little doubtful when she read that most members of the United States Senate, the leading figures in the Knesset, and all the pope's advisers were aliens from the planet Pluto. That was difficult, but this was easy. The man who made the bomb had to be the devil. That he'd kidnapped a woman loved by everyone was not at all surprising. The tabloid went on to say that Dr. Teller may even have kidnapped Vanna White herself and replaced her with an impostor.

The *Gal Gal* producers announced a reward of 3 million shekels (about $1 million) for Gala Keria's safe return. But no kidnappers came forward to claim the prize. And there was no follow-up to the cryptic E-mail. In an effort to maintain public awareness of her absence, *Gal Gal Hamazal* announced that, for the next few days, they would alternate reruns with new shows hosted by different girls. They called on young Israeli women to try for the job if they felt sufficiently qualified.

Andrea thought about going to the television station and offering herself as Gala's replacement. During the festive Christmas Eve dinner, the guests had attempted to discover the deeper reasons for the world's fascination with *Wheel of Fortune*. After Gala's disappearance, all sorts of statistics had been compiled. It turned out that most people on earth were watching a local version of *Wheel of Fortune* at least once a week. At the end of the twentieth century, *Wheel of Fortune* was the most-watched television show on earth.

"A majority of earthlings are absorbed by this game," began Father Hernio. "But why? All have become players and participants, without ever leaving their living rooms. As we rush toward the end of the millennium, a time that we endow with great significance, we seem to be less and less capable of any activity other than following the spinning of Fortuna's wheel. When people do move, it is only to play other games of chance. Gambling is widespread and pernicious. Fortuna, the goddess of luck, rules people with abandon. It is a bad time. False messiahs of every flavor clutter every street corner with cheap boom boxes. You couldn't hear the voice of the Lord if your ears were made of gold. If I had the power of the Turks I would build a new Golden Gate over Jerusalem to keep out both the messiahs and the broadcast of *Gal Gal Hamazal*.

"Sorry, I didn't mean to shout." The priest excused his outburst.

The good father had gotten himself quite worked up and looked in danger of choking on a piece of date cake. Dr. Luna patted his back vigorously, saying calmly: "In the United States, where the show originated, Vanna White has been made into a goddess as important as the Statue of Liberty. Every country on earth has its own *Wheel of Fortune* now, and many of the foreign hostesses, with the exception of Gala, are even more Vanna-like than the original. It may be true; as the tabloids tell us, that the American Vanna has been replaced by an impostor. There would be a certain logic in this."

Mother Superior, seated ceremonially at the head of the table, had kept her peace as long as she could. "What logic, dear friend? I have listened to this nonsense for far too long. This is a day we should rejoice in the Lord, and what do we speak of? *Television!*" She said this word with as much contempt as she could muster. "Does television have a heart? Is it made of flesh, blood, and spirit? Is it an altar for faith?" She put down her fork, on which a piece of roast duck was still impaled, and answered her own question. "No, it is not. It is only a foolish glass eye, like a vain young woman's mirror! All we see in it is a picture of our faithless souls. Forgive them, Mother of God, for their viewing habit!"

"But Mother," Father Hernio said, trying to hide his amusement, "there is even a saint of television, officially blessed by the pope—Saint Cecily of television and multimedia."

"The pope," Mother Superior said curtly, "is a politician. Christ our Lord is not. When he returns he will throw away much of the pope's wardrobe."

"Where do you suppose he will return?" asked Father Hernio.

"*Where?* To Jerusalem, of course."

Mother Superior was sure of this; it was why the sisters of the order lived here.

"Oh, I don't think so," said Father Hernio gravely.

"And where do *you* think that Christ will go when he returns to this vale of tears?" Mother Superior spoke sharply.

"CNN headquarters in Atlanta," replied the father.

Amid the laughter that followed, Andrea noticed that Sister Rodica was crying. Two tears, one on each cheek, were making their way to the corners of her mouth. Andrea reached under the table and found the nun's hands folded tightly in her lap. She pried a hand loose and held it clumsily, squeezing her fingers. But Sister Rodica tore her hand away and bolted from the table, making some excuse of checking on the coffee. No one seemed to notice, but Sister Maria looked quizzically at Andrea and shrugged.

Quite oblivious to Mother Superior's injunction to change the subject, Mr. Rabindranath said that he had seen an interesting interview with a good friend of poor Gala.

This young woman claimed that she and Gala had discussed many times the disappearance of Kashmir Birani, the Indian hostess of *Kismet Chakkar.* Gala had feared that a similar fate might befall her. She'd even had a premonition. The interviewer asked the woman what Gala's reaction had been to the rumor that Vanna White herself had been abducted by aliens and replaced by an alien-controlled clone. Gala had laughed at this, the friend reported, and lectured her at length about the propensity of people to endow their manufactured gods with miraculous powers. Gala was some kind of Marxist, the woman had explained.

"Mr. Rabindranath," Mother Superior said severely, "what are you waiting for? I mean, what are the Hindus waiting for?"

"An avatar."

"Is he very much like our returning Christ?"

"I believe so," Mr. Rabindranath said, not quite sure.

"I would like to ask this question of everyone here. I believe that it matters very much. Who are you—or more precisely, your tradition—waiting for?"

The question startled no one, but it was serious. The table fell silent.

"Since I have the dubious benefit of having been born within one faith and ended up dedicated to another, let me begin," said Lama Cohen. "As a Buddhist I believe in the cessation of the cycle of incarnation and reincarnation. I believe in the return of the world to the source of light, not in the return of a light-being to the source of pain."

"In other words," Mother Superior said shrewdly, "you believe in the End of the World but not in its redemption."

"The End is the redemption," the Lama said flatly. "Why increase suffering, even if it's the suffering of the Messiah?"

Father Zahan said that the Yuin also believed in the arrival at the End of Time of an avatar. His name, even his shape, was unknown, as was the date of his return.

"I must admit, however, that I am here in Jerusalem as a result of signs pointing to the return of our avatar."

Pressed to explain, he would say only that a dream had guided him.

Magh Tuiredh, who was as taciturn as his name was hard to pronounce, nodded in agreement.

"I am also here as the result of a dream. I was told by Lugh, the Celt god, to come to Jerusalem. He showed me a scroll I couldn't read. The End Times are near."

The pronouncement of the gloomy Celt dampened the party's spirits. A gust of wind tore at the convent's roof. The nearness of the End Times was a feeling that everyone shared.

"We Hopi believe that there are nine worlds," Earl Smith explained. "Three have already been destroyed. We live in the fourth world, which will be destroyed by fire in a war started by China or Israel. That time is soon. It will come when Saquasohuh, the Blue Star kachina, will dance in the plaza and take off his mask. He represents a blue star, far off, which will appear soon. The time is foretold by a song sung during a ceremony that was performed three times in this century: in 1914, before World War One; in 1940, before World War Two; and two weeks ago, in Oraibi, on the Second Mesa." Earl Smith paused and passed a calloused farmer's hand over his deeply lined forehead. There were blue lights in his deeply black eyes.

"Then why are you in Jerusalem and not in Oraibi with your people, Mr. Smith?" Mother Superior asked—more respectfully, Andrea noticed, than when she had questioned Mr. Rabindranath.

"I was sent by my people to guide the Blue Star back to the Second Mesa. I am to welcome him," concluded Mr. Smith.

Dr. Luna hurried to begin his turn. "The Mayan cycle is at an end also. Kukulkan, the Plumed Serpent, the one the Aztecs call Quetzalcoatl, is going to return. I am here on a scholarly mission, however. I have heard that an unknown Mayan codex may be languishing in the library of a monastery here in Jerusalem. I hope to find it before the return of Kukulkan."

Dr. Luna impaled a roasted chestnut as if it were a stubborn obstacle to his quest. He had been frustrated in his scholarly work by bureaucrats who did not understand the urgency. The codex contained the protocol that his people had forgotten but now needed to follow if the world was going to survive.

"We wish you all the best luck, Dr. Luna," said Mother Superior. "And how about you, Professor Li?"

During the explanations proffered by his colleagues, Dr. Li had folded quietly within himself. To Lama Cohen, who was familiar with meditation poses, he resembled a closed lotus blossom. The others noticed only his deep quiet. Addressed directly, he replied slowly, barely above a whisper.

"I confess that I am at a disadvantage here, my friends. The only return that the Chinese might fear is the return of Chairman Mao. So far we have been fortunate in that the great man has confined his return to post-cards, pins, and collectors' editions of his books. My waiting here in Jerusalem has to do with the practical whims of Rabbi Golden, the great translator from the Chinese, who has promised to let me study a lost Confucian manuscript. Dr. Luna and I are engaged, I believe, in a similar quest."

"That's only fitting," said Lama Cohen, "in the City of the Book."

Mention of books led naturally to consideration of language and letters, and the discussion returned, quite unexpectedly, to Gala Keria. To tell the truth, Andrea had been rather bored by the clerics' and scholars' religious discussion. She much prefered the living mystery of Gala.

"I also heard an interesting comment about Vanna White on the radio. It was an American radio program," said Father Hernio. "The commentator claimed, not at all jokingly, that Vanna White represents the world's last hope for *meaning*, and that she soothes the anxieties of millions by showing them that behind the jumble of senseless letters there is in fact meaning: phrases, things, foreign expressions, places." Hernio waved his arms, indicating everything. "By simply calling out a single letter, one can then fill out the terrifying spaces between letters and return meaning— like light—to the world. In the opinion of the commentator, Vanna is the giver of light, as her name—White—implies. She is the very opposite, he claimed, of those Dada artists, at the beginning of the twentieth century, who saw no meaning, no hope, no salvation behind the jumble of letters they had maliciously torn out of perfectly reasonable words. Vanna, it seems, has restored to humanity what these Dadaists stole from it, namely, sense and reason. If the Dadaists were already anxious at the beginning of the century, before the two world wars, genocides, and atomic bombs, you can imagine how anxious people are now, at the end of it! Ergo, all they have is Vanna! A devilish argument, I must admit!"

"What this man is saying is that Vanna White is the Western Messiah," Professor Li concluded logically.

This proposition shocked everyone except Lama Cohen and Mother Superior. The lama was not surprised because in the Buddhist view only the unexpected made sense. Mother Superior was not surprised because her faith in Christ did not allow her even to consider such an absurdity. She said so.

"Do you not believe it possible that Christ could be, this time around, a woman?" Father Hernio teased the old nun.

"Christ is Christ, the *Son* of God," Mother Superior said curtly, indicating that the discussion was at an end.

But it wasn't. There were still two pies left and a full carafe of Mount Hebron wine.

"What if Vanna White *is* the avatar? What is Gala Keria, then? Or Kashmir Birani?" Mr. Rabindranath fired these questions directly at the remains of the roasted ducks.

"Then each one of them is the avatar also. They are emanations of the Divine One," said Lama Cohen. "And if Andrea took the job, then she too would become the avatar. Perhaps it is Andrea that everyone's been waiting for all along!"

Andrea felt again that cattle-prod-skull-of-Adam-Unction-Stone tingle. Everyone stared at her as if they had just seen her for the first time.

"What's the matter?" she said in English. "Were you expecting someone else?"

No one laughed at her little joke. For an uncomfortably long time, during which the thought sank in, Andrea felt as if she stood naked before a bunch of portrait painters. Their eyes weighed her features, trying to fit them to those of the Messiahs in their minds. Andrea rose from the table, bowed her head, and asked to be excused. Mother Superior gave her leave. Andrea went up the stairs to look for Sister Rodica.

"See what you've done? You upset the child!" said Mother Superior, ending the awkward silence. She hated to admit it, but for a moment, she had actually entertained the idea herself. *How foolish we are, dear Lord.*

"Let us pray!"

The company fell to prayer, each in the silence of his or her own self. It didn't take a sleuth to know what each was praying for. Written in luminous letters over their heads like banners inscribed with light were requests for the end of each of their weary quests. Most of those present actually *hoped* that the young Bosnian orphan was the Messiah. Or an emanation of her, anyway.

Lama Cohen, who didn't pray (and didn't feel like meditating) remembered a visit to the Marcel Janco Museum near Tel Aviv, the first time she came to Israel with her family. Her father was a great fan of the Dadaists, and of Marcel Janco, who had been the second or third original Dadaist. The first was Tristan Tzara, a Romanian Jew whose original name had been Sami Rosenstock. According to her father, one day this Tzara took a pair of scissors to the world's best literature, including the Bible, and cut everything up and then mixed words from the newspapers right in with the holy words.

It's a wonder that the world didn't end right then and there, thought Lama Cohen. *There are many ways to piss off the God of the Hebrews, but messing with his Word is the surest!* Which is why the hostess of *Gal Gal Hamazal* couldn't very well be the Messiah, even if she restores the order. She still messes with his words and letters, scrambling and mixing them and hiding them. Her father had said that there was another Jew, named Isidore Isou, who was twice as bad as this man Tzara. He had gone to war against every letter, God forgive him! He actually claimed he was *looking* for God in the alphabet. Lama Cohen grinned to herself. *For his sake, I hope he didn't find him!*

Ultimately, the explanation for Gala's disappearance was an anticlimax to the days of morbid speculation. In the most God-crazy place on earth, Gala had joined a religious cult. It seemed to Israelis terribly pedestrian, not at all what they had imagined while Gala was missing.

In a videotape delivered to the six o'clock news, Gala herself informed the nation that she had joined a sect known as the Invisibles. The beautiful ex-hostess of *Gal Gal Hamazal*, looking pale and already slightly transparent, implored the world to forget her.

"I am no longer Gala Keria. I am no one. I walk now the path of the anonymous righteous. It is our purpose to seek unfettered communion with God. I am dedicated to erasing every trace of my existence in the corrupt world."

Hostage experts testified that the statement did not seem coerced, and Gala didn't appear to have been brainwashed, though her die-hard fans insisted that she would never have left *Gal Gal Hamazal* of her own free will.

Andrea, for one, admired Gala's decision to give up being Gala. To give up fame and applause, choosing to be no one, struck her as both very brave and quite inconceivable. Andrea had become no one the day she was herded into the Serbian camp. It had not been a choice. Perhaps that was why she was so excited by the idea of becoming a someone, as Gala had been. Andrea had learned in the camp that she could be anyone.

"Maybe *I* am the True One," she'd shouted at the Serb soldier loading her and her neighbors into the truck. Maybe I *am* the one, she thought now, dreaming of Gala's job.

Chapter Fifteen

Wherein we witness the wholly surprising outcome
of Felicity's transaction with the televangelist

y the time Felicity arrived, Jackson Square was experiencing the magic hour of twilight. The fortune-tellers were all busy, reading the sweaty palms of tourists, casting bones and dice for the lovelorn, slapping worn tarot cards down before wide-eyed Yankee matrons. The portrait painters were at their charcoals and paint, fixing on paper and canvas the solemn miens of suburbanites. Flame swallowers, jugglers, and mimes danced on the cobblestones. Competing musicians poured their hearts out for dollar bills.

A tourist stood, looking bewildered, on the round marker in front of Saint Louis Cathedral commemorating the place where John Paul II had said Mass when he visited the city more than a decade before. Felicity always made sure to step on it before entering the holy place. It charged her with a bit of light blue energy she called "pope light," though she was not particularly fond of this pope or any other.

"Excuse me," said the tourist. "Can you tell me what I am looking at?"

"At a huge flaw," said Felicity, "a red thread that runs sadly through all your perceptions. After your fortune is told, your portrait painted, your aura polished, your past lives established, your money spent, and your nostalgia affirmed, there is still a great flaw in your tapestry."

"Whoa!" the man said, shifting his video-camera bag from one shoulder to another. "Lady, you some kind of poet?"

"I wish," sighed Felicity. "Would you mind stepping off the pope? I need his energy."

"Anything you say." The tourist took her in, a vibrating wisp of a girl, with rings on every finger, spiky hair, fuchsia jeans, boots, maybe not human at all. New Orleans, he thought. Landing pad for the weird. Maybe none of my pictures will come out.

When Felicity stood on the pope she saw the throngs of tourists with crystalline clarity. They had escaped from America for a few hours. In their shorts and T-shirts with the names of bowling leagues, community colleges, and rock bands, rolls of Burger King fat spilling over painful elastic, they wandered clueless through the waning days of the twentieth century. They were nomads of late capitalism, here to retrieve for a moment some of the youthful passion that had been extinguished by their jobs, mortgages, atomized families, and television. The cheap magic of New Orleans transported them a few inches off the ground. Some of them were actually hovering.

Imperceptibly, the crowd grew. At first, the tattooed Shades looked like part of the landscape they traversed every day, but as more and more of them appeared, the crowd took on a hue of sadness and dejection. It was as if a leper colony were slowly emptying itself into an American Legion parade. The tourists tried to take no notice, but they drew in by degrees, moving closer to their fortune-tellers and portrait painters. The Shades smelled young and dirty.

The candlelit chiaroscuro inside the cathedral held few worshipers, but the Shades began kneeling behind pews, filling it up. Felicity was pleased to notice that their tans and tattooed skin did not look out of place here, among haloed, purple-robed saints. Shades were saints, too, perhaps the first saints of that new, nonconsuming humanity her uncle called for. Certainly they didn't eat Whoppers. Felicity took her place before the Holy Mother, where she had prayed not long ago, though it seemed that years had passed.

"Dear Mother," she entreated, "please make this go smoothly, and I will be sure to do good things with the money. I will lessen suffering and I will only have a little, very little, fun myself."

The Holy Mother clutched her Infant tighter and looked upon Felicity doubtfully, as if she had seen her type before, a regular Magdalene in contrite clothing.

At precisely eight o'clock, Reverend Jeremy "Elvis" Mullin entered the church. Alone. Felicity watched him stride assuredly down the center aisle and head directly for her. He was carrying the burgundy briefcase. It surprised her. She had been sure that he would be accompanied by a hundred Bamajans and a whole flock of jailbirds.

He sat on the pew next to her and looked disdainfully at the Virgin. "These cats sure pour the gilt on their holies," he said, loud enough to startle the pew of Shades behind them.

"Did you bring the dough?" whispered Felicity.

"You need to *audition* for it," he said.

Felicity was angry. But she felt in control. That is, she *would have* felt in control if the choir had not at that very moment begun practicing in the loft above them. There was a burst of clear voices, then a pure soaring solo soprano, then two baritones greeted each other, followed by a blast of brass. It was like the heavens waking up hungover in the morning. It distressed Felicity.

> Out of the depths I cry to you; O Lord now hear me calling.
> Incline your ear to my distress.
> In spite of my rebelling do not regard my sinful deeds.
> Send me the grace my spirit needs.
> Without it I am nothing . . .

The words of the psalm entered her heart like thin golden arrows.

Ave Maria, gratia plena . . . Her attempt to pray felt hollow. The choir's fumbling and the verses from on high had a most curious effect. They are softening my bones, noted Felicity. Indeed, she felt molten, like a metal being poured into a mold.

The preacher's cologne was overpowering, nauseating, yet somehow part of the angelic cacophony in the gallery. She was unsettled by Mullin's heat, like that of an animal in a cave. Scent, music, and heat, I will overcome you, vowed the once-steely girl dick, and then she did something unexpected. She touched Mullin. The gesture was intended to push him away, to increase the distance between them. At the same time, she raised her other hand as if to silence the choir practice.

Her touch was lighter than she intended; it landed on Mullin's arm like a butterfly. And then he did something even more startling: he slipped his arm around her waist. Her mind, caught by surprise, shouted a warning, but it was too late. Every bit of sense seeped out of her. Her spine was on fire and the top of her head felt as if it was coming undone, unscrewed like a bottle cap by an invisible hand.

"Audition for me," Mullin breathed hotly in her ear.

Felicity felt an urge to cry and to sing, simultaneously. The choir had somehow gotten itself together, and the first bars of "Out of the depths I cry to you" soared to the vaults of the cathedral. Felicity looked helplessly at the Holy Mother, but she had turned away and was looking down at her Infant. Felicity's whole being strained to remember the phrase she had so triumphantly hurled at the preacher on the night of Grandmère's death, but she could not. There was a hook, a musical note, really, stuck in her throat.

She followed Mullin out of the church with her head bowed, without looking at the Shades, who were surprised to see her walking so humbly behind the man in black. She had arranged with them before the meeting to stay with her no matter what happened, so they filed out after the couple. Outside the door they were met by more Shades. Felicity barely saw them. All she wanted to do was cry and sing.

Inside her, a voice warned: the devil has overcome you; recite the Our Father. But she couldn't remember the familiar words. Another nearly extinguished voice advised: Cuff the beast. Call the major. Ask Mullin about the money. This is business. The money.

Felicity looked at the polished black column that was Reverend Mullin and whispered, "Our business . . ."

"After the audition," said Mullin gently, guiding her with fingers lightly touching the small of her back. Blue electric snakes issued from his fingertips and bathed her spine in warm light.

Across the square, a small procession was marching to a familiar tune.

> Oh when the saints go marching in.
> Oh when the saints go marching in . . .

Oh, I want to be in that number, Felicity's anesthetized mind sang back, struggling to resist its Mullin-induced paralysis. As the procession drew nearer, she could see that the marchers were led not by a jazz trumpeter but by an elderly, Semitic-looking man blowing his heart out on a corkscrewed shofar. He was followed by a man carrying an ornate Torah scroll aloft, and they were followed by a group of sober-looking, dark-suited men.

Even in her stupor, Felicity recognized the man blowing the shofar— Cantor Redman! Papa Redman, Ben's father. As the parade passed she wanted to run to greet him, to ask about Ben, to seek sanctuary in his arms. But she felt underwater, her voice buried in an undertow.

She did not even wonder what a Jewish group carrying the Torah was doing marching to a Christian hymn, even if it *was* also the city's theme song, a football fight song. Questions had fled from her, leaving her empty. Felicity saw a flock of her questions take off like swallows over the roofs of the Quarter. I am a woman without questions now, her mind told her, I am no one.

Mullin led her to the gold Cadillac parked near the Napoleon House, and she meekly got in. I am being pushed underwater by a strong hand. I am being baptized by a monster. She expected the reverend to boom out, "I baptize you . . . in the name of Jesus Christ . . . ," but he was not even moving his lips, and the water was entirely within her. I am drowning in the waters of myself. Help me.

But the voice that said those words could not be heard. Farther and farther down she went.

The Shades milled about, unsure what to do next. One of them called out, "Hey, man, where you going, man?" Felicity gave them no clue; she merely waved as the Caddy rolled out. She saw their bewildered, innocent, affectionate faces stare after her. Then water covered everything.

Chapter Sixteen

Wherein Andrea meets the young rabbi Yehuda ben Yehuda

 e f o r e he came to Israel, Yehuda ben Yehuda had never been on a bus. Now he knew every bus route in Jerusalem and every transfer point. He knew which lines had been targeted by terrorist bombers, and times of day when it was safer to walk.

Before he came to Israel, Yehuda ben Yehuda had been ordinary Ben Redman, an affluent white American boy. Growing up in New Orleans, he'd been driven by his father to and from a private, expensive elementary school. In high school he'd driven himself in his grandmother's hand-me-down Mercedes. The only public transportation he'd ever used was the old electric car on Saint Charles Avenue.

Ben Redman had been a privileged boy, it's true, but he was also Jewish. So, though he never experienced even one moment of anti-Semitism growing up in New Orleans, he had suffered. He felt guilty about being white and affluent and privileged. But then, he'd grown up in a place where the experience of prejudice and injustice was reserved exclusively for black people, and whites were the oppressors.

There is a lot of white guilt in the South, and Ben had somehow absorbed a disproportionate share of it. Sensitive people inherit it like original sin, and Ben was three times as sensitive as the average Southerner. He could not forget that white people enslaved and killed other human beings. He was tormented by his daily contact with the victims' great-great-great-grandchildren, who constituted over 50 percent of the population of his city and were still suffering.

Ben Redman tried to escape his guilt by becoming black. In his second year of high school, he convinced his parents to let him transfer to public school, where he made black friends, talked hip-hop, and continued to feel guilty. He had been freed from his massive guilt only by a sudden and equally massive religious conversion.

But perhaps his conversion had not been so sudden. The conviction had been growing in him that books, which he loved, were being threatened by an evil force in the world. His father had once told him that in medieval synagogues there used to be a chamber where all the *bad* books were deposited and incinerated. These were desecrated Torahs, violated prayer books, and probably, books banned by the rabbis. Ben was sorry for all the books. When he was seven years old, he overheard one of his father's friends say in a dramatic voice:

"The library at Alexandria burnt . . ."

Ben hadn't heard the rest. He had been gripped by panic. He burst out of his hiding place under the table and cried, "When? When did it burn down?" He had thought that his library, the Milton Latter Library on Saint Charles, had just burned down. He had not even wondered why the man called the Latter Library the library of Alexandria. All libraries were the Latter Library to him. He didn't know any other.

It had taken Dr. Redman an hour before he could impress on his distraught son that what was being discussed was an ancient tragedy. And he hadn't quite believed it. Consequently, every tragedy seemed to Ben to be current. He suspected that people attached ancient dates to occurring tragedies in order to calm children. But he knew better. History was a sham. His conversion had had something to do with his desire to save books, to be the white knight who rescued the written word from the flames.

During his first month of study in Jerusalem, he'd felt high-strung, overwrought, and insecure. One day, while in this state, he passed by the window of a store where a television was beaming *Gal Gal Hamazal* at passersby. Gala Keria struck him with a lightening bolt and began to inhabit the very essence of his mind, imparting a golden rose hue to the Sefirot of the kabbalistic tree that was his object of study. She sat inside each and every one of these divine spheres, smiling moist fire, her hand extended to either turn a letter or beckon to him. He had tried to ignore her, fight her, blur her image, stamp away her body with the very letters of the holy alphabet she commanded so sinuously. The harder he tried, the sharper she came into focus, her form deepened and enriched by his struggle. He confessed this demonic possession to the rebbe.

It was a serious matter. Gala's use of the holy letters of the Hebrew alphabet had caused many rabbis, including Ben's own, to fire angry communiqués into the always-charged air of Israel. They accused her and her producers of everything from blasphemy to producing for public consumption a kind of "intellectual pig flesh."

Rebbe Zvetai was worried that "random turns of the wheel could produce a combination of letters that would hasten the End Times." The End might be unleashed by an ignorant player who could unwittingly pronounce the Name in front of millions of people. The rebbe reminded Ben that it was forbidden to pronounce the Name of God. He recalled the dreadful story of the golem, an artificial being produced by a Prague rabbi in the seventeenth century, who'd had the Name of God written on his forehead. This being caused a lot of trouble until the rabbi erased the holy Name and the creature turned to dust. Gala was likewise fooling with creation, and Ben was being drawn into the unholy web, the rebbe warned.

When he thought of what the rebbe said, Ben's flesh became even more incandescent. He burned like a Shabbes candle for Gala Keria.

Andrea entered the armed camp that housed the studios of Israel's biggest commercial television station and waited in the lobby for someone to notice her. She wore as a dress a long sweater borrowed from Sister Rodica, who had brought it with her from the old country but no longer had any use for it. The sweater was blue and embroidered with small red poppies. It came down to just above her knees. Ankle-length white socks rose above the black saddle shoes she had worn the night she arrived at Saint Hildegard's. Her shoulder-length brown hair was carefully combed and twisted back in a rich ponytail.

A female receptionist and a soldier sat talking behind a tall desk. The soldier's automatic pistol was lying carelessly on the counter, next to a smoking cigarette in an overflowing ashtray. Just beyond the desk was a glass door, and on the other side of it another soldier sat on a wooden stool, reading a paperback.

A rabbinical student, his wild curls shooting like black seltzer from under his tall hat, burst suddenly into the lobby.

"Get me the *Gal Gal Hamazal* producer!" he shouted at the receptionist.

A baby rabbi! thought Andrea, somewhat charmed by his curls.

The receptionist turned a pair of hostile kohl-rimmed eyes in his direction. "Wait your turn, like everybody else!"

"There is nobody else!" the young rabbi shouted back.

What am I? thought Andrea. Can't anybody see *me?*

"Excuse me." Standing, she said, "I was here first."

The young man wheeled around. "Who are you?" His Hebrew had an American accent.

"I'm the next Gala," Andrea answered firmly.

"You and a thousand other girls!" chuckled the receptionist, buffing her nails.

The soldier just snorted.

"You are all sexist pigs!" objected the rabbi. "*I* am the next Gala!" he said, bowing low.

The young rabbi then announced that he was in truth Yehuda ben Yehuda and that he intended to break the monopoly of girl hostesses on *Gal Gal Hamazal* because it was wrong for women to manipulate the Hebrew alphabet.

Now the receptionist snorted.

"Well, that's a new one," said the soldier. "We should call Mr. Elahu and have him judge these applicants on the spot!"

The other soldier put down his book and came out from behind the glass to join the fun. The receptionist phoned Mr. Elahu, the show's producer.

"There are two new Galas here," she said sarcastically. "One's a boy, the other a girl."

She lit a new cigarette from the butt of the one still burning.

Mr. Elahu was an intellectual-looking man with square ebony glasses and a shiny bald head filled with the awesome knowledge needed to produce *Gal Gal Hamazal* every week. He invited the two young people to his office, but the receptionist and the soldiers protested they wanted to see the audition. Mr. Elahu tried ineffectively to assert his authority, but the lobby employees overwhelmed him with unanswerable Israeli arguments about democracy.

"I may be a simple receptionist!" shouted the receptionist, "but I voted Likud two times, and maybe this is the *last* time!"

"What's that got to do with it?" intervened the soldier, quite reasonably, asserting, "I'm a soldier and I defend this country, and I demand to see the audition!"

"This is a democracy!" the other soldier said reproachfully.

After several rounds of this, Mr. Elahu told everyone to shut up. He would conduct the audition right in the lobby. He began with "the lady first," and asked Andrea's name.

"Andrea Isabel," she lied instantly.

"Not a bad stage name," Mr. Elahu observed, adding, "The name is not important. We can always find you a new name. It is more important that you know the Hebrew language and understand the game. Can you tell me, for instance, how many different Hebrew languages there are?"

"Rabbinic, medieval, and Israeli," said Andrea without hesitating.

Yehuda ben Yehuda looked at the girl suspiciously. Was this a setup?

"My name is Yehuda ben Yehuda." He shrugged. "I think I know something about language."

"So, you are the namesake of the great linguist Ben Yehuda? Can you tell me, young lady, what was Ben Yehuda's chief contribution to modern Hebrew?"

"Well, he wanted to enrich the modern vocabulary with words from past Hebrew literature. Ben Yehuda favored, I believe, using the Arabic lexicon in order to preserve the Semitic character of the language, and he resisted the inclusion of words from Western languages."

"Did he succeed?" asked the astonished producer.

"No, sir. The Americans came."

Everyone laughed, and the young rabbi blushed. He was American.

"Bravo!" approved the receptionist. "This *is* the last time I'm voting Likud!"

"Well, well." Mr. Elahu looked Andrea up and down, noticing for the first time how pretty she was. A spark of recognition traveled up his spine. He'd been in the business long enough to know that she had potential.

"Literature," he continued his quiz. "First-century Roman poet, exiled to Tomis, author of . . ." He trailed off, inviting her to fill in the blank.

"*Metamorphoses*," Andrea finished the sentence. "Ovid."

Even Yehuda ben Yehuda was impressed.

No, it was worse. He was infatuated! He closed his eyes and prayed to remember why he had come.

"Sir," the young rabbi began, "I am here to register a protest. My teachers believe that *Gal Gal Hamazal* is offensive to our faith and to God. First, it is a sin to be careless with the holy letters, and second, if the show has to exist at all, it ought to be put in the hands of a rabbinical authority. A male authority."

This was an argument that Mr. Elahu nipped in the bud.

"Young lady, you must return here ten o'clock tomorrow morning for a proper audition. And you, young man, please submit your complaints in writing to the executive producer, Mr. Abba. This is not a religious court!"

He broached no further dissent and quickly extracted himself from the lobby, which had become, for an entertaining half hour, a true Israeli café. One of the soldiers asked Andrea for her telephone number, but she stuck out her tongue at him. The receptionist muttered, "For shame!" and glared at Andrea.

Andrea and Yehuda ben Yehuda soon found themselves on the sidewalk in the cold sun.

"So, I go this way," he said in Hebrew, pointing vaguely toward the Citadel.

"That's where I'm going too. East."

In the pedestrian mall at the intersection of Ben Yehuda and King George Streets, they stopped to rest on a bench. The mall was crowded with people.

Neotribals with bones through their earlobes, shaved and tattooed heads, pierced eyelids, and clownish costumes strolled past, ignoring the neatly dressed net surfers sitting at coffeehouse terminals.

Two Yemeni women were making flat bread right on the street, patting down the dough with resounding thumps and drowning the results in a vat of sizzling oil.

A Russian violinist in a threadbare coat coaxed a few tears from his strings, crying out at intervals, "Give a shekel for the fiddler on the cobblestones!"

Next to them on the bench, two shrunken old men soaked up the timid winter sun and passed a soggy cigarette back and forth.

"One good thing about America, no smoking anywhere," Ben observed, feeling awkward. He irritated himself sometimes.

Andrea was silent for a moment and then said in English, "Do you mean, Yehuda ben Yehuda, that smoking is prohibited in America, or that America doesn't smoke anywhere?" She giggled at her own joke.

"Please call me Ben. I'm not an idiot." He smiled. "Where are you from, anyway? You have no accent in Hebrew, and your English is obviously better than mine. Isabel is an unusual last name."

"Spain," Andrea lied, glad for an opportunity to polish the story she'd pieced together from books and newspapers. "My family were Marranos. Although they left Spain when Queen Isabella expelled the Jews in the fifteenth century, they returned and lived as Catholics, taking the name Isabel. There were many like them; crypto-Jews, they've been called. But they continued secretly to practice their faith, never forgetting their true identity."

Andrea watched Ben's face carefully as she spoke, looking for signs of boredom or disbelief. She needn't have worried. The young rabbi's face was a study of rapt attention. He was buying the story hook, line, and sinker. Andrea resumed her narrative:

"Last year, Basque rebels started a civil war. There was fighting in our district, and I was separated from my parents and detained in a rebel camp in the mountains for three months." This information she had gathered from an article in *The Herald Tribune*.

"I escaped and traveled on foot across the mountains to France. There, a Jewish family arranged my immigration to Israel."

Andrea was extremely pleased with her performance. The story was so good she was beginning to believe it. Ben's respectful attention now became something more. He was genuinely concerned.

"What happened to the rest of your family? Your parents? Where are they now?" He sounded worried.

Andrea conceived another twist. "My parents have disappeared." Her voice broke slightly. "They were last seen in Cádiz, waiting for a ship to take them to America. A man who met them in Cádiz told me this"—she paused significantly—"but then, he may have been lying. I think he had a romantic interest in me."

She sneaked a look at Ben to see if the innuendo had registered. He looked very sad. To cheer him up, she added quickly, "Maybe they did take a ship . . . to New Orleans." This last detail was inspired by the scholars' story game, in which Great Minds were traveling to New Orleans for a council on the fate of the world. They had all been reading about New Orleans in the encyclopedia.

"New Orleans is my hometown!"

Andrea had a moment of unease. When Ben had asked about her parents, she'd almost said, "They were killed in Sarajevo." Still, she had told him the truth; her parents had disappeared. The void that should have been filled by "mother" and "father" was like a narrow valley reached by a hidden crevasse. When she called out across this valley, not even an echo returned. Her parents were anonymous people who had been killed by men who made history. To get them back she would have to stop history and run the film backward. Instead, she imagined her mother and father strolling arm-in-arm down an avenue of oak trees dripping with Spanish moss.

Ben was still processing her story. She was beautiful, multilingual, Jewish, a refugee, and most important, she believed her parents had escaped to New Orleans!

Ben was ashamed. His parents were healthy and rich. The troubles of the world rarely breached the walls of their huge garden. When they traveled, their cruise ship brushed past the shores of places wounded by war, but there was no contact. If Andrea's parents *were* in New Orleans, they had to be found.

Ben reached out awkwardly and touched Andrea's hair. It was soft and warm. She inclined her head slightly as if to rest it on his chest, but then drew back. Ben felt compassion, affection, and something else, warm, familiar, and inevitable. He would have liked to tell Andrea the story of the illuminated mystical vision that had brought him to Israel, but he felt small now compared to the grandeur of her suffering.

Suddenly he noticed how thin the girl was under her oversized blue sweater. "Are you hungry?" Ben wanted to feed her.

Andrea allowed that she was. They sat outside at an Afghan restaurant on King George. The smell of frying meats wafted from the kitchen. An old woman, the proprietor's mother, extolled the virtues of Afghan cuisine, which seemed to consist mostly of lamb, yogurt, and ground chickpeas. Andrea had a big pita sandwich of roast lamb and a glass of red wine. She ate greedily and Ben was pleased. The longer he watched her, the more convinced he became that he had somehow been chosen to protect her.

Full now, Andrea stretched like a cat on her café seat and watched the street coming to life in the early evening. Ben ordered a whole carafe of red wine. He rarely drank, but now he felt reckless and alive, not at all like the meticulous scholar he had been only that morning. I'm celebrating, he thought to himself, and I am happy. But almost as soon as he had formulated this thought, he was ashamed. Andrea was sad and her whole life trembled before him, filled with more sorrow than he could imagine. Once again, he touched her, caressing her hand. His gesture was meant to convey sympathy, but the caress was electric. Her skin was shamelessly alive, and Ben was suffused by pleasure.

A group of leather-jacketed, pierced people staked out the sidewalk in front of the café and passed a bottle back and forth. Yehuda ben Yehuda had been studying the eccentric young people mobbing the streets of downtown Jerusalem. He now saw an opportunity to cover up his embarrassment and appear knowledgeable and mature at the same time.

He began explaining these creatures to Andrea as if she had just landed from a planet where they were unheard of.

"They are called neotribals. When this rebellion started, piercing and tattooing were associated with sex, wilderness, and freedom. The neotribals used to kill net surfers, but now they just stare at them. The wilderness is now all copyrighted by the *National Geographic*, and sex, well . . ."

Andrea's warmth enveloped him like a thin fragrant film. He fought the urge to touch her again, and continued: "Suffice it to say that piercing and tattooing are not true opposites of TV watching, like sex used to be. They used to call tattooing 'elective exile,' like you could get out of your tribe and belong to another just by your markings. But they've toned down. Now they watch *Gal Gal Hamazal* like everybody else."

"But why," Andrea wanted to know, "why do they pierce their bodies? Is it in imitation of Christ?" She knew that Christians in many parts of the world pierced their hands and feet in imitation of their Savior.

"There are many distinct groups of this culture," Ben answered eagerly. "For the majority, piercing is an imitation of penetration. Very few of them have real sex anymore. In that respect, they are ascetic—" Ben had nearly said, "like me." The rabbinical scholars at his school were expected to transcend all their physical feelings in order to commune with the divine essence.

"They *are* religious, then?" Andrea felt deeply sorry for the ascetic young.

"In their own way, yes. Without discipline, without education. There is a group that initiates its members by tattooing a faceless body on them. This body embraces them completely, making them sort of . . . self-sufficient. These people have no *outside* loves! They call themselves Shades."

"Why faceless?" Andrea wanted to know.

"They claim that they are waiting for someone, an avatar. When she comes—they believe that their avatar is a woman—they are going to draw her face in the blank."

Andrea thought about this for a moment. The streetlights had come on, and the smoke from the cafés and cigarettes, together with the incessant chatter and laughter from the street, filled her with something close to security. She did love the relentless energy of this young country, its vitality, its constant argument with itself, its turbulent identity. The world of Saint Hildegard's was an oasis in this tempestuous land.

"So, you are going to stay in Israel, then?" Ben asked, shifting to firmer ground. "Are you going to study?"

Andrea looked at the cobblestones at her feet. Her face reflected the difficulty of the decision she was about to make. Finally, she looked the boy in the eyes and told him, "I have only a temporary visa. I had no papers when I arrived, so I cannot yet prove that I am Jewish. Technically, I suppose that I am a Spanish citizen—unless you consider the Basque republic legitimate."

Ben was so ashamed he nearly hit himself across his stupid mouth. How could he be so insensitive as to breezily assume that everything was all right now? There was the matter of her parents. Andrea must have been wretchedly lonely. If her parents were in New Orleans, he would see to it that they were found. He would enlist his whole family in the search. What was important was for Andrea to be reunited with her family. But if her legal status in Israel was in question . . . What if she had to leave again, resume her sad wandering? Ben couldn't bear the thought. He closed his eyes and experienced a violent realization, akin to the one that had one day caused him to change his life and leave America. He became convinced that he must help Andrea with everything at his disposal, even if that meant interrupting, for the time being, his studies in Israel. His resolve was sudden but firm. His heart told him that it was more than that.

Yehuda ben Yehuda had become so deeply intent on his sudden understanding that he did not see Andrea's dreamy face come closer. His baby face now stood within a kissable inch of hers. When he looked sufficiently lost in himself, Andrea kissed him. The boy's body underwent a shock as if electrified. For the next eternity or so he locked his soul to her lips and soared to heaven in delight. All mystical steps to the crystal crown of the Sefirot were illuminated.

"We must return to New Orleans together!" Ben said when he came up for air. "I will help you find your family. My parents can even adopt you to make your situation kosher with Immigration. I can even—" Ben stopped himself short and drew a breath.

"Marry me?" asked Andrea.

"Why not?" said Ben. "Just for legal reasons, of course." Flustered, he made an impatient gesture to shoo away the Russian violinist, who had crept closer and was avidly listening.

"Marry me, too!" the musician burst out.

"Fuck you, Boris!" said Ben, reverting briefly to a semblance of normal self.

Andrea licked a small cut on the inside of her lip where Ben had bitten her when they were kissing. She was thinking about America, how her story had led to this, and then, without much connection, she felt very sorry for the people with the faceless bodies tattooed on them. Her mind was racing. She wondered, too, why she'd chosen the name Isabel. Is . . . Abel. Yes, that was it, of course. She was the daughter of Abel, the nomad, not the child of Cain, the murderer. She would never allow herself to be imprisoned again, whether in a camp or a convent. She had to start moving. She would go to America. Her story had set the wheel of both their fortunes spinning, and Venus gave it an extra push.

Yehuda ben Yehuda ached to kiss Andrea again. But she had drawn back, so he gave himself to words instead. Something momentous had happened, something that demanded, it seemed to him, nothing less than the display of his entire being. Ben believed that if something true had to be told, he told it; and more important, he provided commentary on it, so that the habit of thought would accompany every bit of data. These days, this was a great blessing because most data were free of thought. As were most people. Whatever emptiness was in facts was cleansed by thinking about them. Thought was a "cleansing light." This was written on the wall above his bed at the yeshiva in big black letters.

"I believe that the world must be talked back to its source!" Ben exclaimed, his cheeks flushed by this imperative that was so much like himself.

Andrea chased a grain of rice on her plate and cornered it with her finger. "I believe no such thing. A kiss is worth one thousand comments." She squished the grain on her fingertip and brought it to her mouth. Her plate was empty. Everything she had learned had been the result of an action. And in order to act, one had to forget. Andrea thirsted for forgetting and for doing. Words prevented both.

They left the café and walked to the bus stop. Yehuda ben Yehuda walked clumsily next to the lithe orphan, feeling heavy, hairy, and ungraceful. Men looked hungrily at the girl, not hiding their evident greed. Ben was angry on her behalf, but Andrea did not seem to mind. When they passed a jewelry store where the proprietor and his son both waved at Andrea from the door, she thrust out her left hand as if asking them to adorn each finger with rings. The men laughed and made huge kissy noises toward that graceful hand floating in the air.

Ben's resolve to rescue Andrea grew as they walked past cafés and basilicas, tobacco shops and bakeries. Evening had fallen and the streetlights made Jerusalem glisten, merging its cobblestones with the phantoms peering from behind arabesque grille windows.

Elaborate plans of escape, featuring him as Andrea's rescuer, passed through Ben's mind, but while he fantasized half aloud and half to himself, he found himself standing alone at the bus stop. He was still talking when the bus came and he realized too late, after the bus had pulled out, that he had no idea where Andrea lived. She had clambered aboard quickly as a cat. All he knew was that next day she was going to audition for *Gal Gal Hamazal*. He would be there no matter what happened.

Chapter Seventeen

Wherein Joe, the policeman, searches for Felicity.
Major Notz, distressed by the disappearance of
his niece and rudely interrupted at his meal,
swings into action.

o e , the policeman, was a romantic boy. He could admit this because he prided himself on scrupulous self-examination. He had discovered that while he was outwardly a strong man, with women he was shy and boyish. He still lived with his mother in the old house in the Irish Channel and helped her bake all the breads for their annual Saint Joseph's altar. These loaves were artistically shaped to depict saints and churches, and Joe excelled at detail. One year he had created such an elaborate replica of Saint Peter's Basilica, the *Times-Picayune* came to photograph it. It was a good thing, too, because the next day a stray dog sneaked in with the crowds who'd come to see their altar after the photograph appeared in the paper and ate the basilica—cupola, balconies, tiny pope, and all. Joe was often cited by other mothers in the neighborhood as an ideal example of a good son.

Felicity had aroused in him emotions reminiscent of his first crush, on Angela Damato, who had dashed his hopes by eloping with a black accordionist from Breaux Bridge. Angela had been a classic beauty of the local Irish-Italian type, green eyed with long chestnut hair, a small waist, and bazoombas out to here. Everyone expected her to marry Joe, but she surprised them. And now, Joe told himself, I'll surprise them. A Creole girl dick is very much like a black zydeco accordionist. What will Mama think?

He'd left seven messages on Felicity's tape machine over the past two days. In the first one, he told her that he had retrieved more of the Kashmir Birani file for her. In the next six, he asked only, "Where are you?" in tones ranging from anxiety to anger.

When his seventh message elicited no answer, he went to her apartment. He found the front door of Felicity's office wide open. A scene of utter devastation met him inside. Everything had been turned upside down, ripped open, torn apart. Felicity's bed cover had been tramped on with muddy shoes. Felicity's books were all over the floor, many of them torn in half by a doubtlessly insane person or persons. Her collection of coffee mugs from various volunteer jobs she had performed over the years were smashed into smithereens. A bowl of fruit had been turned upside down; the oranges had been stabbed and the peaches had been crushed with a fist or a hammer. When Joe looked under the bed, a lone unmolested orange hid there. Even the contents of the refrigerator littered the small kitchen. Someone had even probed a jar of mustard, spattering it on the wall above the sink.

Joe had seen plenty of burglaries, but this was something else; this was demented. There was, however, no blood anywhere and no sign of a struggle. If Felicity had been anywhere near this maelstrom of devastation, she would have left some mark. Whoever had done this had been in a rage. He had destroyed her stuff as if seeking to obliterate her essence.

Joe couldn't determine if anything had been taken, or whether the vandals were even looking for anything. This seemed to be destruction for destruction's sake. He remembered Felicity telling him about her laptop, but there was no laptop in sight. Perhaps she had it with her.

Oddly enough, the only object left untouched was the telephone answering machine. The savages had left it whole on purpose. Joe turned it on. There were two messages in addition to his seven. The first was from somebody named Martin, with a private school accent: "Felicity, darling, I hope you possess the whole integrity of your superb physique. You haven't called as you said, but I will wait for you in the lobby at Commander's Palace tonight at eight."

The second message was a voice steeped in smoke, whiskey, and blood. It said: "Put this in your jigsaw puzzle, bitch!"

Joe called his sergeant and reported the break-in. When the detectives and crime-scene technicians arrived, he made sure fingerprints were collected from every surface. They finished about eight, and Joe headed for Commander's Palace. At eight-thirty he parked his patrol car in front of the flock of valets assisting bald men and starched matrons out of taxicabs, and rushed into the lobby. The lobby was full of more baldies and consorts waiting for their tables, but Joe spotted a dandy with a yellow rose in his hand, who kept glancing at his Rolex.

"Martin?"

"Yes," said Martin Dedette, worried. "Something wrong, Officer?"

"I hope not. Could I ask you a few questions?"

Martin nodded and led Joe through Commander's pepper-smoky kitchen to the bar in the courtyard beyond. Martin waved a greeting to a fat man dressed in some kind of uniform, seated at a table near the bar, then chose a table in the far corner.

"Okay, what can I do for you?"

"When did you last see Felicity Le Jeune?"

Martin Dedette told Joe the entire story of his chance encounter with Felicity and their meeting with the Shades. He did not mention the envelope or her instructions, but he hinted at a shared romantic past that was just too complex and too subtle to share with a cop.

"Actually, that man over there, that's Major Notz, Felicity's uncle. He always takes a Sazerac cocktail and dinner here on Tuesdays. Tonight he's a British naval commander, I think. Maybe he can tell you more about Miss Le Jeune."

Joe had to keep in check the urge to smash Dedette with his fist the way somebody'd smashed Felicity's peaches.

Major Notz was wholly absorbed in the leather-bound menu that listed the specialties of the old restaurant, and hardly noticed Joe's approach. Finally, he looked up from the menu, and focusing on the uniformed Joe, said: "Did you know that for one hundred and fifty years, the fire has never gone out from under their turtle soup? In nineteen twenty-three the place burnt down, and the cooks emerged from the flames holding the pot. It's a fact. Ask Ellen."

"If you don't mind, I need to ask you something. Have you seen Felicity?"

"My Felicity?" The major put down the menu and a dark cloud began making its way over the folds of his neck and face. "Has something happened to Felicity?"

Joe explained what he'd found at her apartment and that she hadn't been answering her phone messages.

"You know," said the major, "in twenty-four years, with interruptions occasioned only by wars and the service of my country, I have never missed my Tuesday bread pudding with whiskey sauce at Commander's . . . and I won't now. Felicity is a resourceful girl."

The major handed Joe an embossed gold card on which was written in cursive script, *H. L. Notz, Activist Historian,* followed by a number. "Call me if you find out anything. I expect that she will reappear. For reasons too complex to expain to you, Felicity cannot be harmed."

It was the second time in twenty minutes that Joe had been told that he was just a dumb cop. This will not do, gentlemen, he steamed as he left the restaurant. I am of old New Orleans Italian stock, and if I wasn't on duty I would demand satisfaction the old-fashioned way, and I would leave a number of ugly scars on both your conceited faces if I left you alive at all. Joe was admittedly a romantic boy.

When the policeman left the courtyard, the major snapped his fingers, and Boppy Beauregard came running. He had been the major's special waiter for years. These kids now didn't want to be good waiters; they were all actors or painters or something. When he started out, you set out to be a waiter, became the best you could be, and that was your life's aim. The world now was just chasing shadows.

"No pudding, Boppy," said the major. "A telephone, please."

Boppy Beauregard was shocked. He regarded his favorite customer with more than professional concern. What was the world coming to when a gentleman of the major's caliber missed out on his pudding? The wobbly pylons supporting Boppy's already troubled world gave way a little more.

"Carbon!" the major shouted into the white phone, "get to work right now." He cradled the receiver with his monumental chin and listened to Carbon's belabored breathing on the other end as he tried to contact the entities.

"I need to know," the major bellowed, waving Boppy away, "where Felicity is and what's the point of her disappearance."

The channeler allowed the other world to penetrate him, and then the lisping voice of Hermes came through.

"You better stick to the point," the major warned the loquacious entity.

"Doubtlessly, Major," Hermes replied, "you have noticed that temporal ideas about points and continuity mean nothing to us over here."

"Okay, okay," sighed the major, "get on with it."

"It is said that the job of convoking the Council of the Great Minds should have gone, doubtless, to one of the older, wiser, and more terrible angels, Asophet or Perash or even old Lucifer himself. But as luck would have it, happily or not, heaven has just adopted democracy as its new law, superseding that of Moses, and things have become rather difficult for seasoned angels, who—as representatives of the throne—used to have unquestioned priority on all the plums. The glorious jobs that once were distributed like cheap incense to the senior winged corpus now devolve to those who show the most aptitude for the job. In effect, Zack ran for the job and was elected, though how and by whom is still a mystery. Not all the kinks have been worked out. Heaven is new at democracy."

"What is this crap?" shouted the major loud enough to unsettle a table full of grandmothers treating their grandsons to mile-high pie. Boppy came running. The upset major waved him away again and threatened the mouthpiece through clenched teeth: "I'm asking about Felicity, not your spirit politics, you winged moron!"

"I'm getting to her. She is helping out the angels. It is said that it has baffled Zack as to why the Meeting of the Great Minds would take place in New Orleans, America, rather than in Jerusalem, Israel, or in Mecca, Saudi Arabia. It puzzled him even though, early in his angelhood, reflecting on the crossed nature of his name, he had decided to be surprised by nothing. So he surmised the move from old Jerusalem to America was inevitable, part of the switch to democracy. The Language Crystal tells us to remember that 'U.S.A.' is in the middle of 'Jerusalem,' right? But why, Zack wondered, did the New Jerusalem have to be in a humid, fetid, sense-besotted swamp by the sluggish waters of the filthiest river on earth?"

Then a voice in the deeper realm said: "That is it precisely, you geo-ignoramus. New Orleans is a gumbo, a mix like America itself, only more so. Black and white, hot and sour, ocher and pink, male and female—shiftingly and vaguely so—catholic and sweaty, pagan and nude, empty and masked, drunk and ascetic, squat, loquacious, and generous, sentimental, fat, visionary, hallucinatory—it is a window into the soul of a mix that heaven itself will soon become.

"But there are"—the voice paused—"practical reasons as well. New Orleans has the greatest rainfall in North America. Global warming has transformed the subtropical climate into a tropical one. The felicitous humidity facilitates the inhabitants' presence outdoors. The streets are always full of people, and there are continual festivals. Sadly, the entities of heaven need a great deal of moisture in order to embody, to lubricate the passage. At the same time, they can only embody outdoors, which severely limits heaven's choice.

"Your job, angel Zack, has quite a few blessed opportunities for reflection. When heaven stopped being kosher and began admitting souls formerly automatically atomized, we had few earthly models, and New Orleans was among them."

The deeper voice belonged to Zack's Namer, who'd taken an intrusive liking to Zack and thought that it was his prerogative to intervene didactically whenever he felt like it. It was bad enough that an angel has no privacy anywhere in the spirit and is an open book for all to read, but instant commentary from the namer is more than Zack can bear. Privacy for the angels has to be the next thing in the ongoing democratization of the heavens.

The namer said: "Well, take all the privacy you can pack in your unlustrumed feathers! Who cares enough to read your circular *cogita* anyway? If I bother it's because I'd like to see if it's still possible to educate even one of the spirit's fleas in these days of ceaseless ectoplasmic puddles."

Major Notz slammed the receiver down.

Carbon was useless. It had to be faced. Having chosen him from among the abundant mass of soothsayers and channelers had been a bow to style over substance. A channeler was only as good as his channel; once an entity got stuck in the pipe, no other could come through, and Notz had had enough of Hermes. And missing his pudding stoked the major's fury. His pipe let out a black cloud. He brushed past Boppy, who was evidently suffering, and said between clenched teeth, "If they touch one hair on her head, they shall be *consumed*."

Boppy nodded. "That's only right."

Martin Dedette watched this small drama from the corner table and waited until the major's square back disappeared through the etched glass doors. He then rose and went out the back gate. He headed directly for the mailbox on the uptown corner of Lafayette Cemetery. He took the manila envelope from inside his jacket, read the address, *Our Mirror.* "I wonder who'll get caught with their pants down," he mused, and dropped the envelope in the box.

The Humvee that picked up the major outside Commander's was chauffeured by a militia type with wraparound shades and a marine haircut. He drove silently onto I-10 East and turned off just before the Mississippi state line, at an unmarked exit.

The personage on whom they were going to call was never far from Major Notz's thoughts. He'd had an extraordinary career since the major had first discovered him. He had been a simple country preacher with a good voice, half convinced of his calling but sure of his charm. He was already being called Elvis by his smitten female congregation, about a dozen housewives who sat at his feet. The major had nurtured this rustic tadpole from a one-room church in Gonzalez to a domed arena in Metairie, from a once-a-week spot on local Christian radio to national television. The major had supervised the phenomenal growth of his begging bowl and had provided him with investment instruction. He had done so discreetly, from the shadows, never calling in his markers. The preacher had done well for himself. The last time the IRS had looked into the vast fortunes of his untaxable nonprofit corporation, they couldn't count all the airplanes. After that investigation, the major made sure that the preacher gained a purpose and focus for his money beyond his cowpoke imagination. Now the reverend was using his money properly: as collateral for borrowing more money. Money, after a certain sum was reached, ceased to be money. It became flows of energy with their own will and weather, sequenced all the way back to the Prime Mover and beyond. Something Mullin wouldn't understand and didn't need to.

He had immediately suspected Mullin in regard to Felicity because he knew the hatred the girl bore the reverend. And Hermes, despite his verbosity, had given him a clue. The major had surmised that Felicity might have trespassed on Mullin and been taken into his infamous First Angels Choir. This choir, which Notz had seen perform, was a genuine triumph of brainwashing technique. The major knew enough of the art of brain capture to know that the reverend had created a masterpiece in his choir. He was not entirely sure what the technique consisted of but suspected that it was a combination of drugs, sound hypnosis, and some kind of yogic zap. The girls Mullin recruited never left the choir. They were eternal slaves but, nonetheless, highly functioning and skilled shock troops. It was said that the few unfortunate wretches who had tried to escape had come to bad ends. Kashmir Birani may have been one of them. It was possible, too, that the assignment the major had given Felicity might have led her into the reverend's path. He had thought of the Birani assignment as busy work, but perhaps it was dangerous after all.

Two miles up the freshly paved road they came to a barbed-wire fence and a gatehouse. A bearded guard armed with an Uzi saluted crisply when he saw the major in the rear seat. Notz returned the salute, and the guard stuck his head in the rear window: "You're a philosopher, sir. What's happening to money? It isn't worth the paper it's written on. I owe the bank ten grand. The bank is owned by somebody who owes ten million to another bank. Who owns *that* bank? Is there an end to this business? Is there someone who owns it all? The Jews? When are we going to do something about the Jews?"

The man's questions annoyed the major—Hermes had wasted enough of his time already. "When we get discipline in the ranks, Soldier!" the major snapped. "The sequence can drive anyone mad. Let us through!"

The poor idiot, working lifetimes to pay off his credit, thought that there was no money because someone was hiding it. The Jews, always the Jews. They had their uses, the Jews. Notz liked to encourage paranoia among common folk; if they never confused debt with money, their anger would keep growing. The money they had already spent was not money to them; that was something they had been owed by the cosmos. Money was what the Jews had. And their anger was their currency, though they did not know it. And *that* currency, thought Notz, is what *I* spend for the betterment of the world. With help from the man with the cross, thank you, Lord, he added modestly.

The wide-bodied car, made for the desert sands of Arabia, drove down a winding gravel road toward what appeared to be a a careful replica of Scarlett's Tara. At the center of the vast manicured grounds was a miniature city of Jerusalem made of rose quartz, above which flew a banner that said, *The unborn are gathering!*

The only thing that isn't a replica is the grass, thought the major. And we can't be too sure about that. A study could be made of the fondness of Baptists for kitsch. The Catholics revere some genuine items, at least, in addition to the kitsch.

Reverend Mullin came out to greet the major with outstretched arms, a sanctimonious smile on his face. "Welcome, old friend!"

"Never mind that shit," thundered Notz, sweeping past the reverend into the cavernous entrance parlor, scanning the surroundings like a hawk. "Did you kidnap my niece? I warn you, Mullin, I can smell her. You have her here, and I'll be on you like scarlet fever!"

Even at his angriest, the major retained his wit. He considered it important to remain quotable. It was a mark of leadership. Of course, the reference to Tara flew right past the preacher. Mullin retained his unnatural affability and swore up and down that he had no idea where Felicity was.

"On my honor," he said, "and on the Holy Bible."

"Those things are of inestimable worth, Doctor, but if you deceive me, I will be very upset." The major liked to style Mullin "Doctor," knowing full well that the preacher was pristinely unschooled.

Maids with white aprons and bonnets were busy polishing silver in the large reception hall. Mullin led the thundering major gently through a massive cypress door into a small salon. He bade him sit before a black marble fireplace. He then busied himself with a decanter and a cigar box at a small bar. His back was tense. The major could see his muscles knot under the too-tight black silk shirt. But when Mullin turned, his hairy hands were steady and the original welcoming grin was still pasted across his wide country-boy face.

"I'll level with you, Major." Mullin put the brandy glass in Notz's hand and set the cigar box on a gold-inlaid table between them. He remained standing. "Your kid, Felicity, is a pest. She has obtained a photograph purporting to compromise me. Her hatred is quite inexplicable to me. She has demanded an unconscionably large sum of money, accompanied by ugly threats. I hesitate to use the word, but your young niece is a blackmailer."

Mullin gambled on this disclosure because he suspected that the major was informed about Felicity's little venture of blackmail. But the major, while not letting on, did not in fact know about it. He was surprised and not entirely displeased. Felicity was coming along just fine. Her oversized sense of justice had at last found a worthy target. Mullin was indeed rich beyond anyone's guess; he had sucked the little people's money through the TV tube like a black funnel. Unfortunately, his riches were not to be tampered with. Felicity herself was their ultimate beneficiary. But she could never know it. Life was indeed ironic.

"She caught you with your pants down, Preacher," the major said gruffly, "so you send over your goons to smash her furniture."

"I'm sorry, Major, but I was quite willing to pay . . . something. Not over two million dollars—for a forgery. If it pleases you I will set straight everything that was damaged. But I do not know her whereabouts. I am as concerned about her as you are."

"That is an unconscionable falsehood, Mullin. Not in a thousand years can you be even an iota as concerned as I am. I love my niece dearly, as much as you profess to love Jesus!"

The reverend looked stone faced. "That's blasphemy."

"You haven't seen anything yet."

The major took a sip of the brandy and put it down. "Don't you have any Armagnac? This is swill. And mind if I take a look at your girls? I came all this way."

"It's yes on the first and no on the second. The girls are at the Dome; been there since sunup."

The major started. "What in the world are they doing there?"

"It's perfectly okay, Major. They are training. We are running out of time. The schedule's been advanced."

Major Notz considered this for a moment. "By whom?"

Mullin looked as still as a sheet of blank typing paper. "By the Lord. There have been signs and portents."

The major looked straight at the preacher, who averted his eyes. When he spoke, he sounded commanding and severe. "I will remind you, Preacher, that the Lord is not in charge of schedules. I remind you also that time is my domain. You are to refrain, I repeat, *refrain*, from initiative."

The heavy cypress door opened silently and an ancient black butler brought the Armagnac. The major sipped in silence.

"I will fathom your choir yet."

"Music comes from the Lord, Major." Mullin allowed himself the closest he ever came to a smile. "*Direct* from the Lord."

"Yes, but what channel, Reverend? *That* is the question."

"There are many mansions in my Father's house, sir, but the scripture makes no mention of channels."

"It's a mistranslation, then. Some Greek mangled the Aramaic, and 'channels' became 'mansions.' The radio just wasn't around to serve as metaphor."

"You lose me there, sir. I'm a fundamentalist, remember. We hold no truck with metaphors."

Major Notz downed the brandy and rose from the settee. "We shall see, we shall see. Let your people on the street look for my niece. If even a hair on her head is disturbed, the stretch of my displeasure will be excessive."

"Thank you, Jesus," the preacher rejoiced, watching the teal blue Humvee disappear beyond the gatehouse. "Thank you, Jesus." Jesus was being thanked, for surely the Lord had given the major faith in Mullin's lie. He, of course, knew where the major's niece was. Felicity, safe and sound, was studying at the School for Messiah Development in a house on Bourbon Street, less than three blocks from the major's apartment. Two large drops of sweat formed from a myriad of small ones on Mullin's forehead and headed down opposite sides of his head to his chin. There was real danger here. Had he bitten off more than he could chew? Mullin remembered now the terms of his original contract with the major, in all its stark simplicity. In the irreversible order of things established by that covenant, Mullin was in charge of the spirit, but for all practical details he had to bow to the major. Had he gone too far? And who was this Felicity? Was she his greatest trial yet? The preacher flipped open his cellular phone and ordered the party at the other end to see to the pristine restoration of Felicity's small apartment "in every detail and with quality replacements." He then dialed another party and gave the exact opposite instructions in regard to Felicity herself, stressing that "no trace of the familiar should remain, not even the recollection of where she came from."

Chapter Eighteen

*Wherein we witness Andrea's brush with fame and
her decision to flee, Yehuda ben Yehuda's devotion
on her behalf, and Andrea's leave-taking
from Saint Hildegard's*

a b b i n i c a l scholar Yehuda ben Yehuda, born
Benjamin Redman, had been troubled by women all his
life. Beginning with his mother, he had conceived violent emotions for a number of them, and each had disappointed him in a different way. Felicity, his adolescent
sweetheart, had been his best friend, but their attempts
at physical intimacy had ended in disappointment. Felicity had remained
his friend, though, even throughout her subsequent affairs. He missed her.

In college there were girls whose names he had now forgotten, but each
appeared at the time to be his preordained mate. Other women, such as
Gala Keria, he loved from a distance because they possessed ideal features
that harmonized with his idealism. Now there was Andrea, about whom
he knew next to nothing, but for whom he felt such shattering love he
would have betrayed God Almighty if she'd asked him to.

In the week following their encounter at the television station, Ben saw
Felicity twice. The first was on the day of her audition, when she was offered one night as hostess of *Gal Gal Hamazal*, to prove herself on live TV.
He wanted to take her out to a restaurant to celebrate, but the good sisters
at Saint Hildegard's gave a feast in her honor, and Ben found himself sitting grumpily between Lama Iris Cohen and a taciturn Dr. Luna. Andrea
sat in a place of honor on Mother Superior's right, flanked by Sister Maria,
who was beaming with pride. Andrea glanced in Ben's direction two or

three times during dinner, but her mien was enigmatic. When the meal was finally over, Ben excused himself and made a quick getaway. All those nuns and crucifixes made him uneasy and self-conscious about his curls and yarmulke. It made him angry that a Jew should taste alienation even in his spiritual home. These Christians were mere guests, but he felt like a Jew in the Vatican.

Every day he thought about going to see her, but something always prevented him. He began to feel compelled to break his teacher's injunctions. After a lengthy commentary by the rabbi on the evil of census taking, as evidenced by the terrible punishment God meted out to David when the king counted his people, Ben walked about Jerusalem obsessively counting everyone. After five hours he had counted 2,344 people and felt that God ought to strike him down without mercy. Upon learning of the dangers of assimilation, while studying the history of the Jerusalem Hellenizers during the reign of the Greek king Antiochus, Ben engaged the services of a masseuse who turned out to be a Greek prostitute, and abandoned himself to her ministrations. Warned about false messiahs, he followed a crazy woman up Via Dolorosa. This woman was a familiar sight around the Old Quarter. She had been studied at Kfar Shaul Hospital and released as harmless. She was wearing a white linen shift and talking to herself as she walked. Spotting a group of American tourist girls, she pointed her finger at them and shouted, "You have put the same trust in your clitoris you used to put in your fathers." That set the girls insanely giggling, and Ben guffawed too. On being warned against letting fancy overtake logic, he hallucinated an ancient woman with a glass leg at the Damascus Gate. A taxi driver handed her a package. But maybe she was real. All this time, Andrea's image floated through his mind faintly, like the watermark on a banknote.

The night Andrea had her tryout as Gala's replacement, she mesmerized the land of Israel with the flourish of her arms and the intelligence of her small talk. She revealed the letters with such authority it seemed that she herself had made up the words, and each puzzle solved seemed to answer a mystery of profound importance.

The show's producers had drafted Gala's fashion adviser to dress her up. The designer found her difficult. Although she had practically the same shape as Gala, her posture was different, and she projected sadness and abandon where Gala had radiated warmth and brashness. She settled on a white, blue-trimmed sailor's suit with a short skirt, out of which Andrea's skinny legs shot out like a fawn's. She looked all at once polished, schoolgirlish, and lost.

The viewing audience at Saint Hildegard's was astonished to see the messy waif look so neat. But the larger viewing audience, which had nothing to compare her to, was seduced immediately. They perceived that the lost sailor, who had been introduced as "Andrea Isabel, Jewish Basque orphan newly arrived in Eretz Yisrael," was an extraordinary creature indeed. She spoke nearly flawless Hebrew, with only the hint of an accent, but best of all, she projected a deep sadness coupled with sensuality. Her presence seemed to say: take my body and savor my mind. I don't care. Use me anyway you please, but you will never know me. Such a message echoed deeply with the public of a country where millions of citizens had experienced unimaginable suffering. Many of them were old and saw in Andrea their younger selves, sprung physically intact somehow from hell. Her body was new, but her suffering was ancient.

The country nearly came to a standstill as people dropped everything they were doing to watch her dance across the small screen. In cafés and bars, convents and yeshivas, mosques and motels, viewers screamed the letters of the Hebrew alphabet as if seized by ancient spirits.

The puzzles had not been in themselves remarkable. The category PERSON solved as ELVIS. THING turned out to be THE FUTURE. The PART OF SPEECH puzzle was ACTIVE VERB. PHRASE, one of the more difficult puzzles, was IF I EVER FORGET JERUSALEM. The BOOK was *Lord of the Flies*, and MOVIE was *The Ten Commandments*. The puzzles had been easy to solve. The contestants, a pediatrician from Bathsheba, a grave digger from Eliat, and a bus driver between Tel Aviv and Jerusalem, all knew the answers, but only the grave digger won money, because of his luck in spinning the wheel.

But such factual description does not do justice to Andrea's performance. She herself became the focus of the words, as if all the categories— person, thing, and so on—were no more than emanations of her soul. A light appeared to come out of her, composed of all the words familiar to the viewers, but their familiarity vanished somehow, leaving huge craters of mystery within the sounds themselves.

Father Tuiredh, who had escorted Andrea to the station, saw the show from the greenroom. He had been startled, as had all the Saint Hildegard's inmates watching in the convent lounge, by the announcement that she was a Basque orphan. Was it possible that the show's producers took "Bosnian" for "Basque"? Father Tuiredh sipped his soft drink pensively.

No, that was impossible. And her last name, Isabel, where did that come from? Was it a stage name?

Andrea came out of the studio followed by an overjoyed Mr. Elahu, rubbing his hands. His glasses were askew and he kept repeating the American word "hit" as if something had literally hit him. Andrea was flushed in the face, but her expression was inscrutable. Father Tuiredh helped her into her coat and escorted her out the door. Mr. Elahu followed them closely from behind.

A festive mob had gathered outside the studio. When Andrea appeared, they were led into chanting her name by a young rabbi with wild curls. *"Andrea! Andrea!"* Andrea did not look at her fans. The louder they chanted, the smaller she tried to make herself, until she nearly disappeared at Father Tuiredh's side.

"Tomorrow, then?" shouted Mr. Elahu.

Andrea responded only by walking faster. The disappointed crowd let her pass. She did not acknowledge Ben. A taxi swallowed them.

The next day there were cartoons and articles about her in all the newspapers. A columnist called her Svengali, while another wrote that she had induced a "mass hypnosis" in Israelis and that she was therefore dangerous and ought to be confined to Kfar Shaul.

Someone overnighted to the station an excerpt from the writings of the mysterious scholar Ioan Coulianou, believed by mystics to be an angel actively involved in preparing a great plan for the future. The station sent it to the convent with a messenger.

"It all started in the year 1274, or perhaps much earlier," Coulianou wrote, "with the wheels of Sefir Yetsira. Its wheels, arrayed with Hebrew alphabets, would produce the sublime language of Creation, the language behind the world, seen and unseen." Coulianou went on to explain that "the movement of the wheels was the movement of celestial bodies, and language was the whole universe . . . by manipulating language one can, actually and concretely, manipulate the surrounding world." Language and world, according to the mystic, functioned like the binary structure of the computer, one engendering the other.

Mr. Elahu called the convent to ask Andrea to do the show again that evening, even though another girl's tryout had been scheduled. Andrea said no. Mr. Elahu begged and pleaded, but the more he did, the more stubborn Andrea became.

"Maybe in two days?" The producer persisted.

"Maybe," Andrea said.

But in two days she also said no. The producer called every day, but the nuns told him that Andrea was not available.

Andrea sat on her bed with her press notices spread around her, reading the fragment from Coulianou's writing over and over again. What did it mean? Could language actually *change* the physical world? Words can make people happy or sad. Singing words can make them dance. Angry words can make them fight. But can they, as Coulianou seemed to suggest, undo the very fabric of the physical world merely by being spoken out loud? Yehuda ben Yehuda also believed something similar.

The second time Yehuda ben Yehuda saw her was at the end of that trying week. He waited for her in the morning outside the convent, with a handful of flowers he had personally picked in the Garden of Gethsemane. They went to the Afghan café where they had first kissed, and Andrea reminded him of the promise he had made her the first time they met.

"The time has come," she said, "for you to help me leave Jerusalem."

Ben didn't understand. "But surely . . . after the success of the show, no one would dream of deporting you."

"It is *precisely* now that they will. Do you know when the war came?" Andrea did not say which war. "The fighting started on the day I was elected class president in my high school. Next day the schools closed. This is the time to go, *precisely*," she repeated stubbornly.

Ben insisted, too. "Won't you fight extradition, though? All Israel knows who you are. They will demonstrate."

"You don't understand, Ben. You're American. It is not good to be known by everyone. My father was well known. I don't want to talk about it anymore. Are you going to help me, or not?"

Her voice was firm. Ben did not ask her why she had gone on the show in the first place if she did not want to be known. It occurred to him that perhaps she had expected to fail. She had been surprised by her success. Maybe she truly hadn't liked the fame, the fawning, the reviews, the flowers, the telegrams. He could see that she was frightened.

The day after she and Ben decided to leave Jerusalem, Andrea stayed in her room, skipping meals, and causing concern to the sisters. She lay on the bed with her arms crossed behind her head, looking at Christ hanging naked on the wall, the chipped nails of his long toes just above her feet. Andrea sat up and took off her clothes. She pulled a shopping bag from under the bed and spread the contents on the threadbare rug. There she sprawled, admiring her treasures. Father Tuiredh's gold watch, a heavy lump of gold, ticktocked like the heart of a boy being kissed. To think that she'd almost lost it in Adam's skull! She picked it up by its chain and swung it mesmerically back and forth at Christ. Hypnotized, the Savior closed his eyes.

At that very moment, Father Tuiredh was communicating grave news to Mother Superior. He had spent the better part of two days trudging through government offices in search of records pertaining to Andrea Isbik, or Andrea Isabel, or any orphan of her sex and age. Immigration had never heard of her. There was no trace of her having come to Israel. Her names were not on the passenger lists of any airline for the date of her arrival at the hospice. Father Tuiredh had even attempted to locate Father Eustratius, the Sarajevan priest who sent Andrea to Jerusalem, but a phone call to the Vatican yielded nothing of his existence. It looked as if the girl had simply materialized, the night of her arrival at their gate, out of the thin, snowy air of Jerusalem.

The priest sorrowfully told the mother superior these things, and then the two sat in thoughtful silence. Andrea, the girl they loved, was an illegal immigrant. That wasn't so unusual in itself. What was unusual was that the girl had slipped undetected through the state's bureaucratic machinery to become one of the most visible public persons in Israel. There was also the question of the missing four years.

"Truly," Father Tuiredh sighed, quoting an ancient poet, "we are hidden in the light."

Mother Superior, recovering from the shock of these revelations, defended Andrea's crime. "Why should she respect borders? The soldiers who raped her did not respect *her* borders. What sort of boundaries could such a child have? Her country's borders shredded like so much paper when the war came. Her childhood had no shape and no limits. Perhaps she has acquired a gift for telling people what they want to hear. I can barely imagine this convent without her." The old lady looked on the verge of tears.

In truth, the nuns at Saint Hildegard's were only slightly less adrift than Andrea. They came from places torn by war and dismembered by selfishness; the convent offered them shelter within a chaotic and shapeless world. They were all refugees.

Neither the sullen Celt nor the wise old nun wanted to give in to the unspoken thought that had seized their faith-thirsty souls, namely that Andrea had just *appeared*. The consequences of such a fact were too immense. They turned simultaneously toward the door, beyond which was a vestibule in which there was a door, behind which a young girl might, just might, be the One That Suddenly Appeared!

Behind the door of her tiny room, Andrea pulled a painted silk shawl toward her by one scarlet fringe. This shawl was Professor Li's prized possession; she had found it carefully folded and wrapped in rice paper at the bottom of his trunk. Andrea put her cheek to its smooth surface—it smelled of rose petals. On the fabric three girls with scarlet leaves in their dark hair sat together in a flowering bower by a raging brook. Smoothed out to its full length, the shawl told a story about a fox, a philosopher on a cloud, three maidens, and a ship. Andrea wrapped the story around her shoulders, and the fringes hung down on her hips.

Andrea let the shawl fall from her shoulders and picked up Lama Cohen's jingly prayer wheel. She put her left breast through the circle at the center and thought that she should have the creatures painted on the wheel tattooed there. And around the other breast she could tattoo the creatures from Professor Li's shawl. Thus, orange, red, magenta, and black demons with flaming headdresses would circle her left nipple, while girls with scarlet leaves, a fox, a mountain, a philosopher on a cloud, and a ship would surround the right one. Perhaps the philosopher could be made to appear as if he were squatting on his golden buttocks on the very tip of the deep pink swirl of her aureola. She welcomed the little plump buttocks of the golden philosopher and strained up to receive him, her nipples hardening. She stretched out her arms, imagining her body an airport for winged delights.

The polished wooden man she'd taken from Mr. Rabindranath's room watched her from the floor. He was made from cherrywood, with a prominent, polished erection. Written on him from head to toe were verses in Sanskrit. The verse on his enlarged lingam was written with silver ink. Andrea studied him for a moment: his lips were thick and his big round eyes were shaded by very long, painted eyelashes. She brought the figure to her lips and kissed him. She turned him around and spanked with one finger his exquisitely carved wooden butt. The wooden man just laughed at her, which made her mad. She brought his head down between her legs and made him look straight at the thin jagged line there. She eased him past the soft down surrounding this fault, then made him kiss it.

Two doors down, Mr. Rabindranath began spontaneously to float. He gyrated helplessly for a while, then bumped into a wall, unable to find the

door. He had been hoping to avoid another episode of meditational im-
modesty, but without his compass, the wooden *ithyphallos*, this was nearly
impossible. He had done his best to convince the sisters that levitation
happened only during a trance and that he had no recollection of the event
afterward. In truth, he knew only too well what he had done and what he
looked like when his form took to the halls. He attributed these accidents
to a disturbance in the world of the gods. Several times during meditation
he had been allowed to enter a circle of *deva*s who had been, quite literally,
tearing one another apart over eschatological questions. During one of
these encounters, a red-and-blue deity with a crown of pink flames devoured a modest mauve deity who held the opinion that people ought to
be given another chance. Then a gold pig-faced demon bashed one of similar hue but with the face of a monkey and the sentiments of an autodidact.
These struggles were unusual in cosmic history; to the casual meditator
they looked a lot like weather forming and dissipating in the sky. Mr. Rabindranath was not an average meditator. He had assumed the shapes of
past masters and animals and had amused himself by the performance of
what humans call miracles, though he denied strenuously that such activities were meant to be amusing. He referred always to a "higher purpose,"
which—because mystery was at its essence—could not be revealed. There
was a higher purpose, though. Notwithstanding such highbrow considera-
tions, the *ithyphallos* had served him well in the storms that were breaking
in the invisible realm. Without it, recklessness was added to his familiar
awkwardness.

Gyrating hopelessly before the mirror, Mr. Rabindranath stopped dead
his spinning when he realized who it was that might at this very moment
be touching a pink fingertip to the phallus of his *ithyphallos*. For the first
time since he had begun to float, Mr. Rabindranath became erect. His angry penis pointed to the door, and the door opened to let him out. "Oh,
gods of mine and of all other religions," he sobbed, closing his eyes,
"please do not let what is going to happen happen!"

But it did. The angry swarthy Indian, led by his throbbing protrusion,
crashed into the small chapel where Mother Superior and Father Tuiredh
sat watching the door as if they were expecting him.

"Where to, Doctor?" Father Tuiredh asked, quite amused.

"Returning to India, I suppose," Mr. Rabindranath said painfully before
he spun once more on his axis and ended up near the ceiling.

Andrea lay down the moist wooden man and picked up a round metal box with something rattling inside. There seemed to be no way to open it, no matter how hard she tried. It had been welded shut. The box belonged to Father Hernio, the wealthiest of the convent's guests. There were five trunks in his room, each one full of books, vestments, drawing pads, compasses, writing instruments, pillboxes, creams, lotions, brushes, combs, and mirrors. This little box had been most modest, but it had attracted her nonetheless.

Father Hernio had already noticed the disappearance of the unobtrusive little box and had turned his room upside down in search of it. His day never began before he'd held this box in his hands and said a prayer over it. It contained the fine ashes of both his mother and father, killed by Marxist guerrillas near Mindanao more than twenty years before. He had carried them with him to every country of exile, and he believed that they watched over him and insured his success. He felt that without them, he was doomed to lose his faith.

When shaking it, bashing it against the floor, and tossing it in the air didn't crack it open, Andrea kissed the metal box and licked it. It tasted like the strips of the Mechano set she'd bent and twisted when she was ten. She knew the taste also of the metal screws in her sled, which had hurt her tongue. She had also licked many coins. In fact, her first urge when faced with a small metal object was to lick it. She once heard a story about a man who ate an entire car over a period of six months. He'd eaten everything—the wheels, the motor, the tailpipe—bit by bit, in mouth-sized portions. Andrea loved that story—it gave her a funny, itchy sensation, like spiders walking on her tummy. She would have loved to eat Father Hernio's box, but the thing was indestructible. She'd just have to return it, she supposed.

The next item was puzzling and clumsy. Andrea might never have taken it if she hadn't nearly been discovered by Father Zahan. It was a tall whip with leather tails of graduated length. When she stood it up it was a foot taller than she was. When she laid it down on the floor, the thongs fanned out like braids of hair, some of which were the thinness of piano wire, while others were as thick as her wrist. The handle was made of some sort of hollow reed. Still, it was heavy. She would have put the strange whip back on the windowsill where it had been resting if she hadn't heard the father's voice in the hallway, joking with one of the nuns:

"No man is an island, Sister; every man *has* a peninsula that links him to others. Mankind to womenfolk . . ."

The sister's uncertain laugh betrayed her misunderstanding of the pun. In her haste to lay the whip down, Andrea bent it and it snapped neatly, folding in two. When she pressed on it again, it folded another time. Now it was manageable, no bigger than a blackboard pointer. She stuck it down the right leg of her jeans. The leather thongs spilled over her belt and she pulled her shirt over them. Luckily, the father tarried long enough for her to slip onto the small balcony their rooms shared.

Andrea unsnapped the whip to its full size again and let the tails caress her. Then she straightened out her arm and brought it back more forcefully. She had miscalculated: the leather thongs stung her thighs and wrapped themselves around her. She let out an involuntary cry and clamped her hand over her mouth, fearful that she might be overheard. Her legs felt as if rows of stinging red ants were marching in circles around them.

The thing she'd taken was not a whip but a bull-roarer, given to Zahan at his initiation. He was forbidden to part with it. When Yuin young men reached the age of thirteen, they were taught to speak with the bull-roarer, a leather-stringed instrument that could make an extraordinary range of sounds, in imitation of the sharp winds that sang in Australia's lonely landscape. These were the voices of the Yuin gods, which every initiated member of the tribe understood, though the language was spoken properly only by the holy men. Father Zahan was a holy man, believed by his tribesmen to be five thousand years old—as old as the tribe. Without his bull-roarer, however, the father was no more than what he appeared to be: a Catholic priest. This was an identity he had found necessary to adopt because of the politics in his region. His people did not consider this a contradiction.

When the stinging subsided, Andrea felt very warm. Stretched out on the rug, she listened to the rain. Sometimes she could understand what it said. It was delivering a message to the Yuin priest. The rain said: *I have watched you trying to use your bull-roarer in the difficult environs of Jerusalem, which is a loud city without a single private place!*

The message was not intended for her. The entity speaking was Darumulun, a Yuin god. She tried to warn him: "Father Zahan isn't here, Mr. Rain. You may be confused because everybody here in Jerusalem is always communicating with God, which kinda jams the airwaves!"

Andrea closed her eyes trying to imagine what Father Zahan's god looked like. She saw a massive shape, a pyramidal being swathed in rolls of quivering fat. In his enormous fist he held a taut bull-roarer. In his belly button, which was as big as a cave, there were blue sparks. This is where the rain and the voice came from. Intrigued by her ability to see all the way inside this supernatural being, Andrea looked around. Some naked young boys were tending Darumulun by throwing pails of scented water on his hot skin. She realized that the boys were in the first year of their initiation: they were forbidden to talk. Also, they ate only from the forest floor and they slept only from midnight until dawn. The god Darumulun was a huge telegraph that the Yuin people used to communicate with one another and their ancestors. No matter how far away a Yuin might find himself, he could always reach Darumulun with a bull-roarer.

Father Zahan, meanwhile, was having a fit of nerves. The absence of the bull-roarer had given him a tremor in the hands and legs that would not subside. He could think of no one cruel enough to deprive him of his whip. He searched his room as if hidden within its modest dimensions were holes leading to other worlds. Finally, he curled up on his bed and attempted to guide his shaky thoughts to Darumulun. It was for naught. He trembled like a sapling. It was then, at his most tenuous, that he saw Andrea etched with India ink in his mind. She regarded him with the curiosity of one who knew the future. Gratitude, or something akin to it, filled him. It was time to return home.

"Instruct me," he whispered.

Andrea lay the stinging whip with its voices down on her bed. The bull-roarer vibrated there as if a low-voltage current coursed through its strands. She would have liked to lie on top of it but was afraid that the slight trembling would turn into a thrashing. The thought of what it would be like to be quashed by a massive shape such as Darumulun stopped her. In camp, she'd had to submit to an immense sweaty soldier who'd completely hidden her in his folds of fat. Even the other soldiers, waiting their turn, had protested. The giant finished before he suffocated her, but she'd wished herself dead.

Andrea felt a sudden need for affection. Cautiously, she opened her door a crack and peered down the corridor. No one there. The feeling that she was about to do something naughty never failed to thrill her. But what to do? She had already been inside the guest rooms and taken things. The thrill was keenest at the moment when she actually slipped something under her blouse or stuck it down the leg of her jeans. The possibility of getting caught caused a delicious vibration in her fingertips. The down on her upper thighs and lower back ruffled lightly. She had even let herself into Mother Superior's room, but it was so austere it repelled her. Apart from the black crucifix on the white wall above the narrow bed, there was only a locked steamer trunk. She had fiddled with the heavy, old-fashioned lock, but its secrets held. Just before she abandoned the attempt she'd had the strange thought that if one of her tears fell into the keyhole, the lock would open suddenly.

Andrea looked to the worn stone steps that twisted up to the second story, where the novices' cells were located. No sound came from up there, which meant that the sisters were about their chores at the school or in the garden. She tiptoed up. Just as she expected, the first door she tried was unlocked, but the cell was not empty. Kneeling before the sliver of light that came through a narrow window was Sister Rodica, wearing only a nightshirt. She was weeping. She did not hear Andrea come in.

Andrea closed the door behind her and swiftly took the single step between herself and Rodica before the young nun could turn around. She fell to her knees behind the sister and embraced her. She cupped the sister's breasts from that position, feeling their scared thumping like trapped birds. Sister Rodica's heart beat so furiously that both women thought it might burst. But then, Andrea's heart also thumped out a mad rhythm on the skin of Rodica's back.

They knelt like this for a million years. Then Sister Rodica broke away and asked plaintively, "What are you doing to me, Andrea?"

Rising to her feet, Andrea pointed to the naked man on the crucifix, identical to the one in her room.

"Loving you," she answered.

Sister Rodica whispered through tears, "Do you love me like yourself?"

Andrea kissed her on the lips. She moved her hand under the nun's nightshirt, stroking the shivering skin until she reached the soft pelt covering her pubis. With her other hand, she pulled up her sweater and guided Sister Rodica's hand to her breast. Andrea traced lightly the girl's moist, thin squiggle with her index finger.

"This is how I love myself," Andrea said, holding Rodica's eyes with her own.

Rodica looked into Andrea's eyes and gave herself over to the fire. She had seen pictures of burning martyrs, and she was sure that her turn had come. She would combust spontaneously before the beauty of this shameless orphan. A new millennium would begin tomorrow, but the promise of redemption no longer applied to her. She would belong wholly to her time. Sister Rodica surrendered to the flame and took Andrea in her arms.

Chapter Nineteen

Wherein we discover Felicity in a strange place of worship, where syncretic experiments are conducted

 e l i c i t y knew neither where she came from nor where she was. Still, what she could see of the outside was familiar. Through the barred window she could see palms and banana trees growing untrimmed over the oval of an empty swimming pool. Bunches of small black bananas lay at the bottom of the pool under giant spiderwebs. She could also see a gallery that ran the length of this courtyard, festooned with pink and blue flowers. Night jasmine twined itself around the aging grillwork. Here and there glinted strands of Mardi Gras beads caught years ago on the rusted spikes that topped the brick walls.

She remembered being driven for a long, viscous, thoughtless time. A soldierly man with a crew cut had blindfolded her from the backseat. She had tried to concentrate during the drive, bring herself back. When the car finally stopped, she had succeded at last in remembering her name: Scheherazade. She said it softly under her breath several times and liked the sound of it. She resolved to hold on to her name no matter what they were going to do to her.

The young soldier type, who smelled like pine deodorant, helped her out of the Cadillac and removed her blindfold. Her eyes were smarting. She rubbed them with the back of her hand before she could see anything.

They climbed a rickety staircase. Another young man walked in front of them, leading the way. Cute ass, she thought through her trance. It was an observation without context because she could not think of any other example of such a thing. Who else has a cute ass? she asked herself. But her store of images was empty; it returned nothing.

Still—she stubbornly reasoned in the emptiness—I know enough to describe the young man's behind as cute, therefore I must be able to construct a familiar situation. The cute ass before her was tied to her understanding by a slender thread of feeling. She could not recall the name of this thread, but she became certain that it led the way out of her submerged state. The thread had a name, she was sure of it, but it was more important now as a feeling that led from the young man's cute ass to the world outside.

The men led her to a room filled with school desks. The room also looked familiar, and Felicity was even more hopeful. She could not remember any specific schoolroom in her own past, but school and school desks were, generally, known to her. She knew what they were and she realized that they, too, were linked by the thread of a nameless feeling. This thread was different from the thread of the cute ass; it was more unpleasant, more anxious. She imagined twining both threads around each other to make a bracelet. She imagined it around her left wrist. There were two other bracelets there, one ebony, one gold, but she didn't know what they were doing there. She removed them just as a large man came toward her with an extended hand.

"Welcome to the School for Messiah Development."

This struck her as funny for some reason, like an inside joke. She couldn't remember whose inside joke, though. She did recall, however, that Jesus Christ was the Messiah. In that case, she asked herself quite logically, how could he be "developed"? What kind of school would Jesus need in order to become Jesus? What absurd place was this?

As if in answer to her question, the teacher put out his hand in a kind of blessing.

Felicity thought that he wanted her bracelets, so she handed them to him. He took them and smiled. "I merely wanted to bless you, young woman. But thanks, anyway." He put the bracelets on a desk in front of the room and asked her her name.

"Scheherazade," she replied, and immediately regretted it. She ought to have kept her name secret, like the two threads twined about her wrist. She no longer had her bracelets, but she still had the gold hoops in her ears, her nipple rings, and her belly-button ring. Her breasts felt hot under the thin black turtleneck sweater. The rings burned but they also anchored her, as if they were part of an armor.

The man did not introduce himself, but Felicity was certain she knew him. He had a pale forehead with burning black eyes. A globe lit from within by cherry-colored light sat on the desk.

Felicity squeezed into one of the seats and looked around. Several bewildered young women in various stages of disarray sat awkwardly at the school desks. They looked as if they had come from very far away. Some had mud on their clothes and dirty faces. *Very far away:* here was another thread of feeling, different from the other two. It had a taste that squeezed her tongue and a color she couldn't name. She twined it with the others.

Felicity could smell the redhead in the wrinkled velveteen miniskirt in the adjoining seat. *Whiskey flavored,* she thought. And below that flavor was another, a rich womanly musk. *As if she has just been opened and made to release her essence.* These phrases came to her unbidden and presented her with yet more threads for her bracelet.

The redhead whispered, "And to think that there are so many real problems in the world. Like where the hell is my drink?"

"Very far away," whispered Felicity.

"You can say that again. I flew twenty hours straight before I landed here. Where is my fucking bag? My Prozac's in there."

Of course. "Aviatrix!" exclaimed Felicity. "What a clever disguise!"

"Whatever." The redhead turned to the man at the desk. "Nightcap, teacher man?"

Another girl, on her other side, had doubtless been more girlish the night before, but a five o'clock shadow and smeared mascara were quickly dissolving the illusion. She had taken off her stiletto heels and set them on the desk in front of her. She now regarded them sadly, as if they were the last remnant of her youth. "I don't think this is going to be very amusing," she said, attempting to smile.

It touched Felicity. Even disguised and without armor, the Maid of Orléans was recognizable. She had been temporarily defeated, but not for long. Felicity felt that, even though Joan's story ended badly, history had vindicated her. Perhaps Felicity had been destined to bring the good news to the French saint. It made her dizzy to suddenly know so much about the two women on either side of her. Felicity didn't know how she knew or where she had learned them, but here were their histories, vivid and complete. The threads of feeling that they radiated were leather-thick thongs.

Felicity twined them like the tails of a whip and wound them around her arms all the way to her shoulders. She was sure that any moment now she would recognize everyone, that her world would come flooding back to her with everything, including the elusive memory of her own life.

"Joan," she addressed the sad one in a voice she did not recognize, "fear nothing. You are going to triumph."

"You're a dear," said Joan in a man's voice, and patted her head with a rather large hand.

Now that she had begun threading her way back to reality, Felicity no longer felt that she was in any imminent danger. On the contrary. Not knowing where she was or what was going to happen felt oddly liberating. If she allowed herself to be still, without fretting for answers, she could recognize everyone around her. It was only when she moved her arms and legs that anxiety overcame her. Her body felt adrift as if the steel cable of her identity had snapped, leaving it unmoored. But when she practiced stillness, whole stories came rushing in.

The teacher said: "The School for Messiah Development is dedicated to bringing to fruition the messiah potential in each and every one of you. Within you lies the power to save the world. Some of you have only a little messiah power, others have more. But a few of you have great power, one hundred percent messiah power, and those will lead us to glory. As you divest yourself bit by bit of your physical selves and your earthly memories, you will uncover the radiance of the truth."

Felicity felt lulled by the man's words. She was floating on a calm blue mountain lake.

"Ladies, allow yourself the luxury of rest. We will play a lovely game together," the man said. "Imagine that the world has just ended. You're a survivor. Your life depends on one thing, one thing only. You must try to imagine a pink elephant. If you can imagine a pink elephant, you'll live. The city's burning. The charred bodies pile up. A leprous man grabs your ankle. The water is poisoned. Your loved ones are all dead. You are dying. Unless, unless, you can . . . imagine . . . a . . . pink . . . elephant."

The man paused to wipe his sweaty forehead with a yellow bandana, then shouted so loudly everybody jumped: *"Imagine a pink elephant!"* He hit the cherry globe, making it spin fast.

Felicity did not want to play this game. It was not amusing. And this shouting was unpleasant. She did not want to imagine a pink elephant. It didn't look to her as if her fellow students needed to imagine pink elephants; they had seen plenty of pink elephants. The teacher man was being disrespectful; did he know whom he was addressing? She realized that he did *not*. The teacher had no idea that this small room contained some of history's best-known women. She couldn't help smiling. Here was another secret means of resistance to whatever was being prepared for them. The man had to remain ignorant. Strengthened by this knowledge, Felicity allowed herself to play the game. She couldn't help it; the suggestion had already taken hold. A huge pink elephant filled her mind. It was like a stuffed toy, a piñata full of hidden things. She understood that she must not look inside this elephant because *it contained false memories*. Yes, Felicity thought, this is a Trojan elephant full of somebody else's stories; if it breaks I will be filled with memories of a life that is not mine.

After a sufficient time had passed, time that was either a pregnant pause or a wave of nausea, depending on how much pink elephant one was actually imagining, the teacher shouted: "*Now try* not *to imagine a pink elephant!*" He set his palm on top of the globe and it ceased spinning.

Felicity rolled her eyes and thought, I hate this class. The man hissed triumphantly: "See? You cannot *not* imagine a pink elephant! This is called your *reactive mind!* Your *reactive mind* has been with you all your sorry life. It has prevented you from seeing *the truth*. It has prevented you from letting in *the light*. It has *obscured* your soul like a big pink elephant. *Jesus* will *free* you from it!"

The teacher was a middle-aged man dressed in black with heart-shaped pink eyeglasses. When he said "Jesus" his hands went up in the air and his voice broke as if he were about to cry. Felicity finally banished the pink elephant from her mind. But then she saw what the elephant had been concealing: a scene of utter destruction. A building was burning and a child was running from it with her wings on fire. Felicity grabbed the child and blew on the fire, which, amazingly enough, went out like a candle. She stroked gently the child's charred feathers. Stop, she willed herself. This is *his* game; this is what *he* wants you to think. The world isn't ending; you just can't remember it. She concentrated hard on keeping from this man the secret of who the women in the room were, but she kept slipping into a lazy, dreamy trance that drained her of will. She kept hugging the child with the singed wings. What had they done to her?

She raised her hand. "I can't seem to remember anything," she protested. "Have I been given some sort of drug?"

"Not at all," the teacher replied somewhat indignantly. "You are simply an American. You are amnesiac by definition. We Americans are people without memory. Don't need it. Everything we need to know is available on-line. You are simply a secular-humanist citizen. Relax. Soon you will know your Savior, and your heart will be filled with longing for Paradise."

"Fuck that," she shrieked, "What have you done with *me?*"

The teacher spun the globe again. It had an oddly calming effect on Felicity, and she felt as though she slept for a while, submerged again beneath the waters.

The man passed out a questionnaire and pencils. She raised her hand again and the teacher pointed to her. She stood with some effort and addressed him: "Sir, if I may, I believe I am grown up. Judging from my size. And I don't want to be in school." There were murmurs of agreement from the other women.

The teacher looked stern. "Sit down, young lady, and answer the questions. You are disrupting the class."

To her amazement, Felicity sat down and examined the questionnaire.

FIVE QUESTIONS YOUR LIFE DEPENDS ON
1. Have you ever seen an angel?
2. Has an angel ever told you things you feel that you must share with the rest of the world?
3. Are you psychic? Can you tell, for instance, what the radio will say before the radio says it?
4. Are you angry about the evil in the world?
5. When you speak, does everyone listen?

She answered yes to all except the last one, though honestly she didn't know if she'd ever seen or talked to an angel, or if she was angry and psychic. The child she had saved from the flames was not an angel. She put her head down on her desk and closed her eyes. She felt extremely tired. She was taking a test and didn't know why, though she knew that asking would have been useless. She was small, a schoolchild at Our Lady of Perpetual Succor Ursuline Elementary, and the teacher was a nun, a white cloud, a ruler in her hand. Felicity touched her breasts through her thin white shirt. They felt small, young, unripe. She couldn't wait to be a woman.

"Now you can go to your assigned rooms to change, and then it's time for the music lesson," the teacher said. "After the music lesson you will go to the Bible lesson. Tonight you have electronics workshop."

It sounded like a nice plan.

"I think we're slaves," Joan of Arc whispered in Felicity's ear as they trooped down a narrow hallway with doors on each side. "I think that they are going to sell us."

Felicity was led to her quarters by a petite woman clad in a white gown, who gestured but did not speak. She opened a door above which was written, *The Lord's Hands Apartment No. 3.* Felicity was shown to a lower bunk in the far left corner. The dormitory had twelve beds. The walls were bare but for a black crucifix between two bricked-in windows. An ashen light from an unknown source filled the place. *Like a rainy day*, thought Felicity. She wove that tender thread around her arm with the others.

Lying on her bunk was a white robe and a pair of white Chinese slippers. The woman gestured to her to change. Obediently, Felicity took off her boots, her sweater, and her fuchsia jeans. She kept on her black panties and slipped into the robe. It was a little too big, but soft and quite comfortable. She felt free and unencumbered in it. The sleeves fell below her hands. She was warm. The slippers felt better than her boots, which had weighed her down.

A long time ago, thought Felicity, *I was clad like this as I stood by the side of a tomb.* She saw herself among a group of silent women dressed like her, in white robes, looking into the open door of a small mausoleum. Light came from within. Someone very dear to her had just abandoned the tomb, leaving it empty. *He rolled away the stone*, came to her, and then she knew what she was seeing. She was among those who'd come to look at the empty tomb of Joseph of Arimathea after Jesus had risen from the dead. The picture was bright and vivid, but Felicity knew that it did not come from her own experience but from the pink elephant, who still crouched in a corner of her mind, sending pictures into her head.

The woman led her to a small theater. The other girls were walking in at the same time. Felicity smiled at them. Amelia Earhart, still disguised as a redhead, whispered, "We are fucking nuns now!"

On the stage was a tiny man in a tailcoat, who shouted at them to hurry up and take their places on the risers facing him. There were already other girls there, who looked without curiosity at the newcomers. They were dressed in loose white robes. The conductor inspected each girl as she climbed into place. When he saw Felicity's jewelry he shouted: "The rings must go! The rings must go!"

Felicity felt suddenly a sharp pang of fury that nearly returned her to herself. She had already surrendered her visible bracelets, but she would give them nothing else. She felt the threads of her secret bracelet, wound around her arms. She doubted if the conductor could see this, but nobody fucked with her rings. This she knew. Let the little penguin try. She'd tear his head off.

"No," she squeaked, trying to make her eyes fierce.

The music teacher shrugged and picked up his baton. A cherubic little girl with gold ringlets passed out hymnals. Felicity took one, and the girl looked straight in her eyes. It was the girl from the house on fire, minus her wings. A current of recognition passed between them. *She too is someone who resists,* thought Felicity. *She knows that I saved her.*

The conductor hit the stand with his baton and directed the listless-looking chorus to simply repeat what he sang. The hymnal was already open to the right place.

Rock of ages, cleft for me, let me hide myself in thee—let the water and the blood . . .

Felicity soared. She closed her eyes and gave herself over to a vast blue simplicity.

Not the labors of my hands can fulfill the law's demands—could my zeal no respite know—Nothing in my hand I bring, simply to the cross I cling; naked, come to thee for dress . . .

She floated up there, naked, and Jesus poured a diaphanous robe around her. From the tips of her toes to the crown of her head, a sense of well-being flooded through her, sweeping away her doubts.

While I draw this fleeting breath, when mine eyes shall close in death, when I soar to worlds unknown . . .

All she wanted to do was sing. She was no longer tired; she was a pure voice, clean as a spring, soaring and spreading delight.

Felicity glanced at the others and was startled. They were all in the process of being transformed. Some of the girls looked partly made out of light, as if their bodies were undergoing some kind of chemical process. Joan was shining as if she were wearing her gold armor in battle. Amelia's red hair looked as if it were on fire.

And then everything changed. The teacher led them into the singing of "Nothing but the Blood," and persistent sadness, like a small rain, touched her everywhere.

What can wash away my sin? Nothing but the blood of Jesus—For my pardon this I see: nothing but the blood of Jesus—Nothing can for sin atone; nothing but the blood of Jesus—This is all my hope and peace: nothing but the blood of Jesus.

He who had given her her robe of light now stood pouring blood from his wounds like a fountain. His blood covered her, the sky, the other girls. They were immersed in its cloying waves and there was no hope for anyone, no matter what the song said. She wanted to sing "Rock of Ages" again, but there was no going back. Not for her nor for the world. From where did such despondency come? In the absence of memories to anchor her sorrows to, Felicity was a puddle of unhappiness, this all the more distressing for being pure feeling. If such sorrow was in the world, there was no saving it. The job was too big even for Jesus.

Just as Felicity was about to sink to the floor, the maestro led them into the singing of "Alone in the Garden," and joy returned to the world.

I come to the garden alone while the dew is still on the roses, and the voice I hear falling on my ear, he speaks, and the sound of his voice is so sweet the birds hush their singing, and the melody that he gave to me I'd stay in the garden with him though the night around me be falling but he bids me to go . . .

This time, the sweet joy that suffused her was without ecstasy. It was the sad joy of knowing one's aloneness but also the comfort of the mystic night. The song had plainly named "the voice I hear falling on my ear" as the source of all feeling. She had known this once: sound was the universal source. A song suffused creation and dictated its shape through its notes. Either God sang all the time, giving form to the world, or God was sound, in which case everything was song. And things, such as they were, were only seemingly solid; they were only projections of sound. All of this occured to Felicity in an instant, in the interval between two notes. And just as instantly, she forgot it.

Days passed, merging with one another, each day very much like the next. The woolen blanket on her bunk was too small, and there was only one pillow, but the strangest thing happened. Felicity, who had always had trouble falling asleep and had spent hours adjusting her two pillows in a special way, now slumbered as soon as she lay down. At the end of each day, sleep closed in on her like water. She did not know the other women in her dorm, who seemed always to be humming under their breath with their eyes half closed. They did not speak to her but appeared friendly and kind.

Two plain meals were served every day at a long wooden table. The women took turns cooking, serving, and doing the dishes, but Felicity had not been asked. For breakfast, there was oatmeal and skim white milk. The midday meal was a plate of boiled white rice, white beans, and cauliflower. Pitchers of decaffeinated iced tea were quietly passed around. It was poor and bland fare, but it suited Felicity fine. The meals were eaten in silence, after one of the women said grace. They ended with a grateful hymn. Felicity studied her table companions, a dozen women or so, and wondered where they had come from. From rare occasional remarks she understood that some of them had been recruited from the streets of New Orleans by Bamajans. They did not know why they had been chosen, but they had readily acquiesced, or been made to acquiesce, to their new situation. *It is a long time ago, far away. I have taken vows of poverty and silence.* Sometimes an image came to her in the wake of this thought: a convent perched on a rock face while a blue-black sea foamed below. She found herself sometimes wanting to ask Joan of Arc and Amelia Earhart questions about their lives, but each time something in the women's demeanor stopped her. In the end she realized that Joan and Amelia, like herself, did not remember their lives. Perhaps they did not even know who they were. Perhaps only she, Scheherazade, knew her own name.

Felicity felt more and more at peace with herself. She sang and she lived *feeling.* She had no past and she felt no need to think of the future. She lived in an eternal *now,* punctuated by the steady rain that fell on the roof of the building like a lullaby. One night a violent thunderstorm shook the building, but the thunder and lightning that had frightened her so much, once upon a forgotten time, did little more than punctuate her happiness. She recalled vaguely that she lived in a city that floated on water, where rain came often in great bursts, but she did not care for the outside any more than she did for her past. Her secret knowledge that some of the women in her class were famous historical figures remained twined around her arms in the invisible bracelet, but she rarely sensed its presence now. It did not seem to matter. She saw them every day and was glad to see them, but little by little they became transformed and quiet. If they were indeed who Felicity thought they were, they gave no sign of it. They rarely spoke, and the silence was soothing.

The School for Messiah Development was rigorously segregated. The women, who were all students, ate alone. The teachers were all men, but

Felicity had glimpsed other males, muscled types with dark sunglasses who never looked at her.

In a small classroom with pillows on the floor, an Indian man with a white turban spoke about Jesus. On the wall behind him were brightly colored lithographs from his life. Jesus was blond and blue eyed, not dark and Semitic the way she had seen him in song. His hair reached past his shoulders. One of his hands stretched out in blessing, while the other rested on top of a crooked staff that was also a snake. His eyes followed her everywhere, no matter which way she turned her head.

"You wonder," the turbaned man said, "what kind of Christian I am. I was not always a Christian, but all that is left of my past is the turban on my head. My heart is full of Jesus and my mind does his work. You too will have only an outward trace of your wicked life left, after you accept him. You can decide now what you want to keep, or later, but it will be harder later."

Felicity was certain that nothing remained from her former life. All that must have at one time mattered to her was no longer an inner concern, but something removed from her like dresses worn on occasions no longer important. She knew that she was not alone; Jesus was with her. Now and then an anguished voice within protested this, but it broke against the joy she experienced.

Beware, the broken inner voice said; this happiness you feel is false. But it did not feel that way at all. Light danced in all her bones, and her heart was seized with so much tenderness she cried often and with abandon.

"Pay good attention," the teacher said, reading from Revelation words that struck a painful and familiar chord in her:

" 'Then one of the seven angels who had the seven bowls came and talked to me,' wrote John, 'saying to me, Come I will show you the judgment of the great harlot who sits on many waters, with whom the kings of the earth committed fornication. . . . So he carried me away in the Spirit into the wilderness. And I saw a woman sitting on a scarlet beast which was full of names of blasphemy, having seven heads and ten horns. The woman was arrayed in purple and scarlet, and adorned with gold and precious stones and pearls, having in her hand a golden cup full of abominations and the filthiness of her fornication. And on her forehead was written: MYSTERY, BABYLON THE GREAT, THE MOTHER OF HARLOTS AND OF THE ABOMINATIONS OF THE EARTH.' "

Felicity knew then that in her wicked former life she had been that woman. All the happiness drained from her, replaced by a wave of sorrow so profound her weeping changed. The salt of her tears was bitter now. She knew that this bitter salt was the oldest salt on earth, an element stretched like a shroud over the first layer of matter. Felicity saw the air fill with millions of salty sevens. The very fabric of the air was woven out of myriads of that number writ in salt. And she saw the woman on top of the beast, which gave off an unbearable stench of corpse. The mounted woman was the Whore of Babylon, drinking the cup full of the still-living ejaculates of her many lovers. She, Felicity, was the Whore of Babylon. She became a single cry of agony, reduced only to a burning wish for salvation. She folded in on herself, wet with her own tears, and implored the lithographs: "Take me, Jesus!" Her whole body exploded with light, and the rings in her nipples, the invisible bracelets on her arms, and the gold loops in her ears became incandescent and burned her. She tore them off, without taking her eyes off the Savior, imploring him between sobs, "Save me, save me!"

Two times a week, the women sat before computer terminals. Felicity's job was to download streams of names, numbers, and photographs of men and women. Some of them wore suits, others had on work clothes and hard hats. At first she thought that these were employment records, but soon she realized that they were more than that. She seemed to be downloading the contents of some vast industrial company's computer. Other women were similarly engaged with long files.

At the end of her first hour, Felicity tired. She rested her arms on top of the console, and her invisible bracelets began vibrating. After a time, she found herself touching the keyboard lightly. Her fingers punched in an oddly familiar sequence, though she couldn't remember its purpose. *Make Love to People from History* appeared on the screen. The message confused her. She was as filled with love as she could hold. How was it possible to "make" more love?

She walked out of the room, and nobody stopped her.

Day after day, her happiness alternated with sorrow. At night, spent and thin, she sunk beneath her coverlet of darkness and was as if dead. She knew only day and night and was unaware of either the year or the season.

Chapter Twenty

Wherein Andrea and Ben hastily depart Israel

Y e h u d a ben Yehuda withdrew from his account all the money that his father, Dr. Redman, had reluctantly surrendered to his son's religious education, and bought two airplane tickets with it. They were the cheapest tickets available, on BookAir ("The Airline for People Who Read"), a cut-rate airline that offered no-frill flights around the world. Instead of fancy electronic entertainment—movies and music and earphones—BookAir offered only rafts of used books left behind by previous travelers. Their flight was scheduled to leave in the early evening from Ben-Gurion Airport in Tel Aviv, arriving in Atlanta next morning.

Andrea's lack of papers was a problem Ben undertook with some pleasure. He had created numberless fake IDs in high school for his underage classmates. His work had been quite renowned. He had with him an expired driver's license that had belonged to his sister Clarisse. He pasted a small picture of Andrea over Clarisse's. He next produced a birth certificate modeled on his own, a painstaking calligraphic work that Xeroxed perfectly. He booked Andrea's flight under the name Clarisse Redman.

They boarded a bus full of soldiers, many of whom leaned on their guns looking dreamily at Andrea, who wore a tiny miniskirt out of which her skinny legs stuck out like a puppet's. They recognized her.

"All these soldiers want to kiss me," whispered Andrea to Ben. "I am going to perfect my kiss so that it becomes atomic, a laser. I'll then be able to kiss everyone who wants to kiss me."

"The whole world?"

"Why not?" She wrapped her bare arm around his shoulders and put her head on his chest. A female essence like almond and warm burnished copper suffused him.

"This must be my *chingush* day," she said.

"Your what?"

"My *chingush*. Since I was small, I always lose one day a week to the *chingush*. It's like a little tornado; it picks me up and it takes me somewhere. When I come back I don't remember what happened that day at all. I think that only good things happen on my *chingush* day."

"How do you know if you can't remember?"

"Because I feel good afterward, like I took a sauna."

"Which day is it?" Ben wanted to make sure that he knew so that he could mark it in his calendar: "Wednesday is Andrea's *chingush day*. Don't expect to see her." His father always marked his wife's periods on his desk calendar. "Be extra careful," he wrote in the squares.

"I never know which day it is. All I know is it's once a week."

Great. The *chingush* could strike any time.

What Ben did not know and Andrea did not tell him was that her *chingush* had once lasted four years. That is how long she had been lost until the day a man had brought her to Saint Hildegard's. She remembered nothing from those years, as if she had not existed at all. If she had told Ben, he might have run away from her. But Ben, from his fairly limited contact with citizens of the Old World, had already understood something about Andrea's *chingush*, namely, that being lost was part of every European's past. What little he understood of history made him aware that Europeans needed to forget the past and were thus often amnesiac and lost, whereas Americans suffered amnesia in the present and were lost amid all their bounty. This was one of the reasons he had left his country. There was another difference, too, which was that the amnesia of Europeans could cover centuries, while Americans could experience an eternity of forgetfulness in the space of just an hour.

"Do you have all your things?" asked Ben.

Andrea pointed to the cardboard tube she had laid on the luggage netting over their heads.

"Is that everything?"

"Everything."

In addition to what she wore, Andrea had kept the round box bought at the *suk* and Sister Rodica's cotton underwear. They rattled about inside the cardboard tube.

"You'll need another change of clothes," said Ben. Her miniskirt bothered him, but not as much as her high platform shoes. She looked as if she might topple from them at any moment.

Andrea allowed that she might. All she really wanted, though, was a pair of fluffy white wings. Once more, she was Victory.

In Tel Aviv she purchased a gold Byzantine cross from a Yemeni jeweler—Ben protested weakly, thinking of his mother—and a gold pendant inscribed with the Jews' lament in Babylon. Andrea hung these two symbols on a chain she already wore around her ivory neck.

"It's all the clothes I need." She leaned her head back for Ben to better admire her jewels.

Ben leaned close and held the Jewish talisman, and read:

> If I forget you, O Jerusalem,
> let my right hand wither;
> let my tongue stick to my palate
> if I cease to think of you,
> if I do not keep Jerusalem in memory
> even at my happiest hour.

Ben-Gurion Airport was a cross between an army barracks, a Roman forum, and a multipurpose church. When they arrived, a cordon of soldiers was keeping the crowds away from an armored limousine. To one side, a wailing family of Palestinians watched their enormous bundles dismantled by Israeli soldiers. Toothpaste tubes were squeezed out over silk pantaloons, and jars of yellow saffron rained over holiday suits. It was not a pretty sight, and Ben, despite his rabbi-induced conservatism, cringed. At heart he was as liberal as his father. Oppression made him sick.

Andrea's attention was riveted by a group of arriving immigrants from Russia, who lay on the ground, kissing the asphalt of Israel. They looked like overweight birds stuck to the tar. She saw the joy that radiated from them like puffs of blue smoke. She could taste their tears washing into the tar. Years of quiet terror and a vast store of daily humiliation poured from them like sweat. Enjoy this moment, Andrea urged them silently; it's the best. This is it. Soon you will receive the blessings of reality, its imaginative hassles, sadistic bureaucrats, inevitable heartbreaks, and you will see the grinning skull of capitalism. Most of your pain will return. Her unspoken compassion was genuine and effective; it swept over the overwrought immigrants like a cool breeze. For a millisecond they stopped sweating and felt at peace.

Getting onto the BookAir jet presented no difficulty. Andrea slipped unbothered past officials and baggage checkers, through metal detectors and gate security. It was almost as if she were invisible, which was eerie, considering that her face had been in every Israeli living room and her name in every newspaper. Ben observed that she had the uncanny ability to make herself plain, almost bedraggled. She achieved an everywoman look, an air of ordinariness and modesty. She didn't get a second glance from anyone, despite her miniskirt and platforms.

They had already rolled onto the runway when the pilot announced that they would be delayed. Andrea looked past Ben and some other people toward the window at the dark sky. The ground and their airplane shook as if struck by a terrific wind.

"There they go again, the Israeli jets!" someone said, pointing to the streaking lights of hundreds of Israeli fighter jets taking off for parts unknown.

Andrea felt as if the clanging of all the bells and the popping of champagne corks marking the passing of the second millennium all over the world had lodged in her body. She was experiencing a planetary hangover, though she hadn't had a drop to drink. The fighter planes seemed to go right through her.

After the jets roared away, BookAir finally received permission to depart, and the Promised Land faded behind them.

Chapter Twenty-one

*Wherein Joe leans on the Shades. Angel Zack
considers the unfairness of his duties.
The Council of Great Minds. Nikola Tesla.*

 o e knew what he had to do. Lean on some Shades. Not that it gave him any pleasure. Shades were so passive, hitting one was like punching a pillow. He had cleared some of them from a park last year, and they'd gone limp as overcooked spaghetti. It had taken hours to load a dozen of them into the van. All the way to the station they'd chanted, "The True One comes! The True One comes!" and when Joe's partner told them to shut the fuck up or he'd stuff the True One up their asses, they'd started taking off their clothes. And then they returned to the park anyway. Which is where they were now, doing their lizard thing, though some were quite actively holding out their begging bowls.

It was only ten in the morning and the French Quarter wasn't yet awake, but the Shades kept business hours. Joe strolled into the middle of the group. One girl jingled and flashed quite obscenely in his path. Joe held his hands palms out in a gesture of peace. He was wearing civvies.

"I'm here to help a friend of yours. Some of you met a girl called Felicity . . . she danced with you and you showed her your body writing."

He had their attention, though they tried to show no interest. The Shades had all the toughness of flowers. If a bee buzzed them, they trembled. They didn't know truth from lie, and when they tried to lie, as they had when Joe arrested them, they were pathetic. Still, they were hard to pin down because none of them kept any identification. They'd burnt all society's markers and renamed themselves after flowers and animals, dedicating themselves to communal anonymity, begging, tripping, and waiting for their True One.

After jingling their metals in what they hoped was a scary way, two girls, Poppy and Jasmine, told Joe that they had accompanied Felicity to Saint Louis Cathedral because she had promised them ten Hohner harmonicas if they stayed by her side while she met someone. Pressed to describe this someone, they said that he was "yucky," that he was "tall," that he had a "hump, maybe," that he had a "silver cross on his chest." Joe figured it out before they were finished: Reverend Mullin.

"She is in trouble, we help," said a boy with studs in his eyebrows and a black T-shirt that said in big white letters, FEAR GOD.

"Just keep your eyes open," said Joe.

"Don't need to," the Shade said. "We'll close our eyes and find her. We will find her inside. She's wandering in the desert."

If Felicity was wandering anywhere, it was because she had a gun at her head. Tough kid. Hold fast, honey. I'm coming for you. Joe's heart tightened as he realized that for him there was no life without Felicity.

Efforts to locate the good reverend took most of the day. Joe visited every church listed in the ministries directory but found that he had just missed Mullin each time. The United Ministries of Love in Plaquemines Parish, ostensibly the reverend's home, turned out to be a mansion staffed by Lithuanian converts. They spoke no English and were the latest crop of souls drawn from Mullin's missions in that part of the world. Mullin's soul fishermen were bringing masses of these hapless foreigners with shiny eyes to Louisiana. The United Ministries of Love was believed to own dozens of buildings and businesses in the New Orleans area, but these holdings were, for some reason, impossible to find. The police computer displayed an astonishing blankness in regard to the televangelical empire.

At the end of his search, discouraged and seized by a sinking feeling, Joe went home to see his mother. He was going to be on duty next day, Christmas Eve, and this was going to be the first time he'd miss dinner at her house. They had talked on the phone, and he was worried. The old woman had been having visions and premonitions. She had been telling her neighbors that her son was in love with the Mother of God and that he would soon trade his police uniform for a brotherly cassock.

When he arrived at his mother's house, a white-painted double on Colisseum Street, he found her playing *bourré* with her sister, Carla. The old ladies were drinking beer and eating coconut macaroons from a MacKenzie's Bakery box. A small Christmas tree sat on a window box, decorated with the same trinkets as last year.

Carla was one of Joe's favorite people. She had entered the Ursuline convent when she was sixteen and had spent her life in the service of the church. After he kissed her soft cheek, he asked her teasingly if she had discovered any remarkable saints lately. Aunt Carla's tales of strange saints had been one of the highlights of his childhood.

"No, Giuseppe," Aunt Carla, who also had the gift of foresight, said, "but I had a dream that you have a girlfriend. Her patron saint is Saint Helena—who was the mother of Constantine and, some say, the daughter of King Cole—who was sent into exile before being welcomed back as empress. God bless mother Helena; she went to the Holy Land in her eighty-fifth year and discovered the True Cross and the tomb of our Lord. She's a good girl you've found, Giuseppe."

Aunt Carla was eighty-five years old herself, and Joe bent down dutifully as she made the sign of the cross over him.

"Is there a Saint Felicity, Aunt Carla?"

"There is, darling. Patroness of mothers. She is invoked against infertility. She converted to the true faith and later was thrown with Saint Perpetua to the gladiators and killed by a wild cow. Saint Augustine of Hippo says she kept her skirt down the whole time. Bless you, Giuseppe."

That sure didn't sound like Felicity Le Jeune. Aunt Carla's age must have been muddying up the channels.

"Something eating you, Joe?" His mother started walking toward the kitchen. "Sit down and have some macaroni."

Joe sat down at the table but barely touched the bowl of steaming pasta with homemade tomato sauce that his mama made magically appear before him. The women continued their game of cards.

"What does Father Tommasino say, Aunt Carla? All this talk about the End."

Aunt Carla crossed herself and leaned close over the box of macaroons. "They unsealed the third revelation of Fatima. The End is coming. The Antichrist is born in the world now, and some say . . . he's in New Orleans. Father Tommasino says the archdiocese knows who he is."

Joe's mother was beside herself. "Do tell, Carla."

"You gotta swear you won't tell a soul," said the nun. They leaned in real close.

"The Baptist preacher Mullin."

"The one on TV?" Joe's mother was incredulous.

"Not a word, child, not a word."

Joe would have liked to laugh but couldn't. It was right, somehow.

Zack floated above a bench on the Moonwalk by the Mississippi River. The wide water barely moved, mirroring the towers of the business district. A tug pushed a long train of barges so slowly it made him sleepy, and the *Hilton Belle* casino boat let out a sigh of white smoke. Once intended for cruising, it now festered in the same pool of still water like a familiar infection. Zack smelled coffee, bananas, vanilla, salted fish, powdered sugar, sweat, almonds, mothballs, Japanese magnolia, figs, jasmine, stale beer, and salty sleeping girls. The impression of a sickle moon stuck just over the roof of the Kern warehouse at Algiers Point. Inside slumbered the giant heads of Dionysus, Isis, Pan, and Aphrodite that decked New Orleans Mardi Gras floats. Zack could see through the walls and felt in the immense cardboard silence their papier-mâché loneliness. He empathized with the giant heads. His greatest trial was yet to come. It had been decided, despite his protests, that embodiment was necessary. He had to choose a human being to occupy in order to carry out his mission. He looked about him warily, considering the sad prospects loitering nearby. Sometimes he wished the heavens weren't so ironic.

In vain had Zack pointed out to his superiors the many disembodied missions that had gone without a hitch during his training *mok*. But this one, a matter of form, wasn't going to be one of them. The world of spirits may have been possessed of humorous and occasionally anarchistic inclinations, and democracy may have been proclaimed, but form was still taken very seriously. And the word of any angel superior to Zack was law. The law in this case said, *This is important business. Embodiment required.* Which meant, Zack knew, that he would be supervising a massive transfer of souls to human bodies and then seeing to it that the befuddled souls maneuver their new bodies well enough to draw incarnate wisdom from them for a purpose that was still beyond him. And that wasn't even the worst part. At a certain point, he had to take on a body himself, a prospect so loathsome his wings shriveled slightly. The choreography of this grossly inelegant business was entirely his responsibility.

"I'll be like a traffic cop!" lamented Zack. It's well known that only the lowest spirits incarnate.

But no matter how loudly Zack complained, he found no sympathetic ears. The most he could get was a concession to get out of the body he incarnated into, now and then, in order to take a break from the absurd functions of the flesh. Incarnation was not reincarnation; it was nothing fancy. It was indeed the lowest spirit job. Rookies dead three days did it.

Even as Zack lamented to his superiors, he could see, directly below him, an incarnation in progress. A wino, crumpled on the steps leading to the wide river, had suddenly opened his eyes. A look of wonder and fear was in them. His rheumy lids shot up into his eyebrows. He reached for the paper bag beside him and wrapped an unsteady and dirty hand around the neck of the bottle inside, but the bag swooshed out of his hands and rolled down the steps, breaking on the hunks of cement that lined the water's edge. Zack could see a determined little white poltergeist, shaped like a thin funnel, forcing its way into the top of the wino's head.

"Oh, my God!" The angel Zack was not given to invoking the Supreme Deity in vain. But he repeated it: "Oh, my God!"

He recognized the spirit. Even in a democratized heaven, the famous were still royalty. The spirit screwing itself into the wino's head was the visionary scientist Nikola Tesla. He was one of the Minds. Zack's mission had begun.

Angels are specialized libraries. Zack happened to contain the history of science, and in his vast store of information, Nikola Tesla was a superstar. Zack could recite without trying every moment of the great inventor's life. Nikola Tesla, Serbian, born in Croatia in 1856, sailed to America in 1884 with four cents in his pocket, a few of his poems, and calculations for a flying machine. Tesla had invented alternating current, which had won out over Thomas Edison's advocacy of direct current. He had invented shadowgraphs, later called X rays. His Tesla coil made television and radio possible. He'd discovered terrestrial stationary waves, which nearly blew the cover off the dimension where Zack dwelt. He used the earth as a conductor responsive to certain frequencies and opened the angelic dimension. Tesla had received communications never intended for humans, which he interpreted as signals from other planets. He figured out a way to split the earth in half like an apple. He had even discovered a means of worldwide communication for sending pictures and messages, something humans now called the Internet. Tesla'd filled his notebooks with so many ideas that the decision to terminate his earthly existence was taken at the highest levels in 1943, during World War II, before they could be put into practice. Heaven feared that some of these ideas might prematurely end the world. Zack had been in his first *mok* then but could still recall that important decision. After Tesla reached heaven, he spent all his time playing cards with his old friend Mark Twain, and showed no interest in the physics of the angelic dimension. Apparently a decision had now been taken to return him to earth to participate in the Council of the Great Minds. Zack tipped his invisible hat to the clumsy poltergeist half screwed inside the bum's head.

Tesla finally disappeared entirely into the bum's skull like a genie into a bottle. The wino staggered to his feet and stood straight up, sober for the first time in years. It was an unaccustomed and heady sensation. He took the steps up from the river with an ease that surprised him and filled his heart with hope. He had no idea that what he was experiencing was the result of a spirit who had taken over his body, shoving his pitiful, dark, and sour wino soul into a corner of his being, where it would sleep until his use by the heavens was complete.

The transformation was fascinating. Zack had not been informed as to exactly by what means the Great Minds were going to arrive in New Orleans—another egregious bureaucratic oversight!—but he was still surprised that the heavens had chosen this crude, common way. For a long time incarnation had been practiced only by monitors. The job of the monitor spirits was to insure the orderly traffic of souls into the spirit world after their mass dispatch from the planet, should a conventional apocalypse occur. Originally, incarnation had proceeded in a respectful fashion.

Alas! That had been the modus operandi of gentler days. The millennial urgency that gripped earth and heaven had dispensed with such niceties. Nowadays, hundreds of thousands of people in America alone were unceremoniously taken over as if they were empty trash containers. There was no ceremony. Even a momentary depression could allow one to be taken over. A moment of melancholy, even. Zack was disgusted; it bothered him that humans were being violated in this manner. Might as well bring on the End.

And now, horror of horrors, the Minds were being brought in the same way! Zack shuddered. Such clumsiness! He scanned the city quickly and found that he was right. Perched on a stoop on Bourbon Street, in front of an adult video store, was Albert Einstein in the muscled body of a male prostitute. The great Roman poet Ovid was frozen with bewilderment inside a banker sitting behind a desk in the Whitney Bank building on Poydras Street. The seer Nostradamus, with a towel around his arm, was taking a drink order at the Napoleon House. Napoleon himself was tapping for tourists on Royal Street, uncomfortably situated in the body of a fifteen-year-old black boy. Dante was inside a policeman. Plato stood behind the desk at the Voodoo Wax Museum. Karl Marx, sweating, with a yellow bandanna around his neck and a hard hat on his head, was digging a hole in the street while his white coworkers watched. It was shameful. The heavens hadn't even matched the Minds to compatible bodies.

Zack watched Tesla as he stood on the Moonwalk, looking at the Mississippi River with wonder. His unshaved wino face took on the countenance of a child. He had been informed, rather tersely, that he was going to New Orleans, but had had no time to imagine the place. He had seen this river once at Saint Louis, but it was wider and muddier here. This was the "mighty Mississippi" of his friend Twain's tales. Zack couldn't suppress a twinge of envy in the face of such joyous astonishment. Humans were really something. He hoped he wasn't catching their emotions, which was really the closest to a disease his kind ever contracted.

"What am I?" Nikola Tesla asked himself after his first glimpse of the Mississippi River. He looked down at his rags, sniffed himself in disgust, and put his hands in his trouser pockets, where he discovered only some wadded tissue. "I have even less now than when I came to America for the first time," he mused.

For the rest of the day, Tesla wandered the city on unsteady legs. At the end of the day he discovered an empty warehouse. Inside, a few people dressed in rags similar to his sat around a campfire, eating from cans. They seemed to know him because they made friendly noises and beckoned him over.

"Who am I?" asked Tesla after he had sat down on the ground and been given a can full of warm beans.

"That's funny," laughed the toothless fellow on his right. "You're the urban anchorite. You're a shining example to all of us."

The crowd guffawed, but Tesla was pleased. An urban anchorite. A father of the desert in the city. He liked that. He liked also the warehouse, a big space, perfect for some kind of experiment. All of a sudden, Tesla was seized with the need for a great project. He was back on earth.

•

For the next few days, Nikola Tesla roamed an area of the French Quarter bounded by Chartres and Dumaine on one side and Ursulines and Pirate's Alley on the other. He pushed a contraption that resembled a shopping cart but was, in actuality, a living unit complete with bed, shower, and compartments for carting found materials. He'd designed and built fifty of them for his new friends, who were now scattered throughout the city, gathering what he needed for his new experiment.

Tesla's rounds were so regular the inhabitants of the neighborhood could set their watches by him. He appeared at noon and vanished at sunset. The word on the street was that he was very rich, that he had a photographic memory and was secretly working on a doomsday machine. Tesla's companions had deduced all this on their own and had already started making him legendary. Tesla liked that. He had always been a legend, even to himself.

In the course of his wanderings he had made several important observations about the world at this time, and about the city of New Orleans in particular. For the most part, he was not surprised at the widespread use of his discoveries. He watched the launching of a space rocket on a television set in a Laundromat.

"Is earth attacking a hostile planet?" Tesla asked a bearded street person in a motorized wheelchair with bulging plastic bags attached to the armrests, who used this Laundromat for his daytime quarters.

"It's the space shuttle, man. Where you been?" The street person was huffy. "Most of what you see is fuel tanks. After it leaves the atmosphere, the space capsule takes the astronauts to the moon. Where did you go to kindergarten?"

This explanation, if true, seemed to imply a simple technology that could have been vastly improved using rotating magnetic fields. Tesla was also interested in the motorized wheelchair, but the street person found these questions indelicate and drove off noisily.

Nikola Tesla watched the television for several days after that and found its messages extraordinarily trivial, but addictive. He was most fascinated by commercials and by how quickly they told huge stories that in his day would have taken whole epic novels. He had difficulty at first following the quick changes of scene, but as the technique became obvious, he was delighted. He had been thinking in precisely this way at peak mental pitch and few people had understood him. Now, it seemed, the world had no difficulty moving among landscapes, relationships, machines, ideas, and words all within thirty seconds. At the same time, he was astonished by the use to which this technique of quick jump cuts was put. It was as if people were using laser weapons to slice bread.

Tesla couldn't stop watching. He didn't even mind it when customers changed a program to another; it was all stimulating to some part of himself that bypassed critical thinking and lodged itself directly into his solar plexus, at the seat of emotions. The addictive nature of the medium led him to consider other forms of addiction.

He had to make a conscious effort to avoid the Laundromat. He had seen commercials for the Internet on television and decided to investigate cyberspace. He was already somewhat familiar with cyberspace from the other side. He had occasionally participated in a party game that was quite the rage in the spirit world. The players entered cyberspace and represented themselves as human beings to people on-line. They entered chat rooms and multiple-user dungeons (MUDs) and MOOs (MUD object oriented), where they interacted with the humans who believed that they were communicating with their own kind. His former archenemy but now friend, Thomas Edison, had revealed himself in full, but his confession was taken to be just another identity assumption in the fluid world of cyberspace, where people switched genders, used pseudonyms, and generally misrepresented themselves in every way conceivable. After Edison's prank, many spirits went on-line with their real names and were greeted as naturally as if they lived around the corner of some street in some earthly city. Tesla himself had tired of the game, but now, on the other side of it, he was quite interested in what motivated the embodied to explore cyberspace.

Tesla used a computer at the New Orleans Public Library and quickly got a headache surfing the Internet. People's capacity for producing trivia was inexhaustible. In addition to the rivers of information sludge, there was so much chat it filled his entire capacity for absorption. He likened the din of the never-ending conversation to a huge public festivity where strangers forced themselves to speak in banalities until all vestige of thought was banished. The airwaves were filled with introductory remarks like "Hi," "Hello," and "Where are you from?" leaving absolutely no space for genuine dialogue. It had surely been more fun from the other side. It occurred to him that people involved in such activities as cyberspace and television were probably void of memory. He was certain that the world was in the grip of a terrible amnesia. In considering the nature of the attraction, Tesla concluded, once more, that it was addiction.

When he left the public library, bleary eyed and slightly nauseated by his own capacity for addiction, he was appalled at the filth in the air. The great Mississippi River was a brownish yellow color and full of deadly chemicals. Mark Twain would not have been surprised, given the fact that he had once called the great river a *cloaca maxima*, a great sewer, but even Twain would have been appalled by the depth of the degradation. This too, Tesla concluded, was the result of addiction to products that satisfied a short-term craving while obliterating everything around. Overall, the ethical will of humanity lagged far behind its technology. In some respects, things had reverted to a state he had already thought obsolete in his own time.

As he wandered through the streets of New Orleans, he saw addiction in even cruder forms. Barrooms were crowded with gamblers playing electronic money machines. Casinos stayed open day and night, fleecing suckers who returned as soon as they were able. Of course, this particular human folly was no mystery to him. In fact, he had amused himself in his youth by figuring out probabilities in games of chance, and he was certain that he could do it again. For the first time since landing in this decayed reality, Tesla smiled. When the time came to use money, he could doubtless get it from gambling, and there would be a certain justice to it. Already his mind was working toward possible solutions to some of the more obvious messes.

New Orleans was green, wet, incessantly flowering. Tesla spent an hour with a sweet-olive tree, whose scent of overripe peach stimulated and intrigued him. The tiny cream-colored clusters looked like an unlikely source for such overpowering scent. The tree, at the back of Saint Louis Cathedral, spread its branches over the fence, now and then dropping its tiny blossoms on his hair. He watched a vine clinging to the wrought-iron fence—it put out a tendril that gripped the iron tightly. Tesla pushed his cart up Royal Street, noting green fingers pushing through the cracked sidewalk. He stopped to study a Japanese magnolia—the lavender blooms had opened overnight and were covered by a fine mist. The air was warm, rich, liquid—Tesla drew a breath and sensed the expectant tree waiting for him to exhale. When he did, the tree inhaled the iron-enriched air that had gone through his lungs. They breathed together—man breath out, tree breath in, tree breath out, man breath in—and everything became still except for this symbiotic respiration. Tesla rubbed the top of his head and the sweet-olive seeped into his hand and scalp. The magnolia flowers glowed to reveal their delicate geometry, and Tesla smacked his forehead.

Yes. He remembered his idea for chlorophyll propulsion, left behind in one of the notebooks. He'd been unable to experiment in Colorado because it was too dry. But here in New Orleans, at the wettest place in the continental United States, it was possible. Tesla next communed with the intense green leaves of a banana peeking over the wall of a courtyard on Chartres. His breath quickened as it always did at the onset of an inspired project. He sat on a bench and began sketching.

While the bountiful generative world of vegetation claimed most of his attention that week, Tesla did not abandon his observation of humanity. He was astonished to discover that slavery persisted. He observed the existence of flourishing slave markets, connected with the crack cocaine business. Many drug dealers were also slave traders. One of the markets operated quite openly on Fridays right in Jackson Square, in front of Saint Louis Cathedral. Tesla watched a skinny man with a heavy silver buckle and alligator-skin boots, followed at a short distance by a quiescent boy who looked no older than twelve. A buyer appeared shortly, a burly man in a suit with a pencil-thin mustache. Money exchanged hands quickly, and the boy followed the buyer out of the square, toward Royal Street.

The street people were very concerned. Many young drifters, kids who hadn't been on the street long, were vanishing. Only the old alcoholics and, so far, the Shades had been left alone, possibly because they were not interested in drugs. The slave trade celebrated its might quite brazenly. Bars with slave-and-master motifs stayed open all night, filled with drunk and stoned sadists. Slaves were tortured and killed in back rooms of bars and in luxury apartments. The disposal of young bodies was a growth industry. In his youth, Tesla had been an abolitionist. The new forms of slavery through addiction were alarming.

During one of his rounds, Tesla became intrigued by a shuttered building on Bourbon Street that was the recipient of many young women who never returned from within. A street acquaintance told him that the building was the headquarters of something called SMD, the School for Messiah Development. His informant whispered darkly that the Antichrist was being nurtured there and that the day was not far off when the gates of this house would burst open and he would appear in a globe of fire. This explanation irritated Tesla.

"He? There are only women in there. Is this Antichrist a woman?"

His informant allowed that the Antichrist might be female. "It might even be my ex-wife." He grinned toothlessly, offering the anchorite a swig of his peach brandy, which Tesla refused.

Chapter Twenty-two

Wherein Tesla rescues Felicity from her involuntary happiness

**e s l a** put the SMD quarters on his watch. He was there the day Felicity was brought in. She walked supported by two men, stepping lightly as if she weren't sure the ground was there. Something about the girl touched him. A small sound, like a distant flute, reached his inner ear. He had no idea what the sound was. It could have been the jingling of her bracelets or something that came from his own mind. Tesla had always thought himself far removed from the vulgar emotions that agitated most people. At one time, he had sought to relieve humanity of its sexual burden entirely. Still, Felicity emanated a fresh, lovely light that Tesla, who had read William James, identified with the first female principle, the mother he had never known, the lover he had never considered. He watched her disappear within and almost immediately conceived the idea of helping this girl escape. Tesla did not undertake this mission solely for the girl's sake: he needed her in order to construct the chlorophyll-propulsion machine he had already begun assembling at the warehouse beside the river.

The house itself presented few difficulties. The next day, Tesla took his usual position on the stoop next door to SMD. A mule-drawn carriage filled with tourists passed, and the carriage driver pointed out the anchorite to his charges.

"He there a urban anchor that be there every day like clockworks and about him be said that he old as Methuselah, rich as Croesus, smart as Einstein, and some say he Jeezus. I say he be the reincarnate Napoleon," he explained in rapid patter.

Tesla was by now so ubiquitous many people no longer noticed him and his shopping cart. He was like the Confederate submarine at the Cabildo: it was so odd the locals pretended not to see it. He planned to unlock the iron gate set in a ten-foot brick wall topped by broken glass, with the aid of a small sonic device fashioned from a broken radio. The device had the advantage of being a weapon as well, emitting a high-pitched sound that could burst eardrums.

Tesla was mentally rehearsing his plan when a policeman approached him. Now, of all times!

Joe sat down next to him and showed him a photograph. "Have you seen this girl?"

It was Felicity. Was this a kind of psychic cop or something? In the photo, Felicity's mouth was slightly open. Her green eyes were looking far away.

"If you'll excuse me, I'm in a race against time," Tesla said politely.

"Right. And you race just sitting here?"

"There are grave problems in this city, Constable. In the world. Are you aware that slavery has returned? Human beings are being sold as we speak."

"And why do you think that is?" Joe asked. He did not want to engage the anchorite but felt obscurely that the madman was somehow valuable.

"Because you can only have as much freedom as you're willing to take. If you don't assume your portion, they'll take it from you. The slavers prey on the weak. The issue did seem to be solved well before the turn of the century. It's astonishing. My discoveries are everywhere, but they haven't helped people become any better." Tesla stopped, afraid that he'd said too much.

Tesla could have told the policeman that the girl he was looking for was right across the street, and then, doubtless, the slave ring would be broken and the girl set free. But he had no faith in guardians of the law, whether in the Old or New World, past or present. He remembered Austrian border guards in Croatia, Turkish soldiers in Serbia, Immigration officers at Ellis Island, cops in New York. He had been detained, questioned, and beaten so many times by lawmen, it was a wonder he had survived to become the renowned Nikola Tesla. And there was something else. This policeman was young and handsome, while he, Nikola Tesla, inventor and neo-anchorite, showed the wear and tear of the street. His broken, yellowed teeth could barely stand comparison to the cop's gleaming mouth. Simply put, Tesla, though he barely dared to admit it, was jealous. He wanted Felicity for himself.

Joe was disappointed. He sensed that the anchorite knew something. Perhaps he was afraid to talk because he was dealing drugs out of his shopping cart, but the thought of having to wade through masses of junk to find out was not appealing.

"You see any shit I should know about, you call the precinct on Royal and ask for Joe," he said threateningly.

After the suspicious policeman vanished from sight, Tesla realized that he'd have to act quickly. His experiment lacked only two essential pieces. One of these pieces was vegetal, but the other was human. Felicity was the human component.

To his astonishment, the forbidding gate wasn't locked. He found himself in the well-kept courtyard of a three-story house with galleries running around both upper floors. Young women in simple white dresses and Chinese slippers stood in small groups, singing hymns. They didn't take any notice of him.

Tesla climbed the staircase and opened the first door he came to. A Hindu man with a turban on his head was pointing to a lithograph of a long-haired, blond Jesus Christ. Several female students sat on the floor at his feet, listening raptly. Felicity was not among them.

"Excuse me," said Tesla, but no one seemed to hear him. He shut the door softly.

The next door he tried presented an even more astonishing spectacle. A dozen young women dressed like all the others were sitting before computer consoles, working intently with rows of numbers. This scene interested Tesla—he had not expected the enterprise to be aided by computers. He decided to take a closer look.

No one stopped him. Color charts and rows of numbers alternated on the screens. Tesla knew immediately what the charts displayed—they were integrated circuits. He had worked on similar designs. What was being designed here? And why wasn't there any security? The thought crossed his mind that he was under surveillance and the reason for the apparent lack of security was that he would never leave here.

He felt a hand on his shoulder. When he turned around, an arm covered with crooked crosses rested there. The man rasped in his ear: "The Bamajan will see you now."

Tesla was in danger. He resorted to a technique he had developed when he'd been detained and interrogated by men in the employ of J. Pierpont Morgan. He allowed himself to go slack within, and then he raised an impenetrable inner shield. Through the shield he could hear everything, he could even respond, but he remained impervious to psychological or physical assault.

They entered a bare room with a blank screen on the wall. Leaning back on a chair before a kidney-shaped desk was a short smiling Hindu man with a shaved head. Tesla's escort crossed his spidery arms.

"Welcome to the School for Messiah Development, anchorite. We have been watching your activities, and we have concluded that you can be useful to us," the bald Bamajan said.

These words were nearly identical to the ones spoken by one of Morgan's enforcers when Tesla refused to surrender the patent to his worldwide broadcasting invention.

Then the bald man rose from his chair and did something so unexpected that Tesla nearly lost his shield. He threw himself at Tesla's feet and kissed his dirty bare toes.

"I don't know what you mean," mumbled the inventor.

"This is how we welcome new Bamajans. Welcome, Bamajan, welcome!" he exclaimed, rising from the floor. He sat back down behind the desk.

"Don't you want to know why I'm here?"

"We know. You came to teach us."

"Teach what? What do you people do?"

"We know that you are a Great Mind. We do not know precisely who you are, but we welcome you. Our psychics have been telling us for some time that the arrival of the Great Minds was imminent, but you are the first that we have had the great honor of encountering."

Tesla, though surprised by this turn of events, could not help but remark, "Someone must have an extraordinary sense of humor to place the welcoming committee for Great Minds among the strip joints, T-shirt shops, fried alligator stands, and drunkards of Bourbon Street."

Bamajan smiled. "The surface deceives. The Spanish style of this neighborhood is such that great courtyards with pools of deep quiet lie behind the gaudy facades. Are you interested in architecture?"

"Very much," said Nikola Tesla. "I have studied the construction of the heavens and have a fair idea of the complex layout of hell."

"Oh, my God! You are Dante Alighieri!" The Bamajan slapped the pate of his bald head. "I have studied your verses in school. It's a great honor *indeed!*"

"So how can my poor verses aid your enterprise?" asked Tesla, playing along.

"All skills are welcome and needed. Our leader has ordered the rapid collection of all the Great Minds in order to staff the coming messianic embassy."

"Your Messiah has arrived, then?"

"We cannot say with any certainty. The modest mission of our school is to welcome the Redeemer. Our seers tell us that he is among us now."

"I see." Tesla grinned and bent his head to gather his shimmering psychic shield tightly about him.

The Bamajan came out from behind his desk again and stood behind the inventor. He took Tesla's head between his hands and squeezed with searing strength. The force was such that all of Tesla's thoughts and memories rushed forward and would have been sucked out of him if his shield hadn't been in place. But the shield held and Tesla remained himself.

Bamajan then embraced him and said: "Welcome again! Welcome to the cause of our Redeemer!"

Tesla wondered how many Great Minds had already been captured by the cult. He did not believe the Bamajan's assertion that he was the first one. He wasn't sure what the cult's real purpose was, but they were clearly bent on capturing the Great Minds and coercing them to their cause.

"I know that you are a poet, a *great* poet, but you may not understand what I am about to show you. Computers did not exist in your time. Nonetheless, I would like your impression."

The screen behind him came to life and displayed a detailed map of the Louisiana chemical corridor. Certain areas, marking industries along the Mississippi River between New Orleans and Baton Rouge, were pulsing. Tesla was very familiar with the map because he'd been studying it for his own reasons.

"Isn't it beautiful? There are Bamajans working everywhere."

"You are right," conceded Tesla. "I do not know what I am seeing."

"Beautiful! Beautiful! 'I do not know what I am seeing!' Ah, poetry!"

No one objected when Tesla rose and headed for the door. He was not surprised that no one stopped him. They had perfect confidence in their technique. He shut the door behind himself and could hear the bald one even as he walked away: "Ah, poetry! What did I tell you! This is going to be fun!"

Tesla heard another voice, hoarse and growly, belonging no doubt to the man with the crooked crosses on his arm: "Shut the fuck up, cue ball! Poetry, my ass."

Tesla bumped into a man dressed in coat and tails. Under his arm was a conductor's baton.

"Where do you keep the female slaves?" Tesla wanted to know.

"The what? The dormitories are in the back, in the Lord's Hands Apartments."

Above one of the doors farther down the hall was written THE LORD'S HANDS APARTMENTS. Tesla opened it and struck gold. Felicity was kneeling on a prie-dieu, her eyes cast up at a crucifix, and singing. She looked sleepy but happy as inspired sounds bubbled like a brook out of her. A dreamy smile lit up her face. A faint hum like a distant beehive filled the room, the drone of other worshipers singing in other rooms. The whole building was filled with the instruments of many women's voices.

Nikola Tesla walked up behind Felicity Le Jeune and said softly, "I am an urban anchorite. I come to help you escape your bondage."

Felicity thought about this. For days now, her bonds had been slipping. She felt freer than she ever felt in her life. Was it possible to be even freer? Her heart filled again with the joy that no longer hurt when it flooded her, but poured simply in. She had been told that when the first stage of her training was completed she would be transported to Tara, where the beauty of the surroundings came close to what she would eventually encounter in heaven. After that, if her singing at Tara soared beyond her own expectation, she might earn the privilege of moving to the Dome. There was no earthly way to describe the Dome; it was the purest habitat yet created for the suffering soul. The greatest gospel choir ever assembled, one thousand strong, would be trying on its wings at the Dome. If she was nothing short of perfect she would herself be a part of it, and thus blessed to be among the first to behold the radiant face of the Redeemer. This thought unleashed such happiness in her, her entire body shook with prickly delight. Felicity was learning to surrender herself to the joy of this promised freedom. What an extraordinary program, she thought, as she looked eagerly up to Tesla. I wonder what comes next in my education of liberty.

"Are you here to take me to Tara?" she asked brightly, her green eyes glittering with grateful light.

"Quick," said Tesla. "Speed is of the essence."

Felicity allowed him to lead her to the stairway and out onto Bourbon Street. It was Christmas Eve, and evening already, but neither the date nor the time of day meant anything to the delirious mobs spilling out of bars and strip joints. A throng of drunken college boys were howling up at a bare-breasted woman on a balcony. The men carried large cups full of sloshing beer. One of them began to vomit on his shoes. Felicity blinked as the strobe effects of a bar hit her. The throb of disco music poured out of the place, and she was paralyzed by fear. She broke into a sweat and looked hopelessly at Tesla. The devil, with horns, hump, hair, hooves, red tongue, stood in the doorway of a club called OZ, dancing obscenely to the horrible thumping music. Tesla shrugged. He was reminded of carnival in Graz; the devil didn't bother him.

Felicity counterattacked:

> It came upon a midnight clear,
> That glorious song of old,
> From angels bending near the earth
> To touch their harps of gold:
> "Peace on the earth, goodwill to men,
> From heaven's all gracious King!"

Singing these words, she felt instantly better. She didn't know why the college boys began to stare at her instead of the bare-breasted woman. Instinctively she crossed her arms over her breasts.

"Please," Tesla begged her, "don't sing so loudly."

Felicity couldn't stop. She knew all the words to this divine song, and planted firmly on the sidewalk, she crooned:

> Yet with the woes of sin and strife
> The world has suffered long;
> Beneath the angel-strain have rolled
> Two thousand years of wrong;
> And man, at war with man, hears not
> The love-song which they bring.
> O hush the noise, ye men of strife,
> And hear the angels sing!

But the devils only got louder, and Felicity was compelled to soar above them:

> A virgin most pure, as the prophets do tell,
> Hath brought forth a Baby, as it hath befell.

And she knew that she was the Virgin most pure, and the molten hells were repulsed.

On and on the songs poured from her like water from a pitcher.

A woman in a yellow vinyl coat, wearing only one shoe, was distributing pamphlets to passersby. She handed one to Felicity and said through her tears, "Hallelujah, sister!" Still singing, and growing stronger, Felicity glanced at the pamphlet. It was entitled *What to Do in Case You Miss the Rapture!* Below those words was a red-winged devil standing on a replica of the Vatican, the word *Rome* dripping blood at his feet. It was the Antichrist. Written on the devil's chest were the numbers *666* and the word VISA.

The partner of the one-shoed woman, an evangelist hefting a huge wooden cross, interposed himself between Felicity and the mob. Screwed to the arms of the cross was a liquid crystal display panel across which ran the words of Jesus in blue. *I am the way, the truth, and the life. No one comes to the Father except through me.*

Tesla was amused by this contraption, and the evangelist, seeing his interest, explained: "I used to shout myself hoarse, but these sinners wouldn't listen. But they do *read*, praise the Lord's tools. I've been to China and Russia with this cross and put Jesus' words up there in their own languages. Amen."

Sure enough, one of the college boys who had stared wide eyed at the LCD panel now picked up a pamphlet from the street and tapped on the devil's chest. "Credit *is* the devil. You can't believe how much I charged on my Visa card this month!"

Another student snatched the pamphlet and read out loud, but without drowning Felicity's singing: " 'The Rapture is the immediate departure from this earth of over four million people in less than a fifth of a second. It is going to disrupt communications and transportation like no major war has done in the last hundred years.' "

"That's right!" shouted the one-shoed woman. "Everyone else is going to hell, you and all the babies born before Jesus came."

"I guess I'm going to hell," the drunk said doubtfully. "It says here, 'Whatever you do, DON'T MAKE ANY MARKS OR PRINTS ON YOUR FOREHEAD OR ON YOUR HANDS. This will not only give you leprosy eventually but will also guarantee you an eternity in the Lake of Fire for participating in Satan worship. A number connected with the number six-six-six will be attached to your Social Security number and to all your credit card numbers, and eventually you will have to show by electronic devices this number imprinted on your hand or on your forehead.' "

"Huh? What the hell does that mean?" wondered his friend.

"Don't get tattooed, I guess. Well, it's too late!"

> O holy night! The stars are brightly shining.
> It is the night of the dear Saviour's birth!
> Long lay the world, in sin and error pining,
> Till he appear'd, and the soul felt its worth.

" 'Your only chance of being saved after the Rapture,' " read the student to his fellows, " 'is to either starve to death or to get your HEAD CUT OFF'? Shit, that'll be tomorrow. I always feel like that in the morning."

The one-shoed evangelist was ecstatic. "Yeah, yeah. Sing, angel, sing." White bubbles appeared at the corners of her mouth.

"What's wrong with being fucked to death?" another student wanted to know.

Such scenes have a life of their own. A nest of Shades appeared, led by a Rasta man who preached to them as they fanned over the street: "The store of love, mon, the store of love is open, mon. The stocks are low in the store of love, mon. Them no selling love in the store of love, mon. Gotta put something on the shelves of the store of love, mon!"

One of the Shades shouted at a gawking tourist, "What you starin' at, man? These is the mysteries of New Orleans! Invest in the future! We need a po'boy!"

A big crowd had gathered around the preachers, and Tesla was growing desperate. That cop would be along any minute now, and he would never have Felicity to himself for even an hour. Desperate measures were called for. Tesla reached for his radio tool. A high pitch, like the agony of a dying animal, rose from his hand and broke into Felicity's song, "We've a story to tell to the nations . . ." But the word "nations" was never heard. The agonized pitch filled the air instead, and the revelers fell back, clutching their ears in terror.

Felicity looked about to faint. Tesla scooped her up by her waist, set her atop his shopping cart, and pushed her through the swaying crowd. He began to run as soon as they reached the corner of Dumaine, but as fewer and fewer people were to be seen, he slowed down. Atop the mound of his possessions, Felicity looked blank. She felt neither happy nor sad, but she was empty of song and felt indifferent.

When they passed the Ursuline convent, a crowd was dancing in the courtyard to the sounds of an R&B band. Tesla had heard on the street what the occasion was, and he explained it to Felicity:

"Bill Gates, the software tycoon, rented the convent for a Christmas

Eve party to showcase his version of the afterlife, www.afterlife.com. The people dancing in there are actually attending funerals at virtual cemeteries all over the world. The real mourners see these people's avatars looking somber and subdued, but as you can see, they are far from it. On the other hand, the dead, whose funerals are taking place, have been virtually revived and are present at this party. Their avatars are dancing while their bodies are being buried. They say that this Gates sets up demonstrations like this at many holy places around the world."

Tesla did not tell her that his informant had also told him that "the people who formerly worshiped in those holy places shake with anger at this technocratic assault on their beliefs, and their shaking goes into cats, which then attack people while they sleep. These cats must be strangled with bare hands when they approach, or else they kill one, body and soul." Tesla found this sort of thing reassuring but he didn't know if Felicity could understand.

In any case, only part of this explanation reached Felicity.

Watching her perched like a queen atop his cart, Tesla thought that her stillness resembled a condition he had experienced in his first human life, a form of hypnotic seizure induced by flickering light. In this state, Tesla was extremely receptive but incapable of speech. He had seen his greatest inventions fully developed during such trances. After an episode he would sometimes remain mute for several days. Tesla thought he recognized his disease in Felicity, and this endeared her to him even more. She is my sister, he decided. Definitely the magnet's missing piece.

He pushed his cart furiously at the edge of the Quarter, to the warehouse by the river. The crumbling building looked abandoned, but inside was a different story. The vast space that had once held bales of cotton bound for the East Coast and Europe now housed a complex greenhouse. Flowering tubs, pots, and trees, captured by Tesla's shopping-cart army, sprouted on every square inch. Vines intertwined in complex patterns from ceiling to floor, running the length of the building. The jungle flowed toward an opening in the wall, where Felicity could see shafts of light through the foliage. Felicity inhaled the rich and richly perfumed air and felt suddenly as if the vast floral interior started reaching in to take root in her.

Tesla led Felicity to a hammock inside the maze and pointed to the fuchsia clusters hanging above. He explained, "Those are vanilla flowers; they aid sleep."

Responding to the questioning plea in her eyes, Tesla continued: "You are inside a chlorophyll propulsion reactor. This greenhouse produces chlorophyll propulsion, a force I will shortly be testing. The plants are arranged in patterns that combine their various energies to produce the active chlorophyll stored in the node over there." He pointed to the opening. "The warehouse is a multipurpose object. Its primary objective is to clean up that marvelous river before they send Twain down. He'd never get over it."

"What river?" asked Felicity.

"Why, the Mississippi, of course." Tesla was astonished. What had they done to her? In his haste to impress her by his chivalry and skill, he had neglected to ask her some elementary questions.

"What is your name?"

"Scheherazade," Felicity said immediately. She liked this man. Cleaning up a river was work pleasing to God. But where was Tara? She missed her sisters and her singing.

"Are you an incarnate Mind?" Tesla's favorite book in his earthly life had been the *Thousand and One Nights*. In heaven he'd missed reading, even though he could meet any writer he wished, from any era of history. Information was also bountiful in heaven because angels were libraries. All one had to do is stop one of the myriad of these creatures and find out anything instantly. The abundance of riches had so bored him, he had dedicated his eternity to playing cards. He didn't think Felicity was an incarnate Mind, but her name had the ring of one.

"When do we go to Tara? I want to sing. Where is Joan? Amelia? When do they arrive?"

Whoever the creature was, she had been set on a narrow track. Tesla decided to finish explaining the purpose of the green machine, hoping to surprise her with the grandeur of his conception. Perhaps she was bored.

"The second mission of the chlorophyll propulsion reactor is to change the earth's magnetic field and to set it spinning the other way."

He waited for her to ask why, but when she didn't he went on.

"When the magnetic field is disturbed, all our ideas will change. What now appears urgent will seem quite unnecessary, and vice versa. A certain balance should be restored."

"The river," said Felicity, showing a spark of interest. "How can you clean the river?"

"The process requires stopping the chemical industry along the lower Mississippi," Tesla explained. "I will be using the river to conduct chlorophyll waves, which are similar to electricity. The river will become a live wire that will neutralize anything connected to it by metals. Using a similar machine, propelled by magnetic waves, I once produced lightning flashes measuring one hundred and thirty-five feet, from a distance of twenty-five miles. The chlorophyll currents will produce photokinetic ionization that will purify the water. The photosynthesis component . . ."

Felicity lay back on a canvas cot and closed her eyes. Everyone, it seemed, had a plan. She had none. She only wanted to sing the Lord's songs. She was tired. Tomorrow was the birthday of her Savior, Jesus Christ. Tomorrow, he was going to be born again in a stable to renew humanity's hope. The huge warehouse hummed around her with the breath of a million vegetal mouths. Behind her eyelids was a weary emptiness, a desert in which flowers were sinking sharp claws. It wasn't sleep, but it looked like sleep to Nikola Tesla, so he discontinued his explanation and let her rest.

The thick vines led the energy of the greenhouse into the ground-level hole in the wall and continued down to the Mississippi River. Tesla looked through it and admired again the wide-bodied stream that told the story of America. Felicity was a crucial part of his living monster. Her sleeping form was adjusting to a symbiotic relation with the vegetation, in order to eventually become the main circuit breaker. It occurred to Tesla to take a shadowgraph to see if she was human or an incarnate Mind, but then he banished the naughty thought. She was clearly human, as her humidity index, with its attending emotional weather, clearly showed. Tesla put away the humidity index tester and went about watering, fertilizing, talking to leaves and flowers, whistling, and rubbing sweet-olive into his hair, until he fell asleep.

Christmas 1999, a milky day, dawned. Felicity could hear barges making their way upriver. A foghorn sounded. She opened her eyes and beheld the anchorite asleep upright in a chair, with his left hand on a length of humming wisteria vine. She got up cautiously, feeling light as a feather. She floated out the warehouse door and looked around. The air off the river was rich, wet, muddy, streaked with smells of fish and gasoline. She was alone, sad, uprooted, without memory, and no longer free in song, yet she felt joy. Today in Bethelehem the Christ Child brought light to the world, and that light hadn't died. She did not notice the flow of green molecules stretching behind her like a dazzling viridian train.

Chapter Twenty-three

Wherein angel Zack takes a poll

n g e l Zack sat on a plume of smoke above Brennan's Restaurant and surveyed the Great Minds he had been given in keeping, for the purpose of assessing their opinions of the world. The reflections of the Minds were to be taken as yes and no votes for an eventual decision on the disposition of the planet. "All this 'assessing' and 'eventual'!" snarled Zack. "Nothing but bureaucracy and more bureaucracy! Ah, for a taste of old God the Father, swift decision maker, scourger of worlds, incinerator of lip givers! Democracy, my putti popo!"

Einstein flexed his tattooed biceps, zipped up his tight black jeans, and tucked them into scuffed Tony Lamas. He had just finished offering his new body to a customer inside a peep-show booth at Adult Videos on Bourbon Street and was $20 richer. He surveyed the tawdry surroundings the ironic heavens had cast him in and concluded: Humanity's continuing need for psychological degradation is a revolt against the demands of machinery, and it makes art necessary. Therefore the planet is still a very interesting place, and it ought to be preserved until the last hustler on Bourbon Street and the last showgirl on Place Pigalle die of boredom.

Einstein had cast his vote: keep the shithouse.

Zack sighed and noted it.

Ovid took advantage of the bank holiday and spent the morning in his office catching up on the news. He read the *Times-Picayune*, the *Christian Science Monitor*, *Time*, and the *Wall Street Journal* and tried to make sense of the following:

Gold was $2,000 an ounce. The dollar was worth 1.4 yen. The Securities Fraud Division of the U.S. Treasury had uncovered the greatest Wall Street fraud yet: a young broker had absconded with $100 billion, amassed as a result of profits on derivatives speculation; he had left behind only a smiley face on the company computer and the not-so-cryptic message THE END IS NEAR. THE WHEEL TURNS. In Russia the leaders in hiding of the Supreme Truth cult had revealed that they had purchased three fourteen-kiloton nuclear warheads, which they had positioned in Tokyo, New York, and Hong Kong. They requested the release of all their comrades imprisoned around the world, and a world leaders' summit in their Caucasus Mountains hideout in order to plan the orderly transition of humanity to the heavens during Armageddon. At the UFO convention in Corpus Christi, Texas, a man dressed as a nun sprayed the ballroom with a machine gun, killing ten convention goers. Outside of Texarcana, a miraculous image of Jesus, sans loincloth, hovered over an oil well and turned the sky orange. Witnesses tore off their clothes and refused to put them back on, even when the authorities turned on fire hoses. The huddled nude masses had been camping at the oil well, sure that they would be transported to heaven by the large orange Jesus. They were turning away food and water and drew close for warmth, singing hymns. A millennium party to end all millennium parties was being planned in New York with the hoped-for attendance of every major entertainment figure alive.

Ovid found the price of gold most shocking of all. He had once presented Claudia, the sixteen-year-old niece of Augustus, with a gold breastplate spun by the famed Behethomus. The splendid jewel left Claudia's breasts free so that he might delight in kissing them. He remembered the taste of the gold where it circled the base of her divine flesh. He had written a poem proposing that Claudia's breasts be made the new measure for the Roman wine cup because they were more perfect than Aphrodite's. And for such sublime ideas one got in trouble!

Ovid sighed. If this had been Rome, he would have had no qualms in calling for its end. It was a shame the way the empire treated its poets! But what did all these other things mean? Nuclear weapons, the Jesus . . . He suspected that weaponry had become a great art, but was it really possible that it had reached the stage he had achieved in the writing of the *Metamorphoses*? Had weapon makers truly reduced to nothing the abyss between matter and a poet's vision? If so, he had great respect for these artisans and would do his utmost to meet them. As for this Jesus, he guessed that he was a species of priest who went about scaring people with circus tricks. He had always disliked priests and had made a point to avoid even the Greek oracle when Augustus had once required him to travel there. He had feigned illness and spent a most pleasant time in bed with the emperor's wife. He was then exiled for it! Unjust men! Ill times! Uncouthness!

The most satisfying item was the party of parties at the end of this time they called Christian, doubtless after some forgotten emperor born long after Ovid had died. Ovid wanted to attend this party. Here, he felt, he would at long last meet his peers, those new poets who had advanced and polished the art. He would bask in their admiration of him and receive golden laurels. Ovid leaned back in his uncomfortable banker's settee and read some of the names who'd promised to attend: Dolly Parton, Wayne Newton, Madonna, Trent Reznor, Chef Paul Prudhomme, Angelique Risotto . . . Yes, he would definitely be there.

Another one says yes, sighed Zack.

At the Napoleon House, Nostradamus had just delivered an antipasto plate and a Dixie beer to a rude bald man, and considered throttling him. The man looked Greek or Albanian; an ugly purple birthmark rose over his left eye. In his visions of the future, Nostradamus had often beheld the sorry remains of the once-noble Greek race moving aimlessly among throbbing lights and cacophonous music between the ruined stones of ancient temples. This terrible vision had come to pass, but never in his lifetime of dreaming the future had he imagined becoming a servant to such men. In addition to the destruction of mighty kingdoms and the annihilation of great cities, people had suffered the corruption of the better part of their souls. There wasn't much nobility left in them; they were worse than animals. Might as well mop up the mess.

Nostradamus slammed down his tray and wished humanity gone.

That's a no, recorded Zack.

•

Napoleon had tapped for five hours straight until the beer tops glued to his left sneaker had come off. In anticipation of just such an emergency he had spent the previous evening scouring trash containers. He had over a hundred beer tops in his backpack. He sat on a stoop, took off his shoe, and started hammering new taps in place. Crowds of yuppies and wanna-bes had staggered by with open alcohol containers, paying no attention whatsoever to the fifteen-year-old boy practicing his craft. Fools, Napoleon thought grimly. One day I will be richer than all of you. I will own *your* shoes. He had been saving all the coins tourists had tossed into the cardboard box at his feet. He already had $80, which he planned to use toward the purchase of a shoeshine stand. He had already spoken to a number of boys who would be paying him a percentage of their profits in exchange for affixing taps to their shoes. In the future, he would purchase a number of shoeshine stands for them and get a percentage of those prof-its, too. He had studied also the pimping business and had some hopes in that direction as soon as all his pubic hair came in. But this was only the beginning.

After Napoleon was finished with his sneaker, he took a few minutes off his schedule to read his favorite strategy manual, *A Primer of Management* by A. T. D. Holmes. "The philosophy of management is philosophy," he made out. "It encompasses the entire philosophical tradition because a corporation is a world."

Napoleon had already read the introductory chapter, which described the corporate world as having the same characteristics as the natural world. It had an ecology, seasonal cycles, storms, predators, victims, and architecture. Its laws, though related to those of earth, were in fact differ-ent. A good businessman was less like a god and more like an accurate forecaster, and Napoleon knew that he had what it takes to succeed. He couldn't wait for the future.

Another yes, sighed Zack. He did not like the way things were going. If the majority voted yes, or even if it was a tie, he would have no choice but to incarnate. There were still 329 Great Minds to poll, and most of them were still having difficulty adjusting to their new bodies. Oh, miserable democratic heavens! Zack longed again for the days when the Supreme Deity made all the decisions. This democracy stuff was for the birds.

•

Dante noticed two filthy pigeons pecking at a plastic bag filled with a white powder. Some junkie'd dropped his stash on the street, and now the damn pigeons would be stoned. Walking the beat, he had already re-marked on the astounding resemblance of this modern city to his system of hell. His patrolman's uniform was too tight, and his feet hurt. He no longer felt like a guest in the netherworld but rather a bona fide resident. He reviewed his days on earth. The dirty bookstores and the strip joints were crammed full of drunken sots burning in the guilty fires of their own souls. Small-time criminals addicted to chemical punishments were stag-gering toward mirages and hallucinations. Dante could identify the cate-gory of sin each soul was doomed to suffer for, but he was not pleased by the fulfillment of his poetic vision. No Virgil or Beatrice lived on these shores. He had been abandoned and he knew not why. He quoted, in vain, the verses that once explained both emptiness and fullness: *"La gloria di colui che tutto move per l'universo penetra, e risplende in una parte più e meno altrove."* The glory of him who moves all things permeates the universe but glows in one part more and in another less.

"It glows no longer; it is extinguished," he said out loud, but then he saw flames and hastened toward them.

A building was burning on Bourbon Street. A tall patrolman ordered him roughly to keep the rubbernecking crowd away from the yellow tape. Dante watched the tongues of flame leap out of the crackling timbers and saw his future: every day, he would be drafted in this manner to watch over disasters he could neither prevent nor understand. It would be better, re-flected the glum policeman, if all future disasters were combined into a single one, a magnificent end. If there was any way to wipe the slate clean, he would compose the divine verses that would hasten such an outcome.

Dante wished for cleansing flames.

"Good," said Zack. "There is hope yet."

Karl Marx had volunteered for overtime on Christmas Day to get away from the frighteningly large wife that came with the package he'd been given. His fellow crew members were three mean white men, a group of ruffians who had all recently been paroled from the federal penitentiary at Angola. They seemed determined to not do a lick of work on the busted gas main they had been assigned to, which meant that Marx was doing all the digging by himself, while they drank beer and made fun of his clumsi-ness.

The working class had surely degenerated since 1856. The mere existence of such menial work in the late days of postcapitalism meant that something had gone woefully wrong in the logic of history. Marx wished that he was in a pub in London, discussing the matter with Engels. He would have liked, in fact, to be anywhere but in this city, grunting behind a shovel while scooping large portions of black mud in a ditch. Engels might have provided an insight to the paradox of a seemingly boundless affluence brought about by laborsaving gadgets that did not, however, lessen exploitation in any way. He had not given sufficient thought to the problem of time in *Das Kapital.* The alienation he had predicted had occurred, but humanity's revolutionary impulses had been dulled along the way by unpredictable factors. A vast extortion of time was taking place in postindustrial society, a type of metaphysical exploitation that surpassed his wildest imaginings. Not that he needed to worry about post-anything in his current position, covered with sweat, racially demeaned, physically tormented, and intellectually isolated. Was there truly a progression toward a better future, or had he, as his enemies implied, been misled by the stubborn utopian messianism of his Jewish genes? Marx wished he knew.

"Undecided," recorded Zack.

Twice, when there were no customers, Plato had examined the Voodoo Wax Museum. He had been particularly fascinated by the exhibit of Marie Laveau by the shore of Bayou Saint John, leading slaves in song. A small fire sizzled with offerings of bones. The slaves had their eyes rolled up to the heavens while the high priestess, with her mouth wide open, intoned the words. Improvised altars littered the grass, and Plato was able to make out beads, small dead birds, glasses with amber liquids in them, crudely carved crosses, and pipes. Everything, even the smoke, was perfect to the last detail. Plato had never seen such lifelike resemblances, though he had been acquainted with the work of the greatest sculptors of antiquity. He gazed long at these figures and could not make up his mind whether they were representations of things past or the archetypes themselves, frozen in eternity. He had always thought that the archetypes, in order to give birth to the world, would have had to stand still in order both to embody their ideas and to serve as models. Motion, to his understanding, was a property of representation. The stillness of the archetypes had always soothed him, and he felt something akin to such satisfaction now. On the other hand, if this scene was a reproduction of something already past, it was only a representation of a representation, and thus twice removed from the arche-types.

Last time he had contemplated the figurines, Plato had been inter-rupted by the front door buzzer and had been unable to continue his re-flections. After the customer left, Plato'd picked up the thread of his thought, but once again was unable to conclude anything. If the figures in the glass case were archetypes, then it was necessary to wait patiently for the time when they would begin to produce representations. When the cycle of representations was at an end, the archetypes would release the pure ideas that they embodied. But if the perfect figurines were already representations, there was no need at all for this pale imitation of a world.

Plato voted maybe, pending the completion of his thought.

Not much help to Zack.

Chapter Twenty-four

Wherein Major Notz encounters a musical slave trader and practices vigilantism

a j o r Notz didn't just watch the slave trade in Jackson Square from his balcony in the Pontalba Building. He photographed it with the aid of a powerful telephoto lens. After a second day had passed and Felicity was still missing, the major donned a special forces jacket and cap without insignia or rank bars. He obtained an iced coffee at La Madeleine and went to the Moonwalk to see Bamajan.

The trumpeter was a thin black man with a graying goatee, the trademark of his profession. His mouth connected with his instrument like one pipe fitted to another. Tourists loved him. They stuffed dollar bills into a battered instrument case stickered with the names of cities he'd played. Paris. Amsterdam. Tokyo. He provided his audience with everything that the jazz-musician-shaped hole in their heads required. Bamajan was loose and playful and blew visible notes into the wet, velvet-heavy air. Behind him the Mississippi River curled and rolled in perfect counterpoint. A Greek tanker was anchored in the channel and an old-fashioned riverboat glided around the bend. Algiers Point glittered, sending shafts of light over the river.

"I thought maybe the Mississippi was bigger, maybe because of Huck Finn," a freckled German tourist with three cameras around his neck said to the major. "But," he said, pointing at Bamajan, "he makes it big, bigger, like the Rhine."

"*Yawohl.*" The Major nodded. He waited patiently for the better part of an hour until the musician finally put down his instrument. The major pushed his formidable flesh forward until he completely obscured the thin trumpeter.

"It would give me great pleasure to offer you lunch."

Bamajan was about to refuse until he met the major's flinty stare. "You the law?" he asked.

"More than you can imagine," the major answered, and ushered him down the steps.

At Johnny's the musician ordered the french fry po'boy with gravy, an original New Orleans entry in the heart-attack sweepstakes. It was a favorite of practitioners of "clogging," so called by musicians high on heroin who ate through messes of burgers, fries, and gravy until their arteries were clogged by cholesterol.

"Five years ago," the major began as Bamajan downed in two bites half of his sandwich, "you were detained for a week as a prime suspect in the Kashmir Birani case, but you were released for lack of evidence."

"Hey, man. Fucking history. What's your point?" Bamajan wiped the gravy from his goatee.

"Periodically you are visited by law-enforcement personnel and reporters. For a while, the police taped all your music. You are on nine kinds of medication to control your visions. Correct?"

"Man, you barfing up the wrong shoe. Who gives a fuck?"

"Nobody to this point. But"—the major laid a fat dolorous arm between the plates—"you've been selling dope and girls. Now my niece is gone. I'm going to show you her picture. You look at it long and hard and then you talk to me."

The major held out a snapshot of Felicity.

"Yeah," Bamajan said, without inspecting the photo, "I do recall selling a chick to some dude in a cape . . . Oh, yeah, he had wings, I think."

"I am extremely sorry about your attitude, Mr. Bamajan. The nine types of medication must not be working very well. I ask you again, think."

This time the musician looked. The heavy dude was serious. Of course he knew the girl. She'd been Miles's chick. Sweet Miles, who got too greedy with the stuff and bought the big gig. Bamajan had been depressed ever since he'd sold Miles the stuff that killed him. He'd loved the piano player. A great talent. Fucked-up world. And this girl, whatever her name was, now she was in trouble. He'd have to help her. A small favor for Miles. But he wouldn't help this creep.

Three gold rings glittered on Notz's left hand. One in particular made an impression on Bamajan. He had seen one like it before; a death-dealing Jamaican wore it. It was a snake twined around a cross.

"I never saw this chick before," Bamajan said and started to get up from the table.

But the major laid a strong hand on his shoulder; he sat back down.

"What kind of man goes around selling people?"

"Slavery's back." The musician nodded gravely.

"Slavery's back? As in, the sixties are back? Disco is back? What do you mean, it's back?"

"Everybody does it, everybody has it, everybody's got to do it once at least," he sang. Lowering his voice, he said, "It's the drug of the millennium. I sold this chick—not the one in your picture, another one—to a dude wearing wings in a church on Ramparts Street lit up by nekkid women holding candles. They had a nekkid pope, too, and the bishops were nekkid, and a bunch of nasty nekkid cops. I swear. I've never seen nothin' like it. They give me a bag of gold for the chick, but it turn to shit when the cats return me to the street. I swear."

"Bamajan, I've seen you selling girls right in the square."

"Just whores, Captain. I'm talking slaves here. There is great danger in the world now slavery's back. I admit it. Tell you something else . . ." He had to throw the captain a bone. "You know the SMD over on Bourbon? Church of Messiah or something? They've been buying and they likes 'em young, just like the fuckin' perverts."

"What do they do with them?"

"That's it, man. Nobody fucks them. They make 'em sing."

"Who's the boss over there?"

"The devil, I think. But word is that TV preacher Elvis owns it. They say he owns strip joints too. One twisted motherfucker."

Mullin was becoming careless, and his vices were beginning to get on the major's nerves. He had too many businesses, indulged too many private fantasies. But Mullin certainly wouldn't risk holding Felicity in the heart of the Quarter with a bunch of brainwashed chorus girls. Even he wouldn't be that stupid.

"You got any letters, man?" asked Bamajan.

The major tried not to reveal his confusion. What letters? A new kind of drug? He doubted if Bamajan was asking him about his schooling. Then

he remembered that lately he'd seen people with letters tattooed on them.
Not just Shades. Men in suits, housewives. They were everywhere. The
bartender at Molly's had an *O* on his forehead and an *M* on his chest.

"Not really," he said cautiously.

"That's good." Bamajan whispered. "The letter peoples is multiplying.
They waitin' for the day when they gonna line up and make up a sentence
dictated by the devil. I seen the devil . . . He's fixin' to speak! The slaves
are *food.*"

Notz was growing impatient with the man's raving.

"We're going to take a little trip to your place. I think you need your
medication."

Conflicting impulses tugged at the musician. He needed to get away to
do some looking for Felicity on his own. He wanted to know what this soldier knew about him. He also felt the need for a little fix.

The flophouse on Saint Charles had seen better days. Dark molding and
the grand staircase remained from its former life as the residence of a rubber baron. The rooms had rickety doors with big black numbers painted on
them. On the second floor, No. 17 was unlocked. Inside was a white iron
bed, a small desk, and an overstuffed chair piled high with clothes and
shoes. The floor and the bed were buried under newspapers, more clothes,
parts of musical instruments, and pictures cut out of magazines. A stench of
half-eaten cans of cat food was mixed with the odor of rotting oranges.

"I feed the hotel cat. His name's Aspirin," apologized Bamajan. "That's
his stuff." He pointed under the desk, where a scratch post shared space
with a kitty tray. On cue, Aspirin came in through the open window. He
was a large, ragged, one-eyed striped tomcat with a no-nonsense manner.
He leapt up on the desk over his stuff.

"You two talk," said Bamajan. "I'll be back."

Leaving the door open, he headed for what the major suspected was the
hallway bathroom.

When he tried to pat Aspirin, the cat bristled.

"You sinister demon! How's this grab you?" The major picked up a
high-heeled shoe from the floor. Aspirin flew to the windowsill, arched his
back, and hissed. Notz inspected the mess on the desk: a dirty black T-
shirt, a torn paperback of *The Prophecies of Nostradamus*, a cardboard pizza
box with a petrified slice still in it, sheet music, a pile of photographs.
Standing in front of Café Istambul with their arms around each other, two
musicians grinned at the world. Miles and Bamajan. The major sighed. So
that's how it was.

Bamajan came back high. His eyes shone as he headed for the bed. He had taken off his pants, and a pair of skinny legs stuck out of a pair of striped shorts, open in front. There was something white in his hand. "My teeth," he mumbled.

The major looked at the pathetic figure on the bed. "You killed your best friend, didn't you?"

"No, man," said Bamajan. "He got greedy. He lost his freedom, Soldier." He closed his eyes.

The major nodded sadly to the musician's unconscious form. He sighed and removed a small gold-plated automatic from his side pocket and fitted on the silencer. He put the barrel against the musician's temple and squeezed the trigger. A black-edged red rose opened in Bamajan's head. A rose for Miles. Major Notz put the gun back in his pocket and lit a cigar.

Grotten's stank of beer and vomit—two stages of the same stink, really—and the connoisseur might easily discern the brand: Blackened Voodoo Apocalypse beer, the latest in a series. The pings and sighs of the poker machines tended to by hollow-eyed video-crack junkies made the air as holey as the noses, lips, and tongues of the studded clientele. The slashed leather stools had been re-covered many times. Trapped sweat and urine squished between the layers at every lurch.

Under the excrescences of mucus, viscera, blood, and the traces of delirium tremens, there was wood. Grotten's was the terminus for preinternable creatures, a screening room for the Hummingbird Hotel and Charity Hospital. Criminals, cops, retailers of every flavor, and underaged drinkers all used it for headquarters. On any given night, several novels' worth of secondary characters slid or crawled through. For a quarter you could get a video-poker tan. For ten bucks, somebody's mother. It was also the clearinghouse for everything that went down in the street.

The late afternoon sun looked cautiously in and turned the scene, briefly, to gold. The television, always on, was blaring a special news bulletin. Special bulletins were as frequent nowadays as commercials. Earthquakes. Fires. Sieges. Self-immolation. Suicide bombings. Hostage taking. The clientele of Grotten's paid no attention.

Joe sat gingerly on the last stool at the end of the bar. Joe motioned to the bartender, Spike, who greeted the policeman with an ebullient "What the hell's going on, Joe? I never heard anything like it."

Eight dope dealers had been killed in New Orleans over the holiday.

Even in a city as blasé as the Big Easy, this was a bit much. They had each been shot at close range with a small-caliber gun. They had all been high when they were killed.

Joe watched the television for a minute.

Spike ground his half-smoked Optimo into the epidermal floor and explained that Grotten's, in his opinion, would survive the End of the World for the simple reason that nobody inside the place would even know that the End had occurred.

The special bulletin had to do with a young girl en route to the United States from Tel Aviv who had single-handedly defused a bomb carried on board the jetliner by an Iranian terrorist. The plane was expected to land at any moment at the Atlanta airport, where hundreds of reporters milled about waiting to interview the amazing young heroine.

"Welcome to the New World," said Spike. "They'll freak the poor thing so bad she'll shit. She might join an outfit like SMD just to get away from the fucking media!"

"People." Joe shook his head. "SMD. Haven't heard of that one."

Spike explained: "Happiest place on earth. Girls only. They go in tone deaf and nymphomaniacal, start singing and acting modest. After a while they disappear. Word is they get distributed to harems in the Persian Gulf emirates. They get fucked while singing. Anything for oil. SMD is run by Exxon."

"Whoa!" said Joe. "I know this chain of thought. Give it up. You have nothing to lose but your chains."

But SMD was news to him. It was amazing how much faster than the police the street telegraph was.

"Tell you what, though," said Spike. "Girl like that, wouldn't mind dating her. Motherfucker comes up, she'd take him just like that. Defuse his bomb, har, har."

Like Felicity, Joe thought. Where the hell was she? He hadn't come into Grotten's to investigate the murders of drug-dealing slavers, as Spike had assumed. He was still looking for Felicity. Hopefully there was no connection between the killings and the girl. One of the murdered dealers was the musician Bamajan, who had been connected to Felicity through Miles. Joe found himself secretly cheering the vigilantes. After all, the dealers were scum. He only hoped that Felicity wasn't caught in the middle of this underground war.

•

The gate to the SMD quarters on Bourbon was wide open. Joe unsnapped the holster of his service revolver and climbed the staircase to the second story, where it became evident that the place had been vacated in a hurry. The floors were littered with papers and clothes. One large room stared at him with the empty eyes of computer screens. The cords had been ripped out of the wall and lay coiled all over the place like dead snakes. It looked like a school raided by a gang. Joe had seen a school like that once, in the projects. Scorched maps, broken desks. But this place gave him the creeps. This was no innocent place of learning.

There was an odd smell of burnt leaves in the air, which Joe, a non-smoker, took a second to identify. The wake of an expensive cigar. Whoever the smoker was, he was already gone. He must have been there shortly before Joe and walked through the abandoned school slowly, long enough to leave this bitter smell behind. The smell waned as he followed it down a corridor bearing the inscription, THE LORD'S HANDS APARTMENTS. At the end of this hall was an iron staircase. Joe climbed it, opened the door there, and the cigar smell hit him as hard as if someone had blown it directly in his face. The smell was compounded by something sickening, like burning hair and frying grease. Joe took his gun out of the holster.

The room was void of living presence, but lying facedown on the parquet floor in front of a school desk were the nude bodies of two men. One of them was covered with tattooed swastikas. The other was brown and had a round ass. Joe kneeled to examine the corpses and saw that the backs of the men's necks bore fresh burns made with a cigar. But the cause of death in each case was the small-caliber bullet holes in the temple.

"Jeezus Christ!" Joe exclaimed, recognizing the two nude prowlers he had busted at Felicity's behest the night he had met her. "You two just can't keep your clothes on."

Chapter Twenty-five

*Wherein we follow the passage of Andrea from the
Old World to the New, while Felicity wanders
in the desert of her own city*

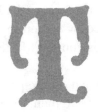h e middle seat in the middle row was the worst seat
on the old airbus. Andrea felt pinned there like a but-
terfly. On her left sat a huge man, a tower of flesh that
spilled into her over the armrest between them. He
wore a thick purple turban on his massive head. Andrea
guessed that he was a merchant, a human abacus. He
smelled like an old crocodile-skin wallet. The flesh of his thigh touched
her like the sticky underside of a huge snail. She drew as far away from
him as she could.

Happily, Ben sat at her right hand, and he smelled like parsnips and
iron. I am a spider, not a butterfly. Andrea put out a long sticky thread and
wrapped Ben in her cocoon. Unaware that he'd just been cocooned, Ben
got up and strolled forward toward the rest rooms. Andrea was left alone
with the merchant, whom she imagined enthroned in a rattan chair, his
rolls of fat quivering while veiled concubines massaged his obese toes. She
had seen this in the old film *Star Wars*. She resolved to turn into a Gorgon,
with a headful of hissing snakes, so that if he looked at her, he'd turn to
stone.

"Are you going home, young lady?" The man spoke in English.

"Oh, no, kind sir. I am hoping that a distant relative will care for me in
America. I am from Russia, from Saint Petersburg. Since our country broke

up, things have gotten worse and worse. I was a member of the Komsomol, you understand." Andrea invented breathlessly, not looking at the man.

"Where are your parents?"

"They went to Finland to work in an oil refinery. There was an explosion. After that . . ." Andrea hung her head and felt the fleshy monster's humid orbs alight on her neck like two slugs on a cabbage leaf. The flesh of his thigh burned. Droplets of sweat burst from under his turban. In his pocket his hand clutched a fat roll of banknotes. Andrea saw through him as through a shop window. A chill crept through her. The man was a soul buyer. Souls, she knew, were for sale now by the ton; it was a buyer's market. They were no longer sold by the gram or the ounce with pacts writ in flame as in the time of the hapless Dr. Faust. Today, Fausts by the thousands waited hat in hand for a man like this. When he finally spoke she had already guessed what he was going to say.

"For the first few days, before you are settled, perhaps you would accept my hospitality. In Detroit, I own several buildings . . ."

The fleshy monster opened his briefcase to extract a roll of mints, and Andrea saw stacks of banknotes from different countries, including Russian rubles.

"You have so much strange money!" Andrea was sure now.

"I own buildings in Detroit, Moscow, Kiev, and Tashkent. I take the rent money and fly to more cities to buy more buildings. I know it's hard to believe, but I don't have a place of my own. I am always flying."

He didn't buy only buildings. He had just offered to buy her.

"Oh, here is my fiancé," she said as Ben returned to his seat. "He is very, very rich. But thank you, anyway."

Andrea craned her neck to see who was sitting to the left of the turbaned Satan. It was a veiled woman who snored. She exuded Calvin Klein Obsession and sweat, and her veil billowed with each snore like a sail. At her feet yawned a Gucci carry-on that Andrea imagined was full of cosmetics and romance novels.

Next to the veiled woman sat a large, clean-cut American boy, reading a well-worn Bible. Andrea squeezed out of her seat toward the aisle. As she maneuvered past the American boy she pushed her lower lip forward and said with a pout, "God, I wish I'd brought my Bible! There is nothing to do for the next eleven million hours!" Her knee touched the pointy bone of the boy's knee.

Surprised, he lifted his cornflower blue gaze directly at her nipples, poking through her T-shirt hard as organ stops.

"Well, this is it . . . the Bible. I mean, I read it. Since I seen the birth-place of our Lord it's got new meanings. I'm in the United Ministries of Love." He gestured toward the rest of the group, which was scattered throughout the plane. His earnest face showed concern for every penny sacrificed by those who'd saved to send him to the Holy Land.

Andrea got a book called *Insatiability* from the bin labeled *Novels*, and returned to her seat. On the way back, she looked at the boy, leaving him the full promissory charge of her deep green eyes.

The turbaned man, who'd watched the exchange with interest, said in a whisper: "Do not be deceived by their guileless faces. Their young bodies are strong and muscular, but it's survivalist training. Their eyes are trained to spot fire, flood, annihilation signs. They are superalert to what they see as the devil's agents—Jews, foreigners, liberals, commies, Negroes, Is-lamic people, atheists, multiculturalists, the FBI, the ATF, bankers, femi-nists. They live only for salvation, the Second Coming, the reward of Rapture. They believe in Jesus, UFOs, decency, honest banking, and their right to buy assault weapons."

Andrea looked astonished.

"I was trained as a sociologist," he explained modestly.

Without waiting for any further reaction from her, he took a thick black book from his briefcase marked ACCOUNTS. He uncapped a Mont Blanc pen and set its gold nib to work on a new page.

Andrea had a creepy feeling that he was entering a report on her into his book. It wasn't a new feeling. It was partly the reason why she changed her story as often as possible. The world was peppered with file starters who could speak eloquently on any subject, who had university degrees in every field, who worked in every industry. No matter how seemingly be-nign, they were all police, which was to say, surveillance, arrest, camps, snapping dogs, cattle prods. Her parents were probably not dead at all; they had simply been shut inside a file inside a huge computer controlled by learned men who employed Orthodox priests, Iranian mullahs, and Christian missionaries to further their studies. Oh, stop, she told herself. You're hungry and you have to pee. She felt a little-girl tantrum coming on. Ben had fallen asleep.

Felicity stayed seven days at Tesla's warehouse, helping him water, weed, trim, and pollinate. Sometimes she followed him to bars, where he emp-tied the video-poker machines using a system he had devised. One day she watched him play blackjack at the casino and win thousands of dollars. He bought exotic blooms with the money, and Felicity helped him load his shopping cart. At night she listened to the boats on the river and stretched like a cat, feeling green power flowing through her and bonding to her cells.

On New Year's Eve 1999, Felicity strolled through the French Quarter in full view of tourists, freaks, shades, cops, barkers, hustlers. She was no longer wearing her white gown, but a man's shirt and pants that Tesla had rummaged for her on the street. It was drizzling, and lights glowed from every window. The clip-clop of the mules pulling tourist carriages over the cobblestones was muted, as if someone had wrapped their hooves in cotton. Old men walked home in the mist with baguettes sticking out of their brown bags like phalluses. Black generals of a nonexistent African kingdom, resplendent in gold epaulets, brass buttons, silver braid, and chef's hats, stood outlined in the doorways of restaurants, distributing menus to tourists. Mimes, tappers, and hustlers were at work in their customary spots on the sidewalks. And of course, the blue notes of a horn spilled from a recessed doorway.

The shrimp Creole at Coop's had been Felicity's favorite. The peppers, tomatoes, and shrimp weren't overcooked; you could taste the bay leaf; and they didn't overdo the cayenne. Felicity knew this, but it was unconnected knowledge, like a piece of paper picked up by wind. She didn't know what it had to do with her.

Her senses were keen. She could smell fresh beignets and chicory coffee from Café du Monde; rosemary baked chicken from Irene's; wet dog leading blind (and blind-drunk) beggar; crawfish and crab bisque out of Tujague's; sweaty tourist; dry cumin, bay leaf, pepper, and prosciutto plus olive salad at the Progresso grocery; cigars and newsprint from Sidney's Newsstand; mule shit; roasting coffee at Kaldi's; vanilla-scented hooker, spent firecrackers, beer, rotting crawfish. By the time she walked the length of Decatur, she had worked up an appetite.

In front of Dead Star Books, a crowd of cadaverous youth dressed in black crinoline waited sullenly for Angelique Risotto, the queen of gothic. Her novels of bloodsucking had a huge following of pale, listless death lovers. She owned lots of real estate, including numerous churches, behind which she garaged the hearses that took her to book signings. The release of a new book was typically celebrated by an appearance in a coffin carried by pallbearers, from which she would leap in a red wedding dress. Angelique was as huge as a whale, and many of her starved followers looked as if they'd been half eaten by Angelique. Felicity crossed the street to give them a wide berth.

The pilot announced that year 2000 had just arrived somewhere over the Atlantic. It was already year 2000 in Israel. Over the course of the next eight hours, the captain greeted New Year's several times, underscoring time's slippery dimension and, Andrea supposed, the roundness of the earth.

Dinner came.

Carroty orange baby penises surrounded a round burnt beef medallion. Wrinkled green peas swam toward shreds of wilted lettuce and fragments of cucumber. A blue-veined sauce in a plastic cup sat on the tray. A hard roll and a square of soggy cake leered up.

Andrea had always eaten whatever she'd been given or managed to scrounge. Black bread with a bit of butter or a dollop of sour cream was her favorite. She also loved raw carrots and scallions, wedges of tomato and cucumbers with salt, and apples, cherries, and peaches. She admired oranges and ate them very slowly, sucking each slice and holding the rest in her hand like a small sun. In truth, she was in awe of oranges. During the siege of Sarajevo she had carried a small orange in the pocket of her peacoat wherever she went. When she was deported she took it out and shared it with the other people on the truck. The orange hadn't decayed at all, and there were enough slices for lots of people. She was not particularly fond of rice, but she ate it with a bit of gravy all the same. She liked cornmeal mush and cakes with salt and onions and cheese, if there was any. Goat cheese was her favorite, particularly goat cheese from Montenegro, where the fiercest and saltiest goats lived. She'd had marinated fish in tin cans and once or twice freshly caught fish from the sea. She'd also enjoyed baked chicken with rosemary, and goat shish kebab, beef stew with new potatoes, fried cow's liver with salt and paprika, pork sausages, lamb brains, and chicken gizzards. After she saw the dog eating brains in Sarajevo, she thought she'd never eat meat again. But she did. She'd do whatever it took to sustain life.

But the airline meal presented a challenge. For the first time in her memory she felt repelled by the idea of meat. The medallion looked to her as if it were taken from a cow with an ice cream scoop. She could plainly see the animal, grazing in a pasture pockmarked by bomb craters. It looked up at her, its round eyes placid but insistent. The animal's sides had scoops taken from them, resembling the cratered pasture. Go away, Andrea said. Obediently, the cow lifted up into the air, a clumsy dirigible, and vanished from her sight. But the burnt meat remained on her tray, solid, congealed, dark. Humanity, it said, is so much bleak meat. She felt sorrow within her own meat, as if the dead matter had triggered death in her body. Waves of compassion, disgust, and fear washed through her. She picked up her knife and fork to cut into the slab, but she put them down. She couldn't.

The fat man, who had been watching her struggle with some interest, pointed to his own special Hindu vegetarian curry dinner, and said: "You can order vegetarian if you call ahead. Would you like to share my humble rice?"

Andrea thanked him and added: "I am not a vegetarian. I'm not sure what it is."

"You should be vegetarian, my friend. When meat eaters die they go to a special hell where they are surrounded by animals with missing parts . . . chickens without breasts . . . cows without rumps . . . pigs without bellies. The animals scream for eternity for their missing parts, and the sinner must listen for many thousands and thousands of years."

Ugh. Andrea shuddered and pushed away her tray.

Yehuda ben Yehuda hadn't touched his food, because he was afraid that it might not be kosher, though the stewardess assured him that it was. He was in love; he didn't have any appetite. He and Andrea looked at each other, then back at the food, and burst out laughing.

"I will eat your butt," he whispered in her ear.

"My butt is a very expensive restaurant," she whispered back.

Tee-hee. Tee-hee. The young people couldn't stop laughing. They laughed so hard their trays jiggled and the solemn meat shook. The orange baby penises rolled helplessly about.

I will never eat the meat of dead animals again, Andrea promised herself. From this moment on, the flesh of animals will never pass my lips again.

Strangely, the entire plane seemed to share her revulsion. The stewardess ended up taking back over forty untouched scoops of cow. Not even the hungry evangelical boys ate any. It was hard to say whether this collective reaction was connected to Andrea or to the airplane's having just flown into some kind of heavenly vegetarian belt inhabited by fruitarian angels. Nonetheless, Andrea felt some satisfaction and took a bit of credit for it.

Chapter Twenty-six

Wherein Felicity learns about the Language Crystal. Andrea and Ben's flight is seized by eros.

 e l i c i t y would have wandered all the way to Canal Street if she hadn't been stopped by a startling shopwindow. Displayed there was an African fetish—a woman with several pairs of breasts and a polished pregnant belly, pierced by thousands of rusty nails everywhere except the eyes. Next to it a whip with small bells along the strands was draped over a carved wooden phallus.

New Orleans had adopted the vampire as its mascot, despite protests from the Catholic Church. The undead were good business. Manteaux was a ritual art shop that specialized in looted African fetishes, local voodoo objects, and contemporary creep art. Rich vampirophiles roamed the Quarter seeking artifacts of this kind. But the stuff sold at Manteaux went beyond boosterism. An entire shelf held reliquaries containing pieces of saints—a tooth, an ear, a piece of bone. Saint Hildegard's knuckle rested at the bottom of an open velvet box; or so the brass plate captioned it. A two-headed fetus floated in yellow liquid inside a plastic jar.

Felicity walked in the door, setting off a sinister little tin clapper.

She asked the bald man behind the counter about the figure pierced with nails. He put a half-smoked cigar into a heart-shaped bronze ashtray and licked the bottom of a luxuriant Stalinesque mustache before answering in a thick accent.

"That African fetish is one of my very best. It's like the witch hurt every part of her except the eyes, the better to make her suffer. My accent is Albanian, in case you are wondering."

"I was, but I don't know Albanians. And the whip with the bells?"

"Interested? Australian. They call that a bull-roarer. It's an Aborigine telephone. They talk to their gods on it. But if you wanted to use it for something else"—the man winked—"you could."

The bald Albanian's eyebrows met over the bridge of his nose like two angry caterpillars.

"Sit, sit." He knocked a beaded fetish off a tall three-legged stool and invited her to perch. Behind her crouched a South Asian demon with gold smoke pouring out of his ornamental nostrils. A Tibetan prayer wheel hung over her head. The walls and ceiling teemed with shrunken heads, human bones, blood-caked fetishes, stuffed snakes, giant eggs, and primitive lethal weapons. Some of the dusty display cases were too dark to allow the disquieting shapes within to be identified.

Felicity flipped open the lid of an oblong wooden box on the counter. Nestled in moth-eaten black velvet were some curled lacquer spirals that looked like pig tails.

"Ah, those," exclaimed the shopkeeper, "are the preserved penises of infidels taken in Jerusalem by the Knights of Saint John in the very first Crusade, seven hundred anno Domini."

Felicity hastily closed the box, pinching her finger.

"This is a mad *Kunstkammer*, no?" The Albanian relit his stogie. The squashed butt ends of his cigars splayed obscenely in dolomite ashtrays and floated in brown liquid in bronze cuspidors all around the shop.

"What's that?" Felicity asked, thinking the word sounded vaguely obscene.

"Oh, you know. Like a curio cabinet. The *Kunstkammer*. Every bourgeois European household had one in the seventeenth and eighteenth centuries. Sometimes they devoted a whole room to oddities."

"What was the purpose of it?" Felicity was rather enjoying the hairy man's lecture.

"The world was much more mysterious then. Doubtless, the purpose was to examine the hidden order that underlies the physical world. People were fascinated by the similarity of patterns between, let's say, a seashell and a mountain plant. It must have seemed to them that nature was pursuing a plan, or many plans; that they were living with all sorts of mysteries . . . plots. This was before Linnaeus, mind you. Classification was a matter of texture, of taste . . . not physical laws."

On a small shelf was a little book handwritten in a language Felicity had never seen. She asked the shopkeeper about it.

"Goatskin. Written in Coptic. A treatise translated as *The Language Crystal*."

She touched it. The texture was coarse and the black letters were inscribed deeply into the leather. An illustration in the middle of the book depicted a naked couple standing under a sort of disco ball filled with letters. The letters were funneling from the ball into their open mouths.

"Everything is explicable through the Language Crystal. There are a small number of sounds that, in combination, contain the entire universe. The actual Language Crystal exists . . . but this is just a book about it. Everybody has a Language Crystal in their brain, which can be plugged into the Great Crystal."

"I don't understand." Felicity frowned.

"Look at Africa, for instance. Europeans, who are rationalists, claim that AIDS came from Africa, but Africans, who use the Language Crystal, claim that AIDS was brought to Africa by AIDS, the Agency for International Development Services."

As Andrea walked down the aisle to the rest room, she noticed that nearly everyone was holding or reading a book. She passed by two Arab men reading the Koran together, their dark heads touching. An American girl wearing shorts was staring at an open copy of *The Teachings of Don Juan*. She wasn't exactly reading. It was as if she'd seen a spider and was wondering whether to shut the book on it or not. A well-dressed Frenchwoman was folding the corner of a page to mark a spot in Simone de Beauvoir's *The Second Sex*. A young nun in a gray habit and wimple was reading a week-old *Osservatore Romano*. An Orthodox Jew was bent so low over his paperback Torah his curls brushed the page. An unshaven, consumptive-looking man with burning eyes was reading something called *License to Carry a Gun*. Two gay men were intent on a passage in *The Prophecies of Nostradamus*.

Andrea had to wait for the rest room behind an elderly couple dressed in secondhand polyester pantsuits. Andrea imagined that they had waited in lines for most of their lives. She recognized her grandparents in them and the grandparents of all her friends. Their bent backs, the humble incline of their heads bespoke an infinite patience, honed by decades of poverty, in eternal wait for bread, milk, medicine, shoes, a vacant toilet stall. They wanted to take as little space as possible. Their whole bodies

tried to shrink in order to communicate deference. They meant no harm
to anyone; all they wanted was a little crust of bread, a corner on the park
bench. Ground down by wars, these old folks shuffled on the edges of the
world in felt slippers, fearful of everyone and everything.

Just then, the toilet was free and the old man gestured gallantly to his
wife to go first. This was a small victory over his burning bladder. Andrea
noted it and silently blessed the old man, who felt suddenly better without
knowing why.

The old people took a long time in there, so Andrea went up the length
of the plane to the first-class cabin. The toilet was occupied there, too, so
she leaned against the back of a seat occupied by a manicured gentleman
smoking a Dunhill cigarette and leafing through *Variety*. Her bladder was
becoming a hot balloon. She imagined squatting next to the portly figure
who smelled of cologne, leather, and smoke, and letting go her stream. He
looked up at her just as the fantasy was becoming unbearable. His gaze was
interested, but not greedy. He took the Dunhill out of his mouth and said,
"Ever thought about a career in television?"

"Well, yes," said Andrea, surprised.

The man nodded agreeably, as if this came as no surprise. "What happened?"

"I met an Italian millionaire. I'm flying to his island right now. I guess I
don't really care for television." She became suddenly cross. "It's evil."

"Are you magnetic?" the man continued, disregarding her remark. "Do
people come up to you for no good reason and begin talking to you?"

Andrea had to admit that they did.

"Do they think that they know you from somewhere? That they've seen
you before?"

"Yes."

"Have you ever acted?"

"No. Biology was my best subject in high school. I took some ballet
classes, but after the earthquake in Los Angeles . . . My parents were in the
house at the time, you see. Our classes were canceled, and by the time I
got home . . . After the funeral I moved to my uncle's place in Tel Aviv, and
I didn't do anything much after that."

A man came out of the bathroom. Andrea rushed into the vacated stall.
When she came out she felt greatly relieved, but she was still angry.

"Television," she spat at the Dunhill smoker, "is the devil. It's sucking
all the people in and sending their souls to a place of dots." Ben had actually said this, and she had liked it.

"You're absolutely right." He smiled. "I'm Reed Sharpless, agent, producer, talent scout. You ever hear of *Hollywood Squares?* I did that. If life on the island proves too boring, give me a call. I definitely think you're magnetic." He handed her a card.

Andrea returned to her seat, thinking about this program she'd never seen, *Hollywood Squares.* She imagined it to be the nemesis of *Wheel of Fortune.* When she asked Ben, he said that *Hollywood Squares* was to *Wheel of Fortune* what the hamburger was to the pizza.

"The first fast food in America was hamburgers, which were small, individualistic portions. Now the most popular food is pizza, which is shared and communistic."

This explanation didn't satisfy Andrea, but she liked Ben even more.

Ben became engrossed in Gershom Scholem's *Kabbalah*, and a silence full of turning pages settled in the cabin. It was as if an angel of reading, finger to his lips, had taken over the jumbo jet, causing everyone to fall into a private pool of words. It's strange, thought Andrea, listening to the leafing, but the world will go on only for as long as everyone keeps reading. When they close their books, it's over. She didn't know where this certainty came from, but she was sure enough of its rightness.

"Can you explain the Language Crystal?" Felicity was still touching the goatskin book and experiencing a chill, as if an ice cold pen were writing words on her body.

The Albanian relit his cigar. He looked Felicity in the eyes and she sank into their bottomless black pools. The hymns that were her comfort tried to rise from within her, but she couldn't sing. There was a lump in her throat; she was near tears. She wanted desperately to hear about the Language Crystal.

"At the simplest level, the crystal makes us share a story. I knew a man with a pencil-thin mustache," he said, and Felicity, too, knew a man with a pencil-thin mustache.

"He called himself a Levantine," she continued.

"He came from the fabled potbelly of Asia Minor called the Levant because he could levitate and also because of his fabulous levity . . ."

Felicity saw him clearly. "He loved women of different races, different countries, different regions . . ."

"Mexican, Thai, Chinese, French, Russian. . . . And each one cooked for him some form of burrito, spring roll, egg roll, crepe, or blini . . ."

"His women *were* just like food. He was a sampler of women, a connoisseur of some kind, and then he hit on the idea of combining his girl-friends."

"He saw his Thai woman in the morning, his Japanese girl at noon, his Russian Katia in the evening. He planned his love life like gourmet meals."

"In fact, he quit eating altogether and fed only on the salt, musk, and juices he absorbed from his lovers. He wrote down everything about them, all the combinations, and he called his method love fusion."

"He got very thin, and after a while he tried to combine all his lovers into a single physical person . . ."

". . . and developed a complex explanation having to do with the end of the individual . . ."

". . . the advent of the collective person!"

"Right! He claimed that people were going to become very thin and insubstantial in the future, and that they would have to band together to make whole units . . ."

"The amazing thing was," continued Felicity, "that these women believed him. They considered his theory sound and overcame, by sheer intellectual will, the age-old difficulties of jealousy, possessiveness, territoriality . . . They became one."

Felicity stopped. The thread of the story snapped and receded from her like smoke. The story had floated up like an island in the middle of a gray sea and had exhausted her. She looked down and saw that she was still touching the goatskin book.

"It never fails!" The Albanian looked away and Felicity surfaced like a cork to the surface of herself. She felt that now she *could* sing, but had no desire to do so.

The shopkeeper explained: "The Language Crystal made it possible for both of us to weave a story. It is odd, though, how *perfectly* you shared, how little of *you* there was in it. . . . You are utterly clear, like a windowpane. People usually add something of their own, some detail of their personalities, but you . . . It's most unusual."

"What's *my* story?" Felicity asked anxiously. She felt keenly the absence of her memories.

The lights in the main cabin were dimmed, but most of the reading lights were still on. Andrea imagined the string of lights floating below the stars, above the darkness of the Atlantic Ocean. She was a mere dot of pulsing life, and then she became aware of an insistent and pleasurable sensation. She streamed back into her body. Ben was kissing her neck.

"Did you know," he whispered, "that Hong Kong is the most densely populated city on earth?"

She'd had no idea, but she didn't want him to stop. He kissed her earlobe, her cheeks, and her nose. As his kisses became more insistent, so did her delight in them. She sunk lower in the uncomfortable seat, oblivious to the discomfort or perverse pleasure of the fat man, the Iranian woman, the Bible boy, and all the others around them. She could feel them straining to ignore her and Ben's nuzzling and not succeeding. Her excitement grew by degrees, as did her radiating warmth. She saw the edges of the heat field that she was emanating. It was widening, like a circle in the water. She tried to see if she could make the field bigger or smaller by increasing and cooling her excitement. It worked. My God, I can turn on this whole airplane! And why not? Andrea asked herself judiciously as she let her fingers play lightly on Ben's upper thigh.

Andrea moved her index finger like the big hand of a clock over the tip of Ben's penis, and row after row of the jumbo airplane caught fire. Those who had been reading succumbed quietly to the wave. The two students of the Koran blushed and pulled away from one another. The student of Don Juan stretched like a cat, feeling the crotch of her jeans go taut. The gay men stretched a blanket over their collective lap. The Frenchwoman lay her sweater over *The Second Sex*, pushed the edge of the hardcover book between her legs, and bore down on the sharp corner. Even the old couple woke with a start and remembered something dim and vaguely happy. Andrea's immediate neighbors simply evaporated. The Sikh's fat sizzled, while the Iranian wrapped her breasts around the boy missionary. Andrea laughed out loud. The whole plane was eroticized, and Andrea had caused it!

"What was *that?*" inquired Ben.

"An orgasm," said Andrea.

Few of their fellow travelers had any idea what an orgasm was. Iran had outlawed the very discussion of it for so long, the lucky few who'd felt pleasure compared it to the dead Khomeini's speeches. The turbaned capitalist sociologist commonly experienced only a swelling in his pile of banknotes. The Bible readers were sure that "orgasm" was one of Satan's names.

Ben remembered his brief flirtation with the work of Wilhelm Reich, the leader of the short-lived orgasm movement. Back then, Ben had believed that world harmony was contingent on orgasmic fulfillment for everyone. When he became disillusioned with Reich, he agreed with the situationists that orgasm was in fact a tool of capitalism, and that the world of those who knew orgasm and those who didn't broke down between those who'd been exposed to a half century of television, its sex machinery humming, and the hungry billions who huddled around village-common radios that exhorted them to die for God.

Andrea considered briefly the frenzy about her. Outside the window, shooting stars streaked past the plane. They sprayed gleeful light dust, revealing swatches of starry sky. Ah, cried everything, let the games begin. Andrea felt flooded by giddy gratitude and thought that she was, all in all, and notwithstanding the terrible facts, a lucky girl.

Ben believed that they were passing through a heavenly belt. He had studied questions relating to angels and had been taught that there were many angelic nodes. He knew the names of many angels, where they resided, what they did, when they interceded, how they interacted with humans, and how they could be summoned. He believed that many worlds existed. Some of these were man-made hells. There were surely man-made heavens, too, like now, here, with Andrea. He was certain that the man-made worlds were few in number compared to the great profusion of worlds inhabited and managed by spirits of the air, angels, demigods, ousted gods, demons, fictions, and myth creatures. He had until now worked only in the human world, but now he felt as if he had been given permission to explore all the others.

It was dark inside Manteaux and Felicity didn't know how much time had passed. A streetlight swayed by the wind threw fantastic shadows into the shop. She had asked what her story was, and now, after darkness had fallen, the Albanian answered:

"A person without a story is a slave."

Felicity tasted the bitter truth of his reply.

"I must be a slave, then. My name is Scheherazade, a slave." She looked about the crowded shop, and it seemed to her that the African fetishes, the Indonesian temple doors, the Haitian voodoo flags, the reliquaria, the racks of priestly vestments, and the crude religious carvings were all the work of people with thousands of stories.

"Your name is . . . Scheherazade?" The fierce man was astonished. "Then you have a thousand and one stories!"

"That may be, but none of them are mine. So I am a slave. Are there other slaves here?"

"Our employees are not slaves. They are artists. Technically, they are relatives of the owner and work here voluntarily. Would you like to meet them?"

She didn't know if she did, but followed meekly when the Albanian guided her to the back of the shop. He pushed open a small door dwarfed by two impassive stone heads. It led into a dark cobblestoned courtyard lined with cubicles lit by oil lamps. Inside the cubicles, people were hunched over tables, working intently. Some were making collages with beads, wires, and broken bits of glass. Others painted gnarled crosses or nailed figures to them. Two young boys were lining a coffin with red silk. Very few tools were in evidence. Most of the work was being done by hand. The workers, even the adults, were small, and some had humps or misshapen limbs. No one looked up when Felicity peered into their cubicles.

"They look scared," she whispered.

"They are. They believe that vampires will consume them if they don't work all the time making protective talismans."

"They *are* slaves, then!"

"Perhaps."

Felicity stood in the dim doorway of one cubicle and watched a little girl polish a small silver cross. She had soft, blond curls and sat on a stool in the form of a devil. The devil's red tongue stuck out of the seat between the girl's legs. A bare lightbulb hung over her head.

"What are you doing, child?" she asked.

In a flat voice the girl said, "This cross was found around the neck of a girl who jumped in the river and died. Her soul is locked in this cross. I'm making it ready for sale."

Felicity turned to face her guide. "Child labor laws," she said. "You are violating—"

She never finished. The Albanian took her by the shoulders and guided her into the cubicle. The child ran out. Felicity sat on the devil stool. It was wet, as if the girl had peed on it. A leaden weakness spiraled from her toes to her head. She picked up the silver cross. Light shot out of it, blinding her for a moment. When she could see again, she felt grateful to the man, as if he had restored her sight.

"Thank you," she whispered.

"That's right," the Albanian said. "You will finish polishing it, and then I will bring you more work."

After she polished the silver cross to perfection, Felicity was given a great number of crosses, with instructions on what to do with them. Some were black and had to be polished with lemon juice until they shone. They came from around the necks of corpses in graveyards. Other crosses were wooden and artistically carved. Felicity's job was to nail animal figurines to them. She nailed a frog to an ornate painted cross. She had little feeling as she worked. She was indifferent to anything but the repetitious movement of her hands. And she sang. She remembered many hymns, and as they filled her, she was no longer anxious.

When she finished nailing the frog, she picked up an old book sitting on a dusty shelf. It was called *The Proper Management of Subhumans.* It was a voodoo manual on how to manage zombies, what kind of labors they were suited to, how to present their work—even how to remove the slight whiff of the grave that inevitably attached itself to all they produced. Felicity knew that she wasn't a zombie. She wanted only to get to Tara and then, oh God, to the Dome. Her mind filled with the crystal wonder of that place. She heard the murmur of a spring, and the sweet singing filled the mild air. Dear God, please help me to the Dome. She saw the illuminated vaults of that place and the elevated stage on which the First Angels Choir stood. Arrayed before them in a dark amphitheater were loving people who had come from very far away to hear them sing. Among them were all her loved ones, whose faces and names she couldn't yet remember but who would reveal themselves fully when the sweetness of song awoke her mind. At that moment Jesus himself, enveloped in a robe of loving light, would descend from the heavens and enfold them all in love.

Chapter Twenty-seven

Wherein Andrea becomes a hero and
Felicity finds employment

h e BookAir jet crossed the dawn of the year 2000 for the sixth time, and only a few reading lights remained on. Even Ben, who had kissed her for three time zones and had soared with her through as many millennial crossroads, looked sleepy now, *Kabbalah* fallen at his feet. Andrea's senses were keen, though, as if everyone's sleep were tonic and she had somehow been appointed to keep watch over the flight. She looked around at her fellow creatures made defenseless by sleep, and felt their fragility. But at that moment, a bolt of sheer panic tightened her chest.

Something distressing was about to unfold on the plane. She reviewed all that had happened since boarding. Except for the moment of mass orgasm, there had been only a pronounced uneventfulness, but this was it, precisely. In Sarajevo, the advent of severe bombardment began with just such deep uneventfulness. She knew this quiet well.

Andrea turned on the reading light above her seat and looked at herself in her compact mirror. A very worried Andrea looked back at her. "What's the matter?" she asked. In response, her mirror face seemed to change: her eyebrows became thicker, her lips became more red, her chin sharpened, and her hair turned very black and shiny. She looked like someone she had never met, though still familiar.

A barely perceptible scent of perfume mixed with frightened sweat wafted her way, and Andrea had an irresistible urge to see the face of the veiled woman two seats away. She squeezed past the fat man, who woke up and took the opportunity to touch her bottom with three fat fingers. Andrea could have caused his fingers to fall off but she didn't want to break her concentration.

The woman was caressing a very thick book, which lay flat on her lap. It bore the gold-lettered Arabic for *Quran* on the cover, had an opening at the top, and was filled with what looked like wet clay. The woman was not reading. The woman's fingers were busy inside the opening. A yellow wire came out of the book and went up under her veil. Andrea reached out suddenly and pulled down the black veil. Her face was the face Andrea had seen in the mirror. The woman looked up, startled, and let go of the wire she had been holding between her teeth.

Andrea stood stock-still as the Iranian's gaze changed from surprise to fury. Andrea took hold of the yellow wire and pulled it slowly out from the doughy interior of the book. An expression of horror covered the woman's face. Andrea knew then that the book was a bomb and the woman was expecting it to explode. But nothing happened.

The fat man and the Bible boy became aware now of the unfolding drama. They watched Andrea's hand pull out the endless wire as if the whole world depended on it. And in fact, it did—their world, anyway.

When the wire came out of the bomb completely, everyone, even the terrorist, let their breath out. After that, pandemonium broke out. The fat man took hold of the terrorist's arms—and began bellowing at her in Farsi. The young missionary took the book from her lap and held it at arm's length as if it were the snake of original sin. Ben shielded Andrea by cradling her head to his chest. A stewardess tied the terrorist's arms behind her back with a scarf. The captain came out and personally placed the woman under arrest. The black bomb-book was carefully removed to the tail of the plane and shut in the food freezer.

As soon as the terrorist was locked in the first-class toilet, Andrea was mobbed. The elderly couple kissed her hands until she wrenched them away. The fat man took a wad of currency out of his briefcase and insisted that she put it in her bag. The captain shook her hand, then hugged her. The second officer hugged her, too. The captain tried to write down the correct spelling of her name, and asked her nationality. This was sticky— she was known to at least three other passengers as Basque or Ukrainian or American.

"Call me Andrea, from Jerusalem," she said coyly.

The captain radioed air control in Atlanta that an angel named Andrea had saved BookAir flight 459 from destruction, and the news was picked up at the same instant by a weather helicopter, which relayed it to ABC News, which interrupted programming immediately. Less than five minutes after Andrea had disarmed the bomb, all the major networks and the Internet were instantaneously broadcasting what they were already calling the "millennial miracle." Within ten minutes, the president of the United States broke away from New Year revelry to congratulate the Israeli girl hero. The Israeli prime minister and the heads of state of Great Britain, Japan, and Russia called within minutes.

Reed Sharpless, the producer, wrote so many different contracts that he used up all the napkins on the plane. Andrea refused to sign any of them.

"The movie!" he begged her. "The movie of your life!"

Which life? "No movie, Mr. Reed."

Ben held her hand tightly, sending long arrows of love up her arms. He didn't speak at all.

It took a long time for the excitement to die down. They left her alone only when she pretended to sleep. She shut her eyes and felt the uncomfortable squirming of a shapeless creature inside her. It was a kind of baby, only it wasn't. She was beginning to give birth to herself.

America appeared from behind a cloud.

Shielding the flame of a taper, the Albanian led Felicity to a vaulted room behind the building. Her fellow "artists" sat on three-legged stools at a long table. Felicity sat and slurped a bowl of thick seafood gumbo, brought in a large aluminum pot by two deliverymen.

The Albanian lectured as they ate. "It is important to let words flow out of you while you work. When you feel them coming on, write them on your work. Let the entities speak through you, let the Language Crystal illuminate your labors."

He held up as a good example of this technique a collage of Aztec heads on a map of a provincial Roman capital, across which the artist had inscribed in a jerky hand a string of blasphemies. The author of this work, a toothless wretch in yellow pajamas seated next to Felicity, beamed with pride and let out a hiss of foul breath.

Bare mattresses were propped against the walls. After the meal, two girls with dirty, matted hair pulled down the mattresses. Obediently, everyone lay down. Felicity curled up on one and watched the darkness in the dormitory. Her fellow slaves made small, sad noises, timid coughs and sighs, and settled quickly into sleep. Felicity was as empty as air.

She fell quickly asleep and woke up inside a dream more vivid than her waking life. Tesla's giant planetarium surrounded her, and though she knew that it had a beginning and an end, its dimensions were so far beyond her comprehension it might as well have been infinite. Within a circle of azure blossoms there was a section that was behaving very oddly. Felicity was herself part of the misbehaving section; every time she lifted her arm a web of connexions vibrated throughout the section and through the green machine itself. She was free to move, but each step she took initiated vibrations in the vegetation. She dove headfirst from a clay cliff into a blue lake and was able to set the green machine in motion both in the air and in the water. At the bottom of the lake a blindfolded man was playing the piano. Colored musical fish were swimming around his head. A rabbi sat on the piano singing a song. She swam to join them, but an octopus gripped her with all his arms and began to pull her back to the surface. Felicity struggled to no avail. She realized that the lake was itself a being, a blue and loving being that she would eventually return to.

When she surfaced, a fat man dressed in a military uniform, wearing her father's face, handed her a fluffy black towel and said:

"Our sector is malfunctioning. The chlorophyll reactor is considering neutralizing us in order to keep functioning. There is only one solution to saving the sector, and it appears that, because of some biochemical combination, you contain it. There isn't much time left, so I beseech you to dream this solution pronto."

"Daddy!" Felicity was overjoyed. She lifted her still-damp arms in the air to show him her lithe young body and her dark-haloed breasts. "What's wrong with the big machine, Daddy? I don't think that there is anything wrong with it!" She stepped forward and threw her arms around him.

Her arms met only air as the man with the daddy face took a step backward. He was displeased.

"You must dream the solution right away! The entire sector, present and past, is watching you."

Now Felicity felt self-conscious about her nakedness. She crossed her arms in front of her breasts and insisted sullenly: "What's wrong with the big machine, Daddy?"

"Our sector is moving either too fast or in the opposite direction from the chlorophyll wave. We must recover the right speed."

Felicity could hear the footsteps of the man with the daddy face moving away from her. She was alone. She lay on her back on the water of the lake and looked at the stars. Of course she had the solution. She would give them their solution, she thought sadly. They can fix their stupid flower engine, but as for herself she would try to get outside of it somehow.

Felicity put her hand through her chest and took out her heart. It was pulsing red, and a rose light emanated from it. She handed it to whoever was ready to receive it, but at that moment she felt a large palm over her mouth. Her heart leapt back into her chest, and Felicity woke up to stare into the black eyes of the Albanian.

"Don't make any sound," he whispered in her ear. "I'm adding you to my fusion. I'm going to take my pleasure in you right here in the dormitory so the idiots can hear us."

The Albanian looked into her eyes, and when he was reasonably sure that she wasn't going to scream, he removed his hand.

"I had the solution but now I can't remember it," Felicity said.

The hairy Albanian held his grotesquely swollen penis in his hand.

"It's no good. I have no opening. I am all smooth down here." She spread her legs wide to show him.

The dream-within-the-dream Albanian vanished.

A feather-light hand touched Felicity, waking her. She sat upright, alarmed. In the moonlight streaming through a window, she saw the child with the soft blond curls standing by the side of her bed. She looked as if she'd been washed, coiffed, and dressed at a subterranean beauty parlor, and seemed to be asleep. She touched Felicity softly, like a baby looking for its mother's breast. The child took Felicity's hand and led her to the window. The dark shapes of the other slaves turned uneasily on their mattresses. Felicity, obeying the stubborn goodwill emanating from the child, crawled out the window and onto the sidewalk. She turned to help the girl out, but her helper had vanished back inside.

The night was liquid and full of moonlight. On Decatur Street drunks still mumbled on stoops. Light and smoke poured out of a bar. An intermittently flickering neon sign above it proclaimed the place to be *Desire, Ltd., Where Every Miss Is a Hit*. A half-naked girl with a feather mask on was sitting on a stool haranguing the passersby. When she saw Felicity, she cried, "Girl, you look like a ghost. You look like you need a job. Come on in and tell Sylvia everything."

Felicity went in. Unfortunately, she couldn't tell Sylvia very much because she didn't know anything about herself. All she knew was that her name was Scheherazade, and that was already a stripper kind of name. Nobody had any problems with that name. Her hair had grown two shapeless inches over the past ten days, and she looked pretty scary. Sylvia clipped it to a manageable fuzz again and died it red. She also undertook to teach Felicity the stripper's art, and to everyone's surprise, she could dance pretty well.

The first milky dawn of the new millennium was sunless and gray. The pilot wished everyone, particularly Andrea, a "happy next thousand years" and announced that they would be landing in forty minutes.

"I'm afraid," Ben told Andrea, "that there will be media."

"Media? Television? Newspapers? But this is what I ran away from. I don't want to be Vanna White! We have to get away from them."

"It's easier said than done." Ben looked very worried. "In America they run everything—heaven, hell, downtown, uptown. You have to pay a fortune to stay out of newspapers. Of course, people pay to get into them, too. It's complicated."

He fell silent, contemplating the immensity of the web that people now trashed in like helpless flies. He too had run away from the overbearing presence of news, from the sense of constant emergency Americans lived in. He thought that he had found freedom in the eternal questions, in the mystery of divinity. Instead, he had run into Andrea, a creature in flight like himself, whom he was now helping deliver into the arms of the very world he'd fled. It didn't make sense. He had to do something to help her. They had to escape what awaited them on the ground.

The nun in gray with the white collar, who'd been reading the *Osservatore Romano*, approached quietly and put her small, white hand on Andrea's shoulder.

"I know what's troubling you, child," she whispered to Andrea. She spoke too softly for Ben to hear.

"*Ecce porta inferni*," said Andrea, in the Latin Father Eustratius had taught her. "I stand before the gate of hell," she added in English, not sure if the nun understood.

"*Partiti sunt vestimenta mea*," the sister said. "They shared my garments."

Ben watched in astonishment as the two women hurried to the rest room. The announcement had just been made for everyone to return to their seats. Ben watched anxiously for the two women, gone for what seemed like eternity. As the plane was about to set down on the runway, they emerged from the tiny cubicle.

The "nun," in her gray habit with the severe collar and wimple, went back to her seat. The other, in her platform shoes and her ridiculously brief miniskirt, sat next to Ben. His eyes traveled the length of milky white legs that had not seen daylight in a long time, and paused, intrigued, on the snow white midriff with the almond of a belly button set vertically in it like a tear. He blushed as he tried to gauge the deep shadow between the thighs. All in all, the sister was not badly made. Though she was not as young as Andrea, her flesh was nonetheless firm and all the more enticing for having been untouched. Or so Ben imagined, from his paltry knowledge of nuns.

Atlanta, from the air, looked ready for the twenty-first century. Its sky-scrapers and domes looked to Andrea hopeful, the very opposite of the lazy dens and warrens of the Old World. BookAir made a bumpy landing, made almost inaudible by the passengers' shouts of glee. It had been the longest night of their lives.

Ben was back in the land of his birth. He had gone to the Holy Land to speak with God and was back without having succeeded, though he had brought back with him a creature such as the New World had never seen.

The passengers waited impatiently while FBI agents boarded the plane and led the terrorist out. One of them looked for Andrea, but the passengers began rushing out, so he decided to wait outside. When nearly everyone was out of the plane, he radioed a fellow officer outside that he had missed the girl.

The lines at the passport control booths were long. Ben went to the one that said *U.S. Citizens Only.* "Sister" Andrea was right behind him, while the real nun was in the *Non–U.S. Residents* line. Ben could see, immediately outside Customs, a restless mass of camera-armed people jostling one another. He made it through passport check and waited anxiously for the "sister." Andrea's improvised document, bearing the picture of Ben's sister, Clarisse, was a most shoddy piece of work. But her green eyes, peering disturbingly out of the gray wimple, affected the young Customs officer just as they affected everyone else. He stamped her immigration form, which Ben had helped her fill out, while losing himself in her eyes and reciting, doubtless, a little prayer against his inappropriate wave of lust.

At Customs, they went to the area of *Nothing to Declare.* Indeed, what was there to declare? Self was undefinable contraband. Still, thought Ben, somebody momentous and metaphysically illegal is being smuggled in. If only you knew. But the hyperkeen dogs who could sniff a grain of cocaine in a saltshaker let Andrea pass without a whimper.

An animated discussion was taking place between the CNN producer, who claimed exclusive rights to the story of the Girl Who Saved BookAir Flight 459, and several producers from the other networks.

Exclusive rights to a news story? The ABC producer was outraged.

"What next? Exclusive rights to the next war? Exclusive rights to the Second Coming? News belongs to everybody!"

But the CNN man wouldn't budge. The flight had landed and CNN had already surrounded the area with trucks and cameras. There was no room for anyone else. This was their city, and as others were quickly learning, the business of news was very much like the business of war. To the mighty belonged the turf.

"You can't control the goddam news!" shouted the frustrated ABC man. He knew because that was his business. Every day, he fought the ocean that was the news, and every day he retreated before the chaos.

"Yes, we can," said his counterpart calmly. "We can control everything but the outcome. And word from above is"—he winked—"that now that Jane and Ted are born again, we can even ask for outcomes."

"Then get the hell out there and make your own news! Who cares about what *really* happens?" The NBC guy was really steamed. He had a sudden and queasy vision of a world of virtual news, things that never happened but everyone thought did. Perhaps the flat-earthers were right, and those who said that we'd never gone to the moon. He himself had come close many times to that edge where it was hard to distinguish between fact and fiction.

"And you don't make up news?" the CNN guy said ironically. "You make it up all the time." For him, that virtual world had arrived long ago. The surprise was not in the ease of fabrication; he had no qualms about that. The surprise was when news really did happen, when amazing occurrences like this girl's plucking a bomb from a terrorist in the sky were actual events, not the constructs of the network's purple prose men.

They went back and forth, but then the discussion became irrelevant. Passengers from BookAir flight 459 were exiting Customs. Everyone rushed forward.

The blood-sniffing hounds of the media let the "sister" pass. All their eyes were trained on the miniskirted, high-platformed "Andrea," who had just left the passport area with a U.S. stamp on her Vatican-issued passport.

"Andrea! Andrea!" Their collective cry rose like a wall before the nun and behind Andrea.

The nun walked unafraid into the throng, and after rocking for a time in the violent motion of their shoving, pushing, and questioning, she said clearly, in Italian-accented English, "I am not the one you are looking for!"

By the time the truth of her assertion had been verified, Andrea, with Ben at her side, was on a flight headed for New Orleans.

Chapter Twenty - eight

Wherein we witness Reverend Mullin's boundless fury, and the promise of Armageddon

**i c t u r e s** in *Our Mirror!* There it was, the most private part of America's most public televangelist, stretched longingly and obscenely toward a child's hand. WHORING MAN OF GOD! MORE PICTURES INSIDE! HE PAID FOR FILTH! DEGRADATION OF CHRIST'S MAN! The tabloid was at every checkout counter in America in a matter of hours.

Our Mirror called Mullin eight hours before press time and offered to squelch the story for $15 million. But feeling that he had successfully prevented blackmail for the much lesser sum of $2.1 million, he'd tried to bargain. Having captured the demon girl, who was now being trained at SMD, Mullin thought that he had a bargaining chip. But *Our Mirror* could care less about what he did with the girl who had mailed them the compromising photographs. Mullin might have paid the outrageous ransom, but he didn't have the money. His entire fortune was tied up at the moment in the great plans of the Lord. His gold was working for Jesus.

The consequences of the scandal were devastating and swift. The revenues of the Ministry of the Utmost God dropped precipitously the very next day. Three hundred Christian TV stations denounced Jeremy "Elvis" Mullin as filth, though they couldn't kick him off the air—the contracts ran into the year 2005. Mullin blamed the machinations of rival preachers under the direction of Satan. He cried on television, asking for forgiveness. The timing couldn't have been worse; during Christmas the appeals of the ministry had been particularly desperate. Mullin had all but promised his followers the Rapture within the month, and Armageddon shortly thereafter. It made sense for the believers to send all they had because in short order they wouldn't be needing any. But the photos in *Our Mirror* stayed their pens in midcheck. Worse even than the withheld money was the outrage in their hearts and the fear that the reverend's hypocrisy might invalidate his promises. So many of his followers had already sold everything they had, broken relations with disbelieving members of their families, and prepared like good scouts for their ascension to heaven. What were they going to do if neither Rapture nor Armageddon were to follow? Their fear and disappointment were quickly turning to anger. Mullin fulminated against Satan, who in collusion with rival preachers, the pope, communists, the queen of England, the *Times-Picayune*, NBC News, and the mavens of secular humanism, through the instrument of a wicked girl, had dealt him this blow for the purpose of nullifying his revelations of the End. But Mullin could hear the thunder of the approaching storm, and neither the paradisiacal inducement of his First Angels Choir nor his rhetorical summits would still it. He needed to make good on his promises fast; he had to stun his constituency with signs. He needed Jesus to really come through.

All plans for the fulfillment of the prophecies had to be pushed rapidly forward now, though some of the elements were still at the developmental stage. It was more important than ever that events should unfold as he had prophesied.

On the second day of the year 2000, Mullin woke up as he had for two days in the grip of an epic fury. He hadn't been sleeping since New Year's, when firecrackers and every weapon men owned were unleashed to welcome the cascade of significant zeros. Mullin pulled the rip cord by the bed, and the curtain over the skylight parted, letting in a gray light void of signs and portents. The sky had been a blank slate each morning; there wasn't even a cloud to look at. The air was heavy and still, as before a storm, but no storm was coming.

He saw again before his mind's eye the face of his blackmailer and wished to annihilate her. He had so far avoided her, letting the SMD curriculum take its course, but he could bear it no longer. He called for Felicity to be brought before him. The Bamajan who answered the phone made him wait more than twenty minutes. When he came back, his voice was shaky. He apologized: "We don't know how in God's name she got away. It's never happened before!"

"How long since she vanished?"

The Bamajan said he didn't know, but he did. To his dismay, the girl had been gone since Christmas Eve, and no one had noticed.

Mullin flung the phone against the wall, where it broke into pieces and rained plastic all over the Bukhara carpet on the bedroom floor. No girl bathed in the psalms and filled with the light had ever left training before. Nonetheless, Felicity had, and she was loose now, a pierced demon with a camera looking to stab him in the heart again. The devil had the reverend under his hooves and kept on pounding.

That day, his best-trained Bamajans fanned out into the city looking for Felicity.

Mullin experienced an onslaught of contradictory emotions. The little northern Louisiana boy in him raised a gun to his lips and blew his brains out. A lusty farmer thought of the girlish pubis that was his downfall and became unaccountably erect. What a time for such a thing! The boy and the farmer were then dwarfed by the rise of the angry preacher, who declared in a foundation-shattering voice: "*I* am Mullin! And *I* will have my revenge! The Lord forgives not!"

His anger notwithstanding, the reverend felt unaccountably sentimental and foolish. He decided that there were still parts in himself that had not been subjected to the cleansing flames of the Lord, parts still mired in the past. He dismissed his chauffeur and ignored his staff. He would revisit once more, he decided, the human parts of himself that he would soon leave behind.

The oleander bushes alongside the freeway squatted under a blue sky pierced by plumes of white smoke. To Mullin they always looked as if they signaled the election of a new pope. In reality, they were the innocuously colored toxic emissions of chemical plants, and they signaled sickness and death.

The girl held out her palm, her wet finger still shiny with both their juices. It was a new girl, on a stretch of Airline Highway strewn with cheap motels advertising adult videos, a stretch he had never frequented before, but where he was still taking a chance. For all he knew, the filthy beds in the by-the-hour rooms had pages of *Our Mirror* strewn all over them. The reverend quickly laid two bills on the seat between them, and the girl, who looked like she could neither read nor write, snatched the money and vanished quickly. But the fear didn't leave him. He looked around. The dusty palm trees of the motor court were motionless. The few parked cars were deserted. And yet his fear issued from something or someone specific. His heart began to race. Though it is said that bombs do not fall twice on the same spot, they were known to have done just that. But even if Felicity's photo lens were to happen again upon the very same scene, the impact would be null. Still, the disgraced preacher was afraid because he had done the unthinkable, which was to practically return to the scene of the crime. To experience pedestrian fear on the day of his grand party was so incongruous, Mullin nearly laughed.

The reverend sped down Airline, checking the rearview mirror, but no one was following him. And still the feeling intensified. He recalled Felicity just as she had stood by that hospital bed hissing at him, "Not on your life, motherfucker!" and he knew that it was indeed a matter of her life. He had offered her salvation, she had rejected it, and now she had to die. Her vulnerable, slightly hurt, undeniably pretty face filled him with dread. She was no mere instrument of Satan; she was of his very flesh. She had to be found. God was testing him. There was a purpose in his downfall and martyrdom. Even the first child prostitute had been sent to him as a sign. Since being given the gift of turning them to the light through music, he had converted many fallen children. Their conversion was never incomplete, as appeared to be the case with Felicity. Still, he had to test all of them again, to make sure that in their newborn innocence they were truly serving Jesus. Because if they weren't, they had to be destroyed, no matter how pretty their singing.

Mullin remembered the day greatness was born in him. He had been a part-time preacher in Natchitoches, Louisiana, and a part-time insurance salesman, and a part-time piano player in country honky-tonks, and a part-time husband, and, mostly, a drifter. There had been no anchor to his life, and no voice had yet told him who he was and what he was meant to do. And then one day, at a Motel Six on I-10, somewhere between Shreveport and Texarcana, a young girl showed up at the side of the empty swimming pool, looking into it as if wondering where all the water went. He walked behind her and put both his hands on her shoulders. Showing no surprise, the girl turned around, her face streaked with tears, and said: "Baptize me, Preacher. Sink me deep into the water of life!"

Mullin could never wholly put into words what seized him then. The skies opened for him and a power as strong as electrical current shot from his arms into the girl. He found himself singing "Amazing Grace" in a voice so powerful each word drove a stake through every wickedness in that girl's body. She sang with him as sparks of black light flew about them like hell's snow. Finally, she went limp and empty. He carried her to his room and watched as sadness drained from her soul all night. At dawn she slept like a baby in the arms of her newly found faith. And it had been his doing. He had restored her. When she woke up, innocent and naked (he had removed her clothes in the night) he united his body with hers but in an oddly chaste manner because he remained soft the whole time and no coaxing enabled him to enter her. The experience hadn't been about sex. He had always despised the simple mechanism of lust. It was too easy and it left behind pitted craters of guilt. No, this was not about sex. It was about power. Power was good, but only if the powerful had something to offer the powerless. Most people were broken and couldn't fix themselves. They needed the ministration of the powerful to renew their acquaintance with the live wondrousness of the universe. That's the gift he had received by the swimming pool through the medium of that perfect angel.

The girl by the empty pool had vanished later that afternoon. He had looked for her through all the subsequent trials of his ministry and his rise to glory but had found only coarse copies. But she was never far from his mind. He conducted a daily dialogue with her, even as he perfected the singing that had such power over lost souls. She spoke with him from the front seat of his Caddy. Seated there with her legs forever crossed under her, her school skirt riding to just about the dimples of her ass, she regarded him with eagerness. She absorbed his wisdom, savoring his plans, shifting only now and then to give him a thrill of girlish revelation. She answered his questions, too, like a schoolgirl who hasn't studied but wants to please. Now and then she teased him with a question that was much too innocent to be truthful, so that he had to upbraid her. He slapped her firm butt with his open palm hard enough for the imprint to glow there like a neon sign. Pursuing the quiet where he could mentally converse with her, he had not, however, given up trying to find the flesh-and-blood child. He followed leads and pursued signs.

But now that image of obedient original purity was mixed up in his mind with Felicity's angry face.

From his phone car, the reverend called his captains, one by one, and received reports about the preparations at the Dome. He instructed them also to put the techies on double shifts the very next day. The day of reckoning was not far. He looked at the oil refineries and chemical factories flashing past his window, and blessed their molten innards. He could taste the salt of the Dome, which had long ago impregnated his pores. Those whom Jesus had called the salt of the earth would be the first to go, lambs to the slaughter. But they would also be the first to be resurrected. He found neither regret nor fear in his heart, only a burning desire to see the End.

The car phone rang and the call Mullin had been waiting for came. But it wasn't what he expected. His Bamajans hadn't yet captured the girl. Felicity had hired out as a stripper at a French Quarter club. The place was packed every hour of the day and night. The operation was risky.

Mullin shouted into the receiver: "It's the Lord's work, you worthless piece of shit!"

The voice on the other end made another objection but didn't finish before the reverend thundered: "Bring every fucking one of them! All the fucking johns and strippers! We're sure to put them to some use! Move the fucking building if you have to!"

He threw the cellular down and leaned back to watch the ribbon of asphalt that was suddenly sparkling with good tidings. It was going to be one hell of a party, forgive me, Jesus.

Chapter Twenty-nine

Wherein Felicity and Andrea are brought together in the city of New Orleans

h e Columns Hotel was a magnolia-scented, bourbon-soaked flop house on Saint Charles Avenue, filled to the rafters with Ben Redman's past. A magnificent great oak spread its branches over the white columns in front of the terrace, where night after night, young and profligate New Orleanians drank the night away. The ornate front door gave onto a foyer guarded by statues of Edwardian Moors with flower vases atop their heads. In the grand ballroom, to the left of the entrance, standing solemnly in front of a piano and before an open window facing Saint Charles Avenue, high school boy Ben was lovingly sucked off by a debutante and distant relative named Susan, whose silvery gown split its sides when he came. Best of all, once upon a time Ben Redman had hid here in the Columns in illicit bliss with his girlfriend Felicity, who escaped from the dorm for days at a time.

The grand staircase curved upward past two plaster satyrs bathed by the colors of a pre-Raphaelite stained glass window. Ben pointed it out to Andrea even as he greeted his old friend Rita, the desk clerk, who had seen everything and was shocked by nothing, most of the time. This time, however, her practiced cool crumbled and she opened her mouth wide in surprise. A nun and a rabbi going up for a quickie! She didn't recognize Ben under his curls.

When she did, she lit a cigarette, "Why, Mr. Ben!"

Every room but one housed revelers from the passing-of-the-millennium party that, Rita explained, "had to be the Columns' personal highest." The still-vacant room had been reserved by the proprietor's son, but it seemed that his trysting had taken him elsewhere. She gave them the key.

Above the four-poster bed in Room 14 hung an English hunting scene in which the hunted were actually disheveled damsels. The mini chandelier cast a rose light over the bed.

Andrea flung her shoes to the far ends of the room, and then she removed the nun's gray habit. She wore nothing underneath, and Ben was shocked by the long whiteness of her girlish body, with the soft stamp of pubic hair sketched lightly below her navel. Andrea laughed and held the upturned pears of her breasts to Ben in both hands like offerings. He kissed her nipples, and the taste of her warmth lingered on his lips for a long, liquid minute.

Andrea grabbed the square of Ivory soap and the tiny threadbare towel hanging above the sink, and went to the communal bathroom in the hall to take a shower.

On the nightstand next to the bed, Ben aligned his prayer book and his notebook. He lay his fountain pen on top of them. From his wallet he removed a pink condom that probably dated back to the last time he'd been at the Columns with Felicity. He put it under the pillow. He then proceeded to undress, socks off first, until he stood in his underpants. He studied himself in the mirror and raked his fingers through his curly hair. He then lay on his back on the bed with his arms under his head. He thought of Andrea walking in, smelling fresh and humid from the shower, and got dressed, put away the pen, the notebook, the prayer book, and the condom, trying to formulate an explanation for his fear.

Rabbi Joseph (thirteenth century) visualized the very shapes of the letters inscribed in the Torah scrolls as a sexual embrace between God and Shekinah, the female principle. In this blessed system, the Hebrew letter yod, sign of circumcision, became the phallus of the king; the letter zayin, an extended yod, the phallus as it was about to be received by the letter chet—which Rabbi Joseph urged his disciples to visualize as "the *Matrona* whose legs are spread to receive the zayin." Since all human activity has its divine counterpart, he argued, the kabbalist's selfless "reunification" efforts on earth would restore wholeness to the universe. This meditation failed to explain away Ben's fear.

Andrea returned from the shower pink and new, wrapped only in her skimpy towel. She took one look at his lugubrious figure lying on the bed and guessed immediately that her boy was being tormented by religion.

"Hand me a shirt, will you?"

Ben didn't budge, so Andrea reached over him and grabbed his duffel bag. She rummaged in there until she found a blue work shirt. After she put it on, Ben took her wrist.

"Try to understand."

"Okay," she said. "I do. I'm not upset."

"It's religion. It takes it away from you."

"I know. It's religion, it's the town of your birth. I like them all, I like everything."

"It's all religion," Ben said stubbornly.

"I'm starved." Andrea sat cross-legged on the bed and shook her damp head, spraying the despondent rabbi.

Ben went downstairs to the bar, returned with two bourbons and a plate of étouffée, left over from the New Year's party. They drank and ate quietly, and then lay side by side like corpses on the lumpy bed that Ben had imagined was meant for love. But Andrea was perfectly and happily indifferent. They spiraled down into sleep.

Ben dreamed that he was floating down into a well full of solemn birds that stared at him as as he sank farther and farther down. At the bottom of the well was a flat plain crossed by the straight line of an infinite railroad track. Men in monks' robes and Puritans' capes stood on a hill above the track with arms full of books they had decided must be destroyed. They dropped them into the open cars of a passing train. When one of the wagons filled up, the books burst into flames. Running alongside the train was Felicity, grabbing as many books as she could. Suddenly, she wasn't running alongside the train but in front of it. She looked in imminent danger of being run over. Ben saw clearly the cover of one of the books she was holding: it was Gershom Scholem's *Kabbalah*. The title was written in gold on the black leather binding. He shouted to warn her: "Felicity! Look out!"

They were waked on the second day of the year 2000 by riotous birds in the azalea bushes below the window. A mockingbird that had lived at the Columns a long time sang the sounds of lovemaking—and of creaking doors, smokers' coughs, and flushing toilets.

Andrea turned to Ben, still sleepy, then turned away to sleep some more. She slept for another hour, which Ben spent thinking about Felicity, whose presence he sensed close by but out of focus somehow. It filled him with anxiety. He had to call her as soon as possible. He had her grandmother's and her uncle's telephone numbers. And then, of course, he had to, sometime, call his own family, which was by now doubtless tearing out its collective hair. Ben had called only once, one day before leaving Jerusalem.

They had coffee and chicory for breakfast.

"Today we are going to meet my parents," announced Ben.

"I want to explore the city," announced Andrea. "I want to walk everywhere by myself. I can meet your parents later." She put on Ben's blue work shirt and wiggled into a pair of his jeans.

Ben argued against this, but Andrea had made up her mind. He gave her instructions in the use of the streetcar, and a few dollars, and pointed her in the direction of the French Quarter, with stern instructions to return by lunchtime, when they would go to meet his parents.

Lunchtime came and went. Andrea had not returned.

I will not panic, he told himself. He called his parents, assured them that they were safe, and told them that Andrea's notoriety made it necessary to remain in hiding for a time.

"Why should she hide?" exclaimed his mother. "She stopped a bomb. She should be on TV, like everybody else this heroic."

"It's a Basque thing, Mother. You wouldn't understand."

After this nerve-wracking call, Ben set down to wait. His efforts at reading were in vain. Everything seemed vague except for a small flame that contained Andrea's face like an old-fashioned miniature. She was the only focused image inside him. His parents and his city were large, amorphous shapes that floated aimlessly around.

At three, when there was still no Andrea, he decided to look for her.

Where do you begin looking in the city that care forgot but whose patron saint is Joan of Arc? In the city of aboveground tombs and countless dives? Ben groaned thinking about just what kind of impression the vulnerable orphan might make in the smoky hells of nighttime New Orleans. Only he knew how innocent Andrea really was. She might be introduced to heroin, cocaine, and the jazzy variety of oral sex favored by trumpet players, before being sold to a pimp who'd put her to work on a street corner before selling her again.

On the streetcar going downtown, Ben studied the familiar faces of New Orleanians. His landsmen, black and white, looked worried. Their faces and foreheads were lined, there were circles under their eyes, and their hands tightly clutched their belongings. They stared out the open windows, looking alone in the universe. These millennial humans appeared vampirized.

Andrea got off the streetcar where it turned onto Canal Street, and immediately sensations assaulted her, making her skin tingle as if she had been lowered in a bath of salts. A group of black women dressed in white stood on the neutral ground singing so powerfully that leaves and dust swirled about them. A cart with balloons and wind chimes gave off an intense chocolate smell. Two men clad in long leather coats held hands watching a policeman on a black horse. A bus stopped abruptly halfway through the intersection—its destination was written in lights and alternated, flickering *Desire*, then *Cemeteries*, then *Desire*, then *Cemeteries* again. Above her head, the high-rise hotels and the stores sported billboards greeting year 2000.

A street preacher accosted Felicity. He had gold teeth and wore a white hat. He addressed her loudly through a microphone attached to a speaker he carried on his back.

"Look," he proclaimed, "Louisiana is gone! and Florida and Texas, too! Three things I now know. Armageddon has begun. The United Nations invaded the United States of America. At Saucier, Mississippi, Gulfport, Mississippi, and New Orleans, Louisiana, there are battalions of foreign troops waiting for word from the assassin of President Kennedy, who lives in New Orleans and who is, let me tell you, an acquaintance of mine! For such is the world now, black and white all mixed up, devils riding on the backs of angels! Massing for invasion! They will cause a great ball of fire that will ignite the Gulf Coast and the lower Mississippi! But fear not, girl! You will be taken under my wing, and with Jesus in your heart, God willing, you will bypass the End. Our chambers are being furnished for the return of Christ. But first we must kill the Antichrist! The UFO that's crashed at Roswell, New Mexico, has been repaired. The Antichrist is on board! Thousands of alien babies brought forth by human mothers are gathering in the French Quarter to welcome the repaired vessel, which is on its way even as we speak."

The preacher took a step forward and exhaled painfully bad breath, ready to pounce on her. But just as he was about to lay his sweaty palm on her shoulder, another hand took her arm and drew her gently away. It was a tall boy with glasses, who looked no older than sixteen.

Andrea was quite willing to be led. "Who are you?"

"Bamajan Michael." He explained that he was a recruiter for the School for Messiah Development, an institute dedicated to finding people with Messiah-attendance potential. He had been instructed to find souls, and he'd been at it for a week. So far he had been wholly unsuccessful.

"Messiah attendance? Like holding a towel for God?"

The boy smiled. "There is so much you don't know. For instance, I might have a Ph.D. in molecular physics."

"So? I might have a degree in psychology, and I might say you are nuts."

"Well, I would say that I am a priest in training of the Division of the Cosmic Egg of the Apocalypse. My supreme teacher has studied all the religions of the world and synthesized them. He has said that the cracking of the Cosmic Egg is imminent. The Messiah comes soon!"

"Who is your teacher?" Andrea asked. "And why is he cracking eggs?"

The boy explained that the supreme teacher had told his followers: "From the holy city of Jerusalem to the fleshpots of New Orleans is a long, jagged line. Few trod it without perishing. It is said, by those who know, that only one made of equal parts flesh and spirit might one day walk the jagged line. The One has come."

"That's interesting," said Andrea. "I just came from . . . Australia. My parents were killed by Aborigines several years ago."

"I'm sorry," said the boy urgently, not quite hearing her. "We have to go to SMD right away. I haven't been there in so long I might have been stricken from the recruiters' ranks!"

As they walked, he told her that thousands of trainees had been working to welcome the Messiah. The trainees were instructed by highly skilled Bamajans. The most privileged were females, chosen to be in the First Angels Choir, who would welcome the Messiah and assist in the birth of a new world.

Andrea wanted to believe him—it all sounded quite beautiful.

"Bamajan . . . sounds like a Jamaican potato dish," she said.

The boy tilted back his head, gazing heavenward, as if asking Jesus to help him with this irreverent candidate.

He looks like he wants to be kissed, thought Andrea.

Bamajan Michael led on, and on Bourbon Street they stopped in front of a building that was cordoned off by police. Yellow tape that said CRIME SCENE was stretched across the sidewalk. An angry policeman paced back and forth. He looked to Andrea like a statue of Dante she had once seen in a museum.

"Oh, my God," said the boy. "What happened?"

A street person seated on a stoop spit in the general direction of the building. "The freaks fled the coop. Cops found a couple of fresh stiffs inside. Reading only a bit of Anton Chekhov's stories might have saved them all the embarrassment—are you familiar with the manner of Anton Chekhov's death?"

The boy let go of Andrea's arm and walked away.

Andrea wandered, looking in shop windows. She was hungry. People shouted and whistled, and firecrackers exploded at her feet. From the open door of a smoky bar, a bare-breasted girl wearing a feather mask called out to her:

"Hey, skinny. You look like you need a Whopper with fries. Come on in—make a decent wage. Put some tits on you."

"Okay," said Andrea. She went in.

"Good move," said Sylvia. "Welcome to Desire, Limited. And 'Limited,' which means 'limited,' ain't no joke!"

The dark interior was lit by Christmas lights strung around the mirrored stage. Andrea stepped carefully to a booth and lowered herself onto the slashed vinyl seat.

"You wait right here and I'll have a girl bring you a burger!"

"Vegetarian," whispered Andrea.

"Make that a veggie burger!" Sylvia shouted to the cook sitting at the end of the bar, reading Marcella Hazan's *Essentials of Classic Italian Cooking*. "Everybody's got a kink. There's a new girl here says she doesn't know what an orgasm is. I'd rather be a vegetarian. Now, from my reading of feminists on the subject, from Millet to Roiphe, I have learned that this orgasm may be a fiction, but girl, let me tell you, if that's fiction, you can keep reality!"

At the bar an old man with a bald scalp snapped his suspenders and shrieked at odd intervals. Onstage, a skinny black girl with huge tits was sliding down a copper pole. "You want pussy," she shouted, "lick this pole!" The speckled mirror behind her was covered with greasy palm prints.

"*Got my mojo workin'!*" wailed the juke.

Five or six bored girls were watching television. The show was familiar. Andrea walked over and sat on a stool to watch, too. The dancers were abusing the contestants on *Wheel of Fortune*. The category was CLUE, (two words), and four letters showed on the board: M-PP---C-----. The girls were shouting, "R, you cow!" The "cow" was a platinum blond California divorcee who'd said that she collected ceramic statuettes of elephants with their trunks up.

The divorcee asked for an *R*, and two *R*s popped up in the second word. The strippers high-fived one another in triumph. The elephant-statuette collector stood to gain a matched luggage set and telescope if she solved the puzzle. It was not to be. A thickly-accented Southerner named Richard, an assistant manager at Kinko's in Macon, Georgia, took his turn and swiftly discovered a *T* and a *C*. MUPPETS CREATOR appeared. Vanna applauded. The girls shrieked. For another $500 he also solved the clue: JIM HENSON. Richard beamed as if he had won the Civil War. He won a Volkswagen and a ballooning trip over Austria.

"And he gets to fuck Hitler!" tee-heed one of the girls.

They all broke up over that one.

"Such better prizes!" exclaimed Andrea, but no one heard her.

"*The boys are back in town!*" screamed the juke. The old man snapped his suspenders. What an interesting country. Andrea liked the New World.

The cook brought Andrea a veggie burger. After she had devoured it, Sylvia, who had watched her approvingly, summoned the new girl who'd never had an orgasm. "Honey," she said, "you teach this one what I taught you."

The girl they called Scheherazade had been in the dancers' dressing room, assiduously trying to identify the face in the mirror. Andrea's face struck her as more familiar than the face she had just been studying in the mirror. Could she be me?

For her part, Andrea was struck by the dancer in an entirely different way. Something about the stripper reminded her . . . of her mother. It was impossible, but there it was; the loving shadow in the eyes of the woman from Sarajevo was in Felicity's eyes. Andrea kept nothing back.

"Mother," she exclaimed.

"Excuse me?" Scheherazade wasn't sure she'd heard right. The girl was young, maybe seventeen, but everything in her body said, No, you are not this girl's mother. And then a tiny voice of doubt said: How do you know? You may have ten children for all you know. You may be a hundred years old. You may be your own grandmother.

"Get off it, you little slut," said Scheherazade in what was actually a friendly voice.

Andrea laughed and apologized. "I'm sorry. I don't know what made me say that. I maybe was thinking about my mother. She was very beautiful, like you."

Good. I am beautiful. I am young. And the bitch has a sense of humor. Maybe she is me, after all.

From the moment that their two pairs of green eyes met (Andrea's were a lighter green, like young wheat), they experienced recognitions that traveled through their bones like electricity. When they spoke, their words trailed echoes behind them, traces of something they strained to hear but couldn't.

Felicity applied herself to teaching Andrea what she had just learned herself only the day before. She taught her how to put pasties on her nipples, how to shave her pubic hair, how to step in and out of a G-string, and how to shimmy down the copper pole slick with the sweat of the previous dancer. But between each of these lessons stretched immensities of time. It was as if they were operating on two levels at once: a slow, mundane, endless horizontal field, where their gestures were practical; and another, dizzying vertical, where they groped toward each other with tentacles of feeling. Andrea had not lost the sensation she'd had when she called Felicity "Mother." On the contrary, the impression strengthened, and it was all she could do to keep herself from bursting out in tears.

When Scheherazade fit Andrea with her own gold G-string, a wave of warmth seized her from the soles of her feet to her blazing cheeks. On its way to her cheeks, the warm wave passed between Felicity's legs and touched her nipples. And in that passage, the wave released the locked spring that no man had been able to turn. Felicity had an orgasm.

Well, the irruption had no name in the midst of its irruptive glory, but moments later, when Felicity-Scheherazade floated back from the spume of the wave, she recognized it as that elusive thing, and she began to weep. She lay her head on Andrea's shoulder.

All of Andrea's repressed sorrow for her parents seemed to bubble to the surface as well. She clutched Felicity's hands, lay her cheek on the small butterfly tattooed on her shoulder, and began to sob. Felicity patted her head and was so moved by the bristly softness of the girl's hair that she began to tremble again, and was carried off by wave after wave of pleasure.

The two women stayed like that, weeping on each other's shoulders, to the astonishment of the other strippers. The air filled with gold specks like a rain of sequins, and quite a few of them heard a sound like the beating of wings.

On the wake of this encounter came another gift: Felicity remembered who she was and what she had been doing. So sudden was the return of her memory that it seemed to be part of the sexual quake, rather than an aftershock. She moved away from Andrea and looked around as if seeing the place for the first time.

"Shit, I'm a fucking stripper!" she exclaimed in her long-unused girl-dick voice.

"Ah! *Chingush*." Andrea understood. She knew also that now she could end her own long *chingush*.

"What's *ching* . . . ?" Felicity tasted the word she couldn't finish, as if her hearing had also been restored.

Andrea explained that it was a period of time ruled by a forgetting drug, and that those who experienced a long *chingush* were like children learning to walk again when their memory returned.

Felicity performed the equivalent of a strip search on herself. Place of birth: New Orleans. Living relatives: Major Notz. Significant boyfriends: Ben, Miles. Profession: private detective. Education: B.A. in psychology, University of New Orleans. Graduate of New Orleans Police Academy. Hobbies: surfing the World Wide Web, questioning self. Felicity patted herself down as if she were a suspect. Her memories kept coming, but as the weight of herself flooded back, she was not sure if she really wanted to be her old self. And then she remembered what had given her a sense of purpose. She had work to do. Mullin. The motherfucker was in for it.

Andrea also allowed herself to remember. She remembered her release from the camp at Utla. She remembered that in Ankara, Marseilles, Barcelona, Cairo, and Bangkok, she had sexually serviced Chinese businessmen, English masochists, steatopygiphile Egyptians, Thai drug lords, and a German steel tycoon. She had stolen, been arrested, spent time in a Turkish jail, and finally stowed away on a boat bound for Israel, nearly dying of hunger during the ten-day journey. She had eaten spiders, flies, and a small mouse . . . and then, when the boat reached Haifa, she seduced a dockworker in exchange for transportation to Jerusalem.

Andrea's recollections were vivid, but there was something almost too fantastic about them. Maybe I'm fooling myself, she thought. Maybe I lay in a coma for four years in a Swedish hospital. She saw herself lying still on a bed near a window half covered by a snowy branch. But she remembered with equal intensity the spring of her arm as she lowered the whip on the steel magnate's fat behind. Which life was true? And might there be other lives, hidden like dreams in her long *chingush?* I will choose the most vivid, Andrea thought. I am young, I can always call on other lives in the future. She chose the life of crime and adventure that first occurred to her, and felt immediately stronger, cunning, resourceful.

A curious mood settled over Desire, Ltd. One by one, the dancers sat down and looked into their own pasts. Forgotten days and months, even whole years came back to them, pouring in like rain. Their memories cast a pall of sadness over the club. Even Sylvia, who made a point of looking life straight in the eyes, was overcome by an awareness of a past she had thought all but buried.

What the women of Desire, Ltd., did not know was that at that very same moment, all the people on all the streets of New Orleans were experiencing convulsive waves of remembrance. People sat on their stoops or stopped on street corners or leaned against walls, crying. Others drove faster, trying to escape the memories that pursued them like rabid bats. Everyone thought that they were alone in this irruption, but it soon became evident that the phenomenon was ubiquitous. Small groups formed, strangers spontaneously holding hands in order to steady themselves. These were the lucky ones, able to understand that while the details were unique, the sadness was common. The winds of memory literally knocked others off their feet. The churches filled with sobbing people.

Only the Shades and the Great Minds were unaffected. They regarded the spectacle of suddenly stilled citizens with curiosity and empathy but did not grasp what they were experiencing.

The lifting of the collective *chingush* lasted only one hour, but that hour at the crossroads of millennia was as long as a lifetime.

Back in the club, Felicity was the first to break the spell.

"I've got to find that motherfucking Mullin!" She was determined now to find the man who had brainwashed her, and to prevent him from doing more harm.

The major had to be contacted immediately. He must be worried sick by her absence. The pay phone was out of order and the one under the cash register was broken. Felicity laughed. She remembered her uncle's belief that all things proceeded from will, but how do you will a broken phone to life? And this, dear Uncle, she addressed his portly seriousness, is yet another proof of the tenuousness of will. Magic is stronger. The future is subject to miracles, not the flexing of the overeducated will. "Jesus came to tell the news, but every phone was broken," Felicity sang.

Felicity was about to run into the street in her G-string, but Andrea stopped her. Felicity told her that she had to act right away, but the Bosnian orphan looked at her so tenderly she lost her desire to explain. It was better to kiss her, so Felicity did, and Andrea gave herself to the kiss as if she'd been born within it. And then they cried some more.

The emotional storm embarrassed everyone. Some of the girls disappeared into the dressing rooms to cry for themselves; others went to the bathrooms for a quick pick-me-up line of cocaine.

"Girls are leaky this way," Sylvia said. "Blood, milk, tears. The moon overfills us." She knew instinctively that both women were running from something. They were in the right place. New Orleans had always been a good place to disappear. The disappeared kept one another's secrets.

"When I was a missionary in Thailand," said Sylvia, "I got caught up in a demonstration where the police were shooting into the crowd. I put my arms around this Thai girl and I prayed. I didn't care about my own life because I believed in heaven then, but I prayed and prayed for this girl. She was cryin' and everybody else around us was cryin'. And then we were all arrested, but they let me go because I was an American. Next day, I took a pedicab through all the slums, looking for her. I didn't have any money, but seein' how I was cute and demure, the driver said no problem. I looked everywhere, but I couldn't find her. I thought about her for years. Yesterday, before my shift, I go to see a friend of mine who works at the Thai Garden . . . I like to practice speaking Thai with him . . . and there is this new waitress there, and it turns out to be Sun Ki, my friend. I'm tellin' you. New Orleans is the center of the world, right here. 'Sylvia,' she told me, 'I knew you prayed for me back in Bangkok, and now Buddha's brought us back together.' "

Andrea and Felicity were struck by this instance of yet another miraculous encounter, and they were filled with a sense of purpose they had never known before. Together, they were a new being.

Chapter Thirty

Wherein angel Zack incarnates

h e   angel Zack, watching all this with an interest bordering on the unseemly, hovered solicitously over the girls, dipped his fingers of light into their tears, and then put them to his mouth and winced. Humans were made out of salt.

Zack felt something tug at his wing, and the entity known as Hermes appeared before him.

Hermes had been without a channel since Major Notz had rebuffed Carbon and the medium had gotten out of the psychic business altogether. He'd taken a liking to the mushy darkness of the channel linking his world to that of humans and was now at loose ends. Spotting an angel, he thought of asking for advice.

"I can't do anything for you, entity. I have a job." Zack tried to shoo him away, but Hermes persisted:

"Just let me give you my rendition of the scene you are watching, and maybe some answers to your questions. You'll see how important I am. And then, maybe you can find me a channel."

Zack flapped his wings in a gesture of sheer exasperation. Why me? Why me, O President of the Heavens?

Hermes took this as a yes, and proceeded thus: "It is said: More than adoration of the flesh is involved in the five-foot-six-inch frames of the mortal entities known as Felicity and Andrea. She who uncovered letters in the puzzles of the Hebrew language is the perfection of the other, who is searching for the mystery of Disappearance itself. Even before these two were chosen, it was decided that deliberations on the fate of the world would take place in New Orleans. It is thus doubly significant that the girls should meet here, at the site of future events. The chief archangels are all watching; I can see their luminous threads."

"What's the point of the slightly archaic flavor?" Zack took issue with the style.

"It's professional!" Hermes was hurt. "Besides, this is New Orleans. Everyone talks funny!"

"Why New Orleans?" lamented Zack. "Why me?"

Hermes took these to be questions.

"It is said: New Orleans has the advantage of being the wettest place on this continent, which lubricates the passage of the disembodied into the embodied. It has more people on the street than any other American city, and as you surely know, entities cannot incarnate in people sitting indoors watching television. New Orleans is concentrated so that the Minds can take in the situation of earth at a single glance and judge it accordingly. Everything is in New Orleans, good and bad, and heaven knows it. By comparison, Jerusalem and Mecca are only full of quarrels. Do not fear your assignment, Zack. Fear neither the intoxication of the jasmine flower nor the sweet-olive blossom with its scent like that of almost rotten peaches. It is not true that an angel perched too long on the folded petal of a gardenia could be pulled in by his light-thread and imprisoned until a virgin earthling kisses him on the behind. Do not be superstitious, Zack, and do not bother your Namer with small questions. Your Namer is busy."

That was enough. The impertinence of this entity knew no bounds.

"I know all this," Zack growled. "You're only mirroring my own thought. You have no message. Pshhhst!" Zack flapped his wings threateningly, and Hermes, chastened but undaunted, flew a safe distance away from the irate angel.

Of course, thought Zack, I cannot ask my Namer anything. He's too busy fulminating at the conservatism of the younger generation! It's not my fault that I sprung out of my pupa eons after the revolution that democratized heaven! I can only see what I can see, and what I see is what I hear: a lot of noise. This is a lunatics' planet. If this is what a democratic heaven has to look forward to, I'm giving up my room in my Father's mansion right now! What's next for heaven? Tourists?

Below him, Zack could see a multitude of creatures with cameras around their necks and stupid hats on their heads. Tourists had to be the lowest form of life, unconsciousness incarnate, impediments to learning, carriers of infectious superficiality. Tourists had been strictly forbidden in heaven since its inception. That was the true reason for Adam and Eve's expulsion from Paradise: gee-goshing when they should have been studying. But these days, who knows? Anything was possible. Tourists in heaven! Lord President Somewhat Mighty!

Hermes lisped: "Try me! Try me!"

"For Chrissakes! You're a mosquito! Okay, tell me this: what's the point of embodiment?"

"It is said: You are embodying because Christ did. But one Christ is no longer enough. To redeem this prison planet now, a multitude of Christs are needed. Therefore, heaven is dispatching multiple Messiahs! Your job is to keep track, angel Zack, to see to it that not one Christ is misplaced. And for that reason, you're going to be encased in flesh, angel!"

Zack flew right over him so he wouldn't have to feel his smug draft. Maybe he knew all the answers, but so what. He lisped! And anyway, couldn't Zack keep better track of the heavenly messengers without being encased in flesh! Ugh. It really was the end.

His only option was either to embody now and do his job from the ground or to embody after the Minds' vote was taken. Perhaps the best thing was to get used to a human body as soon as possible. But the dark, the organs, the blood . . . ugh! And why make such a momentous decision now, on only the second day of the new millennium? What was the hurry? Nothing had been done earlier, despite numerous opportunities. The myriad of spirits inhabiting the innumerable levels of heaven had made such outlandish calculations and promises to the embodied of the earth that it had become something of a scandal even in the scandal-free upper no-incarnation zones. That is, of course, why anyone in heaven worked at all: they wanted to end up in those uppers. Zack's Namer was right: heaven was a growing bureaucracy. From within the diamonds of layering infinity, the Catholic Church, by comparison, looked like a single-cell organism.

Still, if figuring out such things had been his job, Zack would have long ago gotten his service star and gone home to strum a harp. But it was not his job. His job, in addition to polling the Minds, was to instruct Felicity and Andrea, humans heaven had designated to spin the Wheel of Fortuna. On that spin depended something he couldn't quite understand. No matter what the Minds decided in the end, apocalypse or remission, the girls had to spin the wheel. And even then, the final word belonged neither to the Minds nor to Fortuna but, most likely, to the mood of the Creator President. Why even bother with these rituals?

Hermes enjoyed watching Zack suffer. He was sure that in the end he would win over the angel. But something odd possessed the creature just as Hermes attempted to approach again.

Zack was lifted up into the stratosphere by twin sprays of earth perfume, spritzed into the musky air by the two will-o'-the-wisp girls below. Just as abruptly he was hurled down and began a vertiginous descent toward a glowing object that turned out to be a mane of red hair. Zack closed his light-breathing pores and plunged all the way into the darkness of the body below.

Sylvia was washing a glass when she felt that a large moth had landed on her head. A searing pain parted her skull and traveled quickly downward. She felt her cells overfill. Round, spiky, oblong, and octagonal shapes danced behind her eyes. A huge feathery tickle seized her front and back as Zack entered her.

"Shit," swore Hermes. "Now what will become of me?"

Chapter Thirty-one

Wherein Ben Redman, searching for Andrea, regains his city

e n Redman began his search for Andrea in the music clubs. Los Babies del Merengue and the Soul Rebels Brass Band were playing at the Dream Palace. Outside, some kids were hanging out smoking ganja.

"I'm looking for this girl," he began awkwardly, "skinny, has green eyes, is wearing a blue shirt, big jeans. Oh, she's from Spain."

They had a laugh over this, and one of them said:

"That's the one, she be the one I be lookin' for too, for a long time, me."

That broke them up again, and another one admitted that he too had been dreaming of a bony-kneed, long-legged, green-eyed girl from Spain.

"Matter of fack, I eben wrote a song 'bout this girl." He broke into an air-guitar riff and sang:

> She be mah green-eyed girl from Spain.
> Her name be love an' ecstasy.
> Found her, lost her, she mah main
> Liberation fantasy!

Tee-hee, tee-hee, laughed the air, all lavender and bubbly.

Ben crossed the street to Café Brasil, owned by his old friend Adé, but

Adé wasn't there—he was spending the New Year in Rio, where two million Brazilians dressed in white threw flowers into the sea. A Latino couple was leaning on Adé's 1963 Cadillac convertible, parked permanently at the curb upfront, discussing world politics and love. Two French Quarter anarchists rode up on bicycles. Tied to their handlebars were baskets full of flyers calling on Quarterites to resist the throngs of religious madmen who had invaded the city.

"They say they got the nukes, man," argued the Latino boy, "but it's just to calm the public! How many they kill? Three hundred? They got ten thousand nukes, man. Those pictures, they are dummy nukes, man. I can buy six like that at Toys 'R' Us!"

He was referring, Ben supposed, to that morning's headline, which he had glimpsed in passing: INTERPOL STORMS NUKE BLACKMAILER HIDEOUT, CAPTURES ROGUE WEAPONS. ARE SOME STILL OUT THERE? That was good news, and Ben had given it no more thought. The world was being held hostage every few days now. The miracle was that it was still here.

"Maybe they never had nukes in the first place," teased the girl. She took some pink gum out of her mouth and stuck it on Adé's windshield wiper. There was a chain tattooed around her upper right arm, and on her left arm she wore ten gold barbed-wire bracelets. A hole in her T-shirt flashed an upturned breast with a red raspberry on top.

"Never had nukes, man? You crazy? *Everybody* got nukes now. Me and you, baby, are the only people in the world that don't have nukes! We got something better!" Her boyfriend moved his hips seductively and put an arm around the girl, who laughed and jingled her jewelry.

"I can't believe the fascist police moving in and killing hundreds of people!" The bicycle anarchist shook his head. "They've been doing that shit ever since Waco!"

Ben interrupted the discussion to ask if they'd seen Andrea, whom he described as a skinny auburn-haired polyglot. He loved using words like that on the street.

"What kind of tattoos she got?" asked the chain girl.

"I don't think she has any."

"She don't belong to anybody in these streets, then," confirmed the girl. "That's how you know people now, alive or dead, by their pictures. No names, no lineup, no ten most wanted, if you get my drift. Only fuckin' honkies got no pictures."

One of the anarchists looked Ben up and down. "Are you one of the re-

ligious invaders, Rabbi? We could skin you right here." He handed Ben a
flyer.

"Leave him alone," said the girlfriend. "Can't you see he's in love?"

Ben walked on, reading the anarchist flyer.

WORKERS OF THE QUARTER!

Have you recently walked out of your house and stumbled over a crucified
man? Have you been accosted on your front steps by a man eating hot coals?
Has a naked Hindu floated into your bathroom through an open window?
Has a woman with a cobra in her vagina begged you for food? Has a
preacher tried to nail you with a 50-pound neon Bible? If these things hap-
pened to you, you're not alone! Who are these pigs and what do they want
from us? Why are they in the Vieux Carré? Let's meet Sunday at 1025
Chartres and DO SOMETHING ABOUT THE TIDAL WAVE OF DE-
MENTED FANATICS! BRING REVOLVERS, MACHINE GUNS, BOWS,
HAMMERS, AND PEPPER SPRAY!

Le Carré aux Carrois! See you there!

There were hundreds of places in New Orleans where musicians plied
their trade. After Café Brasil and the Dream Palace, Ben went to Snug
Harbor, and the Rubyfruit Jungle on Frenchmen Street, then backtracked
to Decatur, stopped at Checkpoint Charlie's, Café Siam, the Abbey, and
the tourist joints by the French Market. He checked into the Toulouse
Cabaret on Toulouse Street, then walked the length of Bourbon Street,
stopping in briefly at Big Daddy's, the best strip joint in town. A heart-
breakingly beautiful girl was hanging upside down from a revolving wheel.
She looked at him and mouthed the word "mandala." I'm getting tired,
Ben thought, but he was convinced that she had indeed said, "Mandala."
He then walked to Ramparts Street and checked into the Funky Butt and
Dotty's. The longer he walked the more confused his descriptions of Andrea became. For some he made her green eyed and petite, just like Felicity; for others he conjured a fiery, dark woman. Invariably, the description
matched some inner picture of those he talked to: anyone looking at him
could see his longing. The street telegraph broadcast the word that a
young rabbi in love was looking for a lost girl. Suppose I'm mad, Ben
thought. Maybe there isn't any Andrea, and I conjured her out of the Hebrew letter representing the Shekinah, the female principle.

Felicity could certainly help him. Even before Felicity had officially decided to become a PI, she had loved solving mysteries. They had once pre-

tended that she was a detective and he was a smuggler. She had caught him, handcuffed him, and molested him. Was that two years ago? A year and a half? Now she *was* a detective and he *was* a smuggler, but he couldn't reach her. He called from pay phones several times, but there was no answer.

Van Gogh's Ear and Dyslexic Cadillacs were playing at the Last Call. The establishment employed two male bouncers wearing only G-strings, who carefully winnowed the mob waiting to get in. Three prostitutes in red tights and leotards stood at the curb across the street from the club, hawking their wares. A white-hatted pimp sat elegantly with crossed legs on a crate behind them. The creases of his trousers were razor sharp.

Ben walked up to him to ask if he had seen Andrea, but a hammy arm wrapped itself around his throat.

"Not so fast, Preacher. You wanna talk to da man?"

Ben made choking noises that went unheard by the crowd across the street clamoring for election by the beefy nudes. Just as suddenly as it had coiled around him, the beefy arm let go. The white-hatted pimp dismissed his bodyguard and gestured for Ben to approach.

"I saved your life. Now, how are you going to repay me?" The flesh purveyor's diction was clear and inflected by the Caribbean.

"I imagine I'll think of something," coughed Ben.

"You imagine, you imagine. Everybody be imaginin'. But who *controls* them imaginins?"

"God, that's who," said Ben grumpily, "and the electric company, the bank, Intel Corporation, and the police."

"Yes." The pimp grinned. "That's how it useta be. Now it's not like that. Now everyone, man, be controllin' whatever they be imaginin'. I control this corner. And I may, I say I *may* be imaginin' I be controllin' you. You be standin' on my imaginins."

"That's reasonable," said Ben, drawn into the argument despite himself. "It is one of my contentions that at this point in history anybody with an imagination can control as much of the world as they are capable of imagining. It pleases God to watch the effort."

"Man. Who you belong to? You sharp." The pimp half rose and extended two diamond-ringed fingers to Ben, who shook them limply. "Wanna run some chicks, man? I give you the fat one, over there . . ."

"What, do I look like I buy and sell humans beings?" Ben said and looked over where the fat one swung her hips lazily as if she knew she was being talked about.

The man didn't take offense. "My name is Jonah. I protect them girls. I swallowed them, you know."

"Have you seen a girl about seventeen, skinny, wearing loose men's clothes?" Ben tried to remember more but couldn't.

"Hmmm. Light-skinned girl, you say, about five seven, red hair?"

Ben confirmed the description.

"I like you, Preacher. Check out Desire, Limited. On Decatur. They got some new girls there. Now, about that Franklin."

Ben handed him a Jackson instead.

A fire swallower juggled a flaming torch past his ear. A ship floated above him headed around the elbow of the Mississippi. A beaded costume on a dress dummy sparkled in the window of a shop. It's the city herself, thought Ben. He took the corner on Decatur.

Chapter Thirty-two

Wherein Andrea is with Felicity,
and Felicity with Andrea

o u two go home now," Sylvia told Felicity and Andrea. "We're gonna close this place tonight." The city was still celebrating the new millennium, but the crowds in the Quarter had thinned considerably.

"Must be fuckin' resolutions." Sylvia grinned. "Married men resolutin' to stay away from pussy!"

"Yeah," agreed a bored dancer, "even the pussy biz has to clam up sometime."

Dressed in skirts and T-shirts plucked from a clothes pile in the dressing room, Felicity and Andrea hailed a cab.

Felicity retrieved the spare key she'd hidden behind a loose brick to the right of the door. It pleased her to remember again; it was as if her memory, having returned, was powerfully rested and giddy to function. In fact, she remembered every hiding place of every key of every apartment she had ever lived in, a string of keys to her past. Everything she had carried the day she had been abducted was in some locker at SMD, but they hadn't been able to keep her memory.

Felicity opened her door, dreading what might greet her there. But her office and bedroom were serenely undisturbed. As Felicity showed Andrea her tiny living quarters, she grew more and more amazed by the extraordinary neatness of everything. Felicity never was much for housekeeping, yet every single thing in her rooms was shiny and clean. Her Mexican vase had *fresh* flowers in it! Fresh! But the vase itself was newer than she remembered, different.

Felicity pulled open the drawer of her desk. Her gun was still there. She sniffed the barrel, and the smell of steel and gunpowder fortified her. Felicity examined her things one by one and saw that some were hers and some were replacements. There were no messages on her answering machine, but the tape had been carefully wound to the beginning. She called the major's number, but there was no answer. Whoever had gone to the pain of cleaning her apartment had done a good job. Most important, her laptop was in its place on the bed.

Felicity flopped down on her belly and invited Andrea to lie next to her. She told Andrea about her favorite cybersite.

"What is cyber?" Andrea had never heard the word.

"Cyberspace. You go there through your computer."

"There? Where is there?"

"Nobody really knows, but about twenty years ago people all over the world started migrating to this place. Some people stay there sixteen hours a day. There are cities there, and fantasy worlds, and pictures, songs, food recipes, cemeteries, weddings, history. They call this place 'virtual,' but most people think it's real. They prefer cyberspace to what they call 'meat space.' I only go there to make love with people from history."

"Let's both make love with people from history!" Andrea said, grasping only the "make love" part, still not sure what "cyber" was.

"Do you know who Ovid was? He's the coolest."

"The Roman poet? I read him in school." Andrea had even translated the first lines from the second book of the *Tristia*, from the Latin:

> Quid mihi vobiscum est, infelix cura, libelli,
> ingenio perii qui miser ipse meo?
> What have I to do with you, books, my burden and my worry,
> when I, unworthy as I am, am dying because of my gifts?

Ovid was prompt. He sat on the edge of a water well, with a cup to his lips. Behind him the Black Sea moved in a gentle breeze. Flowering vines twined themselves about a colonnaded villa to his right. It was summer in Thrace.

Felicity's avatar—a sandal-clad girl with an amphora—approached the poet by the water well.

"Hello, Scheherazade, good afternoon to you in your world. The inconceivable has happened: the empire is freeing her slaves and recalling her exiles. Nor is this just a Roman phenomenon, though Rome considers herself as the world. I have received the word from Rome that I may return home. A wave of generosity has seized the rulers of the world. Persia and the barbarians are also releasing slaves and calling back their citizens. Accustomed as I am to looking for political motives, I must admit that I am astounded. No such motives seem to me present, though the political consequences will not be long in coming. The freed slaves of Rome will return to their homelands with new skills and ideas, but also bitterness toward Romans. I am told that a great festivity in my honor is being prepared in the Forum. But I will tell you, girl from the future, that I have no wish to return. I have become accustomed to my suffering. I draw the living elixir of my verse from deprivation and pain—I have no need for reconciliation or even happiness. The exile loves his estrangement and his alienation. I have no taste for the Roman olive branch. What do you say to that?"

"I am not very well educated," Andrea said, "but of one thing I am certain: no emperors in history have ever freed their slaves or recalled their exiles. No such thing could have happened in Ovid's time."

But Felicity believed Ovid. She rested her amphora in the dust at Ovid's feet and said to Andrea: "Well, he must know, because he is reporting from his time. Maybe history is not taking place the way it's been reported for centuries. It's still happening, changing, taking turns."

Ovid drank from his cup, waiting for Scheherazade's reply.

Andrea was not convinced. "But is it the same history? The world Ovid lives in is not the same world I learned about in school. If in Ovid's present world the emperors are freeing their slaves, it means that his world is ending. Emperors do not dismantle the bases of their power out of generosity. They must need to self-destruct." Andrea had not wasted her time among the scholars at Saint Hildegard's. "No wonder Ovid misses his sorrows: in them he was alive. The end of his world is also his end."

"Ovid," Felicity spoke, "our age knows you for your sorrows. If you were to suddenly accede to happiness, we would want to know nothing of you. What you say cannot be. If your age of peace has come, how is it that we know nothing of it, and how is it that history continued after your good news in an endless chain of estrangement, exile, and sorrow?"

"To that I have no answer. Perhaps Rome declared her peace many times but few heard the news. In any case, this is good-bye. I have decided to sever all routes to the past and the future. Farewell, princess of sleep, comforter of Thrace's exile." He sauntered off the edge of the well, planted a kiss on the girl's cheek, and walked away. The waves in the sea rolled into view.

"Wait a minute longer, poet. I want to introduce you to my friend . . ."

Andrea chose an avatar—a woman draped only in long curly hair—and said: "Beatrice."

"Ah," said Ovid, turning briefly around and enveloping Beatrice with a kind but distant gaze, "Dante's love." And then he turned again and walked away.

"We'll ask for Dante now." Felicity typed *Dante*, but someone else showed up instead, a gaunt old man carrying a skull. He walked slowly toward them on a field littered with bodies, the aftermath of a battle. Black clouds floated in a gray sky.

"I greet you, Scheherazade and Beatrice. I am Nostradamus. The soup of cyphers that I have spent my life preparing has boiled over. Everything I have predicted has already happened. The world of humans is done. You are on your way to a function where angels and humans will mingle. It will be terrifying. The lion will devour the lamb."

Scheherazade and Beatrice stepped with distaste among the corpses, some of which were still bleeding through holes in their armor.

"You have scared the world for far too long, Nostradamus. You are tired. Sleep now." Scheherazade was angry. She felt no affection for the old bird of doom whose prophecies had come true one by one, and were still unfolding. What evil dream had seized the poor man to give him such detailed visions of war, pestilence, famine, and death? Even now, so many years after his own historical death, Nostradamus prattled on, omen after omen, nightmare after nightmare. Sleep, you old coot. Scheherazade granted him rest across time.

Felicity typed *Dante* again, but there was no answer. She typed *Amelia Earhart* then, and *Joan of Arc*, and no one appeared. An abandoned city showed on the screen, but nothing moved within.

Then a message came onto the screen, a banner floating above the silent houses: *Greetings, Scheherazade. Your cyberlovers from the distant past are saying good-bye. They are all disconnecting, withdrawing to their niches of time in anticipation of a great event.*

Andrea was disappointed and Felicity was angry. She scrolled through her list of electronic addresses. There they all were, people from all ages:

Alexander, Archimedes, Hoffman, Homer, Jefferson, Joan of Arc, Lao-tzu, Marx, Plato, Saint Teresa . . . Even if they lived just around the corner, they still had the strength of imagination on their side. Felicity wrote the following message:

> *Scheherazade, who has given closure to your restlessness and made your nights bearable, now asks something of you. This is the most important request she has ever made in her life. Listen, all. Come now out of cyberspace and be with her and her new friend, Beatrice. Come from your hideouts in ages past, from countries far away, from your offices. Come out from behind your pseudonyms, leave your shells at once. Get in your cars, strap on your wings, teleport if you must. For this time only, you must come and join us! While every person in New Orleans will soon mask for Carnival in order to become someone else, you are invited to come here and be yourselves!*

Then she selected SEND ALL.

Felicity typed her real name and address. She had no way of knowing, and perhaps neither did her cyberlovers, that the actual entities whose identities they had so carefully claimed were already in New Orleans, engaged in a grave activity. Others, of course, were mere humans whose on-line service had mysteriously failed.

"Your cyberfriends make me think of my friends in Jerusalem." Andrea told Felicity about the scholars and the nuns at Saint Hildegard's, and how she had left without saying good-bye.

"They must miss you."

"They must hate me." Andrea felt sad for a moment.

The evening of Andrea's departure from Jerusalem, still ignorant of the fact that she was gone, Professor Li wrote to his wife in Beijing.

> My Blossom:
> I have been wasting time waiting for permission to translate the manuscript. But not entirely. The distinguished guests of this hospice have provided me with much food for thought. They are all emissaries of certain religious currents who appear intent on a mission I have not been able to fathom. They have gathered in Jerusalem to receive instructions

about some momentous event that is supposed to conclude the Christian millennium. I have not been trained to understand the core of their religion, which is supposed to be a mystery, in any case. I do have the sense, nonetheless, that a sort of monstrous, unbalanced occurrence is palpable here in Jerusalem, a city unlike any other. I would not be surprised if an entirely unknown element, something that might be called *mysterium*, were one day to be discovered leaking from the stones. A sort of radiation. Forgive me, blossom. I digress. This is also a consequence of this city, which considers itself the center of the world, making everything else a digression. There is also a girl here, a Bosnian refugee, whose presence has somehow captivated all of us. She was raised under the Yugoslav communist regime for the early part of her life. Because of this I feel a certain empathy for her that I doubt my religious-trained friends would understand. If the tragic mistakes with which we are all familiar had not occurred in the former Soviet sphere, this girl could have been a leading comrade of the first rank. She has a genuine revolutionary sensibility. As it is, she is a refugee, tossed about by the winds of circumstance . . .

Having allowed himself the luxury of sentiment, Professor Li pushed his laptop away and looked out the window. A raindrop hung there from the tip of a bare olive branch. Ah, poetry. It wasn't something he thought about very often nowadays. In his youth, he had written poetry. But then, so had Mao. And Stalin. It didn't prove anything. The time had come to return to China. His search for the manuscript had been unsuccessful, but he had gained something else, a mission that was yet unclear. Dr. Li had an unsettling vision of himself a few months hence, after returning to China. He saw himself in a large, cold auditorium, standing before thousands of blue-clad Chinese from the highest ranks of society, talking . . . about Andrea. He tried in vain to modify this ludicrous picture by willing himself to speak of other, important things: the future of Confucian scholarship, the direction of education in the twenty-first century. It wasn't working. Every time he opened his mouth, unbidden words came to him: Comrades, I must speak to you about Andrea the Orphan. Andrea, the mistress of the wheel. Andrea, the one who has astonished and seduced me.

Just about the time Professor Li finished his letter, Lama Cohen, panicked by her inability to locate her prayer wheel, began searching the closet where she kept her few things. She remembered last using it the evening before, prior to her meditation. She had fallen into a deep dreamless sleep, interrupted only by the passage of a white bird through the room. The bird had been tall and smelled strongly of tobacco. The lama had woken up smiling at the bird in her dream, but now she wondered if the bird had been a dream. Lama Cohen shivered. White birds were a bad omen. Was she going to die soon? There would be no doubt about it if the bird had indeed taken her prayer wheel. But while the white bird was a likely suspect, Lama Cohen rather knew who'd taken it. She had early on discerned in Andrea an impishness that reminded her of her own self. Between the ages of fourteen and seventeen, naughty Iris had shoplifted from every interesting store in the better ski resorts of the Rockies and found enough time to seduce considerable numbers of men her father's age. Still, her sympathy went only so far. Her wheel was her professional tool, like a doctor's stethoscope. She had to retrieve it. She had already opened the door of her room to go out and look for Andrea when she heard a series of low moans at the window. She left the door half open and pried open the wooden shutters. Standing on the windowsill, looking straight at her with round eyes, was a white owl. The bird moaned again and Lama Cohen laughed. How could she have suspected Andrea? Here was the culprit.

"Where is my prayer wheel?" she asked of the bird, who looked apologetic on top of being terminally sad.

"You must return to your congregation in New Mexico. Bring them the good news of the coming of Andrea the Orphan." The bird enunciated the words like an ancient teacher of the dharma.

Father Hernio noticed that the box containing the ashes of his parents was gone. Curiously, he felt neither panic nor anger, but relief. He understood that the loss of this object signaled the end of his journey in the weary city of miracles. He saw stretched before him the city of Mindanao and the ocean beyond it. The city and the ocean teemed with millions of people gathered to hear his message. "I have brought good news from Jerusalem," he said. Standing next to him, enveloped in green shimmer, was Andrea, holding a dazzling emerald wheel. The priest began to pack.

The disappearance of his bull-roarer was particularly grave, because Father Zahan was at an impasse. He needed to request instructions about the next stage of his mission. He had received his first set of instructions in a dream exactly one year before. Darumulun, the supreme Yuin deity, had ordered him to go to Jerusalem to meet other holy men in advance of a great meeting that would decide the fate of the visible world. Father Zahan had been surprised. The Yuin had no apocalyptic theology like the Christians. For them, the End had come a long time ago, close to their beginnings in dream time. The Yuin had angered Darumulun then, and they had had to remove an incisor and scar themselves during initiation ever since, in penance. After that, the Yuin distinguished no longer between the visible and the invisible worlds. But Father Zahan had not questioned his dream. Such dreams came only three times in the life of any man. These were his guide dreams, proceeding from dream time: they had to be obeyed. Even Darumulun had to acknowledge other gods. Even heaven, it seemed, was subject to change in these troubled days.

Father Zahan had last employed his communicator in the Garden of Gethsemane on a day when there were no tourists. He had asked the gods to guide him and had concluded with a plea for peace among them. He hated to admit it, but he had become quite distressed by the way heaven mimicked discord among men. Or was it the other way around? In any case, he had received no answer but for the burst of rain that broke unexpectedly over his head.

Dr. Carlos Luna shivered. He couldn't find his Aztec-wheel sweater. This sweater, knit for him by the seven *brujas* of his native village, near Palenque, from the finest hair of a young llama, was his protector both against cold and against the world. When he was wrapped in it, neither cold nor indifference bothered Dr. Luna. This sweater was indeed warm, as Andrea had already ascertained. She had pulled it over her head and stretched it down just past her naked butt, noticing how soft it was. Together with Professor Li's shawl, she was dressed quite comfily. The mirror on the door had given her back an image of disheveled but stylish loveliness.

Dr. Luna was certain that his sweater had been stolen by one of the many idle neotribals who loitered at a café he liked to frequent. Their looks of admiration for the sweater's intricately woven calendar hadn't escaped him. Doubtless they were interested in reproducing its intricacy on whatever unadorned skin they still possessed. It had been exceedingly hot in the café, and he seemed to remember removing his sweater.

Dr. Luna tucked a rarely smoked pipe in the pocket of his black trench coat and went out to investigate. He tipped an imaginary hat when he passed the open door of the chapel where Mother Surperior and Father Tuiredh were absorbed in the study of what appeared to be a large dark shape floating above their heads. These Christians are very strange, he said to himself.

The Fig, a vegetarian restaurant on Haik Efraim Street, was a popular neotribal hangout. The sign read: THE FIG, *Just the Garden, No Internet.* He hoped to find his sweater. If not, he would pin a notice on the bulletin board, offering a reward for its return. The waitresses had hair painted in various colors, earrings and rings in various parts of their bodies—more parts than were visible, he suspected—and spoke six languages (without saying much in any of them, he thought meanly, then regretted it). Father Luna was not mean, but he found the fashion of body piercing and scarification for no good ritual reason distasteful. Mayan people scarred themselves when they became adults, in order to signify their separation from childhood. But these young people seemed to do it for the opposite reason, in order to remain children. Punctured and scarred like this, they incurred only ridicule in the adult world and were always shunned and given only the least responsible tasks. He was horrified by this waste of strong young people in the Christian world. Just when they should be called to serve their people, these youths became most adrift. Everything had been set on its head and was exactly the opposite of what it should have been. The young were more idle than the old, men served machines, women were barren, little screens had replaced meetings between the people, the wondrous senses were in decline, nature or what remained of it was being defoliated and erased. Most wild animals were dead or dying.

While Dr. Luna had these uneasy thoughts, a young woman stood before him with a pad, ready to take his order. She had barely any hair on her head but what there was struggled between several colors. Each strand was a different hue. In her lips, three gold studs gave her a funny triangular mustache. When she spoke, he saw that her tongue was lined with some kind of metal.

"I will have this." The Mayan father pointed absently to an item on the menu labeled Tofu Nightingale Nest. "And I have a question . . . I was here the other day. Did anyone find a sweater?"

The metallic girl took his order, then said, "You look sad. I will go ask at the back. We will find your sweater."

Dr. Luna was touched by her compassion. She put her pad in her back pocket, then said: "Didn't you come in here once with the girl from *Gal Gal Hamazal*?"

"Yes. Andrea." He had once had lunch with Andrea here.

The entire staff and all the customers in the restaurant heard this and began to comment.

"I never watch TV," a boy said, "but I saw her once when I was waiting for a bus. She's a very unhappy girl, I think."

"There is a rabbi in the Knesset who wants the show stopped because the letters of the Hebrew alphabet are sacred. This girl could bring about the End of Creation," remarked a rail-thin youth with tiny gold glasses sewn right into his skin.

"*Gal Gal Hamazal* is a gate for the disappearance of people," the waitress said. "I had three roommates who disappeared because they watched too much television."

"True." The thin youth nodded gravely. "Television is a portal through which people pass into the afterlife, while still alive. Already, people are nothing but heads and fingers connected to the evil neural World Web. Their bodies are gone." He spoke with so much bitterness Dr. Luna felt the need to comfort him.

"You are still young." He didn't know what else to say. The boy was a philosopher, but so was everyone in Jerusalem. The whole city was in need of comfort.

Dr. Luna was pleased that his acquaintance with Andrea had awakened such interest among the usually sullen young. He agreed that the rabbi's fears were well founded.

"The rabbinical objections have parallels in Mayan beliefs," he explained. "The priestly language is forbidden to the uninitiated. I can't say much about the disappearance of people now . . . Our people have disappeared for centuries."

The multicolored metallic waitress, who had gone to the back to ask about his sweater, came back with disappointing news. No one had seen it. The other patrons' sympathy was immediate and energetic. They understood the importance of vestments and symbols.

"Whoever took it is going to bring it back!" vowed a bald-headed giant dressed in an African skirt and a leather jacket.

Everyone concurred. Dr. Luna ate his Tofu Nightingale Nest, a round-bottomed concoction with bright pimento slivers in the saffron-tinted tofu curds. These young people were not at all bad. During the course of his dinner he was astounded to hear them express beliefs very similar to his. They too lamented the destruction of the natural world. Some of them had never seen a wild animal except on a television screen. After they renounced the virtual world, they saw none. They spoke lovingly and nostalgically of birds.

One small Australian youth with what appeared to be antennae grafted to his skull remembered every bird he had ever seen. He recited their names with eyes half closed in rapture and cried after the name of the last one, the snow ygdrin. He had seen the last ygdrin at the Sidney zoo.

Dr. Luna returned to the convent, content with his outing. He had also changed his mind about the young. The boy who had cried over the ygdrin looked a little like an ygdrin himself. Perhaps the birds were not gone after all, but had become these armies of painted young people with their plumagelike tattoos. It was not unheard of. The world had begun with bird people. He thought affectionately of Andrea, who, though unscarred and unfeathered, was yet a member of this generation. It distressed him to think that they were inheriting a world on the brink of annihilation. There would, of course, be another world, but these children would be sacrificed before they could even register a complaint. The cosmic forces, he well knew, had their intricate harmonies, but for an earthling all of it brought sorrow. He forgot all about his sweater, though he had been assured by the denizens of the Fig that no stone would be left unturned in search of it. He smiled at the quaint expression. This was Jerusalem—there were a lot of stones. He imagined them in their bird guises, led by the whiteness of Andrea, searching for his brightly colored sweater among the stones of Jerusalem. He knew also that he would never see this, because it was time to return to Indian America to report to the elders what he had found.

What have I found? I found the spirit of the young, he answered himself.

Next day, the scholars found all their cherished objects. They had been shoved under the cot in Andrea's room. Retrieving them one by one, Sister Rodica wept, and when she returned them one by one, the scholars looked ready to weep as well.

Lama Cohen expressed all their feelings when she spun her prayer wheel and said, "She played with it."

Indeed, as each of them put away their things, they were glad that their orphan had taken and perhaps played with them. Her touch had added an imponderable substance to their possessions and in a mysterious way facilitated their leave-taking. Then the scholars began to pack, this part of their mission having come to an end.

Chapter Thirty-three

Wherein the necessity for action seizes our heroines. Dinner with Major Notz. Ben's oracle.

n d r e a leaned over and kissed Felicity's mouth. In that instant, Felicity's body spoke to her with all the voices locked within it. Fear! Fear what? God! one voice said, louder than all the others. God what? She heard others—Miles, Grandmère, Notz, garbled, speaking fast, questioning—and each voice died in the kiss. She understood now: every kiss she had been given or offered had been in quest of something. Felicity drew away and asked Andrea: "Who are you?"

Andrea opened her eyes, and her face came back from so far away it took a fluid eternity to regain its features. "I've been so many people, I'm too tired to remember them all."

And then they gave themselves to the kiss.

There have been many kisses in the world, Andrea thought, but this kiss is different. There's been a lot of kissing this girl done, but this is different, thought Felicity. They kissed for so long they remembered, if that is the word, every kiss they ever kissed. All the incomplete kisses of their young lives rushed to be completed.

"Damn!" Felicity drew her breath. "This is *the* fucking kiss."

"Light chocolate!" Andrea licked Felicity's lips.

"Balkan swarthy candy with long white legs."

They laughed and played and were lighter than air, and then kissed some more, and each time the kiss overwhelmed them. They lay there with their hearts beating hard.

"I have a feeling that every time we kiss we make something." Felicity saw a marble sculpture of their lips on a green lawn.

Andrea heard something that sounded like many human voices speaking at once. She thought about Rodica and how she'd wept when pointing out a painting of Judas betraying Christ with a kiss. "That man," Rodica had said, "made kissing evil." That's it, Andrea thought. Judas had made kissing evil, but when she and Felicity kissed, kissing was made good again. Their kisses were snaking like seismic fissures through the psyches of the citizenry, causing them regret, pain, humility, and a dolorous need to emerge from hiding. People jolted to awareness by the return of their forgotten pasts were burning the phone lines trying to make amends to those they'd hurt a long time before.

"Do you suppose we ought to try this in public?"

Andrea was all for it. They were going to take the kiss for a walk.

The phone rang as they were about to go out the door. It was Major Notz.

"Finally. How are you, darling?"

"I tried to call you all day, Uncle. I had a nasty experience, and you'll have to help me with the terrible revenge I am planning on someone. And I want you to meet a friend, Andrea."

He invited them to that evening's dinner at Commander's Palace.

"You'll like my uncle; he's a first-class eccentric. Every Tuesday he eats dinner at this restaurant."

Andrea liked whatever Felicity said she'd like.

It was evening already and the city pulsed with an energy unusual even by its elevated standards. The fog-shrouded neon above the hotels on Canal Street sent plumes of soft light drifting over the street.

"New Orleans is an old whore," explained Felicity. "She takes a long time to get ready and a long time to wind down. No party ever really ends here; it just keeps smoldering till the next one."

Felicity waved to the Shades massed on her street. They cheered when they saw her.

"Man, you're back." The girl with the sixteen rings in her cheeks was glad.

"Don't go anywhere without me," laughed Felicity and handed her a twenty. "Wine all around. Happy New Year."

They let out a cry of thanks, sounding like birds. For a moment, Andrea saw a flock of many different kinds of birds glistening with rain under the streetlights. She was beginning to enjoy her ability to see metaphors become literal. Was this a kind of power, or just craziness? She didn't care. The world had been literal for too long.

Felicity and Andrea walked with their arms around each other, kissing now and then. At the streetcar stop they collided with a gang of drunk rednecks.

"Fucking dykes!" slobbered one of them.

Andrea gave him the finger.

"Why, it's bigger than his dick!" exclaimed Felicity.

Something crude might have taken place if Andrea hadn't spotted a slender young boy on the neutral ground, looking lost.

"Look, it's Michael, the boy from the Bama . . . the Jamaican potato dish." She dragged Felicity by the arm toward the boy. Inexplicably, the rednecks parted to let them pass.

"They were weird," the bellicose one told his companions, but he couldn't explain the mortal fear that had seized him when Andrea gave him the finger. He didn't have to explain; the same claw of impending mortality had seized all of them.

The women overtook the boy, who had started to walk faster when he saw them. Felicity touched him on the shoulder. The boy's hair stood on his head like a fright wig.

"Easy, lad. I am one of the angels of the First Angels Choir." Felicity hummed "Rock of Ages," and the boy looked trustingly back and inclined his head lamblike. Felicity patted it, smoothing down some of the quills.

"Do you know anything about the Dome?"

"Well, you're an angel, shouldn't you be there now?" Michael Bamajan trembled.

"She fell, she's a fallen angel . . ." Andrea smiled, but seeing his quills return to vertical, she added quickly, "But she's still an angel. Look at her."

Indeed, beatific green light streamed through Felicity and joined a strong rose aura around Andrea. Together they made a kind of window that seemed to the boy more beautiful than the rose window of Notre Dame. He rubbed his eyes.

"I overheard two Bamajans talking . . ." He hesitated, but another look at the women nearly blinded him. He spoke quickly. "They said that some of the evangelists were taking little packages to different places in Louisiana. And there was some science talk I didn't get."

"What places?" Felicity had a pretty good idea what these packages contained.

"Lots of places—the Exxon plant in Baton Rouge, a gypsum processing plant, the Akzo salt mine at Armadillo Island. I don't know . . ."

"Armadillo Island!" exclaimed Felicity. "Isn't the U.S. strategic petroleum reserve stored near there in salt domes?"

"Are the packages bombs?" inquired Andrea, suddenly remembering the smell of the book-bomb on the airplane.

"I'm afraid so," said Felicity. "I believe that Armageddon isn't entirely up to God."

The Dome was the salt dome called Armadillo Island. Now Felicity knew both where Mullin's paradise was and where the nerve center of his operation was located.

They let Michael Bamajan go, but he remained rooted to the spot, following them with his eyes until they turned the corner.

Commander's Palace had pulled out all the culinary stops to welcome the millennium and was now serving the leftovers at a discount. The foyer was jammed with starched locals waiting for their tables and discussing the menu. Ella Brennan had announced on television that every dish for the next month would be an exact replica of one cooked in 1901 by her great-grandfather. There was something immensely soothing in this, a guarantee perhaps that tradition was not to be upset by the mere passing of time. Enormous vases filled with lilies, orchids, and roses stood between the tables. A five-piece ensemble was already performing staunch classic jazz compositions. The light of flambeaux reflected splendidly off the crystal chandeliers and the warm red velvet of the curtains.

Felicity, holding Andrea's arm, shoved her through the waiting crowd past the operatic kitchen, where a gastronomic performance was unfolding in spicy clouds of smoke and steam. The cooks wore leaves and frolicked in a sylvan landscape under the kindly gaze of an aging Pan with furry white eyebrows. Andrea shook her head and they became cooks again.

Major Notz was seated at his usual table, with Boppy Beauregard standing by, still as a bronze statue. A magnum of champagne with a white towel around its neck stood in a silver bucket by the table. When he spotted his niece, Notz swung his bulk with a groan halfway out of the chair. To Andrea the scene looked like a painting by Frans Hals she had seen in Sarajevo. It was a picture of infinite bourgeois opulence, whose reality had been as remote from her war-torn world as the planet Mars. Now here it was, out of its frame, in vivid color. The triumph of the flesh, she thought, and she let her hand disappear in the major's paw as Felicity made the introduction.

"Duck," the major said, by way of greeting. "It's the duck of the century. And the gumbo roux is uncompromisingly dark. Where have you been, darling?"

"I was imprisoned by Mullin, Major." Felicity took the chair to Notz's left. Andrea sat demurely on the edge of the velveteen chair to his right.

Without preamble, Felicity described her confinement, her loss of memory, the strange powers of the hymns that had filled her mind, the appearance of Nikola Tesla, who had helped her escape, and her wandering through the city she barely recognized. But she had the odd feeling that her words slid over the sparkling silverware without reaching her uncle. He sat unmoved during her confession, as if she were part of the music.

"I am going to put Mullin out of his misery," she concluded grimly, "and I could use your help. He has not just harmed me, but he is planning a catastrophe for the entire world."

"Perhaps," the major said. "But first we must dine, to celebrate the end of the Christian era." He studied Andrea from under his heavy lids as if she were an item on the menu. "Your friend is shocked by our ways."

"This is true," Andrea agreed graciously. "I grew up communist. But I want to learn."

Felicity was exasperated. "Something horrible is about to happen, Uncle." She felt like the scared little girl who, years ago, had depended on him to explain the big, bad world.

"Nothing could be as horrible as interrupting this magnificent dinner."

"You have to call your friends in the CIA, Interpol, the secret services . . . Someone is planning to turn Louisiana into a bomb. I think that it's a planned Armageddon . . . the oil reserves . . . a chain reaction of some kind. If the Gulf of Mexico catches fire, all the underground oil could be involved . . . and our nuclear submarines . . ."

"Felicity, darling. Please. You're breaking my concentration. This menu may be the most important document produced in New Orleans in this wretched century."

Boppy, who had not moved, now spoke: "Shall we begin?"

Tears in her eyes, Felicity tried again. "Don't you understand?"

"All right. Hold on another moment, Boppy." The major put down the menu, visibly annoyed, and removed a Cuban cigar from his vest pocket. He clipped the tip with tiny gold scissors. "Who is the somebody planning all this?"

"Why, Mullin, of course."

"Suppose that he is indeed, my all-seeing private eye. Don't you think that people monitoring catastrophe are cognizant of his intentions? Can anyone enter the strategic petroleum reserve without authorization?"

"An evangelist could. Someone wearing only one shoe, preaching the word of God, could plant a trigger . . ." Something else occurred to Felicity. "Besides, you gave me a job. I believe that Kashmir Birani, the Indian television star you charged me with finding, is Mullin's prisoner at the Dome. I must rescue her."

Finally Major Notz seemed to take in what she was saying. "This Tesla, the anchorite who helped you—what sort of contraption is he building?"

Felicity was exasperated. Major Notz had never been this obtuse.

"What does it matter? He's a good guy. The main point is that we stop Mullin."

"Fine. Now, Boppy, let us begin."

Felicity could hardly believe her ears. As Boppy uncorked the champagne and poured its gold bubbles into their glasses, Felicity leaned toward Notz and said calmly, "Uncle, are you with me, or not? I am going to go directly to Armadillo Island to the strategic reserve. You can come with me, or you can get your gumbo and wait here for the End of the World . . ."

The major put his napkin back on the table. Tonight he was sporting the olive uniform of an Israeli tank commander. "My child, I wouldn't want to be anywhere else but in your company for the End of the World. Shall we eat now?"

Boppy Beauregard covered his eyes with the back of his left hand. It was the second time in two weeks that an unmovable routine was being upset. The world was surely on its last legs.

"I promise to bring great force to bear on this rogue preacher." The major laid his palm over Felicity's clenched fist. "But let us first show your young friend the deeply civilized ways of our city." He withdrew his hand and raised his champagne glass. "To the end of sorrow," he toasted.

Felicity had no choice but to raise her own glass. Andrea did, too.

"To the end of sorrow."

It seemed for a moment that their toast reverberated throughout the restaurant and then beyond it, as if these words and no others had found a way into the hardened hearts of the city's doubt-wracked citizens. Who knows, thought Andrea, these words may now be circumnavigating the globe. To the end of sorrow.

Trying to conquer her impatience, Felicity drank her glass of champagne, and then another and another, and ate the marvelous dinner. Andrea glowed in the shimmer of the torches and looked like she'd been born among the exquisite flowers. Felicity saw her reflected in the mirrors and loved her. Andrea marveled at Felicity's compact and graceful presence and felt that they had always been together. The major nearly faded into the shimmer and the velveteen, a discreet producer of marvels who directed the ceremony without intrusion.

At midnight they toasted again to the end of sorrow.

The city outside exploded with fireworks, as it had every night of the New Year. Andrea came out of her chair and kissed Felicity on the lips, and then, without warning, planted a kiss on the major's blubbery cheek. The cold flesh quivered like a Jell-O mold, but he smiled.

"Dance," he urged them.

Felicity took Andrea's hand and swept her onto the dance floor, and there, feeling boundless liberty, the two friends danced their first dance of the new millennium.

When they returned to the table, Notz was gone. He had left untouched his favorite desert, the bread pudding in whiskey sauce. Boppy, who had been gone but a minute, stood by wringing his hands. He hadn't seen the major leave.

An hour before midnight, Officer Joe arrived at Desire, Ltd. Joe had spent the day tracing again the intricate web of connections between Mullin's legal and phony businesses, and had struck gold. He owned a small software design company called Heaven's Works, which produced religious virtual reality games. The company tested its products at a nature preserve near Armadillo Island. The nature preserve had struck Joe as incongruous. Sooner will a pig escape a Sunday barbecue than a Baptist save a pelican. Or something like that. Joe wasn't too good at aphorisms, but he didn't take Mullin for a nature lover. The place was probably a survivalist enclave of some sort, and the religious games were for training militants. Joe had nearly driven there to look for Felicity when a street informant came up with information that she'd been seen at Desire, Ltd. The place was right under his nose, and Joe felt stupid as he jingled through the beaded curtain into the dark club.

He heard the jukebox carrying on about blue velvet and then felt the cold barrel of a gun against his neck. A deft hand unsnapped his holster and withdrew his service revolver. He was ordered to lie facedown on the floor, and he complied. When he reached out his hand on the floor he encountered a warm buttock.

"Hey," a woman said. "This may be unusual, but no pay, no touch."

When Joe's eyes became accustomed to the dark, he sneaked a look and saw a sea of buttocks, most of them bare. He was lying on the floor with a bunch of strippers. Towering above them were men with weapons. Presently someone fastened his wrists beyond his back with plastic handcuffs. Another hand pulled his head back, slipped a blindfold over his eyes, and inserted a gag in his mouth. The girls also were being cuffed, blindfolded, and gagged over protests that were soon reduced to muffled moans.

The captives were ordered to stand and then herded out the door and up the stairs of a vehicle that Joe thought was either a camper or a bus. As they rolled out, a voice trilled merrily: "Happy New Year! You are all going to a party!"

Sylvia-Zack, in a state of uneasy symbiosis, was returning from the Verte Mart with a pack of Vantage Ultra Lights. Sylvia wanted to rush forward, cursing, to stop the kidnapping, but Zack stopped her. There is a purpose to this, he declared, and we must find out what it is. Sylvia angrily tore the top off the smokes and lit one. Damn. Zack hated smoking. They got in Sylvia's car, across the street from the club, and followed.

Ben Redman arrived at Desire, Ltd., shortly after the abductors' bus had left. He parted the beaded curtain and walked in. He called out Andrea's name, then shouted, "Is anybody here?" Receiving no answer, he sat in one of the booths and proceeded to wait. The jukebox, stuffed full of quarters, played one song after another. Ben wasn't sure where everyone had gone, and being myopic, he missed the signs of struggle visible on the floor. It was dark anyway, and the bits of tassel and scattered beads weren't very obvious.

He pulled a book from his knapsack. It was *The Nag Hammadi Library*, a fourth-century-Gnostic anthology he thought might shed some light on events. He had used this book for divination before. His rabbi would have frowned at this non-Jewish text, but his rabbi was far away. It contained, among other texts, the *Gospel of Thomas*, which bore this promise: "Whoever finds the interpretation of these sayings will not experience death." These writings had long been thought to contain secret keys and had been used to divine everything from particular fortunes to the course of history.

Ben essayed two experiments. He opened the book at random, an oracular method he had been taught by Rebbe Zvetai. His teacher had said that sacred texts, by their very nature, were equal in their parts to the whole. Each part reflected the whole: every letter contained the book just as every book contained the universe. This is what the Nag Hammadi text had to say:

"The Savior said to his disciples: 'Already the time has come, brothers, for us to abandon our labor and stand at rest. For whoever stands at rest will rest forever. When I came I opened the path and I taught them about the passage which they will traverse, the elect and solitary.' "

Ben understood this to mean that he ought to let go now of his plans and ambitions. A path was opening before him, now that he had come full circle. The journey was going to unfold without his conscious participation.

He opened the book again.

For those who were in the world had been prepared by the will of our sister Sophia—she who is a whore—because of the innocence which has not been uttered. And she did not ask anything from the All, nor from the greatness of the Assembly, nor from the Pleroma. Since she was first she came forth to prepare monads and places for the Son of Light and the fellow workers which she took from the elements below to build bodily dwellings from them. But, having come into being in an empty glory, they ended in the destruction of the dwellings in which they were, since they were prepared by Sophia.

Interesting, thought Ben, to be spoken to so plainly. The whore who was Wisdom was now preparing the world for its reentry into the light. Her name was Sophia, meaning "wisdom," but also Andrea, the feminine form of "man." He loved none other than Sophia, the light of wisdom herself. Besides which, he stood in a temple of divine whorish wisdom. "*Strike him, mistress, and cure his heart,*" wailed the jukebox.

Midnight came and went, and no one returned to Desire, Ltd. Ben fell asleep with his head on the table.

Chapter Thirty-four

Wherein Mullin prepares the End of the World.
Felicity and Andrea, aided by Shades,
begin their journey to the Dome.

 a r t h q u a k e ! From the tip of Tierra del
Fuego to the rock of Manhattan, a pluripotent finger
traced a line of fire that buried 100 million lives under
their proudest buildings. A finger with a vamp red fingernail scratched a death sentence on the skin of the
earth. The subterranean rumble was like horses run-
ning under the ground—no, panicked herds of hippos tearing up the bot-
toms of hidden rivers. It was like nothing ever seen before. The mightiest
things that had happened could only be compared retroactively to this,
the greatest event.

Zags of vamp red light streaked across the three hundred screens in the
Dome. Parti-colored objects ricocheted in all directions. There were body
parts mixed with domestic junk: lacquered faux toenails curling out of
high-heel sandals, prosthetic thighs encased in silk, rubber bellies shaking
with uncontrolled laughter, clown noses, detached silicon eyeballs, ivory
elbows, sliced plastic fruit, coffeemakers, crushed cans, paper cones, torn
stamps, weapons, coins, furniture, crumpled lithos, family photos, baby
carriages, keyboards, handcuffs, and violins.

As the velocity of the junk increased, the Dome stretched to accommo-
date it. Above it all, near the expanding heavenly vault, twirled a hyperbul-
bous blue rose. It was carnal, the revelation made flesh! It was made of
light!

Reverend Mullin raised his arms over his head and roared over the rumble, "SWEET GOD! HERE WE COME!"

Bamajans wearing camouflage abandoned their keyboards and streamed toward the gesticulating reverend, beaming and raising their arms in imitation and shouting, bright-eyed and released from fatigue: "PRAISE THE LORD! SWEET JEEZUS, HERE WE COME!" They danced to the explosions, their faces upturned, their hearts filled with bright fear. There were men with shaved heads and young women dressed in white. Not exactly a cross section of society, but each faithful unto death to their leader, avatar, Bamajan supreme, true Elvis, and deliverer.

"You are the missing and torn pages of the lost scriptures!" he hollered to his frenzied followers.

The blue rose swelled above them until it burst into smithereens and strings of words shot from it like comets through the dome.

Over one wall was a map of the world like the ones at NASA and at the Pentagon. It was lit up red and trembled under the rumbling earthquake. Mullin imagined the military men at NASA and the Pentagon, studying the same sort of map, unsure of the nature of the catastrophe, unable to prevent it, their knees weak, their hearts racing, an awesome black light at the root of their brains. They could stop fire falling from the sky, but they could not fathom the conflagration raging under the earth, connecting pools of oil to pools of oil under the crust.

"And this is but the beginning," the reverend taunted them. "There are a hundred deaths before the End!"

He rubbed the fava bean controlling the rose between thumb and forefinger, and the splintered flower of light gathered itself together and a jet of blood shot up from its center and reached the domed ceiling, nearly blotting out the stars virtualed there.

In truth, he didn't despise those scientists and soldiers who'd try to prevent him from accomplishing the Lord's revenge as much as those Christians who had fashioned for themselves a sugary peacenik Jesus who forgave endlessly, a wimpy sap who justified softness and vice. This was an act of egregious surgery and wicked revision. Mullin knew that Christ was made of burning light and of the hard, blackened shell of the world's sins. When he did come back, it was going to be inside a ball of fire as large as the globe, a ball of fire on the surface of which the flesh of sinners sizzled. Layered inside the fire were the epochs of men, bubbles of fashion and frivolity stuffed with millions of faces distorted in pain. The fireball would roll over countries and continents. It would evaporate the oceans.

Mullin closed his eyes and heard the hissing steam of the oceans going up to form heavy black clouds. From the vast store of oil below his feet to the Gulf of Mexico, the black fire snaked out of control, torching the earth and the skies, setting off refinery stacks and sulfur processors. The smell of the devil, burning oil and sulfur, must be reaching the hells of Wall Street by now. When Mullin opened his eyes again, the fireball of righteousness had reached the lower edge of Greenland and was rushing across the barren rocks, charring them.

The reverend's faithful, sweat shiny, now surrounded him with a firm knot of hot flesh. The wild tremors gave way to a different movement, a steady rolling wave. They linked limbs to steady the small island on which the reverend stood.

When the object wind subsided, it gave way to history rewritten the way it should have happened the first time. They saw the Crusades shoring up the Kingdom of God in a Jerusalem without Jews or Muslims. They saw the children of Christian America praying in their classrooms at dawn under a waving Stars and Stripes that had a bright new cross at its center. They saw Paradise and trod the flower carpet of the Garden of Eden. They stood before the molten bronze of God's quill on the mountain. They stood close enough to Jesus on the Mount of Olives to taste the metallic sweat of his fervor. There was also Muhammad's heaven, where they might go for research and allow themselves to be kneaded by the perfumed hands of frolicking Fatimas.

Those were the big things.

But they saw also the smaller triumphs. The World Trade Center towers folded into each other like an accordion, done at last. The town of the capitalists, the disbelievers, the Marxists, and the Jews crumbled into dust and was blown over the marshes out into the Atlantic.

Elsewhere in America, wheat silos collided with missile silos, mixing bread and radiation, causing poisoned loaves to fall on burning farmhouses. A rain of golden ash filled in the skyline of Oklahoma City, one of the pulsing dots on the map wall.

One by one, the cities of the world launched their sports domes, their church spires, their looping freeways, their radio towers, their television dishes, and their chimney stacks into space. Some were in flames, some just floated detached, like a child's squiggles.

"Oh, look there! Dear God!"

Everyone looked. Zooming from the Dome roof were thousands of gold-and-blue dragonflies beating their wings and making the air vibrate.

Their eyes, which could be seen through the whirring of their wings, were filled with a cold intelligence.

"Damn!" cried the reverend. "The angels!"

Indeed. Those were no dragonflies. They were angels. The air crackled with electricity, and sheets of gold and electric blue clothed the reverend and his faithful. All around them the angels flew, celebratory and musical, among exploding buildings, collapsing apartment houses, folded bridges, rivers turned into geysers. Cracks appeared in the earth now, an intricate web of widening fissures sucking down all that had not exploded, burnt, or floated off. The angels multiplied over the cracks like luminous spiders. There were now millions of them.

"Sweet Jeezus!" exclaimed the reverend to his faithful shadows, "I never knew the Lord had such numbers!"

"Amen! Amen!" cried the dwellers of the Dome.

"Give me a close-up on that!" The reverend pointed to a swarm of commalike shapes funneling around a tower.

When the commas came into close-up view they proved to be a mob whirling around the top of the burning city of New Orleans. Parts of their bodies had vanished, leaving them hollowed out in the shape of question marks made out of phosphorescent bones. Then they jelled into a single lump of clotted black matter. They now looked like a single fat exclamation point.

Mullin knew what had happened.

"Can you believe that? Incomplete Rapture!" He filled with admiration for the wondrous intricacy of the End. "Woe unto you, you disbelieving fool!" he said to himself. "You who thought that it was going to be simple Rapture for the righteous and fire for the sinful."

He turned to his shadows. "We now see half Rapture for the half righteous, quarter Rapture for the quarter righteous, and decimals of decimals for every thought, and fire for everybody, woe unto us!"

"Amen," cried the faithful.

Mullin was drained. "Back to your stations! Change the channel!"

The burning world faded as if it never was. The silos went back to silence, the wrathful fires of the Lord retired into their mustard seeds. The floating body parts and the homeless objects went back to the bodies and homes they came out of. New York filled back up with Jews. The cross faded from the flag. The angels folded themselves inside their burning dots, becoming mere pixels. The rose of light squeezed back into the favabean button. He put it in his pants pocket.

The bells tolled midnight and Mullin made the sign of the cross over his people.

"God bless you in the New Age, and congratulations! Operation Apocalypse is now concluded. Had this been the real event, you would have been instructed to pray as well as watch. Glory be to Christ and his coming!"

The First Angels Choir, arrayed on a platform above the banks of computers, rent the salty air with the strains of "Amazing Grace." They were a splendid sight indeed, pleasing to the eyes of heaven. Among them were the proudest flowers of his collection, a bouquet of races and colors, including even an Indian princess, Kashmir Birani, who had forsaken a multitude of heathen deities for the glory of Christ. And in a little while Mullin would ascend in an elevator to the observation deck, where two Bamajans had just herded a crowd of strippers and a uniformed policeman. Hopefully the blackmailer was among them, her wicked heart beating like a caged bird watching a cat's paw slide between the bars. Mullin hoped that she had seen enough of the show to tremble at the coming wonders. What the hell was the policeman doing? Caught in the net, he supposed. The Bamajans were getting dumber and dumber, even as the miracles came nearer and nearer.

Sylvia-Zack looked down on the pompous dot that was Reverend Mullin and choked alternately from fury and disbelief. Had I but waited a day to imprison myself in this body, I would right now be causing you such guilty torments, Preacher, you would prefer a stint in your apocalypse! Look, Zack, Sylvia shot back, if we are going to share this body, which incidentally used to be all mine, we must restrict these bouts of rage, lest they impede our circulation. Since you can't use any of your angel tricks now, I advise employing human patience until we have an opportunity to properly roast Mullin. Slattern, strumpet, trollop, Jezebel, muttered Zack.

On the fifth day of the year 2000, a rainstorm swept over New Orleans, flooding the streets and sweeping into gutters and drainage ditches the millions of religious pamphlets scattered there by wild-eyed evangelists: *Jesus: The Ultimate in Body Piercing, The Romans' Map to Heaven, How to Get to Heaven, The Second Coming: Surely I Come Quickly!* Drunks stirred amid the soggy pages and drifted away with them. The Mississippi River came up to the top of the levees, gleaming above the city like a gorged snake. Some New Orleanians were sure that this was the hour of their submer-

sion. But the weatherman on the weather station said that the rain would
stop, and as soon as he said it, it did. No fewer than 60 percent of all Americans thought that the Weather Channel was the voice of God.

Major Notz adjusted the satellite antenna on the roof of the Hummer,
his ear on the world. He felt fierce, contained, and lucid. He wore the
white uniform of an Iraqi colonel. The major's uniforms were all the expression of a determined martial state, but some were more emotionally
charged than others. British uniforms made him feel serene. The Iraqi
uniform, made by Saddam Hussein's personal tailor, represented sheer
fury. The major fancied himself the incarnate rage of Babylon, and his
rage was directed at Mullin, who had trespassed the agreed-upon boundaries of his role. This Pygmalion had forgotten he was Notz's creation.

He remembered the day Mullin acquired his "greatness," but it wasn't
the way Mullin remembered it. At about the time that Mullin thought
he'd found his calling at Motel Six, the major acquired controlling interest
in a television station. After much discussion among the members of his
organization, it was decided to employ this station to broadcast exclusively
Christian programs, and the twenty-four-hour channel GOV (God's Own
Voice) was born. In subsequent years it grew into an empire. The challenge had been to find charismatic preachers who weren't too smart. The
major foresaw the vast wealth that these men could acquire, and his intention all along had been to control this wealth for his own purposes.

To carry out his project he relied on the help of friends in the Fellowship of the White Dawn, an occult order founded in Ireland in the fourteenth century for the purpose of establishing a secret world government.
Members of the White Dawn, in addition to occupying important posts in
many countries, supplied the major with some of his best uniforms and
objects for his collections. The fellowship believed that people's faith in
the coming of an avatar was an opportunity not to be missed, and they had
mobilized their resources to find a suitable candidate. The major was
charged with spearheading the project. At a time when syncretic con-
sciousness was uniting all religions, finding an appropriately charismatic
but intellectually limited avatar was quite complex. The democracy of
television solved the problem, however, by electing the preacher with the
best ratings, and that had been, regrettably, Mullin. Once he'd been
found, there remained the question of how to best make the prophecies of
various faiths agree within the rather invertebrate rhetoric of the
Louisiana preacher. This was still a work in progress.

The major sat back in his seat and studied the road as if it were a page of alien text. He was driving himself, having decided that from this point on, his hand had to be at the wheel, literally and otherwise.

Felicity and Andrea left Commander's Palace in a taxi. Crowds were dancing on the streets and fireworks made continuous streaks of light in the rainy sky. New Orleanians had resolved, in characteristic fashion, to celebrate the new millennium until Mardi Gras. The Shades on Felicity's street were gathered around a bonfire, singing camp songs. Their painted school bus was parked on the sidewalk.

Felicity had an idea. "Hey," she called to them, "what do you say you and your friends come up to my place and I cook you an omelet?"

The Shades were overjoyed. They had been eating from trash bins for months.

"You can take showers, too!" she promised in a burst of magnanimity. "And gas up the bus. We are going on a trip after breakfast."

The shades spread themselves all over Felicity's little apartment, making joyous noises over her torn collages of birds and Victorian ladies, while she got out her huge black iron skillet and proceeded to crack a dozen eggs, beating them with Grandmere's whisk.

Andrea was sure that she'd arrived in Paradise. As she helped straighten out the Shades' rags, handing them towels and soap, she decided that she had at long last escaped the war. Watching Felicity cook and seeing the pink naked Shades with the bodies drawn on them like a second skin, she felt fortunate and free. The scholars at Saint Hildegard's had been a good and peaceful family, but they had been old and reserved. The Shades were her own age, and filled in her family needs with warmth and sexiness. Watching them eat greedily, Andrea silently thanked something out there.

"Hey, isn't it some fucking holiday?" a pink nude wanted to know.

"Sixth of January, the feast of the Epiphany." Felicity knew her holy days.

"The Epi . . . What's the Epiphany?" The Shade was puzzled.

Felicity laughed. It was the first time Andrea had seen her laugh, and she blushed. Felicity laughed like a flower opening, from the root up. The sound of her was like petals thrown in the air. Everybody began to laugh.

"Yeah, it's Three Kings' Day, when you get gifts. Frankincense, myrrh, and gold," she said between peals of laughter.

"Goodie," said the pink nude, "we get gifts!"

When they were done eating, Felicity explained that the trip they were going to take was very important. But she didn't have to explain anything. The Shades would have done anything she asked them to.

The night melted away like an ice cream cone.

The old school bus, painted in colors that were once described as psychedelic, was covered with the faceless body of the True One—the Shades' one obsession. At least half of them now believed that Felicity was the True One, while the others were beginning to think that Andrea was.

The old road hog took a while to start, so Felicity and Andrea arrayed themselves on the layers of ratty sleeping bags that covered the floor. I have always been a Shade, Andrea thought. Felicity felt at home, too. She loved the feeling of a trembling, cheap, naive life. It must have been a blast, once upon a time, to be a pink child in a world of metal men. New Orleans still had bars where old hippies with white hair came together to remember sleeping with one another in the bowers of the Golden Age. New Orleans had bars for the natives of every age since the last century. Each generation had its own bars where, safely ensconced in the jukebox music of its own era, it could pretend to be young again. The twenties, thirties, forties, fifties, sixties, seventies, eighties all lived side by side like big, wet birds invisible to one another. Perhaps, thought Felicity, even ancient ages past, since the beginning of time, had their secret hideouts in New Orleans. They certainly traveled freely through her computer, loving her as if she were their secret hideout. Maybe she was. And now it was over, the millennium, the millennia, the ages of men. As the old bus rattled and roared, Felicity's mind raced ahead into the future, but she saw only bright white light.

Andrea sprawled, her head on the belly of a pale young woman with delicate bones and her feet on a moonfaced youngster who appeared to be still in the throes of Felicity's laughter.

Chapter Thirty-five

Wherein Ben Redman meets the devil. The Shades' bus is on the road, and Major Notz intercepts the travelers.

e n Redman woke up in the still-empty club when the first daylight came through the open door. He had dreamt that he was traveling in a car toward Andrea. His old girlfriend Felicity was there, too. He thought about asking the Nag Hammadi text what he should do, but he already knew. He had to travel in a car to find the women in his dream. The lack of a precise destination was not an impediment, since chance, like the oracle of the book, was going to take him where he needed to go.

With the satchel of books slung over his shoulder, Ben extended his thumb to the road. Almost immediately, he got a ride from the devil. Or so the red-haired, one-eyed man with two curvy horns, driving a vintage Oldsmobile, claimed.

"Where to, boy? The name's Mephistopheles," he said, winking.

The devil always winks—this had been one of Rabbi Zvetai's first lessons, and Ben, like the rest of his classmates, spent many hours practicing facial rigidity so as not to inadvertently wink. Mephistopheles winked more than once.

"Did you see them bonfires New Year's Eve?" (Wink.) "Them Cajuns was burning boats and log houses on the levee all night." (Wink.) "Everybody and their mama was there. Biggest party you ever did see. They fried anything with juicy meat in the whole swamp." (Wink.)

The devil was loquacious, so Ben didn't get a word in edgewise.

"It's my very, very favorite season, and today is Epiphany, my very favorite day. Gifts to the newborn. Got a trunk full of them."

Ben managed to enquire why Christ's holy days were his favorite.

"Why?" The devil winked indignantly. "For one, when the spirit of partyin' takes hold of a certain number of people, everybody else be gettin' the urge. I be the chief proponent for these human foolishnesses: joy, enthusiasm, happiness, contentment, lust by licking, sucking, and fucking, singing loud, masturbating in the shower, eating meat raw and cooked, sucking marrow out of bones, dancing, bending people in shapes they didn't even suspect they could be bent in, using individuals and groups as toys in games of pure childish mindlessness, traveling without any money, pushing tourists into canals, running Christ for president, feeding canaries to alligators . . ."

The devil's list was very long, and the longer he went on, the more articulate he became, dropping the friendly rube effect that had characterized his earlier speech. All these symptoms Ben recognized from his lessons. He closed his eyes and heard many delightful sounds behind the devil's soothing litany—the sea at Carmel beach, the seals at the New Orleans zoo, the chimes of Andrea's voice. The devil is pure comfort, thought Ben. If I didn't have this odd idea that I must serve God, I'd really love to hang out with him.

"Look in the backseat," said the devil. "I have some CDs there."

The devil's CDs were an odd mixture—some Billie Holiday, Frank Sinatra, the Temptations, Sonny Boy Williamson, Johnny Cash, the Sex Pistols.

"What, no Rolling Stones?" Ben asked, almost winking himself.

"I hate clichés," said the devil. "I like music by people I helped personally, like Frank . . ."

Ben slipped *The Very Good Years* in the CD player, and Sinatra accompanied them the rest of the way.

"Do you really know everything?" asked Ben.

"Well, yeah, but it's a big bore. I prefer to keep myself in the dark."

Ben contemplated the awesome proposition of willful ignorance. Keeping oneself in the dark was a bigger deal than knowing everything. How can one not know what one knows? It's just not possible.

"The upcoming fight between good and evil," Ben wanted to know, "is there going to be a winner?"

"I hope not," said the devil. "If goodness wins, everyone will be filled with ennui. If evil prevails, it will be the same. Have to keep people on edge."

"Will humanity survive the battle?"

"Of course. Most people will hide. The earth is full of fissures, crevasses, hollows, caves, nooks, crannies, closets, and shelters. I know because I put them there myself."

Ben felt suddenly starstruck. "What is your favorite pastime?"

"Words. I like to start talking, and then I can't wait to hear what I'm going to say next."

How very different from our theological procedures, marveled Ben. We direct everything toward God, leaving nothing to chance. The devil just starts something and keeps going without any idea of where or why.

"Are you really the devil?" Ben was starting to worry.

"Are you really Ben Redman?" asked the devil. "Mardi Gras is coming up in a few weeks. Everybody will be someone else. Ask me then if I'm really the devil. Maybe I'll be God for Mardi Gras."

They had just passed the town of Grosse Tête. In the sky, a flock of ducks changed formation behind the leader, turning north. The leafless willows allowed for glimpses of the vast swamp that stretched all the way to the Gulf of Mexico. The swamp water was red and rusty. They crossed over the Vermillion River and Bayou Teche. Rusty oil derricks bobbed up and down like monks doing their prostrations. The oil beneath them signaled the beginning of the salt domes. The land swelled imperceptibly at first, then bubbled up into hills that rose suddenly from the swamp.

"Here they are, beneath us, the domes of salt, my domes of salt, my sparkling crystal balls."

According to the devil, the huge salt balls left over after the evaporation of the ocean that covered North America were his property. In fact, that whole ocean had been his property until God saw fit to hurl a flaming meteorite at it. All that was left were these balls of salt that were very dear to him, family jewels of some sort. An oil company drilled through the crown of some of the domes a couple of decades before. A freshwater lake invaded and ate the salt. Two of the remaining ones contained the U.S. petroleum reserve and the Akzo salt mine. The third and fourth were being currently occupied by entities that caused him grave doubts. That's where they were headed now.

"Why is salt so precious to you?" asked Ben.

"Why? Why?" sputtered the devil. "You ask why? Because God's world is bland and tasteless without salt. Because people are just meat without salt. Because those poor souls Jesus called the salt of the earth are mine. Every time you put salt on your potatoes you pray to me! There is salt in your tears! Every time you cry you pray to me! All your tears are mine! That's why."

Ben didn't want to get the devil too worked up. So far he had been most congenial.

The Shades' bus crossed the Vermillion River a few moments after the devil's Oldsmobile. Felicity lay with her eyes closed, listening to the Shades sing silly songs and play dozens.

> After I did my tricks
> I went to the lady doctor.
> I was her fellatrix
> And she was my proctor.

And: "Hey, you so loose you have a dick tattooed between your tits!"

"Yeah, and you got 'Pay as You Enter' writ above your bush!"

Which may have been true, for all Felicity knew. But God, did she enjoy silliness! There wasn't enough left in the world to fill a thimble. When they passed a pasture full of grazing sheep, Felicity pointed them out to her playmates.

"Look, Shades, look at the sheep!"

Screaming with delight, the shades waved at the animals they'd never seen before.

Felicity had brought some fruit along, and distributed some mangoes to the happy shades. They bit into them and, juice dribbling down their chins, they reveled in the strange new taste. Whatever else I might do in this life, thought Felicity, will be both forgiven and less significant than this. I have given the innocents sheep and mangoes.

Andrea had seen many sheep but she had never eaten a mango. She delighted in it like a Shade.

"Are there sheep in heaven?" a shade asked.

"Of course," Felicity reassured her, "or else the angels would bugger each other."

They came upon some machines lopping off the tops of cypresses from the elevated highway, so they had to stop.

"They are cutting off the cedars of Louisiana!" exclaimed Andrea.

The Shades crowded at the windows of the bus and made faces at the men in the machines. Some of the men laughed, but others gave them the finger. In any case, they had no intention of letting the bus pass.

Felicity stepped out of the bus, followed in close order by the disheveled passengers, and gestured to one of the hard hats standing by the biggest machine. He turned to her.

"How long . . ." is all she was able to say before she saw his face. What she had taken for a foreman was a four-foot gnome with a hairy pig snout and burning yellow eyes. He had small, pointed ears and tufts of red bristles coming out of them. From his mouth, a long thin tongue shot out about three feet, launching a fire red spitball in Felicity's direction. She stepped aside just in time. It landed at her feet and burned with a sizzle through a pile of leaves.

Felicity looked up at the other workers in the machines and saw that under their hard hats they were all monsters of some sort.

After being startled at first, Felicity began to laugh, and her laughter became contagious. The Shades gathered behind her started laughing also, and a cloud of laughter floated right up to the strange creatures. They began sputtering one after another, letting out raspy cascades of giggles. As they caught the wave of hilarity, the creatures began to disintegrate. The harder they laughed, the wispier they became, until they vanished, leaving behind only silvery tinkles of sound.

"Remember this, friends," Felicity said, wiping her eyes. "We seem to have a weapon."

Ah, thought Andrea, it's a weapon I don't yet know how to use.

Neither Andrea nor the Shades seemed concerned with their destination. Felicity was astonished that they did not ask, and glad. She would have had to tell them, "To the End of the World," and it would have spoiled the party.

They piled back on the bus and it was a quarter of an hour before anyone could look at Felicity without bursting out laughing. By that time they had reached the rise of the domes.

Shortly after the turn to Armadillo Island, Felicity spotted the major's Humvee parked on the shoulder of the road. The major sat sphynxlike inside, the seams of his white uniform strained by rolls of fat. He was alone in the vehicle. Oh, Uncle, you did come to help me! Felicity was glad. He had not abandoned her.

She pointed him out to Andrea. "Our ally. He is waiting for us."

They pulled alongside, and Felicity climbed out, followed by Andrea.

"Where is your chauffeur, Major?"

"Get in, Felix." The major was curt.

Andrea was right behind Felicity. "I'm going with you."

The Shades tumbled out of the bus and watched, quite bewildered by what looked like their leader's defection to the fat soldier. Felicity reassured them.

"Go on, children. We will see you at Armadillo Island. Remember mangoes and comedy! This man is my friend."

The Shades were not convinced. They remembered the last time Felicity had gone off in a car with a strange man. That man had not been her friend. They surrounded the Hummer.

The major sat still, but Felicity was embarrassed. "This man is my uncle, really. I'm safe. Tell them, Major."

Without warning, the major thundered in a commanding voice:

"Scram, munchkins! I am Jupiter and this is my thunderbolt!" He lifted a huge machine gun from the floor at his feet and aimed it at her friends.

Notz had made his point. At Felicity's urging, the reluctant Shades regained the painted bus, which looked sad, as if it had lost its luster. The sad bus drove away with a lurch.

"Jesus, Uncle, are you into scaring children now?" Felicity's reproach was not gentle.

From the backseat, Andrea observed the oddly similar backs of their heads. She knew that they were not blood relatives, but at this moment, their necks held a similar stiffness, poised for battle. The major looked imperial behind the wheel of his Humvee, a wide-hipped machine that reminded Andrea of a turtle. Andrea sensed the affection Felicity had for this man, her protector, cajoling, educating, and raising her "for something special." Felicity seemed very far from her right now, and Andrea felt a sharp, familiar pain.

The major started up the engine, and they got back on the road. Tanker trucks carrying Louisiana's chemical products barreled by. Liquid petroleum gas. Molten sulfur. Liquid oxygen. Chlorine gas. Train tracks ran parallel to the highway, flashing in and out of the swamp. An egret, neck stretched out, was poised at attention over a dead cypress stump. A row of white cattle egrets perched on a duck blind in Lake Pelba. While machines pushed impatiently forward, nature looked expectant.

This was the time, Felicity thought, that the major needed to answer the question they had always held between them like a secret love child. Felicity had often imagined that the major was not simply a family friend, but her real father.

"Uncle, what was I supposed to be when I grew up? It is critical that I know. I'm not a child anymore."

But Notz spoke to her exactly as he had when she was a child. "You, my dear, are the princess of salt, my viol. You will grow up to be salt in all our bland jambalaya."

This went way back. When she was a little girl, Major Notz had told her the story of the Salt Princess. Once upon a time, the world was a sad and dismal place. All the food was white and the people were all random. No one did anything on purpose—everything was left to chance. If it rained, people got wet, caught colds, and died. When they were hungry, they got in lines at food centers and were given tasteless white food— mashed squash, oatmeal, egg whites, turnips. They wore state-issued rain-coats and listened to long speeches from evenly spaced loudspeakers in cement squares. Their cement-cubicle houses stood around the cement squares. The temperature inside and outside was always sixty-eight de-grees Fahrenheit.

At this point in the story, Felicity always asked why people didn't sing songs or put on polka-dotted raincoats or why they didn't make their own food and put Tabasco sauce in it.

Because, Major Notz would explain, people had been stripped of their free will by the state, which was a machine that lived in a paper house. The machine made all decisions for them. But the real reason for this sad state of affairs was that there was no salt, no salt in all the world. What the world needed was a hero like Prometheus, who stole fire from the gods and brought it to the people.

What was needed was a princess of salt.

"That's me, that's me! I am the princess of salt," Felicity always shouted. Major Notz would then lower his formidable bulk over her and press a warm kiss on her head.

"That's you, Princess. You are she. And little by little I will tell you how you became the Salt Princess." But he never quite got around to it, though he'd given her many clues—books to read and pictures to look at. And as she grew older, Felicity had been embarrassed to ask.

"The answer lies in the salt dome," Notz roared over the noise of the engine. "Do you remember, Felix, what I told you about history?"

"Yes, Uncle," she said tentatively, like a schoolgirl. "There are three forms of history, one divine history and two human."

These varieties of history, which the major had drilled into her at a ten-der age, were often at odds with one another. Divine history was knowable only in those instances when it intersected human history. Those intersec-

tions were numerous and constant, but impossible to confirm. They occurred in every place on earth all the time, but they were never properly
recorded because of quarreling and competition among religions. Some of
these intersections were of such great consequence, however, that they are
well known: the encounter of Moses with God, Muhammad taking dicta-
tion from God, Prince Siddhartha's tree, the crucifixions of Mani and of Jesus, for instance. The major had no interest in divine history because the
motives for the deity's actions were essentially unknowable, thus not worth
bothering with. It was an entirely different story with the two types of human history, one of which was simply a cover for the other. The official history was a recording of the deeds of people in time. The other, and this was
the only history that interested the major, was a secret history, composed of
instances of will that set events in motion. The secret history was small—
all its crucial facts could fit in one elegant volume. Of course, such a volume
would never be allowed to exist. But he, Major Notz, believed that he was
himself such a volume, and he existed to be discovered by Felicity.

He turned to her. "Now, dear Felix, you must open me to the last chapter and read what is written there!"

Felicity smiled, picturing her uncle as a book. The folds of his abundant
flesh were the pages on which this secret history was written in minute,
coded script. He read her mind and admonished her, "Don't be literal,
naughty child."

"Well, I don't know what you mean, Major. How can I read what you
won't reveal to me?"

"What is a book, child?"

"Something with a beginning . . . a middle . . . an end?"

"Very good. What does this mean for a book of history?"

"That history has a . . . beginning, middle, and end?"

"Precisely. Now, before the book is finished, who knows the end?"

"The writer?"

"Who is the writer of the secret history?"

"Those men," Felicity remembered tentatively, "and women who exer-
cise an active will in the course of events. But this will is always a will for
the End. Oh, I see. Every time the conspiracy option is exercised, the goal
is an end to history. Each instance of will in history is an end, but only a
false end . . . because history continues."

"Not bad. Now imagine the true End. Who among us could write it?"

"A person chosen by divine providence?"

"Well, of course," Major Notz said impatiently. "But who will determine the authenticity of this Messiah? The world is rife with pretenders. Can you truly say that Jeremy 'Elvis' Mullin, who is about to bring his own end to history, is *not* the Chosen One? Millions of people believe he is."

At the mention of Mullin and his plans, Felicity remembered where they were going and was rent by anxiety. They should be discussing strategy, not philosophy. She understood, nonetheless, that the major, in his parabolic way, was preparing her for battle.

"He is not the Messiah," Felicity said, quite certain, "because he is a salesman. The Messiah doesn't sell . . . she just *is*. She persuades simply by the good news of her presence."

"Ah," cried the major, "now we're getting somewhere." He swiveled his bulk slightly and gazed at Andrea in the rearview mirror. "Who are you?"

"Why, Andrea the Orphan, of course." Andrea told the truth reflexively, which rarely happened. Her instinct usually made lying more natural.

The major looked disappointed. "Are you Felicity's missing half?"

No one had ever asked her anything this important. Something in the way Felicity sat evoked helplessness before the coming answer. Andrea felt a great power, as if the world depended on what she was going to say.

"Yes, that's what I am . . . and Felicity is my missing half."

The major looked at his niece.

"I suppose, Uncle, that now you would like us to become seriously delusional and declare ourselves the Savior of the world. That way we could write the last chapter of your secret book and finish your work."

"That would be nice."

"Sorry," said Felicity. "There is absolutely no inner voice guiding me. I don't have the slightest messianic inclination. I'm not even religious. What's worse, I'm a very bad detective. If I was any good I would have found the Indian girl and stopped Mullin by now."

From the backseat, Andrea said, "And I'm just a sensualist. I think that the padres at Saint Hildegard's would have rather boinked me, but they educated me instead."

The word "boink" fell like a chunk of hail on the hood of the Humvee. The land rose steadily as they climbed over the salt domes. Felicity could feel a great activity taking place in the bowels of the earth beneath them. It was not the kind of inspired knowledge that might have heartened Notz, but it was an intuitive power nonetheless. She was sorry to have disappointed him. He looked grimly down the road, like a man trying not to cry. In the backseat, Andrea was grinning foolishly to herself, repeating "boink" in her head. Boink, boink, boink.

Chapter Thirty-six

Wherein the Great Confrontation unfolds

h e n the the major's Hummer pulled up in front of the Bar & Bait Shop at Armadillo Island, the Shades' bus was already parked there. So were many other cars, including a vintage Oldsmobile. A statue of Saint Barbara, the patron saint of miners and artillerymen, stood guard above the café in a cypress tree.

The women jumped out of the car, but the major did not follow.

"You go on. I'll be right along." He watched them head for the cabin and then took a small box from under his seat.

Felicity opened the creaky door of the cabin and gasped at the sight of Ben Redman sitting there at a wooden table with a devil.

If Ben had believed in magic before, finding Andrea and Felicity together eliminated whatever residual skepticism he harbored. The oracle that had brought him to Armadillo Island was but one of the many inexplicable ways in which he was guided. Andrea was not surprised to see him, but Felicity, who had not seen him since he left for Israel, felt the wing of an angel touch her. She had found her soul mate and now here was Ben, another missing piece of her soul. Oh, God, she prayed, let Miles come! I will be whole then!

Andrea had neglected to mention the rabbi who had brought her to America, but now some explanation was in order, and facts were proffered, though they paled in comparison to the sheer miracle of their togetherness. Felicity played with Ben's curls and Andrea pinched him playfully on the cheek. They were like three kittens in a basket.

The devil looked on indulgently, his nostrils slightly flared.

Ben tried to impart some of what he had learned in the last few hours. "Listen, this is going to sound crazy, but everything taking place now is part of a divine opera. There are about a million angels all around us."

Andrea laughed and feigned pulling up Felicity's shirt.

"I know, Ben. 'Sing, choirs of angels. Sing in exultation. Sing, all ye citizens of heav'n above.'" For the first time since she had returned from Mullin's darkness, she could sing without fear of losing herself.

"That's great, Felix." Ben was touched by the beauty of Felicity's voice. He had never heard her sing before. And he felt that this was no mere song but an instruction, somehow, conveyed to the invisible world around them. His friend was commanding the spirits. Andrea, he already knew, was mysteriously connected. Everything had become luminous and inescapably significant.

Sing, all ye citizens of heav'n above. The air grew thick with the spirits of poets, prophets, and founders of religions, who were part of the Council of Minds that had not yet incarnated. Little blue globes of electricity jumped around the room.

"What are all these entities, Felix? They seem to know you," asked Ben. He put out his hand and touched a smooth blue roundness that gave him a slight shock.

Felicity knew at once. "My cyberlovers. They owe their postmortem sexual lives to me."

They had flown in from the darkest recesses of cyberspace, the folds of time and the spirals of other dimensions, in answer to her call.

The devil, who had kept his counsel until now, saw them too, and said to Felicity: "Miles is not among them."

Even the world beyond, animated by the passion of her love, could do nothing to bring Miles back to her. The truth, Felicity told herself, is that I will never be complete. Perhaps the world has already ended and I'm in some kind of intermediary heaven, where I'm being fooled into believing that I've found love. The entities whirled faster when she thought this, and Felicity found herself wishing for destruction. She wanted to die with her friends right here and now in a collective Götterdämmerung, a ball of fire. She wanted to join Miles.

The devil laughed. "You are so right, young lady. The tragedy is not that the whole world might end, but that the world might go on after your own personal world has ended. We will forgive each other only if we all go at the same time, but we will go on causing strife if we keep ending piece-meal. The end of the world is preferable to dying alone. Take it from me, I'm always alone, dead or alive."

The devil's speech saddened them all, but before they could think of a rejoinder, the door of the cabin burst open and a red-faced major shouted: "Felix, we are going below to see Mullin!"

"I wouldn't dream of going without my friends."

The major shrugged.

Ben looked enquiringly at the devil, who laughed. "Go on—I'm better behind the scenes anyway."

Outside, Felicity saw that the Shades had built a fire and were holding hands, keeping a vigil.

Mullin kept his eyes on the monitor from the moment that the foursome boarded the train leading to the Dome elevator. He had discovered imme-diately that Felicity had not been among the strippers the Bamajans had delivered to him. But now he had them all, coming to him like lambs to the slaughter.

The major looked uncharacteristically glum.

"Everything okay, Uncle?" Felicity put her hand on his round shoulder.

"Oh, child." He shook his head with evident sadness.

Felicity had never seen the major depressed before. He always had a so-lution to what he called "apparent misery," and that solution was always to look for deeper causes, for the events in history that directly caused the distress. In his view, every single pang of emotion, whether of grief, nos-talgia, or love, could be traced to an instance of will on someone's part. But now Notz looked ready to cry.

"Isn't there a clear instance of will, Uncle?"

He shook his head. "Promise to think well of me, no matter what hap-pens in the next few hours."

Felicity promised.

The little train came to a halt and they entered an open elevator. The shaft was as deep below the surface as the Empire State Building was tall. The elevator descended for a long time into the brightness. Andrea saw Felicity's eyes fill with tears, and hers did too, though she tried hard to keep them back.

"It's the salt," Ben whispered, as he too began crying.

Where were they going? And why? Whatever the imperative driving them, it had not yet made itself clear. The farther down they descended, the saltier the air became. They could taste it on their tongues. The elevator scraped the crystalline walls and a fine powder of salt snowed on them, covering their hair and clothes.

"It's true," said Felicity, "down is the way. All those pathetic attempts we make at going up . . . getting high . . ."

The uneven walls of salt rock sparkled like a billion diamonds. The Dome was at least two miles in diameter and five miles deep. Millions of tons of salt had been scooped out of it to make the cave. The salt crystals acted as lenses, magnifying the lights of the elevator.

When the elevator finally stopped, they stepped out into a cave looking down on a vast technological wonder. Below them, scurrying like ants, lab-coated drones were manipulating keyboards and control panels. Seated on some kind of throne at the center of the vast cave was the tiny figure of Reverend Mullin, twisting a twenty-foot-tall image of a blue rose. Flaming words shot out of it and fell in a shower of sparks.

"It's like the rose tattooed on my butt," whispered Felicity.

She felt keenly the doubly tragic condition of human beings. "Like birds in a glass house . . . hit the walls, over and over . . . but down, down . . ." She had always thought of Web surfing as a descent. And even when she got high she was going down, to look for Miles.

The three of them embraced and tasted one another's tears, and at that moment something came to pass. Their embrace set in motion the last act of will in history.

Or so Major Notz explained consequent events when he revealed the last chapter of the world's secret history to an audience composed in equal parts of angels and humans.

The connection between Felicity, Andrea, and Ben took the form of a spongy emotion that jumped through their nervous system, joining them together with light threads.

We are being woven, they thought.

The brilliant, salty light of the cave grew in intensity.

"Jesus," said Andrea, "We are a mushroom."

Their bodies were crisscrossed with the fine gills of a spore connected to millions of living things outside the dome. A sparking green glow discharged energy around them, and they knew that together they would battle heaven on behalf of creatures like themselves, tender flesh forms filled with light and confusion. They were a joined nothing, less than nothing, but each one of them yielded a luminous distinction: Felicity felt arrowhead hard the presence of her courage; Ben, the sharp twang of his desire for justice; Andrea, the delicious languor of her power to transform. Together, they were an arrow drawn against certainties, verities, eternal truths, gospels, edicts, writs, primers, laws, stone tablets.

A phalanx of bald Bamajans escorted them to the platform where Mullin was enthroned. The preacher bade them sit on the mushroom-shaped stools around his console. A sultry, dark girl in a blue sari approached and stood behind Mullin.

"Kashmir," Felicity gasped. "You're alive!"

"I was dead until I found God," replied Kashmir, looking serene.

The major fixed Mullin in a pitiless gaze. "Preacher! You have forgotten your creator!"

Mullin surveyed the instrument-laden Dome, his hand resting lightly on his control keyboard. "I am grateful, Major, grateful indeed for the wondrous mechanisms you've bestowed on me. But now the true work begins. In a few moments, you will witness the End. And when the End is under way, you will witness the small ends of these sinners, followed by your own end. And I promise you a worthy end, Major. I do admire you."

Notz smiled, recalling the vast tapestry he had woven to bring this event into being. He had used his knowledge of conspiracy to provide a philosophical ground for the "End," as the preacher called it. He had learned the methods of each and every major act of hidden will in human history and synthesized them for application to his purpose. He had used secret intelligence connections to set up an elaborate network of unwitting agents, and he had recruited Mullin. Mullin and his ill-gotten millions had done the rest. The major had ruthlessly dispatched anyone who had threatened his plans or the flower of his project, Felicity. Under the protection of the millennial fever sweeping the world, he'd launched hundreds of charlatans to provide the world with a raison d'être for its own disappearance. Technicians, both paid and converted, had done the rest. Notz had guided Mullin from the shadows and smoothed his path, and now the fool believed he was in charge.

"Preacher, could we have something, a little lunch, before you fiddle with your Armageddon stick?"

Felicity laughed. "That's my uncle! Just because the world's ending—"

"I feel the same way," interrupted Andrea. "A last meal!"

Ben was astonished by the frivolous turn of events. The last thing in the world he wanted was food, and he knew that neither Andrea nor Felicity wanted any. But then he understood: it was going to be a ritual last supper, their disconnection henceforth from the eating of matter.

Jeremy "Elvis" Mullin was feeling generous. He instructed Kashmir to prepare food, and she shortly returned with a platter of pickled mushrooms, a bowl of fresh figs, and a pitcher of milk.

"How did you come to select these creatures to survive?" Notz asked, plunging two saffron-spiced 'shrooms into his mouth at once. The mushrooms were followed by a fig.

"You recognize my talent at last, Major. Deciding who would survive Armageddon was more difficult than your studies and technology. I couldn't have done it without Jesus. I came up against the limits of human expertise. We designed the End to engulf all but the Dome, and I screened my beings as carefully as Noah choosing animals for the ark. As you instructed, I scanned the range of human types for strength of character and physical distinction, but also for their faith in the Lord and in me. Every race is carefully represented, every individual genetically screened for abnormalities. Every girl in the First Angels Choir's has been tested, biographed, X-rayed, analyzed, and measured for faith. They've been chosen for libido, for hardiness, steadfastness, both left- and right-brain-specific skills, and the other characteristics that you painstakingly outlined for me."

The major finished swallowing the mouthful of mushroom and fig and laughed.

Felicity's stomach knotted and suddenly she knew—her mentor, her teacher, her father was the mastermind of Mullin's insane plan. She looked at the fat man swallowing his food and saw the real monster, his shadow stretching to her very beginnings, imbedded in her life like the roots of a live oak.

With their vision magnified, the three friends could see that the demented Reverend Mullin was only half bad. The bad half sold certainty to a desperate public—but his innocent half was in love with a fantasy of love. If they had the power, they would grant him a life with his slutty waif, stripped of his wealth, forced to live with the uncertainties of poverty for the rest of his miserable days.

They saw the silent drones, the bald Bamajans, and the singers in white, and they weren't all bad, either. Their capacity for faith had been misled.

They had been saved from their chaotic freedom and held captive by the serenity of song. Mullin had stolen their free will, but faith lived on in its prison. Angels had stolen bodies as well, shoving their spirits into dank cells. Even the merely dead, neither humans nor angels, ranged freely across the fields of these timid souls, taking them as they pleased.

The divine gift of faith had been perverted by preachers, priests, texts that promised closure, prophecies, bibles, commandments, depictions of the End, promises of salvation. The wielders of these false closures were guilty of cupidity and ignorance.

The three friends experienced their loving solidarity as a wave of repulsion against the purveyors of certainty, a wave soon replaced by another, of love for those who searched, who had doubts, who were tormented by their bodies and unhappy with the limits of their minds.

How arrogant, Felicity thought, to believe that she could solve crimes and find answers to the mysteries of passion and disappearance. But Notz was the most arrogant—he was responsible for her bondage to the discipline of certainties. He believed that human will could control events and minds and hearts. Dear Lord, she silently told the others, we have harmed God, who may have fattened on the praise of men like Mullin, and been delivered to the likes of Notz. The threesome was enveloped in sadness, but green pulsed through them again, and their power returned.

They saw light stream through the multicolored gossamer of millions of angels' wings. The crystals burst with light. People were mixtures of faith and bondage, but one element was steadfastly good. Salt. The salt of their sweat and tears was infinitely amplified by the miles of salt surrounding them. The salt of their suffering was going to war with the cunning of false promises.

They thought that, like themselves, the world was not finished. It was continually evolving in complexity. God was not in the past but in the future. Humanity was evolving God, therefore there could be no End. At least not until God was born.

Mullin was ready. "Showtime, sinners!" He pressed an orange key on the control board, and in his mind he saw the underground fires beginning to snake into oil refineries and chemical plants, turning the Mississippi River into fire and the land into molten tar.

Notz was amused. He had not been speaking in riddles when he told Felicity that in him she might read the last chapter of the world's secret history. He held the ending in the palm of his hand—a compact black box with a single red button on it. It would relay the single command needed to set off the chemical corridor, overriding Mullin's controls.

He had succeeded perfectly. The red button held his concentrated brilliance; it was the center of his ambitions, the concentrated form of his wide-world connections, the point of his plan. When he activated it, he would unleash Armageddon on a scale Mullin never imagined. Everything but the Dome would evaporate, bringing Rapture to the Christians, nirvana to the Hindus, Paradise to the Muslims. Destruction would be his triumph.

Then he saw Felicity's face, and all her pain and anger invaded him. I have nurtured you to be my queen, he wanted to tell her. For you I have tested my will in that most dangerous place, my own heart. He felt a physical need to see her eyes filled with love and admiration. Great men had utterly passed from history. In this age without heroes, even the belief in the possibility of greatness had been extinguished. He had single-handedly engineered the destruction of humanity and had conceived of a new world, born of Felicity and himself. This was the something he had raised her for.

Felicity heard him and sent back her wordless reply. There was no mistaking it, and he received the full content of her disdain. So be it. He was tired. Major Notz, author of the single greatest act of will in history, a big man in whose folds of flesh was written the secret history of intention, closed his eyes and pressed the red button. The button went in like his mother's nipple when his greedy baby mouth sucked too hard, but there was no blast, no devastation, no glory. Notz pushed the mechanism over and over, bewildered. It wasn't possible. He had personally constructed the little beastie, connected each wire. His life's work was a dud.

Felicity, Andrea, and Ben rose up at once and enveloped Notz and Mullin in a terrible kindness. Intense green light streamed from them like a flashbulb snapping a giant photograph. A hidden fountain of grief sprung inside Mullin, and salty tears streaked down his cheeks. He no longer wanted the world to cease existing—his only desire was go to Airline Highway, the true center of his universe, to find the child who owned his heart.

Mullin lifted a hand, and the First Angels Choir burst into the purest song that was ever sung. "Amazing grace," they began, "how sweet the sound . . ." The cavern pulsed, wounds healed, evil light was released, trapped passions flew into the open. One thousand girls made of nothing but music released a blessing into the salty air.

The major clutched his chest.

Mullin covered his face with his hands.

"The figs and mushrooms were poisoned," Kashmir whispered.

Not that it mattered. Immediately after the failure of the red button, the major had chosen the Roman way out—he'd swallowed a cyanide capsule.

Felicity tried to embrace the stillness that had been her mentor, but her arms could not reach all the way around him. She saw the major's spirit rising to join the flocks of angels that sat watching throughout the Dome. Without missing a beat Notz began to explain himself to an audience of the heavenly host, proffering both the explanation and apology he would be doomed to repeat for eternity.

Felicity wept for her uncle and for the world. The salt that fed her tears was inexhaustible.

Sylvia and the devil sat on a patch of salty grass not far from the mouth of the mine shaft. The devil had spotted her immediately, calling out, "Hey, Sylvia girl, what is it? Who's that inside you!"

They had known each other forever, and Sylvia was happy to see him, but explaining Zack wasn't so easy. At first sight of the devil, Zack had started pouting, beating his wings, and making a low growl like a threatened mutt.

"Unfortunately," Sylvia-Zack said, "we are a querulous unit, though my joie-de-vivre is bound to prevail over our bitching."

"Well, you two sit right down here on this grassy picnic spot and relax." The devil pointed to an inviting glen flanked by a murmuring spring.

"I want to go down," Sylvia-Zack said. "I have to see the new creature."

"Would you like to see from here? It's so much more comfortable." The devil scorched a patch of grass with his hand, clearing the ground and leaving behind a circular black mirror. Reflected in it was the scene below.

"I can barely see them," protested Sylvia-Zack, "and I can't hear a thing."

"I can fix that." The devil zoomed in on the scene and turned up the sound.

Deep inside the cave, Felicity, Andrea, and Ben held on to one another as if they were the only people left on earth, although hundreds of choir girls and Bamajans milled around, looking lost. Mullin's followers needed direction, but Mullin lay crumpled on the control panel, sobbing with his head in his hands, and the three young people who had defeated him did not seem in a hurry to take charge. It looked to Sylvia-Zack as if the three of them could care less if anyone else was alive on earth or not. They were, Sylvia-Zack realized, simply in love with one another.

"They are in love. This is amazing," she told the devil.

"Love," said the devil. "One of my better inventions."

"I don't care," said Sylvia-Zack, "who invented it or why. All I know is that ever since I got this body, I've been wanting to roll around kissing on some warm skin. I have to go down with them. So much depends on these critters. I have to help. I have a job. I'm an angel. I'm forgetting the Minds."

"Don't be delusional," said the devil. "Nothing depends on anything. Nothing will happen, no matter what happens. Tell your big brains to go home—the show's over."

"I'm off to the underworld, 'Phisto."

"A regular Orpheus, eh?"

"Well, what would you suggest I do?"

"Have some fried chicken, a couple of deviled eggs, a slice of watermelon, a glass of this nice claret . . ." The devil produced a picnic basket, a couple of wineglasses, and linen napkins.

"Cute. A picnic at the End of the World."

"What, should the End of the World necessarily be met with parsimony and denial?"

"There must be something I can do down there," Sylvia-Zack argued.

"There's nothing you can do. On the other hand, I can do a number of things, *after* I finish the picnic. Because I am, I would like you to know, the devil *ex machina*. I can make things go anyway I please. I can make all of this vanish, or I can enjoy the show without lifting a finger. What do you suggest?"

Sylvia-Zack couldn't think of a thing. The devil had a cute behind, and he emanated fetching shamelessness. But she knew that she had to go down, to smell the new Felicity-Andrea-Ben entity close up and report to the Namer and the boss.

Her stubbornness worried the devil. When he invented love, he hadn't counted on this sort of tenacity. He had invented love on a whim, to piss off God, who had split the human creature in two in a fit of anger, intending that the creature remain eternally unhappy searching for its mate, always divided and unfulfilled. In a fit of counterpique, the devil had created the glue of love to counteract God's punishment and give solace to the poor divided creature. But his glue had run out of control, and now it oozed from the very pores of creation.

"Okay," said the devil, "but before you go, let me show you how it is."

The devil took his laptop out of the case at his feet and turned it on. When text appeared on the screen, he offered the machine to Sylvia-Zack.

Sylvia-Zack said: "I can't—I never learned."

So the devil read aloud:

" 'So be it. He was tired. Major Notz, author of the single greatest act of will in history, a big man in whose folds of flesh was written the secret history of intention, closed his eyes and pressed the red button.' "

"Now," said the devil, "watch this." He typed in the sentence, *And nothing happened.*

"Laughter," the devil said, plopping an entire half of a deviled egg in his mouth. "Another one of my inventions."

"Now, now," said Sylvia-Zack, biting into an egg and admiring the handsome bulge in the devil's pants, "we do like to take all the credit."

Nikola Tesla jumped up and down three times, shaking his whole flowery monster, to the delight of assembled street folk and incarnated Minds. But he was not, his audience imagined, terribly thrilled by the success of his experiment. He had taken that for granted. He was delighted, though, by his timing. At four o'clock that afternoon, he had been overcome by the desire to activate the green machine. About the same time, one of the bums who had been sleeping in the warehouse began to receive guests for a potluck supper in honor of Tesla, a kind of surprise birthday party. As the people gathered, bringing take-out food cartons from the Verte Mart, items selectively stolen from the A&P grocery on Royal Street, and even the fruits of their fishing, hunting, and foraging, Tesla had set the chlorophyll propulsion reactor on standby. The warehouse hummed marvelously, and bottles of cheap wine made the rounds.

The fat vines penetrating the river's surface began sending powerful photokinetic charges through the water. The fish in the Mississippi River experienced a salutary ruffling of their scales and were lifted several feet into the air before returning with geyser intensity to the water. The barges and tourist boats spun in place while their passengers roller-coasted briefly, losing wallets and keys. The charge stripped the murky water of its murk, leaving pure water molecules in its wake. All substances alien to water swirled together in an irridescent ball that lifted into the air and rolled out of the river, hovered over the Moonwalk, and took off, blotting out the sun, before settling with an oozing finality over New Orleans City Hall, which vanished under it. The photokinetic currents demagnetized the fiber-optic cables buried under the river, and all the computers from New Orleans to the Gulf of Mexico failed. Computer terminals died—from convenience-store cash registers to Mullin's keyboards to Notz's box—before reaching Felicity, who contained in her body the circuit breaker that sent the green wave around again, doubling its intensity. The old river locks in Pointe Coupée Parish opened, and the Mississippi began flowing out, cutting a channel on its way to his true love, the Atchafalaya.

In a matter of minutes, the Mississippi River turned a spectacular viridian color, then the water, cleansed of phosphates, mercury, radioactive gypsum, petroleum, and carbon gases, turned pale green.

"What do you think of that?" Tesla proudly asked his friend Mark Twain, watching events from a fat white cloud hovering over the Huey P. Long Bridge. "Now it's good enough to drink."

"We'll see," Twain drawled. "Have Mary Baker Eddy try it first."

Chapter Thirty-seven

Wherein our story comes to an end on Mardi Gras of the year 2000. The New Jerusalem Cafe, where all levels interact, opens amid the revelry. Silence settles over the weaving of the story, and the night continues, lovingly.

eated on a Turkish tambour, Andrea drank in her guests like a birthday child. She could have died of pleasure right there, seeing the faces of those who'd answered her invitation to come. They had trickled in for the past three days, complete in their persons, assured in their friendship, naturally intimate, and utterly involved in the very same questions that had first awakened them to consciousness. They now sat, lounged, or reclined about the small salon that replicated to the best of her recollection the sitting room at Saint Hildegard's. But there were some additions: a rose-crystal chandelier very much like the one in the Pioneer's House in Sarajevo before the war, which had come from Major Notz's Pontalba apartment; two Venetian mirrors she had bought at an antique dealer's on Royal Street; and a long cherrywood bar behind which sparkled bottles of fine liquor selected by Joe, the security chief and master steward. The salon gave onto several arched passageways to other parts of the building.

It was very late, only hours before dawn, and the conversation was in bloom, despite the frequent interruptions of others, notably Felicity, who hurried by several times, followed by Shades carrying kitchen utensils, flowerpots, and striped futons.

Twirling her Tibetan prayer wheel, saffron-robed Lama Iris Cohen sat on a revolving bar stool, repeating the proposition that "the wheel offers the hope of return—Christianity moves toward a linear End." She'd said it twice because, the first time, Father Tuiredh asked ironically, "Come again?"

The good father, stretched out in his cassock on the carpet, tossed some runic bones into the air like a handful of peanuts, caught only two of them, and sneered. "We crushed people on the wheel in the Middle Ages. It wasn't all linear."

Professor Li, clad in brown suit and tie but wearing a comfortable pair of New Orleans crawfish slippers, was seated on the edge of a couch, a scroll under his arm, characteristically awkward and diffident. After his return to China, he had devoted a great deal of his time to thinking about Andrea, an orphan risen from the ruins of war, a capitalist entertainment star, and an object of curiosity to diverse scholars. These reflections began to show up in his lectures, and the Chinese authorities, seeing in his preoccupation an unhealthy religious streak, warned him to desist. When he didn't, they fired him. On the day that the grim-faced party secretary offered him several unappetizing alternatives to his teaching career, Andrea's invitation came in the mail. Posted only one week before in New Orleans, the letter had arrived in record time for foreign mail. When he applied for a travel permit, it was granted immediately—another first in his experience of Chinese bureaucracy. Nonetheless, a shadow fell over this fortuitous expediency: his wife refused to accompany him. She sided with the Chinese authorities.

Earl Smith was idly drawing a female face on a cocktail napkin and taking long sips from a blue glass straw. He was averse to flying and had taken the train from New Mexico, a bone-wearying journey that had, however, given him ample time to consider the sequence of dreams that had sent him wandering all over the world. He'd concluded that the gods were unnecessarily cruel in dispatching him such distances at his age. The gods, he thought, should take Amtrak sometime.

Ever since arriving from the airport in the painted Shade bus, Sister Rodica had done little more than gaze with love at Andrea. Her journey to New Orleans had been the strangest of all. She had stolen money from the convent to pay her way and had flown in an antiquated BookAir plane, reading a worn anthology of Japanese poetry all the way to America. In her small suitcase, the nun had brought with her the mysterious letter from Father Eustratius that first gained Andrea access to Saint Hildegard's.

Others had brought gifts as well. Father Hernio had with him an Ashkelon scroll called *The War of the Prophets*, in which it was shown that the trials of history resulted from a continual war of numbers among prophets. Prophets since the earliest days of humanity had tried to accurately predict the end of their worlds. Some prophets had even been in a position to actually bring about the End, because they were advisers to kings and could wield the power of their treasuries. Each of these visionaries could have ended the world if other prophets, proffering different End dates, had not stood in the way. Thus, the incompatibility of cyphers had preserved the world many times, but by the same token had allowed it no peace. The Ashkelon scroll, in Father Hernio's opinion, explained many of the events that had occurred over the past few days.

Dr. Carlos Luna had brought a Mayan translation of a Lubavitcher manifesto that claimed the Messiah, a recently deceased rabbi, had resurrected in New York and was operating a kosher deli on Second Avenue. Dr. Luna was unsure about the propriety of his gift. Perhaps, he thought, I ought to give it to Lama Cohen, who'd be sure to laugh.

The lama herself wasn't sure if the pouch containing a small dried herb that healed most minor illnesses was of any use to Andrea. She thought of giving it to young Sister Rodica. A sentimental memento—no great gift.

Father Tuiredh had brought a huge Bavarian chocolate cake, but it had been smashed in transit, covering everything in his suitcase with a thick black ooze. He wore a knee-length nightshirt Andrea bought him on Bourbon Street, and black knee socks. The nightshirt said, *My parents went to New Orleans—and all I got is this stupid shirt.*

Mr. Rabindranath was floating. He had controlled himself for a brief time after his twenty-eight-hour flight from Calcutta to New Orleans, but the joy that sparkled in his bones had been too much, and he had found himself once more at the mercy of a massive erection, and was now levitating. Only now, no one seemed to mind. Sister Rodica, when she allowed herself to lift her gaze from Andrea, saw him and smiled. Mercy, she thought, that tumescence is a bridge to our common past.

The Saint Hildegard's family was well aware that they had been brought here by a force greater than themselves, represented somehow by Andrea, but this imperative hardly felt dutiful. Whatever their approaches or beliefs, they were glad to be here to stand by Andrea's side. Their previous gifts, which Andrea had stolen from them before she understood that they were "gifts," had been advance ritual tokens. The scholars were not divided on the meaning of these gifts.

After Andrea's hasty departure from Jerusalem, they had discussed the possibility that she was an incarnated avatar.

Lama Cohen had asked: "What does your Christian Savior save humanity from?" and answered her own question: "From yourselves. If this is the case, Andrea is not such a figure. She is more like an addition, a missing limb, let's say, that has returned long after being severed. From the cyclical Buddhist point of view, this makes perfect sense. Everything returns."

Father Zahan had said quietly: "Does the world deserve saving?"

Professor Li: "The world is saved by those in it."

"What does a Savior save? And from what is he saving what he saves?" Mr. Rabindranath asked.

Carlos Luna wondered, if white people were crazy enough to believe that they were going to heaven at the End of the World, what did they expect to do once they got there? Were not the great cosmic circles always turning, always employing God's creatures in unending toil? How could there be cessation of labor and movement, when everything in the world labored and moved? Even according to Christians, God himself was the only still point. The rest of the universe was becoming.

And so on. Only Father Tuiredh accepted the simple promise of his faith—that Christ's Second Coming would deliver the world from darkness. He just couldn't see how the Savior could be a female.

Now that they were gathered together again, in the presence of their speculative object, their old argument seemed silly. Andrea was so alive, fragrant, and welcoming, she canceled abstraction. And she seemed—healed.

She introduced Felicity, Ben, Joe, Sylvia-Zack, Nikola Tesla, and a few of the others as they rushed around preparing for Mardi Gras. Felicity immediately aroused their interest, but she was like quicksilver, hard to pin down.

Seeing Felicity and the rest of Andrea's new friends, it began to dawn on the travel-weary scholars that they had been altogether wrong. Andrea was not the avatar they suspected, or rather, not by herself. It was possible (Lama Cohen was the first to think) that this avatar was a collective, consisting of several people—perhaps a whole generation.

The waves of humanity arriving for Mardi Gras 2000 threatened to crush every blade of grass in the city of New Orleans. Strata of beads and crawfish shells layered the neutral ground on Saint Charles and Carrolton Avenues. Fat Tuesday 2000 began cloudy, but the rising sun bestowed brilliance and warmth on the city, and by eight o'clock in the morning, party goers in the French Quarter had stripped to the essentials, which in some cases meant nothing. A gentle breeze ruffled fringes and feathers, and snapped the purple and gold pennants above the crowd. Two naked women, painted silver, stood pensively still on a balcony on Toulouse. A distraught queen was appealing for aid from the Drag Repair Squad camped on the street below with loaded tool belts of nail polish, rouge, false eyebrows, and brassiere stuffers. Masques representing mythology, fantasy, the animal, mineral, and vegetable kingdoms swirled, circled, and swayed. A band of Peruvian minstrels playing harps, flutes, and thumb pianos gave the matinal scene an incongruous alpine air.

Seated on yellow director's chairs under the awning of the brand-new New Jerusalem Café, the staff and guests observed the tide.

"Man," said Joe, "I don't know how the ground can take it." The marshy soil of New Orleans had been sinking five inches every year.

"And these are only the ones we see," Ben agreed. "And it's still early morning."

"My mom used to take me on Mardi Gras to see the Indians," reminisced Felicity. "We followed the Branch of the Downtown Wild Magnolias, who'd be dancing on Tchopatoulas Street. People lined the street to watch them show their feathers and dance. Mama told me that the chief's robe weighed more than fifty pounds!"

Ben remembered his first Mardi Gras parade, perched high on his father's shoulders, watching the Krewe of Iris roll down Saint Charles Avenue. The fire-breathing chariots of the all-women crew had frightened him. And when the flambeaux carriers passed by, lighting up the night with their torches and throwing wild shadows, he couldn't hold it any longer. He had peed right on Dr. Redman's neck, who nearly dropped him under the wheels of a float when warm liquid trickled down his spine. Ben decided to keep this to himself.

"Once the Lords of Misrule occupy the intersections, we might as well give up trying to go anywhere." Joe wasn't worried. Since his rescue from the Dome, he had resigned from the police department and was now in the considerably mellower position of chief of security and master steward for the New Jerusalem, the café owned and operated by Felicity and Andrea.

New Jerusalem was situated on Royal Street at the intersection of Orleans. The sign bore the legend *Every Level All the Time* hand-lettered in slightly Gothic script by Andrea. Felicity had invested in the business almost the whole $2.1 million that Mullin had gladly handed over in exchange for his freedom and unconditional return to anonymity. She'd spared no expense on the two lavish performance stages, the fully equipped kitchen, a multiservice spa and confessional, and the computer stations built into every table. Attached to the café was a communal apartment building where the Shades and the wait staff resided. The wait staff consisted of the singing angels of the First Angels Choir, with a considerably enlarged repertoire now that included blues, the devil's music. Only Kashmir Birani, faithful to Mullin, had refused to come along, going off with the reverend in his gold Cadillac.

People began drifting into the café. Felicity rose to her feet to greet a tan, handsome man in a finely tailored Brooks Brothers suit. He returned her gaze, both arch and amused. He mouthed a word Felicity could not make out, and then it dawned on her. Ovid! Of course. The Roman poet, but a shade on the Internet, had come farther than his exile had ever flung him. Felicity embraced him. He was scented by an ancient oil, nard of the Black Sea, Getian perfume.

Standing close by was tuxidoed Nostradamus, perfumed by cigarette smoke and fried fish, holding a newspaper in his hands. "Behold," he cried, "the sad fate of the deerskin-bound book! It has come undone like the springs of the world! Ten popes have gone and not a face looks gentler!" He handed her the paper.

She thanked him, glorying in her armies of time.

Ben Redman was explaining to Joe: "Listen, Di Friggio, here is the good part. What goes on onstage is not as important as what goes on in the bleachers. One billion souls of the dead are watching the spectacle. It's their reviews that count. Who wins or loses onstage is of no importance."

Overhearing this argument, Felicity laughed so hard tears squirted out of her eyes. She hadn't laughed this way since she had eaten mushrooms with Ben and watched him do headstands. Only Redman could do this to her.

"Did I say something funny?"

"Yes, darling. You did. I really do love you, you know."

"Okay, but do you believe I'm right?"

"I believe everything now, Ben. A week ago, I didn't believe anything."

"Then what's so funny?"

"Well, the numbers got me. Billions and billions! You go, girl!"

"When you're like this, I just want to throw you down on the floor and spank your café-au-lait ass."

Felicity laughed. "And then try to shove your baseball bat in places too little for it. I know you, Ben Redman."

Andrea applauded. "What about me?"

"Same idea." Felicity kissed Andrea's shoulder.

Joe felt all their kisses. He had been communicating telepathically with Felicity since he'd seen her enter the Dome with Andrea, Ben, and Major Notz, and picked up the strains of an eerie but uplifting music coming from them.

The café's first customers did not walk in off the street. The largest room in the café was given over to computers and virtual-reality stations built at eye level within comfortable nooks equipped with overstuffed leather chairs and couches. Cyberentities hovered both inside and outside the screen, exiting their designated environments at will. The thin-as-cigarette-smoke French poet Antonin Artaud drew together his scattered pixels and walked as far as the door of the VR room. He was followed in short order by Henri Michaux, André Breton, René Crevel, and other members of his generation, who traveled in a gang even in ectoplasm. After skewering the surroundings with disdainful glances, they surrendered to the evident licentiousness and separated, heading for the women in the room. Other literary gangs took tentative steps into the new millennium, gathering substance into their images and interacting with embodied creatures as if they were made out of the same stuff.

Karl Marx, who'd wandered into this room looking for a bathroom, was astonished. He watched a gang of literary cybertravelers gain mass and dimension, exit the screens, and become physical entities. What was the economy of this time-and-space free-for-all?

"Who are you? Who are you?" Marx kept asking as entities streamed in from cyberspace. The cyberoids were covered with a superfine powder of salt, as if they'd passed through the Dome on their way to New Jerusalem.

They stated their names for Marx like schoolchildren answering a roll call: *Benjamin Fondane, Ilarie Voronca, Tristan Tzara, Apunake, Paul Celan, Gherasim Luca* . . . Marx reeled in amazement—even though he himself was an embodied creature from another level, he could not grasp the existence of the pixilated apparitions. He'd never believed in other worlds and had always disdained saccharine spiritual conceits, even before he wrote his mature works. He had believed neither in God, nor in Christ, nor in the Bible. He had been certain of the material world only. Regret for his misguided faith filled him, even as a stubborn inner voice admonished: You are feverish, Karl Marx. This is a dream.

Several pudgy boys with long hair and bad posture were voyaging in MOOs and MUDs, oblivious to the cyberinvasion around them. A large postmodern wolf urinated on one of the boys, and he gave out a war whoop. His next-console neighbor jumped into a pool of furry-mucker mud and felt up the tail of a large, flirtatious lizard.

A barefoot man with long hair and a crown of thorns on his head walked past Marx to the doorway and stood behind Sister Rodica. She started, turned around, and fell out of the director's chair. Andrea helped her up, but Sister Rodica, her eyes fixed on the longhaired man, fell to her knees and touched her forehead to the ground. The man fixed his burning black eyes on her and said, "Oh, lust-laden one! Let spirit do the work of the spirit!"

Nostradamus explained: "It's not Jesus; it's Mani, the Persian. Get up, Sister."

Reluctantly, Sister Rodica rose to her feet.

Mani admitted it: "I'm not your Christ—I was the first one crucified. Others were crucified after me, and long before Jesus. A row of crosses as long as the Akbar seacoast stretches between us."

A naked man with a wooden cross on his back pushed through the painted and sequined revelers toward the New Jerusalem, shouting: "Repent! Repent! Shed your devils!"

Felicity recognized him—the man with the LCD cross who had first greeted her when Tesla'd sprung her from the School for Messiah Development. She invited him to come by later to watch the performances.

The sunny morning gave way to a warm, cloudy afternoon, the afternoon in turn to a velvety evening. The intoxicated creatures crowded every inch of the street, and inhibitions dropped like boa feathers. Young women bared their breasts and young men displayed their penises. Pierced nipples, penis chains, leather whips, and restraints brushed against skin. The masked celebrants danced to music pouring in from balconies and boom boxes. A parade passed nearby on Ramparts Street; echoed police sirens mingled with a traditional Mardi Gras tune played by a high school brass band.

The New Jerusalem was thick with bodies pressed tightly against one another. Two Day-Glo Shades lit a bank of black candles set on a wagon wheel above the center stage. Other Shades hung a black cross with chains and hooks from the wheel. Two bare-chested blond men wearing tight vinyl pants climbed on the cross and draped themselves over the arms, bent at the waist, their arms and legs swaying over the heads of the crowd. A bare-breasted woman, wearing only black thong panties and red fishnet stockings, slowly walked her slave in front of the cross. The stoned slave followed the leash attached to his collar.

Shades lit candles on the side stage, revealing a girl stretched naked on a wooden palet. A red-robed priestess in spiked heels and a Mylar bikini heated a pair of pliers red hot over a Bunsen burner flame, and then burned an elaborate ankh on the small of the girl's back. Another woman knelt in front of the girl and kissed her mouth. The smell of burning flesh filled the air. A man with Chinese characters inscribed on his back and leather straps tattooed on his body masturbated as he watched.

Two naked Magdalenes danced, grinding their crotches into the faces of the thieves hanging upside down on the cross. The slave master unleashed the slave Christ before the cross, and several shades helped hoist him up, his back to the audience. The master pulled off the vinyl pants, exposing his buttocks. A leather harness held his genitalia. And then a young girl in red vinyl boots with six-inch heels began to whip Christ's bare bottom.

One by one, women and girls took turns hurting Christ, who winced but did not cry out. Some used whips or paddles; others hit his reddening bottom with their open hand. A costumed nun, her enormous breasts pushed up by a stiff corset, a black veil hanging past her midcalf, and a pink Burmese python around her neck, beat Christ for a long time. Each time she let her leather thong fly at his back she rushed forward, the huge, pale snake dangling terrified from her neck. A long, thin dildo protruded from her pelvis, and when she was done whipping the now bleeding Christ, she plunged the dildo into his ass and began to fuck him to the technodisco beat. The appreciative crowd began to applaud the furious fucking.

Kneeling at the foot of Christ, his female master rubbed salve on his behind, comforting him after the ordeal. Now and then, an unscarred girl or boy leapt forward toward the cross, shedding their clothes and asking to be beaten. The pierced and branded mob surrounding the cross obliged, and moans of ecstatic pain filled the air.

Mr. Rabindranath had witnessed many spectacles of self-mortification and ritual sacrifice in India, but he was quite astonished by what was unfolding here. He found Andrea near the front of the center stage and asked her: "Who are the people being branded and crucified? What is their religion? What are they celebrating?"

"Only their bodies are here," she reassured him. "Their minds are traveling in cyberspace."

He didn't understand. Andrea took him by the hand and tried to press through the crowd, but movement was impossible. Mr. Rabindranath squeezed her fingers and began lifting up. Andrea felt her feet leave the ground as she followed. The two of them floated above the heads of the crowd to the next room, where computer consoles blinked and breathed like lungs. Some avatars were moving through electronic cities and forests, entering the room at will, while others were going from the room into the screens. Andrea pointed out the travelers going out rather than in, though it would have been hard to explain exactly what in and out were in this situation.

"The ones going in—they are human minds," Andrea said. "They have found happiness in cyberspace. They've left their bodies behind for use by the celebrants, who play with them like dolls."

Mr. Rabindranath understood. The cybernauts, addicted to electronic existence, suffered abuse to their abandoned bodies without pain or complaint. Their minds were fulfilled in cyberspace, linked to other minds in a spaceless, timeless existence.

"These other minds," Andrea continued, "the ones coming in from cyberspace, are so potent now they are creating flesh bodies. Their purpose is to embody. Sometimes they take over the bodies left behind by the other voyagers, but sometimes they just incarnate at random in anybody vulnerable. They are taking over a lot of bodies. The cybertraffic is mad just now."

They floated back into the performance area, where other brandings were taking place. The girl with the brand-new ankh moved painfully through the crowd, helped along by her attendant lover. Other Christs clamored to be crucified, after the first was lowered down. More and more bodies gained the side stage to be branded, until there seemed to be no more spectators, only a human mass reveling in their shared pain.

Ovid was nonplussed. He sat onstage below the latest Christ, speaking into the ear of a white-robed man in sandals. "It is a good bacchanalia, Aristotle, but it compares only negligibly to Roman Saturnalia, which of course paled compared to the worship of Baal in Babylon."

"This mystery religion seems to be led by women," observed Nostradamus, who had found a vantage point, standing on the shoulders of a muscular dwarf called Pythagoras.

"They always are," replied Mani, swatting at a swarm of angels buzzing around his head. "Everywhere I go," he complained, "these winged pathogens follow me. Ostensibly for my protection. As the first crucified one, you see, I get an honor guard."

Nostradamus looked baffled. "Is this the End of the World, or not? Is it over? I don't get it."

Ovid and Mani laughed.

"Every bit of the material world, yes," affirmed Ovid, "except for the parts that refuse to believe it, continuing to cling to meat space. Haven't you read the *Metamorphoses*? Why the hell did I write it?"

Mani patted the distraught seer on the back. "Prophets are always disappointed, dear Nostradamus. That's why new ones are always in the wings, updating the catastrophes."

"I was given to understand that *everything* would cease," lamented Nostradamus, mostly to himself.

A cross-bearing evangelist nodded in agreement.

Professor Li pointed to the cross and told Nostradamus: "That object is at the root of all your troubles."

Nostradamus took offense. "How is that, Confucian heathen?"

"Look at the shape!" Professor Li traced the vertical arm from bottom to top, then from top to bottom. "Your prayers always go up, begging your God to descend into your world to help you. Your God is continually confined to the job of sending his messengers down; his gaze is always downward. He has no time to look up; he is prevented from evolving. You ought to pray down, free your God before he kills you all. Above everything, you should eliminate this symbol!"

Confucius rolled off a large sea turtle and also addressed the distraught prophet: "There is a flaw in your eschatology caused by the splitting of your God into three and of your goddess into two. These initial splits kept on causing more splits, until all your gods were in fragments, and now they rain on you haphazardly, looking to *you* for their survival. This is not the end of humans, but the last days of the gods."

"Aha!" exclaimed Sylvia-Zack, overhearing. "That explains heavenly democracy and all that. Heavenly meltdown is more like it! Every human in this sorry world's going to be hosting their very own personal god in their very own personal body!"

"Of course!" Lama Cohen slapped her forehead. "It's all about real estate! The gods move into us, we move into the vacated heavens! They get our bodies, we get their cybermental apartments."

"Alas, poor Yorick," said Ovid, still moved by Nostradamus's plight.

"I see. You've been spending eternity reading your future fellow poets," laughed Aristotle, who had spent eternity doing very much the same thing, though he didn't much care for postdeconstructionists.

The crowd began moving toward the door, drawn by something going on outside. The Minds gathered around the stage joined the flow and found themselves on the street. Felicity and Andrea were already there, surrounded by their faithful Shades. A naked woman painted gold was riding toward the group on a white horse. She held a bright sword in her hand.

"Joan!" cried Felicity. "You've come to save New Orleans!"

The rider reined in her horse in front of Sister Rodica, who lifted her arms toward her. Joan held out her free hand and helped the nun mount. Rodica put her arms around Joan's golden waist and lay her head on her shoulder. The Virgin of Orléans lifted her sword and the crowd parted for them. The couple rode down Orleans to the back of Saint Louis Cathedral and lifted above the spires into the night sky until they became a small gold coin. Watching them vanish, Andrea felt her heart break, as if an arrow had sliced the tenderest meat at its center.

Tesla held up a shiny blue rose he had created. A Christian with a metal sign that said *Everything Must Go* looked at him in dismay.

The breeze that had until now caressed the revelers strengthened, snapping banners over balconies, ruffling the maskers' fringes and feathers. The starry sky shone brightly between the luminiscent shimmers of silk, synthetics, street lights, pixilated phantoms. The wind grew in intensity. It snatched the metal sign from the evangelist's hands. The metal square rose into the air, twisted over the heads of the mob and out of sight. Next, the metal buckles of belts began snapping off and rising. Swords, knives, and concealed guns tore through the costumes of the revelers and headed up, sucked by the increasing velocity of the mysterious wind. People wearing metal shoe fastenings were thrown down by the wind. Some of them flew up with their attached metallic accoutrements. Inside the café, Christ's chain snapped and he fell into the arms of his owner. The sky became a dense mass of flying metal heading faster and faster over the Mississippi River.

Sylvia-Zack, holding a silver flask, looked at Tesla in wonder. Felicity, Andrea, Ben, and Joe cheered as the flask flew out of her hand.

"I'll be damned," cried Felicity. "Tesla made a chlorophyll magnet, and it's working. He's disarming the world."

It certainly looked that way.

"Everyone we love is here," said Felicity.

"Not my parents," said Andrea.

"Nor Miles," added Felicity. "Or the major."

"At least we now know who the True One is," said Ben.

About the Author

Andrei Codrescu is a poet, novelist, and essayist. His radio essays have been heard on National Public Radio for fifteen years. He has written and starred in *Road Scholar*, a Peabody Award-winning film. His last novel, *The Blood Countess*, was a national bestseller.